THE BURNS DEFIANCE
THE FIRE SALAMANDER CHRONICLES BOOK THREE

N. M. THORN

N.M. THORN

THE BURNS DEFIANCE

THE FIRE SALAMANDER CHRONICLES • BOOK THREE

The Burns Defiance

By N.M. Thorn

Copyright © 2019 by N.M. Thorn. All rights reserved.
nmthornauthor@gmail.com
This is a work of fiction. Any resemblance to actual persons living or dead, businesses, events, or locales is purely coincidental. Reproduction in whole or part of this publication without express written consent is strictly prohibited.
Cover art design by www.originalbookcoverdesigns.com

PROLOGUE

* * *

November 1916
Saint Petersburg, Russia.

"They are not going to kill me! You're lying! I've heard this prophecy once before. How did you find out about it… Things have changed, and they wouldn't dare! I have the ear of the Tsarina herself. She'll kill them all for me."

The man was pacing in front of a large silver mirror that was hanging on the wall, throwing angry glances at his own reflection from time to time. After a minute, he stopped, leaning heavily on a small table. He glowered at the mirror like it was his worst enemy, breathing hard. His electric blue eyes got glassy and his black pupils widened, coloring his eyes black.

He slowly lifted his hand and brushed his fingers over the smooth surface of the mirror. "What are you saying?" he asked drowsily even though it appeared there was no one else in the room but him. For a moment he fell into a deep trance. Then he shook his head and his pupils returned back to normal size. "Yes, you're right. I know what I need to do."

The man pushed away from the table and walked to the opposite end of the room. He lifted a curtain and found a small button hidden in the wall. He pressed it and a small trapdoor cracked opened. With his height of six-foot-four he had to almost double-up to walk inside.

The small room behind the trapdoor was submerged into darkness, but the man knew his way around. He moved his hand to the right and found a half-burnt candle that was sitting on the small shelf next to the door. He picked it up and touched it with his index finger.

"Ignius," he whispered, and a small flame ignited on the wick of the candle, illuminating the tiny room with a flickering yellow light.

The man proceeded inside, careful not to hit his head on the low ceiling and sat down on a single chair that was positioned next to a table. A few large books in leather bindings were scattered all over. At the far end of the table stood a bunch of new candles, and a number of different jars and cans filled with liquids, crystals and powders. Chemical scales with a set of weights were sitting next to the candles. The wall above the table was partially concealed by bunches of dried up herbs.

The man picked up one of the books and read it, slowly moving from one page to the next. Then he closed it and pressed his lips into a stubborn straight line. "I'm still missing one ingredient. I still need that apple. But this will have to do for now."

He got up and took an empty jar. Carefully he measured a spoon of powder and placed it inside. Then he picked up a bunch of dry flowers and plucked a few petals off, dropping them inside the jar. Slowly mixing everything with a wooden pestle, he poured a few different liquids and put everything in the metal holder above the candle.

It took a while for the liquid to come to a boil, but the man wasn't in a rush. Once the liquid finally boiled, he took the jar and placed it on the table. Slowly he started to chant, clearly pronouncing each word. A dark mist rose above the jar, shimmering in the light of the candle. He kept at it until the liquid turned bright red. Once he noticed the change, he stopped his enchantment. The man took the jar off the holder and carefully placed it on the table. After the potion cooled down slightly, he picked it up.

"Na zdorovie," he muttered and downed the contents of the jar in a few large gulps. He placed the empty jar on the table. A few drops of the red liquid trickled down his thick mustache and his long untidy beard, but he didn't bother wiping them.

He found a clean piece of paper, a stylus and an ink bottle on the table. Pulling everything closer, he dipped the long stylus into the ink and started to write.

"I write and leave this letter in Saint Petersburg. I feel that I will leave life before January 1st. I wish to make known to the Russian people, to Papa, to the Russian Mother and to the Children what they must do."

He wrote and stopped, thinking, his black pupils fluctuating in size. He picked up the stylus again and continued. He was writing fast, like he was afraid that he would forget to include something.

"If I am killed by my brothers, the Russian peasants, then you, the Russian Tsar, have nothing to worry about. You will remain on your throne and keep your reign. And you, Russian Tsar, don't need to worry about your kids. Their reign over Russia will continue for hundreds of years."

He stopped writing again and put the stylus back into the ink bottle. Wiping perspiration off his face with the sleeve of his shirt, he re-read again what he wrote so far and picked up the stylus.

"But if I will be killed by boyars and nobles, and they will spill my blood, then their hands will remain soiled by my blood, and for twenty-five years, they won't be able to wash their hands clean. They will leave Russia. Brothers will rise against brothers and they will kill each other. And for twenty-five years, there will be no peace in the country.

Tsar of Russia, if you hear the bell ring, telling you Grigory has been murdered then know this: if it was one of your own blood who wrought my death, then none of your children will live for more than two years..."

He dropped the stylus on the table, spilling some ink and got up. For a while he paced in front of the table, the sinister words of his own prophecy making his blood run cold. "I have no reason to worry. Nothing of it will come true. They can't kill me now that I have taken the potion, it's impossible." He nodded, feeling reassured by his own words and sat back down, picking up the stylus, dipping it into the ink.

"Russian Tsar, you will be killed by Russian people, and the people will be cursed and serve as a weapon of the devil, killing each other and spreading death through the world. Three times for twenty-five years, the servants of Antichrist will destroy Russian people and the Orthodox faith..."

Once he was done, he looked over the letter and re-read it a few times. Satisfied with his work, he signed his name *"Grigory Rasputin"* and sealed the letter.

* * *

December 10, 1916
Saint Petersburg, Russia.

IT WAS past midnight when Rasputin walked into the Molika

palace of Prince Felix Yusupov. The Prince met him at the door, expressing his delight and quickly ushered him into the basement room of the Palace. The basement was just as lavish and bright as the rest of the palace and the table was served for a late-night feast. The sweet scent of cookies and cakes filled the air, giving it a welcoming, homely atmosphere.

Rasputin sat down, relaxing in a soft chair. He didn't wonder why he was invited into the palace at such a late time. It wasn't the first time for him. Felix Yusupov filled his cup with tea and placed a slice of cake on his plate, the smile on the young Prince's face just as sweet as the dessert he offered.

Grigory took the cup into his hands and felt a light touch of heat on the wrist of his left hand. He glanced down. One of the stones on his bracelet changed its color from black to dark red. The stone indicated the close presence of a poison. A wide smirk stretched his lips. The young Prince was trying to kill him. Well, let him try. He had nothing to worry about. Confident in the elixir of immortality he took just a short while ago, Grigory brought the cup of tea to his lips, observing the Prince over the rim of his cup.

The eyes of Yusupov lit up with impatience and hope. He looked like he was ready to pour this poisoned beverage down Grigory's throat himself if he wouldn't drink it fast enough. Grigory slowly sipped his tea, taking large bites of the poisonous cake. The stone on his bracelet became hotter, counteracting the effects of the poison. Grigory smiled, complimenting his kind host on his hospitality and delicious dinner.

"Some wine, perhaps?" asked Felix rising, his pale face glistening with sweat. "I have a nice bottle of Madeira in my study, waiting for a good reason to be opened."

The Prince forced a smile and walked out of the room. He came back a few minutes later with a bottle of Madeira in his hands and filled Rasputin's glass. Grigory knew the wine was poisoned even without the amulet in his bracelet telling him that. He smirked and raised the glass.

"Za zdorovie," he said and downed the wine, placing the empty glass back on the table. He wiped his lips with his hand, staring at the Prince with a mocking smirk. Then he took the bottle and filled his glass again, demonstratively lifting it to his mouth and swallowing its contents in one giant gulp.

"How is it possible?" whispered the young man, his eyes bulging. "It's not possible!"

Rasputin cackled, staring down at the young Prince with scorn in his eyes. He filled his glass one more time and drank it to the bottom. Felix backed away, crossing himself, whispering something incomprehensible. As he stepped back, Grigori moved closer, his imposing frame towering over Felix. Prince Yusupov drew his revolver and shot Rasputin in his chest point blank.

Grigory pressed his hand to his chest, bright red streams of blood gushing between his fingers. With shock, he gaped down at his own blood spilling down his chest, dripping to the floor. The sickening smell of it made his head spin. He swayed, fell on his back and blacked out.

When he regained consciousness, the first thing he heard was the voice of Prince Yusupov.

"This can't be," said Felix, "I shot him in his heart!" Grigory felt someone's hand tearing at his shirt. "Look at all this blood on the floor, but there is no bullet hole! I couldn't have missed! I shot him point blank."

Rasputin slowly opened his eyes. His vision was hazy, but he recognized Prince Yusupov standing over him. Right behind him he saw Grand Duke Dmitri Pavlovich and the right-wing politician Vladimir Purishkevich.

Rage surged through him, providing him with much-needed strength. Grigory leaped to his feet, his face contorted into a devilish grimace. All three conspirators gasped in horror, staggering away from him, but Rasputin reached the young Prince and seized his neck, shaking him.

"You're a bad boy. Bad boy!" he growled, continuing shaking the Prince. "I'll tell everything to the Tsarina!"

The Prince whimpered, struggling helplessly against his grip for a few seconds before he gave in, hanging limply in his hands. Rasputin finally dropped him and rushed toward the stairs, thinking about only one thing – escape to safety. He needed to walk out of this house and cross the palace's courtyard, and then he'd be safe. Tomorrow he would tell everything that had happened to the Tsarina and she wouldn't be merciful to those who dared to harm him.

He made it all the way to the outside door and burst through the door of the palace into the cold winter night when he heard the sound of two loud gun shots, one after another. He felt a sharp pain in his back and in his side. Grigory cried out and fell to his knees but managed to get up and kept running toward the exit from the courtyard. He didn't listen to the agitated screams of Felix Yusupov and his co-conspirators. He didn't care. All he needed to do was run out onto the street. They wouldn't keep pursuing him there and the immortality potion would do its job, healing his wounds.

Grigory almost felt the taste of freedom on his lips, which were smeared with his blood, when he saw another man standing in front of him, blocking his only way to freedom. He'd never seen this man before. Young and well-built, the man was slightly taller than him. He was dressed in an expensive suit of a nobleman. His long gold hair fell below his shoulders, down to his waist.

"Regular bullets can't kill him now," said the stranger calmly, addressing Prince Yusupov. He raised his hand and Rasputin saw a revolver. The weapon was glowing with a soft shimmering light. Staring directly into Rasputin's eyes, the man pressed the trigger without blinking.

As if in slow motion, Rasputin saw the bullet erupt from the revolver's barrel, followed by a bright red flare and swirls of white smoke. It shimmered with the blue light of magic, a tiny glowing rune engraved on its tip. He felt a push into his head and clasped his hands to his forehead. Pain the likes of which he had never felt before forced him down to his knees. He swayed and collapsed on the snow. He was still alive, but he couldn't move, he couldn't open his eyes, he couldn't make a sound.

"Is he dead?" He heard the voice of the Prince.

"No," replied the stranger, his deep voice laced with sadness. "Unfortunately, I was too late and now it won't be easy to kill him."

"What should we do?" asked Purishkevich. "How can we kill him then?"

"You need to submerge his body into frozen water," replied the stranger. "You do that, and I'll do my part. Pray that the Dark Nav can keep his soul from rising."

A few minutes later, Rasputin felt someone's hands move his body, tying his arms and legs with thick ropes. Then they wrapped his body into a cloth and lifted him.

Who was this man? Was he privy to the dark arts? He had to be, otherwise he wouldn't know any of it, Rasputin thought desperately. *I have no idea who he is, but I swear to God, I will rise again. And when I do, there won't be a place on this Earth where he can hide from my wrath.*

The icy waters of the Neva river closed above him, pulling his body into its frosty embrace.

CHAPTER 1

~ ZANE BURNS, A.K.A. GUNZ ~

Modern day. Somewhere in Florida... Probably...

The roars of a demon were supposed be scaring him but mostly annoyed him. Gunz watched as the demon carelessly launched his whole bulky body into a frontal attack and rolled his eyes. The monster was over six feet tall with a massive body wrapped in a thick layer of muscle.

The demon obviously thought highly of himself, sure in an easy victory, but Gunz knew better. No matter how much muscle-power this monster packed, how impenetrable he thought the shield of his iron muscles was, there were always a few weak vulnerable points on his massive body. Besides, compared to Gunz, the demon was extremely slow.

He watched the demon's fist sail by his face and took a quick step to the side, meeting his opponent with a powerful strike to his neck. The monster choked, losing his balance. He fell down clutching his neck, his eyes bulging. In a split-second, Gunz reached him and pulled him into a sitting position. He wrapped his arm around his neck and clasped his hands, his forearm set firmly into the demon's back. He pushed with his forearm and yanked his hands, applying a brutal choke.

The demon was thrashing in his arms, struggling against his hold. Gunz squeezed harder, putting the monster to sleep. Then he got up, dropping the unconscious body on the floor and turned around, staring through the net of the cage at the raging crowd. He found the eyes of Mr. Kogan, the man who owned all supernatural fighting pits in Florida and watched him turn his thumb down.

A cold smirk split Gunz's face as he kneeled next to the demon and drove his fist through the monster's face all the way to the floor. Blood and brain matter splattered all around the place where the demon's head used to be. Gunz rose, staring down at his dead opponent with disdain.

The crowd exploded in carnivorous screams. The referee opened the door into the cage and approached Gunz. He seized his wrist and yanked his arm up, blood – demon's blood – slowly trickling down his forearm. Gunz pulled his arm out of the referee's grip, wiped the blood on his cargo pants and walked out of the cage.

He headed to the backroom where he could clean up and relax for a few minutes before leaving. As he walked with his head bowed down, the roar of the crowd followed him. He felt a few hands touch his arms and shoulders, but he didn't react. It wasn't his first fight and he got used to ignoring everything, never paying attention to what people around him were doing or saying.

Gunz made his way into the backroom and dropped down on the bench. The room was small and dark, a tiny electric light bulb hanging from the ceiling, illuminating the room with a fluctuating yellow light. The thick smell of sweat and blood seemed to be permanently rooted into everything within its walls. A small dirty sink was installed in the far corner of the room and even drops of water were falling from the rusty faucet.

He leaned forward slightly and rested his elbows on his lap, hiding his face in his hands. He wasn't tired – the fight was over so fast it hardly spiked the adrenalin in him. He felt hollow inside, indifferent to everything, inwardly wishing that the late demon put up a better fight.

He heard the phone ring and snapped his head to the side. Gunz reached for his bag and pulled the phone out, staring at the screen. *This is exactly what I didn't need,* he thought with a sigh, but answered the phone.

"How did you get this phone number, Agent Andrews?" asked Gunz coldly.

"And hello to you too, Mr. Burns," replied Jim, ignoring his tone. "Where are you and what are you doing?"

"A little preoccupied at the moment," muttered Gunz, unwilling to get into a conversation with his boss.

"What are you doing, Gunz?" repeated Jim, softer notes in his voice. "You disabled the GPS tracker in your watch and just fell from the face of the Earth. This is the first time in months you answered my phone call. Even Aidan can't sense you. What the hell are you doing, man? There are people here who actually care about you!"

"I'm doing my job, Agent Andrews," replied Gunz dryly. "You wanted me to bring the ring of supernatural underground fighting down? So, I'm doing just that. I'm trying to get you all the names and information you need to make it happen. I concealed my fire energy because I'm undercover. I believe you know what it means to be undercover, sir?"

"But Gunz—"

"I got to go, Jim. Try calling me in a few hours," Gunz interrupted him as the door into his room opened.

He hung up the phone and looked at the woman who walked inside and halted in front of him. She was tall and slim, dressed in the latest style black dress and high-heels. Her wavy blond hair was styled to accentuate the soft oval of her face and her skin was covered in a generous layer of makeup to conceal her true age. Gunz lowered his head, not willing to meet her eyes.

"Gunz, you were as magnificent as always today," she purred, her hand resting on his shoulder, slowly moving down along the shape of his bicep. "I love watching you fight, darling. You're an untamed brutal beast. I can't believe you're just a wizard."

"Um... Thank you, Mrs. Kogan, I guess..." replied Gunz without looking at her and carefully took her hand off his shoulder. "I'm covered in blood and sweat after the fight, ma'am. I don't want you to get your hands dirty."

Mrs. Kogan squatted down in front of him, pulling her elegant black dress up just enough to expose her shapely thighs. She glanced up, searching for his eyes and reached forward. Her hand wandered down his bare chest, tracing the shape of his muscles.

"Mmm," she purred. "What can be more exciting than a young handsome sweaty savage."

Her eyes were dark with lust and her hands seemed to be restless, traveling down his stomach. Before he could say anything, her fingers found the button on the waistband of his pants and pulled the zipper down. Gunz wrapped his hand over her wrist and gently pushing it away.

"Your husband, ma'am," he said frostily, flicking his eyebrow at the door where a tall man was standing with his hand on the door handle.

"My husband? The thrill is gone. He doesn't excite me anymore," she replied, not paying attention to anything except him. "Just like I don't excite him. We live in an open marriage and he wouldn't mind if I had a taste of this." She grabbed his crotch and squeezed slightly. "I wonder if you're just as mighty in bed as you are in the cage."

Gunz grunted, his aggravated gaze meeting the eyes of the man in the doorway. The man in his late fifties was tall and thin, dressed in an immaculate business suit and a blue shirt underneath. With his gray complexion and deep, dark circles around his yellowish eyes, he wasn't exuding a healthy vibe. Mr. Kogan watched his wife's fruitless advances with an uneven smirk on his hollow-cheeked face.

"Clarissa, darling," said the man, approaching his wife, and pulled her up to her feet, "go get your busy hands into someone else's pants, preferably with someone who doesn't mind the intrusion. I need a few minutes to talk to our undefeated fighter here."

Mrs. Kogan pivoted on her high heels and sauntered away, swaying her hips. "I'll see you later, darling," she promised Gunz, blowing an air-kiss to him as she walked out the door.

Mr. Kogan waited until his wife had left the room and shook his head chuckling. He put his hand in the pocket of his pants and pulled out a wad of cash held by a money clip.

"Your cut," he said, counting out a few hundred-dollar bills and offered them to Gunz.

"Thanks." Gunz took the bills and threw them into his bag without counting.

"Oh, no, thank *you*," replied Mr. Kogan, a wide grin on his face. "You're my biggest moneymaker after all. I'm sorry about my wife's behavior. She can be a little forward."

Gunz smirked. "She wants my body. There is nothing more to it," he said with a shrug without lifting his eyes. "And I don't give a damn."

"I know," replied Mr. Kogan nonchalantly and waved his hand at the bench. "May I?"

Gunz finally lifted his head and glanced at him. Then he nodded and lowered his eyes again.

Mr. Kogan sat down next to him. "Why are you doing it, Gunz? Why are you fighting every night, risking your health and possibly your life?"

"I need money," replied Gunz evenly.

"You don't care about money," objected Mr. Kogan sharply. "I watch you every night and I'm sure that you couldn't care less about money, or vanity, or women. None of it. You make enough money fighting in these pits to live in a five-star hotel in any city we travel to, but you choose to live in a cheap fleabag motel. So, what drives you inside that cage?"

Gunz didn't reply. He didn't even change his position.

"Well, allow me to ask another personal question then," continued Mr. Kogan. "You look like you're in your late twenties – early thirties, but I've been around the supernatural community long enough to know appearances can be deceiving. Magic slows down the aging and there are enough immortals roaming this world who don't age at all. How old are you, Gunz? Are you really as young as you look?"

Gunz nodded. "Yeah, I'm twenty-nine…"

"I wonder what made you so cold and cynical at such young age?" asked Mr. Kogan quietly. "I see the way you kill your opponents in the cage – you don't care whether they live or die. When you fight, it's like you're begging for trouble. You're a wizard. You undoubtedly know how to use your magic, but I saw you using it only once. It's like you're inviting the pain or possibly even death."

Gunz remained silent, staring unblinkingly at his hands, covered in blood.

"Fine," said Mr. Kogan rising, "then let me do something unusual for you. After all, whatever drives you into this shithole makes me richer. Usually the Heads of the Houses don't socialize with their fighters – not even with unattached fighters, but I'd like to treat you to dinner tomorrow night. Would you be open to that?"

Gunz lifted his head and glanced at Mr. Kogan, slightly surprised. The Heads of the Houses not only didn't socialize with the fighters, they hardly even noticed them, treating them as low-level scum, which most of the fighters were. They were the rogue demons, vampires, werewolves, dark wizards and other monsters who were trying to either make a few bucks or satisfy their thirst for blood without getting into too much trouble with local authorities.

"Thank you," said Gunz.

"Thank you yes or thanks but no way in hell?" asked Mr. Kogan chuckling.

"Yes, thank you," replied Gunz quietly. "Just please, don't ask me any personal questions, sir."

"I'm wondering what bothers you more – the questions I ask or my wife's groping technique," he muttered and laughed. "Don't answer that, please. Is there anything I can do for you tonight, Gunz?"

"Yes, sir," replied Gunz rising. "You can get me one more fight tonight."

"Are you serious?" asked Mr. Kogan with a tone of shock in his voice.

"Deadly serious," said Gunz. "And if they don't have a strong enough opponent for me, get me in the cage with two fighters. Or three. Whatever will get you more money."

"I'll see what I can do," said Mr. Kogan heading out of the room.

* * *

ONE HOUR LATER, Gunz was walking toward the cage again. The crowd was shouting, chanting his name. Everyone was staring at him – women with lust, men with blood-thirsty hunger in their eyes. Women were reaching to touch him, but he saw nothing, felt nothing, thought of nothing as his eyes locked on the two monsters inside the cage.

Carefully he probed them with his Salamander senses and wanted to laugh. One of his opponents was a demon. Just like the demon he fought earlier today, he was tall and bulky. The second opponent was a dark wizard, and out of all the magic tricks he could pull out of his hat, he chose to use fire magic. Both of them were at least a few inches taller than him and they glowered down at him with arrogant smirks on their faces.

The bouncer opened the door of the cage for him, ushering him inside. Gunz stepped on the blood-splattered floor of the ring, a frosty lopsided smirk on his face.

"I'll wipe that smirk right off your face, wizard," hissed the demon. He exchanged a boastful look with his partner and they both nodded.

"Please," muttered Gunz dryly. "Do your worst."

The bell rang announcing the beginning of the fight and the demon charged him at once. The shouting of the crowd dimmed down and disappeared as his mind immediately was set to a high alert.

Fire Salamander – go! Gunz thought as he drove his fist into the demon's face, knocking him out cold in one punch.

CHAPTER 2

~ ZANE BURNS, A.K.A. GUNZ ~

Gunz walked into the dark hotel room and threw his bag on the floor. He hated coming back to this place, small and musty, but it had something his house in Coral Springs didn't – solitude and isolation. He needed it. Being next to people who cared about him was dangerous for them and he didn't think he could survive losing another person he loved.

He stopped in front of a cracked mirror and carefully pulled his shirt off. He explored the dark bruises on his ribs and chest with his fingers and winced. That dark wizard had been better than anyone he had fought since he dove headfirst into the dark swamp of underground supernatural fighting. The damn wizard actually managed to land a few punches and kicks on him.

Gunz didn't like using his magic during the fight and resorted to it only when he had no other choice. Today had been that day. This dark wizard's magic was potent enough so Gunz had to use his shield to counteract his attacks. The asshole had brought a dagger, the deep laceration on his shoulder testimony to the fact. On the bright side, at least the wizard put up some fight. They had a whole two rounds before Gunz dropped him to the floor with his neck broken.

He headed to the tiny bathroom and came back with a first aid kit. He pulled out a few sealed packages with alcohol gauzes, a few large band-aids and a surgical kit, placing everything on a small cabinet next to the mirror. Then he grabbed an opened bottle of vodka from the table and took a few large swigs. It wasn't going to help him with the pain, but he hoped it would numb his senses at least a little.

With habitual quick moves, Gunz ripped the sealed package and cleaned the affected area with an alcohol gauze. He grabbed the surgical stapler from the box and checked his wound again. *No more than five staples,* he decided, pulling the edges of the laceration together. He finished closing his wound as quickly as he could, clenching his teeth to stop himself from screaming every time the metal staple penetrated his skin. Once finished, he placed a waterproof band-aid over it.

Just as he was ready to go into the bathroom, he heard a soft popping noise and Mishka, his wyvern, materialized between him and the mirror. The wyvern peered down at the bloodied gauzes with disgust and shook his flaming head.

"Why are you doing it, boss?" he asked, landing on the cabinet.

"Doing what?"

"This." The wyvern pointed at the surgical instruments with his paw. "All you need to do is revert into your natural state and you'll heal yourself. No mess, no blood, no pain."

"I can't revert. It'll create a huge magical energy spike," explained Gunz, heading toward the bathroom. "No one here can know that I'm a Fire Salamander."

"Well, that's kinda stupid," muttered Mishka. "What's the point of being the Fire Salamander if you can't actually use the perks?"

Gunz decided the safest course of action would be not

answering. He opened the hot water and stepped into a questionably-looking bathtub. The water was slightly above room temperature at best which added to his overall misery. He gritted his teeth and quickly washed the blood and dirt off his face and body. Still shivering, he toweled himself dry and got dressed for the night.

He turned the light off and lay down on the bed. His whole body was sore and buzzing with exhaustion. Although he closed his eyes, sleep eluded him as always. Mishka landed on the bed next to him and gently sprayed him with fire, channeling some of his elemental energy through him.

"It's not going to heal your wounds," said Mishka, "but it'll take the edge off your pain, so you can get some sleep."

"Thank you, my friend," said Gunz, petting the wyvern's back. "I don't mind physical pain… It numbs down the other one…"

"What other one?" asked Mishka, cocking his head.

"The pain that's here… always…" mumbled Gunz, pressing his hand to his chest.

"People are such strange creatures…" Mishka muttered with a half-shrug of his wings.

With the wyvern's help, he slowly started to drift off to sleep when his cell phone rang. *Who the hell is calling me at this late hour?* Gunz cursed, searching for the phone with his hand without opening his eyes, as aggravation spiraled through him. He found it and checked the screen. He saw Jim's name and sighed. He was just starting to fall asleep, too. *Why me? Dammit, Jim!* He swiped his finger across the screen, answering the call.

"Jim, do you know what time it is?" he mumbled drowsily, closing his eyes again.

"What's the difference? You're not sleeping anyway," replied Jim dryly. "And I would rather be in a dental chair right now than be calling you, asshole!" He took a short pause, breathing heavily into his phone. "Anyway, there is someone here who wants to hear your voice. Hold on, I'll put you on speaker."

A soft knock announced that Jim put the phone on a table.

"Gunz?"

Gunz heard Mrak Delar's voice and cringed. "Mrak? What are you doing in Jim's office?"

"Where are you, Gunz?" asked Mrak Delar. "Why can't I sense you anywhere in this world? Why do I have to use this mundane device to communicate with you?"

"Because I don't want to be found," replied Gunz, remorse twisting his heart. Mrak was his friend; one who truly cared for him. "I'm okay. Don't worry and don't look for me."

"When did you learn how to hide your elemental energy signature?" asked Mrak Delar, the surprise clear in his voice.

"I guess all those hours in different libraries paid off. I learned many interesting things."

"Gunz, you must come back," insisted Mrak Delar.

"No. I'm not coming back until I'm done. You can't force me, Mrak."

"Yes, I can. I'm a Master of Power, Gunz, and you know that I can control you," said Mrak Delar calmly, but his voice was infused with suppressed anger. "I will find you eventually, and when I do, mark my word, I'll twist you into a pretzel for what you did to Kal."

"What the hell are you talking about, Master? I didn't do anything to Kal," yelled Gunz, the leftover of his sleep gone now. "How about what he did to me, Mrak! Jeez, man, do not make me hang up on you!"

"Hang up?" asked Mrak Delar, sounding lost. Gunz heard Jim's quick explanation on what "hang up" meant and Mrak came back to the phone, his voice a low growl. "Don't you dare hang up on me. Kal blames himself for everything that's happened. For the loss you suffered, for your disappearance, for your pain. For everything, you jackass! You need to go back to Kendral and at least speak with him."

"I can't, Mrak, I'm sorry. I need to finish what I started first," replied Gunz. "I'm getting close—"

"Close to what? What is so important that you dropped everything and everyone who loves you and disappeared without a word?" yelled Mrak Delar. "Even Akira doesn't know where you are, and you swore to her that you'd find her son! Since when did you stop caring about your friends! It's been six months since you disappeared, Gunz. Six goddamn months!"

"That's exactly what I'm working on!" shouted Gunz, jolting off the bed with the phone in his hand. "I am searching for Akira's son. And tomorrow I have a private audience with a person who might help me find him. I need you to back off and give me time and space to do my goddamn job!"

"Where are you, boy?" growled Mrak Delar and Gunz heard him slamming his hand on the wall. "You can't do it alone. And most importantly, you shouldn't be doing it alone. Yaroslav is not a newborn. He's an ancient vampire and quite a capable fighter. Whoever managed to hold him captive is extremely powerful and dangerous. Please, Gunz. You know that I'm not the type to beg anyone for anything, but right now, I'm begging you… please… let me in. Let me help you."

Gunz fell silent, uncomfortably twisting the phone in his hands. He heard Jim talking to Mrak Delar, explaining to him that there was no way he could find him using mundane methods, saying he already tried, and failed.

"Mrak," called Gunz.

"I'm here…"

"Mrak, can you please tell Kal you spoke with me? Please tell him I don't blame him for anything. He did what he thought was right." Guns swallowed hard, sadness gripping his chest. "Tell him he is the only Father I've ever had, and nothing can ever change that. I'll return to him as soon as I can. Can you tell him that?"

"Yes, of course, but—"

"Tell Akira I'm not coming back without Yaroslav," continued Gunz. "I gave her my word and I intend to keep it."

"But, Gunz—"

"No buts, Mrak," said Gunz firmly. "I'm here undercover. Jim can explain to you what it means. And if everything works out well tomorrow, I may need to go deeper down this rabbit hole. If I do, you won't be able to call me on this phone anymore."

"Gunz, don't be an idiot!" Gunz heard Jim's voice. The agent sounded terrified, which was unlike him. "Please tell me you are not trying to find your way into the captive circles. Please, Gunz, if that's what you're planning to do, you need to stop. There is no way out of there."

"Don't worry, Jim, I'm not planning to do that," said Gunz and cursed quietly at how unconvincing his voice sounded.

"He's lying," said Mrak Delar flatly.

"No shit," muttered Jim.

"Yes, I am lying," confirmed Gunz, shame coiling within him, "and I'm sorry about that. I'm lying because I have no idea what I will need to do to find Yaroslav, and if penetrating the captive circles is what needs to be done, I'll do it."

"No, Gunz! That's an order!" yelled Jim. "The only way you can get into the captive circles is by becoming a captive fighter. One thing is you going undercover as an unattached fighter, but captive? No! You hear me? NO! You have no idea what that means and what you will have to endure to survive it!"

"Jim, you can't order me. I'm not one of your FBI agents," said Gunz bluntly. "Mrak, I was happy to hear your voice. Please talk with Kal for me and I'll be back in Kendral as soon as I can. Now, I need to try and get some sleep. Don't worry about me and don't look for me. I'll be fine."

He hung up the phone before Mrak Delar or Jim could say

anything else. For a few minutes, he sat on the bed, staring at the dark screen of his phone, feeling numb and tired. Then he put the phone away and lay down, folding his hands on his stomach.

Can someone knock me out? I need some sleep...

CHAPTER 3

~ ZANE BURNS, A.K.A. GUNZ ~

Gunz ran his fingers over the stubble on his chin. It felt soft, more like a beard than a stubble. He pulled out a razor blade and shaving cream, thinking he should probably shave for his dinner with the Head of House. As he squeezed some of the shaving cream on his fingers, he caught his reflection in the mirror and shuddered. He could hardly recognize the man staring back at him – a hardened face with icy blue eyes, a deep vertical crease between his eyebrows and mouth set in a hard line.

Eight months had passed since the fight at Mount Karasova. Eight months since he had lost Angelique, yet he still couldn't forgive himself for what happened to her, reliving the horrors of that fight over and over every time when he closed his eyes. She wasn't dead. He couldn't force himself into believing she was. If Death himself couldn't find her soul in any of his domains, she still had to be alive. Nevertheless, all the research he had done, had brought no results.

Was she still alive somewhere? He couldn't find a definitive answer to that question and it was tormenting him day and night. He couldn't find a way to counteract her spell and separate her essence from Zmey's either. On top of it, he was tired of listening to his friends who were telling him it wasn't possible, that he must take his time grieving and move on.

Gunz had never been a social butterfly. He would much rather spend his time alone on a canal or lake with a fishing pole in his hands than at a noisy party. However, he had a few people in his life who he considered his friends and he treasured their company and attention. After what had happened at Mount Karasova, he wanted to be alone, so when Jim asked him for help in penetrating the ring of underground supernatural fighting circles, he jumped at that assignment.

The only way to numb his constantly aching heart was to get busy and submerge himself in his work. He did enough fighting with monsters while he was patrolling the streets of the city anyway, so fighting with the monsters inside a cage wasn't that much different. The only difference was that the fights in the cage were scheduled and consistent. In the cage, he would get what he needed every day – silence around him and oblivion, even if for a short while only. During a fight, you couldn't think of anything but the fight.

But that wasn't the only reason he took this assignment. Akira, the powerful queen of vampires, lost her son, Yaroslav. Gunz had an unorthodox relationship with the Scarlet Queen. It had all started with her offer to teach him sword skills, but with time it turned into something closer to a friendship. Besides, both Akira and Yaroslav helped them to protect the city during the attack eight months ago. As strange as it sounded, the Scarlet Queen was trying to keep her subjects in check and humans safe in her territory.

And now, when Akira's son was missing, he couldn't leave her without help. Gunz and Akira had done a lot of digging and both had come to the conclusion that Yaroslav was taken by one of the underground supernatural fighting Houses. In the Unites States, there were fifty major Houses – one in each state. Each House had two types of supernatural fighters working for them – unattached and captive.

The unattached fighters were free to come and go as they please and they were always searching for better fighting events where they could make more money. It wasn't unusual for them to move from House to House, as long as the Heads of Houses would take them in. The captive fighters were treated more like slaves, completely subjugated and powerless against their captors.

Some of the Heads of Houses were pureblood humans, but others were members of the supernatural community with magic of their own. Human elite and some rich people with supernatural abilities paid huge sums of money to watch the fights and bet on their outcome. The Heads of Houses were basking in money. Cold and indifferent to everything besides their bottom-line, they didn't care how many supernatural fighters were killed during the brutal combats. After all – the fighters were nothing but low-life monsters no one was missing, and the Heads of Houses thought they were doing humanity a favor by keeping them off the streets.

If Yaroslav was held captive, Gunz couldn't leave him in this situation. After a few months of fighting in the underground pits as an unattached fighter, he had finally heard something that made him believe Yaroslav was indeed fighting as a captive fighter for the California House. It was nothing but some stories and gossips about an undefeated California captive who was a tall vampire with long blond hair. The fighters were whispering it in dark corners, repeating it over and over and every time the story seemed to change a little. It was all Gunz had for now, which was better than nothing.

Now, getting from the Florida fighting pits into California's and penetrating the captive circles, that was another matter entirely and he wasn't sure he could easily do it. Also, he wasn't a hundred percent sure that the fighter he heard of was indeed Yaroslav and was hoping to confirm this thought during dinner with Mr. Kogan.

Gunz took a quick shower in unpleasant cold water and got dressed. Just as he finished, he heard a soft knock on his door. He opened the door and found Mr. Kogan's bodyguard towering in the doorframe, his square shoulders covering most of the view. The bodyguard glanced down at Gunz with a smirk and stepped aside.

"Gunz?" he asked.

"Yes. Were you expecting someone else?" *As if he doesn't know*, thought Gunz, suppressing the desire to wipe the arrogant smirk right off the face of the giant.

"Mr. Kogan is expecting you." He pointed at the black limo parked on the parking lot in front of his motel.

It was quite unusual to see a new car, much less a limo, in this area, and Gunz decided to move quickly so he wouldn't attract too much attention. He followed the bodyguard to the limo where the giant jackass opened the back door for him with the same arrogant smirk on his face and it took Gunz all his resolve not to knock his teeth out.

Gunz went into the limo and sat down across from Mr. Kogan. The Head of House was dressed in an expensive pinstripe suit and a white shirt with a black tie, looking as immaculate as ever. He glanced at Gunz's plain black jeans and shirt and a light smile crossed his face. Gunz noticed that and cringed inside.

"Sorry, sir, I don't own a suit," he said calmly. "I hope the way I'm dressed is not a problem."

"No problem whatsoever," said Mr. Kogan, chuckling. "At first, I was going to take you to a restaurant, but then I thought that you would feel a lot more comfortable if we had dinner in the privacy of my mansion. I hope you don't mind."

Gunz noticed that whenever Mr. Kogan felt uncomfortable, he chuckled. "I don't mind, sir. After all, it's your treat, your choice of venue. But since we're outside the pits and there is no one here, let's be honest," said Gunz with a lopsided smirk. "The real reason you decided to take me to your home is because *you* would feel uncomfortable being seen in the company of one of your fighters. Am I correct?"

Mr. Kogan stared at him for a moment, his mouth open, then he chuckled again, shaking his head. "A fighter who has brains. Go figure," he muttered, giving Gunz a quick tap on his shoulder. "I do like you, Gunz."

"Thanks, I guess," replied Gunz, leaning back against the soft leather seat.

"Let me ask you, Gunz, where did you learn to fight like this?" asked Mr. Kogan, also relaxing in his seat. "I've never seen anyone as powerful and brutal in hand-to-hand combat as you are. And that's without using your magic."

"Many different places, sir," replied Gunz evasively, lowering his eyes.

"Have you served?"

"Yes, sir."

"I thought as much," continued Mr. Kogan with a light flick of his hand. "The way you address me, the way you move. It shows. Is that where you learned to fight? The military?"

"No, sir. I did learn a few things while I served, but mostly – in many different places."

"I guess, you're not going to let me ask you any personal questions, are you?" Mr. Kogan chuckled again, but it wasn't his usual uncomfortable chuckle. His smile seemed to be genuine and openhearted.

"You can ask all the questions you want, sir. I can't stop you," replied Gunz with a shrug, "but most likely, I'm not going to answer."

Mr. Kogan raised his eyebrows, staring at Gunz with amusement. "You know, I've never had such an interesting fighter working for me," he said folding his arms. He was about to say something else when the car came to a screeching halt.

Gunz heard a light noise outside and frowned. The noise was so soft that a normal person wouldn't notice, but to him it sounded like an alarm bell. "Are we at your house, sir?" he asked quietly. Mr. Kogan peeked outside and shook his head no, his face a sickening gray color.

Gunz extended his senses probing the area around the car. He could sense three people standing in front of the limo and one at the front passenger side. He didn't have a lot of time for more observations as the dry click of a cocked weapon reached his ears. He seized Mr. Kogan's shoulder, roughly pushing him to the floor.

"Stay here and don't move until I come back for you," he hissed. Reaching into his pocket, he pulled his knife and turned it into the sword. Gunz opened the door on the driver's side and quietly slipped out of the limo. He opened his sight and registered that the attackers weren't human. All four of them were demons.

Stealthily, he moved along the length of the limo and carefully peeked inside the driver's window. Both the driver and the bodyguard were dead, their throats cut so skillfully that they didn't have a chance to scream, let alone fight back.

Gunz walked out into the open and halted in front of the car, touching the nearest demon with his sword. All three of them spun around and glared at him. He felt the nauseating touch of their demonic energy as they scanned him, and identical wolfish snarls stretched their lips. One of them whistled and the fourth demon joined them.

"What do we have here?" said the fourth demon, stepping

closer to Gunz. "An itty-bitty wizard who brought a knife to a gun fight. Hey boy, your magical energy signature is so feeble, I wonder if you even know that you're a wizard. Well, let me be the one to tell you – you're a wizard, Harry!"

Gunz cocked his head, staring at the demon with a crooked grin. "Thanks, bro, I had no idea."

He extended his clenched fist forward and slowly unlocked his fingers, one at a time. An energy orb, crackling with blue electrical discharges, twirled in the palm of his hand. The demon gasped but had no time to react. Gunz pushed the energy orb through the demon's chest. The monster yelped and collapsed, a bleeding, gaping hole in his chest. A dark shadow separated from the dead body and shimmered into the ground.

The other three demons shouted all at once and charged Gunz, their rage making them forget about caution. Gunz touched the blade of his sword and whispered, *"Ignius."* The blade went up in flames and he laughed, basking in the energy of his element.

He swung his flaming sword, decapitating the nearest demon. With his arms outstretched, one of the remaining two demons jumped on his back, dragging him down to the ground as he landed on his shoulders. Quickly regrouping, Gunz rolled to his side and conjured a fireball. As the demon started to rise, he propelled the fireball at him. The fire reached the target, setting the demon ablaze.

The last demon stared at Gunz, his eyes wide with fear. He took a step back and raised his hands up. Gunz quickly closed the distance between them and seized the demon's shirt with one hand, lifting him slightly off the ground.

"Who sent you?" hissed Gunz, putting the tip of his blade under the demon's jaw.

"If I tell you, he'll kill me," the bug-eyed demon managed to say.

Gunz laughed coldly. "And what do you think I'm going to do if you don't tell me what I want to know?"

The demon squirmed in his grip, and Gunz applied some pressure on his sword, drawing a few drops of blood.

"Sorry, but he's a lot scarier than you," hissed the demon. The dark shadow separated from the body and the demon shimmered away, leaving the silent dead body behind.

"Dammit," Gunz hissed, dropping the corps to the ground.

He found Mr. Kogan still crouching on the floor of the limo. When he opened the door, the older man gasped and turned around sharply, his face locked in fear.

"It just me," said Gunz, shaking the dirt off his clothes. "You're safe now, sir, but both your driver and your bodyguard were killed by the attackers."

Mr. Kogan climbed out of the limo and walked around. He stopped in front of the car, observing four dead demons in disbelief.

"You killed the four of them? Alone?" he whispered, raising his eyes at Gunz.

"Yes, sir," replied Gunz. He pulled the bodies of the bodyguard and the driver out of the limo and looked at the Head of House. "What do you want me to do with the bodies? I can burn them."

"That won't be necessary," mumbled Mr. Kogan. "Just pull them into the shrubbery and I'll send the cleaners over."

Gunz touched his sword, turning it back into a knife and hid it in his pocket. Then he pulled the corpses to the side of the road, camouflaging them in the shrubbery and headed back to the limo. He opened the back passenger door, gesturing at Mr. Kogan to get in.

"Have a seat, Mr. Kogan," he said with an encouraging smile. "Seems that tonight, I'll be your driver and your bodyguard."

"If you don't mind, I would prefer to ride in front, with you," said Mr. Kogan, still a little shaken after everything that had just happened.

Gunz silently opened the front passenger door, letting him in. As he started to drive away, Mr. Kogan pulled his phone out and made a call, ordering the cleaners. Then he gave Gunz the directions to his house and finally relaxed in his seat.

"Sir, do you know who would want to send four demons after you?" asked Gunz without looking at the Head of Florida House.

Mr. Kogan shrugged. "Competition. Possibly, someone from the other House wants to encroach on my territory." He thought for a moment and then stared at Gunz with narrowed eyes. "Or it's possible that these demons were sent after you, not after me."

"I'm no one," said Gunz, shaking his head. "Why would anyone want to send assassins after me?"

"Maybe you *were* no one, but not anymore," objected Mr. Kogan. "I'm sure word of your victories in the pits and your fighting style spread around. Any Head of any House would love to have you as their captive."

"Captive?" Gunz frowned.

"Yes, a captive fighter," repeated Mr. Kogan. "A fighter with your skills is priceless as a captive. Just think about it. Fights in the captive circles are a lot more profitable. Besides, I don't have to pay the captive fighters, and I don't have to worry they will leave me to work for my competition. So, yeah... A fighter like you is worth his weight in gold as a captive."

So is a fighter like Yaroslav, thought Gunz, furiously squeezing the steering wheel.

A few minutes later, Gunz drove through the gates and stopped the car in front of the entrance into a large Victorian style mansion. With his thoughts on Yaroslav's situation, he threw a quick glance at it and smirked, rolling his eyes at its splendor. The Head of Florida House didn't feel shy about showing off his wealth, built on blood and sweat of his fighters. He walked around the limo and opened the door for Mr. Kogan. The man walked out of the car and gave him an appraising once-over.

"I've never thought of you this way, but I'm sure many would kill to have you as their captive." He chuckled and headed toward the entrance.

CHAPTER 4

~ ZANE BURNS, A.K.A. GUNZ ~

"Would you like to change into something... fresher?" offered Mr. Kogan as soon as they walked inside.

"No, thank you," replied Gunz, giving a quick once-over to his reflection in the large mirrored wall. "I just need a few minutes to clean up."

"First door on the right," said Mr. Kogan pointing in the direction of the washroom. "My butler will show you to the dining room once you're done."

Gunz walked into the washroom, which was bigger than his entire motel room, and stopped in front of the mirror. His shirt was covered in road dirt. He pulled it off and cleaned it the best he could. Then he washed his face and his hands. The dirty brown water ran down the sink, marring its pearly-white surface.

He wiped his hands and face with a paper towel, throwing it in a garbage basket and stared into the mirror, thinking about everything that just happened. Mr. Kogan's words flashed in his mind, resonating with shock. Since the last few months he spent fighting in the pits, he knew there were captive circles where fighters were treated as slaves and if

Yaroslav was there, he was willing to do almost anything to get him out.

Nevertheless, it never crossed his mind that someone would try to capture him. Possibly because he was a young modern man, the idea of slavery didn't feel as something real to him. Even though he knew that slavery was still a real problem in this world, and not only in the illegal supernatural fighting pits, it was still hard for him to accept.

"I've never thought of you this way, but I'm sure, many would kill to have you as their captive." Gunz remembered the words Mr. Kogan said and shuddered, wondering if he was truly safe in Mr. Kogan's house now that he thought of him as a possible captive fighter. Would the Head of Florida House cross the line and betray his guest's trust? Gunz wasn't sure, because as nice as Mr. Kogan was to him, it was possible. After all, it was money that ruled his world, not honor. People like him were capable of pretty much anything.

I better watch my back, decided Gunz, heading out of the washroom.

THE DINING ROOM WAS A LARGE, sunlit space with tall windows adorned by light chiffon panels and valances. An enormous glass dining room table stood in the middle of the room with a contemporary stylish crystal chandelier hanging above it. The dining table was large enough to sit at least twenty people, but it was set only for three.

"Please, sit down, Gunz. Make yourself comfortable," offered Mr. Kogan rising and gesturing at an empty chair on his left. "We just need to wait for Clarissa a few minutes. You know how women are… They never have anything to wear and their makeup takes forever to put on."

Gunz smirked, thinking that Mrs. Kogan would probably

prefer wearing nothing when in his company but wisely decided not to say anything. Mr. Kogan noticed his reaction and his colorless lips stretched into a stiff smile. He chuckled uncomfortably.

"I know what you think, Gunz. I don't really care what she does. So, if you want to, you can give her what she wants."

"That would be hardly appropriate, sir. Even if your wife's morals are flexible enough to openly cheat on her husband, mine are not."

"Spoken like a true warrior." Mr. Kogan chuckled his uncomfortable chuckle. "Anyway, Gunz… Sometimes I wish I knew your real name."

"You do," replied Gunz with a shrug. "Gunz is my real name, not something I came up with for the fighting pits."

Mr. Kogan gaped at him for a moment, his eyebrows slowly climbing up. "I've been in the world of supernatural fighting for years, and I must tell you – you're quite a unique young man." He lowered his eyes for a moment and then continued, "Anyway, Gunz, as you're well aware, my bodyguard is dead, and I was wondering if you'd like to take that position. I would feel a lot more comfortable with you by my side. Of course, I will compensate you generously."

Now it was Gunz's turn to get surprised. "I thought I was your biggest moneymaker."

"You are. But what good is money if I'm dead?"

Gunz thought for a moment, all sort of different thoughts and scenarios flashing through his mind. Being the Head of House's bodyguard wouldn't get him where he needed to be. Mr. Kogan never travelled with his fighters outside the state, instead, sending his representative anytime they were challenged to a fight elsewhere. If Yaroslav was indeed a captive fighter in California, he needed to travel there, which would become impossible if he was tied up to his boss in Florida.

The other problem, the captive fights were highly-secretive

lockdown events. Only people who paid to attend, the Heads of Houses or their representatives, and the captive fighters were allowed to be present during the fight. Bodyguards or any other service staff weren't allowed inside. To buy a ticket for this kind of event wasn't easy either. On top of being absurdly expensive, a person had to be recommended by someone with the right reputation to get an invitation in the first place.

Out of all his friends, the only person who possibly had a chance to get invited to this kind of event was Aidan McGrath. He had a certain reputation in the supernatural circles and enough money to afford a ticket. Based on his past experience, Gunz didn't want to get any of his friends involved. This could get messy and he couldn't risk the wellbeing of people he cared about.

"I appreciate the offer, but I have to respectfully decline, sir," he said finally. "I want to remain in your House, fighting for you. But if you ever need my services outside the pits, you can always call me."

"Why don't you think about it a little more, Gunz. Sleep on it," said Mr. Kogan rising.

Gunz saw Clarissa Kogan walk into the dining room and also got up. She wore a long silver dress that seemed to expose more of her skin than it was covering. She circled Gunz, running her fingers over his shoulders as she passed by and approached her husband giving him a quick high society airpeck on his hollow cheek. Mr. Kogan pulled a chair back, helping his wife to sit down and waved his hand at a young man who was standing by the wall. The server brought the soup, placing the hot bowls carefully on their plates.

"Well, darling," he said to his wife, dipping the spoon into his soup, "I was just asking our guest why he is so set on continuing to fight. After all, one day he may meet an opponent who is faster, better and stronger than him. Meeting an opponent like that could cost him his young life."

"Young?" Clarissa glanced at Gunz undressing him with her eyes, a hungry smile on her lips. "Yes, darling, I would like to know that too."

Gunz shrugged. "Death doesn't scare me. I've being looking for an opponent like that since I started fighting in the pits. So far, I haven't found one, but I've heard of a fighter on the west coast. California House, I believe. A vampire who never lost a fight, so far. I would love to meet him in a cage one night. I'm sure a match like this would bring a lot of money and fame to your House, sir."

"If you win," pointed out Mr. Kogan dryly. "I think I know which fighter you're talking about—"

"Is he talking about... Alucard?" whispered Clarissa, her fingers squeezing the napkin on her lap. Mr. Kogan gave her a warning stare.

"Alucard?" repeated Gunz. "Like a Netflix cartoon character? Or that vampire from the Castlevania video game?"

Mr. Kogan frowned at his wife, shaking his head reproachfully. "Yes, something like that. I've heard of this fighter too. He's an ancient vampire, tall with long blond hair and his weapon of choice is the katana. So, the nickname Alucard seemed to be appropriate."

Yaroslav... It has to be him...

Gunz took a deep breath to keep his emotions at bay. It wasn't easy for him to constantly keep his power shadowed and when he became emotional it was even harder.

"Is it possible to set up a match between Alucard and me?" he asked, hoping he looked calm and indifferent enough not to arise any suspicions in Mr. Kogan. "I would love to try my skills against a worthy opponent like him."

"No," Mr. Kogan cut him off, switching his attention to his meal. His mood seemed to decline drastically. He tried his soup and threw the spoon back into the plate, splashing the liquid around. He turned to the server, frowning. "This soup is too hot. It's impossible to eat."

Gunz smirked, putting a spoonful of hot soup in his mouth. "Seems okay to me."

Mr. Kogan chuckled nervously. "Always trying to prove your superiority, aren't you?" he asked, waving at the server to stay back.

"Not at all, but this soup is delicious," replied Gunz, nonchalantly. "So, why can't you set up a match with a fighter from out of state? We had matches before with the Georgia House and with the fighters from Texas. Why not with California?"

"Multiple reasons," replied Mr. Kogan, twisting the spoon in his fingers. "But the main reason why a fight like this is not possible is because Alucard is a captive fighter. You two are fighting in different circles. You'll never meet him in the cage, Gunz. Get this idea out of your head."

"I understand, sir." Gunz nodded and bowed his head to his chest, appearing crestfallen.

"And if you're thinking about going to California and approaching the Head of House, don't," warned Mr. Kogan. "The only way you will ever fight Alucard is if you become a captive fighter, and from what I hear, the new Head of California House is quite brutal with his captives. You don't want to experience that kind of abuse, trust me."

Clarissa got up and walked around the table, halting behind Gunz's back. She put her hands on his shoulders, gently massaging him. Gunz stiffened under her touch. He threw an uncomfortable glance at Mr. Kogan and lowered his eyes.

"Why, darling," purred Clarissa, staring at her husband. "You got our guest so upset. I believe the match between Alucard and Gunz is possible. All Gunz has to do is become *your* captive fighter. If he agrees to that, you can always approach the new Head of California House. I'm sure, he wouldn't object to the idea, as both Gunz and Alucard have quite a reputation in their fighting circles."

Mr. Kogan waved his hand at the server, asking to bring the main course. "Gunz, don't listen to her," he said, frowning at his wife whose hands sneaked under Gunz's shirt and were now slowly traveling down his chest. "I actually like you, young man. I wouldn't want to submit you to a life of a captive fighter. You're making tons of money for me as an unattached fighter. I'm happy with that and don't want to change anything."

Gunz seized Clarissa's exploring hands, taking them off his chest. "I understand, sir. You don't want to take a chance with your bottom-line."

"Darling, come on. Make it happen," whined Clarissa, her hands back on Gunz's shoulders. "I would love to watch him fight that blond vampire. Imagine that... Two wild beasts, tearing at each other's throats. Ahhh... It would be a breathtaking show." Her breath quickened, her fingers with silver manicured nails digging into Gunz's shoulders in ecstasy. "Just imagine how much people would pay to see the two best fighters of the country clash in mortal combat. Two monsters enter, one monster leaves... You and that new Head of Californian House, whatchamacallit... never mind. Between the entry fees and the bets, you both would make millions on a single fight, regardless of the outcome of the event. Tell me, is it not worth the risk?"

"Dammit, Clarissa!" yelled Mr. Kogan, slamming his hand on the table. His fork and knife jumped up and landed with a loud jingle. "You really want to get into his pants so much? If you want to screw him, just tell him and pray he wouldn't mind giving you want you want. Don't push him into slavery!"

"Ugh!" Clarissa stamped her foot and marched back to her chair.

Gunz averted his eyes and got busy with his food. They finished the main course in silence with Clarissa throwing angry scowls at her husband. After the dessert, she slammed her napkin on the table and turned to Mr. Kogan, aggravation in her every move.

"I don't understand you, Robert," she shouted, her hands on her hips. "If he wants to fight Alucard, then make it happen. It would be great exposure and money for our House. If you're so afraid to submit him to slavery, then don't. Just make it look like he is your captive for the outside world. No one needs to know what you do with him behind these walls. You can treat him like a member of your family for all I care! I want to see him fight that vampire!" She stomped her foot, pouting like a little girl and stormed out of the room.

Mr. Kogan sighed and threw his hands in the air. "She can be impossible when she wants something. And I hate to admit it, but she has a valid point." He sighed. "So, what do you think, Gunz?"

"I don't know what to think," replied Gunz, taking the napkin off his lap and carefully placing it on the table. "I'll be honest with you. I do want to fight that vampire, but the word *slavery* terrifies me, sir."

"Since we are on the honest streak here, I will disclose everything you may need to know before making the decision," said Mr. Kogan rising. "Follow me, please."

They walked through the house into the garage. At least ten cars were parked there, varying from antique models to modern vehicles that cost more than some people's houses. Mr. Kogan sat down in a golf cart, asking Gunz to join him. For a while, Mr. Kogan drove him through the dark park that was surrounding the mansion. He stopped in front of a small enclosure which looked like an oversized toolshed.

Gunz followed Mr. Kogan inside the toolshed and his jaw dropped. He was standing in a small room filled to the top with state-of-the-art modern technology and security devices. Two giant security guards were manning the equipment, staring unblinkingly into the monitors. They didn't move and didn't turn away from the monitors even when their boss walked in.

Mr. Kogan waved at Gunz to come closer to the monitors. Gunz peered at the screen and his throat tightened. On every monitor, he saw a small room with a man inside. Each room was sparsely furnished, just enough to attend to the basic needs. Although the rooms didn't look like cages or musty dungeons and there were no chains or handcuffs, there was no mistaking in what they were – prison cells designed to keep the inhabitants securely locked in.

"These are my captive fighters," said Mr. Kogan quietly. "I don't love the idea of treating the fighters as slaves or animals, even though some of them are true monsters. But I wouldn't be able to hold my position in the House if I didn't have a solid representation in the Captive circles. So, I do own a few captive fighters, and I try to treat them as humanely as possible." He turned to the guards and ordered, "Let us in, please."

The guard pushed a button and a small door opened up in the left wall of the room. Mr. Kogan walked through the doorway, asking Gunz to follow him. He went down a narrow staircase and ended up in a large underground facility with multiple locked rooms. Each room had a see-through wall designed like the mirrored window in police interrogation rooms. A few guards were stationed inside the facility to monitor the fighters day and night.

Gunz walked closer to one of the see-through walls and touched it. Then he turned to face Mr. Kogan. "You run tight security here," he said quietly. "At least you don't keep them in chains…"

"I do," objected Mr. Kogan. "But with these monsters, you can't use mundane restraints. The chains we use are magical, and since I promised full disclosure, allow me to show you."

He headed to the table where the guards were sitting. "I need a controller for fighter #303, please," he said to the guards. The guard gave him a small plastic device that looked like a TV remote. "Fighter #303 is a wizard, but unlike you, his strength lies in the dark arts. Nevertheless, he's been serving my House for a number of years and I trust him a little more than the others. I'm going to use him to show you what I am talking about."

He clicked the green button on the controller and the door into one of the rooms unlocked. Mr. Kogan walked inside and Gunz followed him. As soon as they walked in, the man inside got off the bed and lowered himself to his knees, bowing his head to his chest.

"Master," he said, without raising his eyes, "what can I do for you?"

"No need to kneel, Rand." Mr. Kogan approached him with a friendly smile and helped him up. "This is Gunz, my unattached fighter, and I wanted to show him a few things."

Rand threw a heavy look at Gunz and a hardly visible dark smirk curved his lips. Mr. Kogan seized Rand's chin with his fingers and lifted his head up. Now, Gunz could see a thin metallic collar around his neck.

"What do you sense, Gunz?" asked Mr. Kogan.

Gunz carefully scanned Rand with his magical sight. "He is a powerful dark wizard, sir," he said flatly, "but I don't think he can access his magic. It seems to be blocked."

"That's correct," confirmed Mr. Kogan. "This collar, in combination with four bracelets locked around his wrists and ankles, keep him under control and his magic locked."

"Wait," said Gunz, cold sweat running down his back. "Are you using gray stones to lock his magic, creating an inverted pentagram? Is that how these devices keep him under control?"

Gray stones were a powerful natural artifact that could drain magic and power out of anyone who came in contact with them, and the more powerful the person was, the worse these stones affected them. Gunz shuddered as the memory of his first encounter with gray stones magic popped up in his mind.

"You're quite knowledgeable for your age, Gunz," said Mr. Kogan, giving him a narrowed-eye stare. "Yes, I'm using gray stones, but not full ones. That would be too painful for my captives. I'm using dust of gray stones and trust me – it works like a charm." He showed him the controller he was holding in his hands. "Depending on the settings of this controlling device, I can change the effect of gray stone magic on the fighter, giving him a certain level of access to own magic or removing it completely and bringing him down to his knees. Watch this."

He pushed on a button on the very left side of the controller and Gunz could feel the magical energy rise around Rand. The fighter closed his eyes and inhaled, visibly enjoying the feeling of magic rushing through his body. His face, disfigured by multiple ugly scars, relaxed as the dark aura of his magic rose around his body like a glowing cloud.

"Now, watch what happens to him when I bring the magic of the stones to the maximum." Mr. Kogan moved his finger to the very right button on the remote.

"No, please!" Rand and Gunz yelled at the same time, but Mr. Kogan had pressed the button already.

Rand screamed. His body convulsed like from an electric shock and he dropped to the floor, his face contorted by pain.

"Please stop," said Gunz, his hands tightened into fists. "You didn't have to show this to me. I already know how the inverted pentagram with the gray stones works. I saw it before and experienced the effects of gray stones magic myself."

Gunz turned around and walked out of the room. As he approached the desk, he planted both of his fists on it, and lowered his head, breathing heavily. He knew that if he decided to become a captive, it wouldn't be a walk in the park, but seeing the horrors of it firsthand, made his resolve waver.

Oh, God, is that what is done to Yaroslav? I need to get him out and back to safety, no matter what.

He felt a soft touch on his shoulder and straightened up, slowly turning around. "Is that how you force them into submission?" he asked, his voice painfully hoarse.

Mr. Kogan nodded. "Yes, and there are some other methods. I don't utilize them, but most of the other Houses do. Take for example this vampire you want to fight, Alucard. From what I've heard, it took the owner of the California House over a month to break him. Trust me, the methods he used were a lot more brutal than just gray stones. You probably don't want to know all of that."

Blood drained from Gunz's face and his eyes widened as he thought of the possible torture Yaroslav went through. Mr. Kogan observed him with his attentive eyes and pursed his lips. "Let's get out of here. We'll finish our conversation at home." He threw the controller on the desk and pulled Gunz toward the exit.

A FEW MINUTES LATER, Gunz was back in the dining room. The butler offered him something to drink and without thinking, he asked for vodka. The butler silently disappeared and came back right away with a shot glass filled with the clear liquid. He placed it on the table in front of Gunz and just as silently, disappeared from the room. Gunz brought the shot glass to his lips and flipped it upside down, swallowing the contents in one gulp.

Mr. Kogan walked back into the room and sat down across the table from Gunz. "Well, Gunz, you saw it all," he said calmly. "If you still want to fight the vampire, the only way you can do it is by becoming a captive fighter. So, what do you want to do?"

"Can I ask you a few questions, sir?" Gunz looked up at the Head of House, fighting his doubts.

"Of course, you can ask anything you wish to know, and I promise to be honest with you," said Mr. Kogan, leaning forward and lightly touching Gunz's hand.

"Let's say, I agree to become your captive fighter, would you keep me the way you keep the others? Imprisoned?"

"No, not all the time," replied Mr. Kogan with a half-shrug. "Just like my wife said, we will have to keep up the pretenses to the outside world, but once we're back on my property, you can pick any room in my mansion and stay there."

"To keep up appearances, what would I have to do?" asked Gunz, not quite sure he was ready to hear the answer to this question.

"There are a few conditions you'll have to agree to. You'll have to wear the collar and the bracelets. That's unavoidable. If you don't, no one will believe that you're my captive fighter. However, I will keep the influence of the stones on you to the minimum and will never use the controller on you," started Mr. Kogan. "Also, before the fight, the representative of the opposing House may visit me here and ask to see you. In that case, you will be locked up in the underground facility, like the rest of the fighters. For the duration of the visit only."

Gunz nodded, biting his lip. "Anything else?"

"You will have to participate in training with the other captive fighters. At least a few hours every day."

"That's not a problem," Gunz managed to say.

"When we're in public, you must address me and my wife as your masters. You saw the way Rand did that. And you must comply with all our orders."

"Dammit," muttered Gunz, rubbing his face tiredly. "You want me to kneel before you?"

"Only to keep up appearances when we're in the fighting pits or in front of people involved in the underground supernatural circles," replied Mr. Kogan with a dismissive wave of his hand. "I would never ask you to do something like that otherwise."

"What else do I need to know?"

"I think, that is it," said Mr. Kogan. Then he thought for a moment and added. "And my offer to take the bodyguard position is still open. Some of the owners do use their loyal captives as bodyguards. And even though it is quite rare, it's not unheard of."

"After I fight Alucard, if I survive this fight, would you set me free?" asked Gunz, everything inside him stretched to the limit.

"Of course," replied Mr. Kogan right away, notes of empathy in his voice. "I'll set you free at any time you wish, before or after the fight. All you need to do is ask for your freedom. After all, you're not going to be a true captive fighter. It's just going to be a pretense to get you this fight and get my wife off my back."

Mr. Kogan fell silent furrowing his brow, and Gunz was wondering what the Head of Florida House was thinking about. He shifted uncomfortably, not willing to interrupt the heavy silence in the room.

"Answer one question though," Mr. Kogan continued as suddenly as he stopped talking before, "and please answer it truthfully. After all, if we go for this deception, I will be endangering everything I built so far and more."

"Sure," replied Gunz, feeling numb all over, "what would you like to know?"

"Why is this fight so important to you? Why do you fight?"

Gunz hid his face in his hands and closed his eyes. Then he raised his head and sighed, quickly deciding to stick to the truth as close as possible.

"The only woman I ever loved was killed a few months ago. I failed to protect her," he said, the pain slowly flooding him. "Mr. Kogan, since that day, I can't live my life. I can't sleep and I can hardly eat. The only time I don't feel this gut-wrenching, all-consuming anguish in my soul is when I fight. And the more brutal the fight is, the better I feel… So, yeah… I am addicted to fighting like some junkie who's addicted to painkillers. I need an opponent who can stand his ground against me and give me these few minutes of peace."

"Oh, you poor boy," mumbled Mr. Kogan, sympathy reflected in his sunken eyes. "Sure, I'll do what I can to keep you fighting and to get you the fight with that vampire. Before I can set up the fight with Alucard, however, you'll need to win a few fights in the captive circles, so you'll be fighting a few nights every week. It'll keep you busy."

"Thank you, sir," said Gunz rising. "Can I think about all this before I give you the final answer?"

"Absolutely, take your time. After all, I'm completely satisfied with our status quo. If you wish to remain as my unattached fighter, I'll be more than happy to keep everything the way it is," said Mr. Kogan with a dismissive shrug. "I'll see you tomorrow after your fight and we can continue this conversation then. In the meantime, I'll get my other driver to take you to your motel."

Gunz thanked him one more time and followed the butler out of the mansion.

CHAPTER 5

~ ZANE BURNS, A.K.A. GUNZ ~

Gunz sat on the bed, hiding his face in his hands. This was the first time in the last few months he wished he had his friends with him. He knew what he had to do. He had been researching underground fighting circles for months and had come up with nothing until his recent conversation with Mr. Kogan. Now he was sure – the only way to get anywhere close to Yaroslav was for him to become a captive fighter.

But trusting a Head of House with his freedom and his life? That was crazy. No one in their right mind would trust a mobster who made money on the death and suffering of others, even if those others were supernatural monsters, most of them ruthless killers themselves.

"Mishka," Gunz called, lying back on the bed. The broken springs moaned under the weight of his body, poking him in the ribs.

"I'm here, boss." The wyvern was hovering above his face.

Gunz lifted his arm, inviting the wyvern to land on it. Mishka didn't make him wait, gently landing on his forearm. He softly stroked the wyvern's hot back with his fingers.

"What's going on, boss?" asked Mishka, shifting closer to Gunz's face. "Your unusual tenderness is unsettling."

Gunz sighed. "I'm about to do something extremely stupid and reckless," he said, closing his eyes.

"So, what else is new?" huffed the wyvern, his red eyes igniting with fire. "That's all you've been doing since I've met you. *Stupid and reckless* should be your middle name."

Gunz sat down, lowering the wyvern on the bed next to him. "Mishka, I am afraid," he said quietly. "I'm truly terrified of what I'm about to do."

"Let's circle back to the *stupid* part," muttered Mishka. "If you're so terrified – don't do it."

"I have no choice. I can't leave Yaroslav in the situation he is in right now," replied Gunz. "Unfortunately for me, this is the only way to save him."

"What's so stupid about saving a friend?" asked Mishka snidely, sarcasm overflowing. "Even if your friend is a few hundred-years old vamp who probably killed more people than you can count?"

"Ahh, Mishka, as usual, you're not helping," muttered Gunz.

"Was I supposed to?"

Gunz decided not to reply and continued, "The stupid and reckless part is that I have to trust a Head of the underground fighting House with my life and my freedom. And I'm scared because I know where drinking this Kool-Aid may take me."

Mishka flew off the bed, hovering up and down in front of his face. "Are you out of your friggin' mind, boss? You'll end up enslaved, fighting for the amusement of rich assholes, humans and otherwise! And what's even worse, you'll end up pulling me down with you."

"Aren't you a ray of sunshine," muttered Gunz, shaking his head. "Way to go, Mr. Positive."

"Let me ask you something else," continued Mishka, angrily spitting tiny fireballs with every word. "Let's assume for a moment this low-life mobster is not going to betray you and sell you to the highest bidder – which is very unlikely I must say. But for the fun of this conversation, we'll assume he keeps his word and you end up in a cage with Yaroslav. You'll be facing each other in mortal combat. It's a kill or be killed situation. Did you think about what you are going to do in that situation? Or are you planning an uprising of captive fighters, Spartacus?"

"Dammit, Mishka," said Gunz, throwing his hands in the air, "are you going to allow me to talk at all?"

"No," spat Mishka angrily. "I like you much better when you're silent."

Gunz sighed. "Okay, I promise to shut up as soon as I tell you why I called you."

"Fine," grumbled Mishka. "Just try to make it as painless as possible."

"Mishka, tonight, after the fight, I'm going to accept Mr. Kogan's proposition," he said quietly. "He's going to put me under his control by using the gray stones magic."

"Jeez, Gunz, it's going to be—"

"I know, Mishka. The pain is going to turn me inside out. This is why I can't demand that you follow me there. All I can do is ask you to help me. I hope you will choose to remain with me, well-camouflaged. When the time comes, you'll be the only way for me to send a message to Kal and ask for help. Would you do it for me, my friend?"

"You had to ask?" asked Mishka, giving him a light slap on the shoulder with his wing, an irritation flaring in his scarlet eyes. "You're lost without me, ignoramus. How can I leave you alone to deal with the consequences of your own stupidity?"

"Thank you, my friend." Gunz chuckled, taking his shirt off. "I can't keep you in my watch. I'm sure that I'll have to give up everything I own to Mr. Kogan. So, we need to hide you in a different way. Remember a while ago you showed me that you could camouflage yourself as a tattoo on my body?" Mishka nodded. "I can't have a new tattoo on my body. Mr. Kogan saw me without my shirt, so he knows I have only one tattoo. So here is the question, can you hide in the special forces tattoo that I already have?"

Mishka vanished from the room and a moment later, Gunz felt a burning pain in his shoulder. He grunted, clasping his hand over his tattoo. He walked to the mirror and looked. Within the shield that was a part of his tattoo, he could clearly see the outline of a wyvern.

"Perfect," muttered Gunz. "Now come out. There are a few more things I need to tell you before we go."

* * *

THE FIGHT WAS over before it had even started. The werewolf lay on the dirty floor, motionless and defenseless. Gunz stared down at the knocked-out opponent, wondering why Mr. Kogan agreed to this fight. It had been too easy. The werewolf wasn't a pureblood and it wasn't a night of the full moon. So, even though he was stronger and faster than a normal human would have been, he still had no magic or special abilities to defend himself. Besides, his fighting skills had been below average too. He had stood no chance against Gunz.

He had no idea how and why this man had ended up in the underground pits. After all, he wasn't a purebred werewolf, it meant, he was a monster only three nights a month. He didn't look like a trained fighter either, so why did he risk his life? Did he need money to feed his kids?

Gunz surveyed the room through the net of the cage. The crowd was screaming, pointing down at the defeated man, demanding his blood. He shuddered inwardly as the bloodthirsty mob reminded him of all the movies he had seen and all the books he had read about the gladiatorial fights in ancient

Rome. For the first time since he started fighting in the underground pits, he felt remorseful about killing his opponent.

Gunz found Mr. Kogan's eyes, meeting his frosty stare, and shook his head slightly, mouthing the word *no*. Mr. Kogan arched his eyebrows and extended his arm forward, thumb parallel to the ground, still deciding the fate of the defeated fighter. Gunz froze, drilling Mr. Kogan with his burning gaze, his chest rising with heavy breaths.

"Please," he mouthed silently.

Mr. Kogan rose, observing the bloodthirsty crowd and a thin smile stretched his pale lips. Gunz stiffened, his heart beating somewhere in his throat, as he expected the Head of House to flip his thumb down, ordering him to kill the defeated warrior. So, when Mr. Kogan slowly moved his thumb up, he could hardly believe it. As expected, the crowd responded with boos and screams of disappointment. Remaining unfazed, with the same fake smile plastered all over his face, Mr. Kogan raised his hands up, asking for silence.

"It is our last fight of the night and I feel merciful today," he said. "This werewolf wasn't ready to face our undefeated wizard. I believe he can give us a much better spectacle after I train him a bit." He waved at his bouncers and pointed at the cage. "Take him."

Gunz watched silently as the two bouncers lifted the limp body of his opponent and carried him away, followed by the angry screams of the mob. Following them, the referee walked inside the cage, announcing the winner of the match, raising Gunz's arm up.

Gunz couldn't get away from the cage and the shouting crowd fast enough. He walked briskly toward the backroom with his head bowed down, ignoring everything around him. He kicked the door into the backroom open and almost collapsed on the bench. His hands were shaking, and he had a hard time suppressing his fire power. As his stomach twisted, he leaned forward to deal with the nausea.

"Gunz."

He heard Mr. Kogan's voice and raised his ashen face. Taking a deep breath, he said, "Mr. Kogan. Thank you for sparing the life of that wolf."

"Don't mention it," said the Head of House with a light shrug. "So, Gunz, did you make your decision?"

There was so much impatience and hungry anticipation in the older man's voice that Gunz did a double-take. "I thought you didn't care about that either way?"

"I didn't," replied Mr. Kogan a touch too fast. "I mean I still don't. No matter what you've decided, I'll be on the winning side, but I'm curious, you know?"

Gunz nodded, wiping cold sweat off his forehead and dropped his head, staring at his trembling hands. Mr. Kogan stepped closer and put his hand on his shoulder.

"Listen, Gunz, I don't want to pressure you into making any kind of decision," he said, softly squeezing his shoulder. "I can see you're not ready. Let's just forget it and leave everything the way it is. Go home. Relax and don't worry about anything." He tapped Gunz on his shoulder and headed toward the exit.

"No, Mr. Kogan, wait," called Gunz, rising. "I made the decision. I decided... I'll fight as your captive under the conditions we discussed yesterday."

Mr. Kogan stilled, then slowly turned back. "Are you sure?" he asked calmly.

"I trust you to keep your word," said Gunz, picking up his bag.

"You trust me? I'm flattered, indeed," said Mr. Kogan, an uneven smirk playing on his colorless lips. "But Gunz, I thought you knew that trusting anyone in our line of business is the single biggest mistake one can make. Nevertheless, I'll make sure that as long as you're in my House, you're not going to be abused. Follow me, please."

* * *

HALF-HOUR LATER, Gunz was walking to the second floor of the mansion, following Mr. Kogan and his butler. The butler stopped in front of one of the guest bedrooms and opened the door, letting Gunz and Mr. Kogan in. The room was spacious and generously lit by the wall lights, but Gunz could hardly see anything. He dropped his bag on the floor, turning around to face Mr. Kogan.

"Are you going to be comfortable here?" asked Mr. Kogan, gesturing around the room. "If you need anything else, please let me or Stephan know. Anything you need, you'll have it."

"Thank you," said Gunz. Noticing that his voice was breaking, he cleared his throat and forced a smile. "It's perfect. I'll be as comfortable as I can be with a collar on my neck."

"Oh, Gunz, you know that all this is just a deception. A show you and I are going to put up for the outside world," said Mr. Kogan, shaking his head. "Even with the collar on your neck, you're still a free man."

"Before we start, can I have one hour alone?" he asked. "I'm going to stay in this room, you can even lock it. As you can see, I'm a little nervous. I just want a few minutes to calm down."

"Take all the time you need," replied Mr. Kogan. "We don't have to do anything right away. When you're ready, call Stephan – the intercom is on the wall." He pointed at the white plastic panel with multiple buttons and walked out of the room, carefully closing the door but not locking it.

As soon as he was sure he was alone, Gunz carefully explored the room, searching for any surveillance devices. To his surprise, he didn't find any hidden bugs or cameras, but just to be on the safe side, he cast a quick spell to disable any magical or mundane listening and video devices. Once done, he placed his usual fire-proofing spells on everything inside the room and also a few different wards to contain his natural state. Just in case...

All of that took him about an hour. Once he was done, he pressed the button on the intercom, telling the butler he was ready. Mr. Kogan showed up almost immediately, accompanied by Stephan and one more man whom Gunz had never seen before. Stephan approached him and placed a silver tray on the bed stand. A silver collar and four bracelets were lying on the tray, reflecting ominously in its shiny surface. Gunz tensed, involuntarily taking a step back as the memory of his last encounter with the gray stones flashed through his mind.

Mr. Kogan noticed his reaction and gave a sign to the other man to stop. "Gunz, are you sure you're ready?" he asked with a calm smile. "Nothing has to be done today. Or at all, if you don't think you can go through with it."

"No, I want to get it over with," said Gunz flatly. "What do you need me to do?"

"Okay, as you wish. First, let me tell you that applying the gray stone jewelry for the first time is extremely painful," started Mr. Kogan. "I don't want you to suffer any pain, so I brought this."

He waved at the man and he stepped forward, showing him a syringe with a hypodermic needle. Gunz peered at the needle and swallowed, feeling blood drain from his face. He wasn't afraid of the injection – for him it was nothing. He was afraid of what would happen if he wasn't in control and reverted into the natural state of the Fire Salamander, reacting to the pain. Mr. Kogan chuckled, noticing his reaction.

"This is a twilight sedative. It'll put you to sleep for about an hour," he explained. "The more powerful the person is, the more painful the application is going to be, and the longer the aftershocks will last. I don't think you have that much magic, so from my experience, I would say it'll take about fifteen minutes for you. But I want to make sure that you're not going to be in pain. When you wake up, the worst part will be over."

"Thank you, but I don't want it," said Gunz, taking another step back. "I can deal with any pain, as long as I'm in control of my actions."

"Are you afraid of needles?" asked Mr. Kogan, flabbergasted.

"I'm not afraid of needles. I'm afraid of losing control," explained Gunz honestly.

"Fine, we'll do it your way." Mr. Kogan nodded to Stephan and he brought a glass of water, offering it to Gunz. "Okay, drink some water and then I'll give you a mouthguard. Just to be safe."

Gunz took the glass and drank the water without stopping until the glass was empty. As he returned the glass back to Stephan, he felt a strange wave of weakness spread through him. The world spun around him and he swayed. The butler caught him, gently lowering him on the bed.

"Did you drug me?" hissed Gunz, panic assailing him.

"Yes, I am sorry," said Mr. Kogan. "I just can't put you through this procedure without any sedation. I promised you were not going to be abused in my house."

"Oh God," whispered Gunz, fighting the fatigue. "Mr. Kogan, please listen to me and do as I say. In my bag, find a bracelet with a single red stone. Lock it on my wrist and don't take it off until I regain consciousness. Do you understand??"

The room became blurry and his eyes started to close, but he fought the sedation, struggling to stay awake. Mr. Kogan, alarmed by the urgency in his voice, rushed to the bag. A few seconds later he came back and locked the bracelet over Gunz's wrist. Gunz sighed in relief, as the bracelet locked his fire deep within his body.

"Gunz, open your mouth," said Mr. Kogan, gently pressing down on his jaw. Gunz didn't fight him, allowing him to place the mouthguard. "Now you can relax, just let it go. When you wake up, it'll all be over." Mr. Kogan gently patted his hand with the red-stone bracelet.

Gunz closed his eyes and let the sedation take over.

* * *

WHEN GUNZ REGAINED CONSCIOUSNESS, he was still lying on the bed in the same room. The electric lights were off, but the room was glowing with the yellow-pink colors of sunrise. When he tried to get up, dizziness and weakness washed over him, and he fell back on the bed. His every muscle was painfully sore. He lifted his arm and saw the silver bracelet locked around his wrist. He moved his hand up and touched his neck. The collar was in place. He was a captive fighter now, his freedom gone. Gunz moaned and closed his eyes.

A few minutes later, the door opened, and Mr. Kogan walked in. Gunz turned his head, watching the Head of House cautiously approaching him as if he was expecting Gunz to jump off the bed and attack him at any moment.

"Gunz, you're awake. Finally," he said sitting on the edge of the bed next to him. "How are you feeling?"

"Like I've been to hell and back," whispered Gunz, with surprise noticing how sore his throat was.

"You probably were." Mr. Kogan chuckled, rubbing his hands together. "This was not the first time I had to install the gray stone jewelry on a fighter, but I'll be honest with you, I've never seen anything like that."

"What did I do?" asked Gunz, mortified.

"You were tormented for a full hour, and the aftershocks continued for another three hours," said Mr. Kogan, shaking his head. "I had to give you more sedatives. It was terrible..." His voice trailed off and he remained silent for a moment, biting his lip. "I thought you were going to die... And then at some point, your whole body lit up with a red glow and fire broke through the skin on your arms. What are you? You can't be just a wizard – the stones had been feeding on you way too long."

"I am a wizard," said Gunz quietly. "A very powerful wizard. Fire magic is my strength." He pulled the red-stone bracelet off his wrist and gave it to Mr. Kogan. "This bracelet locks my fire magic within my body. When you sedated me against my will, my first thought was that without my control, you would get hurt… I'm sorry, I didn't tell you before."

"You have nothing to apologize for. When you feel better, you can go anywhere you wish within the borders of my property. Stephan and all my staff are instructed to serve you just as they would serve me. Just don't leave the property," said Mr. Kogan, rising. He picked up Gunz's bag and started to walk out of the room.

"Mr. Kogan," called Gunz and the man stopped at the door. "My bag. Can I keep it, sir?"

"Sorry, but no. Captive fighters do not own anything. What is in this bag that you want? Your phone?"

"No, I destroyed my phone yesterday," replied Gunz. "My wristwatch. It's a gift from—"

"I see," said Mr. Kogan. He opened the bag, pulled the wristwatch out, and carefully examined it, reading the inscription on the back and sighed. "Sorry, Gunz, but my security staff told me that your watch has a GPS tracking device installed. Even though it's disabled, I can't let you have it, but I promise I'll keep it safe for you until the time you're a free man again. Rest today. Your training as a captive fighter will start tomorrow."

He put the watch back in the bag and walked out of the room, leaving Gunz alone.

CHAPTER 6

~ ZANE BURNS, A.K.A. GUNZ ~

As soon as Gunz regained his strength, he got up and left his room. Just like Mr. Kogan had said, no one tried to stop him. He met Stephan next to the front door and the butler opened it for him with a light bow. He spent most of the day exploring the property and learned that his collar had some features that Mr. Kogan failed to disclose, like a GPS tracker that was connected to an electroshock device that was installed into the collar.

Since no one had warned him about it, he had learned it the hard way. As soon as he approached the outer gates, a powerful electric shock pierced his body. He cried out, his body arched, and he collapsed on the ground. Stephan found him a few minutes later and Gunz had to wonder if the butler was following him.

"I'm sorry, Mr. Gunz," he apologized, helping him to his feet. "I guess Mr. Kogan forgot to warn you about this. I know he mentioned that you can't leave the property, but he didn't explain why. With this collar on, you're bound to stay within the property walls, unless Mr. Kogan widens the permitted radius."

"Nice. What else did Mr. Kogan forget to mention?"

muttered Gunz. "Does it have an anti-bark detector installed too?"

"Not that I know of, sir," replied Stephan in full seriousness. He inclined his head, hopped back into his golf cart and drove away.

Gunz followed him with his eyes, biting his lip. "Woof-woof," he murmured, starting on his way back to the mansion. "Enslaved dog is at your service."

Mr. Kogan's mansion had a large library. Gunz browsed the shelves for a while, then he picked one of the books and spent most of the evening in his room reading. At eight o'clock, Stephan served him dinner in his room. Since he wasn't in the mood to see his new *"master"*, Gunz was happy that Mr. Kogan had decided to leave him alone for the night.

Next morning, he was summoned for his first day of training. Stephan provided him with a training uniform and walked him to the modified toolshed where the guards escorted him down into the underground facility. Gunz wasn't surprised to find a large training room equipped with everything necessary for martial arts training and an MMA octagon cage. Besides the training equipment, the room had a variety of weapons, some of which Gunz had never seen before. With remorse, he thought about Mr. Kogan taking not only his bag, but also his Swiss army knife, leaving him without his sword.

As much as he had hoped for the best, everything happened exactly as he expected, and not in a good way. Mr. Kogan owned ten captive fighters who had been serving him for a number of years. As soon as Gunz stepped on the floor, he was drenched in the muddy wave of silent hostility. Not sure what to do next, he stopped at the door, just to be pushed inside by a pair of strong hands.

Gunz staggered forward but managed to keep his balance. He spun around and saw a herculean figure of a purebred werewolf obscuring the entrance. The man was at least six-foot-five and his shoulders seemed to be disproportionately wide. His lips curled into a ferocious snarl as he took in Gunz's appearance.

"I guess you're the new captive," he noted, folding his massive arms over his hairy chest. "I don't know why master is wasting his time and money on you. I don't see you surviving a single round in the cage. What's your name, little man?"

"Gunz."

"No, seriously," growled the werewolf, taking a step closer to him. "I'm not in a mood for smartass jokes."

"My name is Gunz," repeated Gunz calmly, holding the furious gaze of the werewolf.

"Do not lie to me, jackass!" snarled the werewolf, swinging his arm to slap him.

Gunz quickly stepped aside, easily avoiding the strike, which seemed to infuriate the werewolf even more. Werewolves weren't famous for their ability to keep their cool and this one wasn't an exception. One of the fighters stepped forward, holding his hands up. Gunz recognized Rand, the dark wizard.

"He's telling you the truth, Sensei," said Rand quickly. "Master introduced us a day ago. I met him when he was still an unattached fighter. I assure you, he is who he says he is."

The werewolf came closer to Gunz, demonstratively bending his knees to get down on the same level as him and gawked at him for a moment before he barked laughing. "Rand, are you saying this tiny wizard is the undefeated warrior of the unattached circles?" He shook his head with disapproval. "The unattached fighting is truly going down the drain if a small wizard with hardly any magic in him can fight for months and never lose a fight."

"I saw him fighting once," stated Rand with a shrug, "and I hate to say it, Sensei, but his reputation is well deserved."

"Let me be the judge of that," rasped the werewolf and headed to a small table that was positioned next to the cage.

Gunz glanced at the table and his heart thundered in his chest. Besides a few strange devices, he saw multiple controllers lined up on the table. *Kogan said he'd never use the controller on me,* he thought desperately as he watched the werewolf fumble with the devices. After a moment, the werewolf turned to Gunz and frowned.

"Where is your controller, boy?" he demanded, planting his fists on his hips.

"Now, why would I know that," replied Gunz with a shrug. "I guess you should ask Mr. Kogan."

"To you, he's not Mr. Kogan. He's your master and owner. Do you understand, asshole?" growled the werewolf. "And on this floor, I am your lord, your commander and your god. You will obey me, and you will respect my every word. Am I clear, little wizard?"

Gunz raised his hands up, a sarcastic grin on his face. The werewolf caught it and grunted, frustrated.

"I will teach you respect, boy." He slammed his fist on the table, scattering the devices and controllers all over the floor. "If I see the tiniest spark of disobedience or disrespect in you, I'll make sure you'll curse the day you were born. Do you understand?"

Gunz shrugged. "You know, if every time some dumbass said those words to me, and I actually got scared and gave in, I would have been dead a long time ago."

The werewolf's eyes bulged, and he charged Gunz. "Oh, shit," mumbled Gunz, getting ready to fight.

He easily avoided a few strikes and responded by just pushing the werewolf around without doing any serious damage. For a couple of minutes, he danced around Sensei, avoiding every single attack, which only made things worse, igniting the blinding fury in his opponent to overwhelming strength. The werewolf howled and partially transformed, launching at him again. Gunz let him slide past and kicked him under his knee. However, when his opponent dropped on the floor, he just stepped away.

For a moment, the werewolf stood on all fours, his yellow eyes burning with hatred. Then he got up, laborious breaths expending his enormous chest and transformed back into his human form. With a malignant smirk, he waved at the other captives.

"Take him and hold him down," he ordered.

The remaining ten fighters didn't wait for a second invitation. Gunz knew he had no chance fighting on his own against ten men who were trained just as well as he was. Punches and kicks fell on him from every direction, and he was surprised he was able to stand his ground for at least a full minute before he was pushed down and pinned to the floor by the weight of a several bodies.

Two fighters twisted his arms behind his back, forcing him to his knees and a third fighter grabbed his hair, tilting his head backward. As the werewolf approached him, he backhanded him without holding back. Gunz's head jerked to the side as a white light exploded in his head, and the metallic taste of blood filled his mouth. The man that was holding his head up let go and Gunz dropped his head to his chest, a thick dark liquid dripping from his mouth to the concrete floor.

"Hold him up," ordered the werewolf and the fighters pulled him up into a standing position.

For a full minute the werewolf used him as a punching bag without giving much thought on where his strikes were landing. When his initial wave of fury started to dim down, he stopped and stepped back, observing the results of his handiwork. After a moment, he seized Gunz's chin with his meaty fingers, forcing his head up.

"So, boy, did I put the fear of God into you or do you need more?" he asked snidely.

Gunz laughed. Blood splattered from his mouth, running

down his chin. Every move radiated with pain, but he raised his eyes and met the werewolf's taunting gaze.

"Not even close," he hissed, "keep going, asshole, if you have the stamina for it."

For a moment complete silence enveloped the training room. The fighters stared at Gunz, some with respect and others with bloodlust in their eyes. The werewolf roared, clenching his massive fists. Gunz braced himself for a mighty punch and closed his eyes.

"Stop what you're doing at once!" Gunz heard Mr. Kogan's voice and opened his eyes. "What the hell is going on here?"

Mr. Kogan stopped in front of him, taking in his bloodied face and frowned. He waved his hand at the fighters who were holding him, and they lowered him into a kneeling position. Mr. Kogan seized Gunz's hair, lifting his face up, quickly checking the damage that was done to him and shook his head.

"Master, you need to get rid of him," drawled the werewolf. "It'll be hard to break this man. He'll never be what you need him to be. Give me your command and I'll break his neck right now."

"No," said Mr. Kogan, his voice shaking with fury. "I didn't tell you anything about breaking him, did I? I told you to train him, so he was ready for the captive events next week. And what did you do?" He pointed at Gunz. "Now, it'll take a week for him just to heal and be ready to return to fighting!"

"I'm sorry, master, I misunderstood you," pleaded the werewolf, going down to his knees. With shock, Gunz realized that the huge monster was scared of the tiny, skinny man in front of him.

"Master," said Gunz, almost choking on this word. Mr. Kogan turned back to him, observing him with curiosity. "It's not Sensei's fault, master, please forgive him. I did provoke him a little." The werewolf turned his head, gaping at Gunz bug-eyed. "I'm fine, master, and I'm ready to continue training if you allow me, sir."

"Are you sure?" asked Mr. Kogan, squatting down in front of him and gently touching his face where the dark spots of bruises slowly started to swell. "You look like you're about to collapse."

Gunz nodded, his body responding to his every move with a jolt of pain. "I'm fine. I can continue training."

Mr. Kogan rose, observing his captive fighters with severity. "I don't want any harm to come to this fighter," he said pointing at Gunz. "No pain, unless it's necessary for his training, should come his way. And definitely no bodily injuries. Did I teach you all nothing?"

"Yes, master," replied the werewolf. "May I ask you for his controller? I need to be able to control his magic if I want to teach him how to use it effectively during the event."

Gunz gave him a mortified stare but was relieved when he saw Mr. Kogan shaking his head.

"All along, his collar was set to zero, meaning he had full control of his magic," explained Mr. Kogan, iron notes in his voice. "Yet, I didn't see him use his magic to fight your cowardly attack, did I? Eleven trained fighters against one and none of you got hurt by his magic. I assure you, he's in complete control and handling him with the controller is absolutely unnecessary. Just tell him how much of his magic you want him to use and he'll comply with your request. Am I correct, Gunz?"

"Yes, sir," replied Gunz but then caught Mr. Kogan's arched stare and added, "Master."

Mr. Kogan left without saying anything else. As soon as he was gone from the training room, the werewolf approached Gunz and took one knee in front of him.

"I don't think you can train today," he said, carefully probing Gunz's ribs with his fingers.

Gunz winced and chuckled. "No, I don't think so either."

"Then why did you lie to the master?" asked the werewolf straightening up.

"I didn't want you to suffer," replied Gunz quietly. "I didn't want master to punish you or the fighters, so, I lied. Will that get me in trouble with you?"

"No," answered the werewolf and turned to the other fighters who stood quietly behind him. "Help him up. Gently. And let him lie down on the mats. He can rest until the end of training today."

* * *

AFTER TRAINING WAS OVER, Gunz barely made it to his room. The fighters couldn't leave the underground facility and he had no help. He walked into the room and shed his blood-soaked uniform off. Standing just in his underwear, he surveyed the damage. His body was covered in angry-looking blemishes and lacerations.

His nose was broken, and dark bruises spread under both his eyes. His lips were split and still bleeding. He quickly reset his broken nose, stifling the scream. He leaned on the dresser panting as pain wreaked havoc in his head.

The door into his room opened and Mr. Kogan walked in. Gunz turned to him and sighed, dropping his arms at his sides. He wasn't dressed, but it didn't bother him. At the moment he was too tired and hurt to worry about that.

"Mr. Kogan, please tell me," he said quietly, "since I wear the collar on my neck, is the basic courtesy of knocking before entering no longer extended to me... master?"

"Gunz..." Mr. Kogan rubbed his forehead tiredly. "I'm sorry, you're right. I should have knocked first, but I was worried about you and wanted to make sure that you were okay." He fell silent for a moment. "And you don't have to call me master when it's just us here."

"Sure," replied Gunz, wishing for this man to be gone so he could finally lie down. "I'm fine. I'll be ready for training in the morning and in one week you can start booking me for the fights in the captive circles."

Mr. Kogan stepped closer and ran his fingers over a deep laceration on his chest, muttering something under his breath. "Do you need me to send a doctor to your room?" he asked after a moment. "You may need stitches."

"No." Gunz backed away from him. "I just need a good night's sleep. I heal fast. Your bottom-line is not going to suffer because of this little squabble. I trust you're not going to punish your Sensei or any of your captive fighters?"

"Punish? Of course not!" exclaimed Mr. Kogan, seemingly terrified by the thought.

"Are you saying you never punish your captives?" asked Gunz, unable to hide his disbelief.

"I do reprimand them if they deserve it, but I never resort to physical punishment, Gunz," said Mr. Kogan. "Why in the world would you think otherwise?"

"Because of the look on your Sensei's face when he thought he angered you," replied Gunz flatly.

"I purchased him a year ago from an abusive master," replied Mr. Kogan with a dismissive shrug. "I guess he still didn't get over his past experience. Well, if you don't need my help, I'll leave you alone so you can rest. Good night, Gunz."

Purchased from an abusive master? This conversation was rubbing him the wrong way. Mr. Kogan talked about his captive fighters like they were nothing more than his pets, animals who were there for his entertainment and could be easily disposed of at any time. Yes, most of them weren't human. And Gunz had not forgotten that the majority of the captive fighters were the true monsters whom he often had to fight on the street of his city. Nevertheless, humans or monsters, no one should have this kind of power over another being and their supernatural origins didn't give anyone the right to treat them as debilitated pets.

As soon as Mr. Kogan walked out, Gunz groaned and bent forward, wrapping his arms around his ribs. All this time he had been suppressing his pain, struggling not to show how he truly felt. Slowly, he managed to get to his bed and lay down.

"Mishka, are you still with me?" he whispered, brushing his tattoo with his fingers.

The wyvern manifested above him and sighed audibly. "Almighty Fire, what the hell is wrong with you, Salamander," he yelled in a high-pitch voice. "If I didn't know any better, I would say you're enjoying the pain. And now you're going to tell me you can't revert and heal yourself!"

"I can't revert and heal myself," repeated Gunz dutifully. "I was wondering if you could share some fire—"

"That's it!" shouted Mishka, hopping up and down above Gunz. "I had enough of this. I'm going back to Kal and I'm telling him everything you're doing here! How can you be so stupid! They are going to break you and I don't think I want to associate with a broken Salamander. Kal needs to find me a new Salamander to guard, one with brains."

"Pretty please?"

"Ugh!" Mishka landed on his chest, but this time instead of spraying him with the fire energy, he conjured a large fireball and thrust it through Gunz's chest. The energy of fire surged through him, energizing him and healing his injuries to a degree. Gunz moaned and relaxed as the pain slowly gave up its hold.

"Thank you," he whispered, his eyelids too heavy to keep his eyes open.

"Sleep now," said Mishka with a sigh. "Your wounds are not healed completely, but you'll feel better tomorrow."

Gunz nodded, feeling a soft burning on his shoulder as Mishka camouflaged himself in his tattoo.

* * *

He was awakened in the middle of the night by a soft touch to his shoulder. Without moving, he opened his eyes. The room was still dark, but he could see the silhouette of a woman by his bedside.

"*Ignius*," he whispered, conjuring a tiny flame in his palm. The shadows shied away from the dancing light of the fire, and he recognized Mrs. Kogan. He extinguished the fire, cringing. *Oh, no... Please, God, I don't have strength to deal with her on top of everything else.*

"Mrs. Kogan, what are you doing in my room this late?" asked Gunz realizing with horror that he was almost naked, lying on top of the blanket.

"Call me Clarissa," ordered Mrs. Kogan, her hand landing on his inner-thigh, her manicured claws making their way up his leg.

"Fine. Clarissa, you shouldn't be here at this time," said Gunz, gently removing her hand.

"Why not?" she asked innocently. "You're perfectly well undressed for the occasion, lover..." She leaned over him, trying to kiss him, but he turned his face away.

"Mrs. Kogan, please—"

"Clarissa—"

"Yes, Clarissa, what do you want from me? I'm tired. I'm hurt. And I can't—"

"Aw, Gunz, don't play coy with me. You know exactly what I want. Am I not attractive enough for you?"

"You're married enough for me, and I won't sleep with a married woman. Especially since your husband extended his hospitality to me," growled Gunz, shifting away from her as he pulled a side of the blanket over his body.

"Oh, please! Did someone knock your brains out in the cage?" Mrs. Kogan rolled her eyes. "He didn't extend his hospitality to you. He enslaved you. He is nice to you right now because it suits him, but if it comes to a choice between loyalty to you and his bank account, he'll choose the latter."

"Be that as it may," said Gunz with a sigh, "I'm not going to go against my conscience and sleep with you."

"Are you afraid to take a sin on your soul, love? Is that what it is?"

"Clarissa, really, it's late. I need to sleep because training is starting in the morning and I'm still hurt," mumbled Gunz. "It has nothing to do with religion and sin. It has everything to do with my honor. So, please, have mercy and leave me alone."

"Slaves have no honor," hissed Mrs. Kogan angrily.

She seized his collar, forcing his face up and crushed his lips with hers. He stiffened, fighting the desire to grab her and throw her out of his room, but hurting the wife of his "owner" didn't sound like a hot idea. His split lips started bleeding again. He was sure that she could taste his blood but didn't acknowledge it.

She finally let him go, her lips red with his blood, and smiled a drunk smile. Then she carefully wiped his blood off her lips with her finger and put her finger in her mouth. He grunted and turned away, the sight of her making his stomach churn.

"You're bleeding and hurt, slave," she said sliding off the bed, "so I'll cut you some slack tonight. Rest and try to remember for the next time – as long as you have this collar on your neck, you're my property and I can do whatever I want with you. You have no choice but to do as you are told. Am I clear, slave?"

She kept repeating the word "slave", rubbing it in.

"Crystal clear," growled Gunz, anger slowly rising up in him.

Clarissa swung her hand and slapped him across his face. "You must address me as your mistress, slave!"

That brought Gunz to a boiling point. He jumped off the bed, ignoring his bleeding lips and soreness of his body. Before she could say anything else, he grabbed her by her wrist and threw her out of his room, slamming the door in her face.

"I understand you just fine! Fuckin' Mistress!" shouted Gunz, pushing the back of a chair under the door handle to keep her from entering again.

Tomorrow I need to talk to Kogan about that and ask him to install a lock on my door. Goddamnit! As if my situation wasn't complicated enough without this bullshit.

Enslaved dog and a whore... Can it get any worse?

CHAPTER 7

~ ZANE BURNS, A.K.A. GUNZ ~

Gunz hardly slept for the rest of the night, waking up at the tiniest sound. He got up with the first rays of the rising sun, quickly took a shower and got dressed. The mansion was silent. Even Stephan was still asleep. Gunz walked outside and inhaled the fresh morning air. His body was still sore, and he hoped it wouldn't prevent him from training today. He spent an hour just strolling along the endless trails in the park and by the time he returned back to his room, he felt recharged and in a better mood.

However, his spirit plummeted when he found Stephan waiting next to his door. The butler inclined his head greeting him and announced that Mr. Kogan would like Gunz to join him for breakfast. Gunz had no choice but to follow the butler. To his surprise, breakfast was served in a small breakfast nook next to the kitchen. Mr. Kogan was already there, sitting at the table with an iPad in his hand. As soon as Gunz walked in, he put away the device and smiled, pointing at a chair across the table from him.

"Good morning, Gunz, I hope you're feeling better today?" Mr. Kogan started the conversation.

"I'm fine, thanks," replied Gunz dryly. "I'm getting back to training today. Don't worry, by next week, I should be ready to start making money for you, sir."

Breakfast was served right away, but since Gunz had to start training in one hour, he resorted to a cup of coffee and toast. Taking a sip of his hot coffee, he thought about everything that had happened last night, wondering what the best way would be to address this sensitive situation with Mr. Kogan.

"How can you drink this coffee?" asked Mr. Kogan, chuckling. "It's close to boiling."

"Fire magic is my strength," replied Gunz, absentmindedly.

"I can see that something is troubling you," said Mr. Kogan, leaning across the table. "Don't be afraid… Give your thoughts a voice."

"I was wondering if I can ask you for a favor," started Gunz.

"Why not? What do you need?"

"A new lock for the door to my room," said Gunz quietly, "so I can lock it from the inside. At least at night."

Mr. Kogan frowned and reclined back in his chair, folding his arms over his chest, scanning Gunz with his attentive eyes.

"You are not asking for the lock because I walked in without knocking," he stated. It was clear to Gunz that it wasn't a question. "It's Clarissa, isn't it. What did she do?"

"Mr. Kogan, she is your wife," said Gunz, lowering his eyes. "I don't want to—"

"She came to your room last night and made certain demands of you, didn't she?" hissed Mr. Kogan. His face lost all color turning sickly yellow.

"Yes, sir," replied Gunz, uncomfortably fumbling with the edge of the table cloth. "I didn't want to tell you. I just want to have a lock on my door, so I can get a good night's sleep. The training is exhausting, and I need—"

Mr. Kogan pursed his lips, frowning. "Stephan," he yelled, his voice infused with fury. Gunz tensed, not sure what infuriated the Head of House – the favor he asked for or his wife's behavior. The butler silently came into the room. "Stephan, as soon as Gunz leaves for training, I want you to install a lock on his door. When he comes back, give him the key and make sure no one else has the key to his room." Stephan bowed and disappeared just as silently.

"Thank you, sir. I appreciate it," said Gunz, throwing a quick glance at the wall clock. In fifteen minutes, he should be in the underground facility. "I have to go now, sir. I don't want to anger your Sensei by being late."

"Before you leave, Gunz, I need to make something clear," said Mr. Kogan rising. "I'm going to talk with my wife, but I can't guarantee she'll listen to me. I have known Clarissa for many years and when she wants something, there is no way of stopping her. The lock on your door is not going to keep her away. And I hate to say it, but you are in a vulnerable situation. To everyone besides myself, my wife and Stephan, you are just another captive fighter. You have no rights and you must obey your masters, no matter what they ask of you. And I may not be there for you every minute of the day. Do you understand?"

"So, what you are saying is that rape is not considered to be an abuse, is that right, Mr. Kogan?" said Gunz evenly, struggling not to raise his voice. "You swore that if I trust you with my freedom, I'll never be abused in your house."

"Do you consider the attention of a beautiful older woman an abuse?" Mr. Kogan chuckled. "Why don't you just give her what she wants, and she'll leave you alone. Like you said before – it's just physical. All she wants is your body."

Gunz threw his hands in the air. "I must go… master." He turned around and walked out of the room.

* * *

AFTER THE FIRST week of training, Mr. Kogan started to book

Gunz for events in the captive circles, two-three times a week. They were smaller events and didn't have the grandeur of the bigger fights he needed to participate in to give Mr. Kogan the opportunity to challenge the California House. Nevertheless, Gunz didn't lose any of his fights and Mr. Kogan was happily counting the piles of cash after every event.

He continued training every day with the rest of the captive fighters. After what happened during his first day of training, Sensei warmed up to him slightly, but the fighters never accepted him as their own, holding him at arm's length. However, the general atmosphere of hostility was gone, making it tolerable for him to train. Except for the use of the controller, Sensei didn't single him out in any way, treating him the same as any other fighter in his group.

As promised, Mr. Kogan installed the lock on the door to Gunz's room, which allowed him some privacy. At least at night. Clarissa never bothered him again. In fact, she completely avoided him, and it made him wonder what kind of conversation Mr. Kogan had had with his wife.

Once in a while, Mr. Kogan requested his services as a bodyguard. Gunz didn't mind as it allowed him to leave the property. His mood was growing worse with every day he had to spend in captivity, and these brief interludes were a welcome change. But every day, he counted the minutes until Mr. Kogan would finally set up a fight with the California house.

Almost a full month past when finally, his patience was rewarded. After the last fight, Mr. Kogan walked into his room and announced that Gunz's reputation had reached the ears of the Head of the California House and he agreed to stage a fight between Gunz and one of his fighters. As good as it sounded, it wasn't what Gunz wanted to hear.

"One of his fighters?" he asked without hiding his disappointment. "There is only one fighter I care to fight in the California House."

"It doesn't work like that," replied Mr. Kogan patiently. "To have the honor of fighting his best captive fighter, the Head of House wants to see you in action, fighting against lesser opponents. That's a pretty standard approach."

"Fine," agreed Gunz, shaking his head. "I waited longer. I can wait for a few more events."

"Attaboy!" Mr. Kogan chuckled his uncomfortable chuckle. "Anyway, a week from today, the representative of the California House will be coming here to discuss the arrangements for the event. I'm sure he would want to see you."

"That's fine—"

"I just want to remind you that for the duration of his stay, you will be locked down in the underground facility like the rest of my captive fighters," warned Mr. Kogan. "It shouldn't be longer than a couple of days."

"Doesn't look like I have a choice on this matter. Do I?" muttered Gunz.

"No, you don't," answered Mr. Kogan frostily. "For these two days, you'll be treated just like a real captive fighter. It means that if the House representative would want to use the controller on you, I will allow him that."

Gunz tensed at the mention of the controller, his hand slowly rising to his neck. "I hope it won't come to that."

EXACTLY ONE WEEK after that conversation, the representative of the California House arrived. Even though he was staying in a hotel, Mr. Kogan decided it would be safer if Gunz remained in the underground lockdown for the full duration of his visit to Florida. One more time he reminded Gunz that it was done to keep up proper appearances. After all, it was also Mr. Kogan's business and reputation on the line and he didn't want to risk anything.

Gunz was sitting on the hard bed in his room in the underground facility when he heard the click of the lock. The door opened and Mr. Kogan walked in, accompanied by a tall Korean man in a business suit. The man was holding a phone in his hands, but he wasn't looking at the screen. There was something unsettling about him. Possibly it was his flat face, void of any human emotions or the venomous look in his glacial, angled eyes.

"Mr. Park," said Mr. Kogan, giving Gunz a pointed stare, "this is the fighter I was talking about."

Gunz realized why Mr. Kogan was throwing killer-looks at him and lowered down to both knees, bowing his head obediently. "Master," he said without raising his eyes.

Mr. Park peered down at Gunz, his lips curving in distaste. "He doesn't impress me," he said to Mr. Kogan and turned back to Gunz. "Stand up!"

Gunz got up and stood with his head bowed down, tensed to the limit. Mr. Park approached him, staring down from the top of his height and shook his head. "Take your shirt off," he ordered after a moment.

"Do it," Mr. Kogan confirmed the order.

Slowly, Gunz pulled his shirt off and threw it on the bed, feeling numb all over. Even though he wasn't completely naked, he felt exposed and vulnerable. Mr. Park approached him and checked his biceps and chest muscles. Then without any warning, he pulled his arm back and punched Gunz in his stomach. Only the heightened Salamander senses allowed Gunz to catch the movement fast enough and withstand the punch.

"Well, Mr. Kogan, your fighter is too small, but he's well-built for his height and he has decent reaction," said Mr. Park, wiping his hand with a handkerchief. "Having said that, I don't want to reject him right away just because of his height. I believe tonight there is one of those tiny captive events?"

"Yes, Mr. Park," replied Mr. Kogan eagerly.

"I would like to see him in action," said Mr. Park, his angled, narrow eyes traveling up and down Gunz's body. "I hope he is fighting in this event?"

"Yes, Mr. Park. He is in the last fight of the night," replied Mr. Kogan, sugary. "Would you like to meet for dinner in my mansion after the event is over? We could discuss the arrangements over a nice glass of Bordeaux…"

"Fine, I'll see you after the fight," replied Mr. Park and walked out the door.

* * *

IN ALL THE months of him fighting in the underground supernatural fighting pits, Gunz had never been as nervous as he was this night. He wasn't worried about losing the fight. He was worried he wouldn't get a strong enough opponent to show off his fighting skills.

Mr. Kogan probably had exactly the same concerns, because he rearranged the fighting itinerary slightly, paring him with two opponents – a massive demon and an older vampire, which would give Gunz the opportunity to show off his skills. It took him only two rounds to knock both fighters out. He stood in the cage, waiting for a sign from Mr. Kogan. Instead, Mr. Park got up and approached the cage. He waved his hand, gesturing at Gunz to approach the net.

"I want you to kill them by ripping their heads off. With your bare hands, that is," he ordered frostily and flipped his fist thumb down, commanding him to proceed. There was nothing but emptiness in his cold voice and his snake-eyes were as expressionless as his voice. "You manage to do it, little wizard, and I'll report to the Head of House that you're worth his time."

"Yes, my lord," replied Gunz, "as you wish."

Gunz approached the fallen demon and seized his head, planting his knee on the demon's back. He channeled a tiny amount of his magic toward his hands and ripped the demon's head off in one move. The dark shadow of demonic essence separated from the beheaded body and disappeared into the floor. Gunz got up and slowly headed to the vampire. He repeated the same procedure with him, watching the body disintegrate into a pile of ashes.

As soon as he was done, the guests of the event clapped, talking softly and discussing everything they had witnessed over a glass of red wine. The bouncers unlocked the cage and escorted him into a small cell where the fighters were supposed to wait for their owners to collect them. Since it was the last fight of the night, he was locked in the room alone.

He expected Mr. Kogan to come in and give him instructions on what to do next. Instead, Stephan walked into the room and asked Gunz to follow him. He drove Gunz to the mansion and escorted him to the underground facility where he locked him in the same room. The only thing he said was that Mr. Kogan will be busy entertaining his guest and he'll be with Gunz as soon as he can.

With nothing to do and his nerves stretched to the limit, Gunz paced the small space he was locked in. The longer he waited, the more he was positive something wasn't right. His intuition raised one red flag after another in his mind, but there was nothing he could do. There was no clock in the room, and he had no idea how much time he spent bouncing from wall to wall. Finally exhausted by all the events of the day and by constant worry, he lay down on the bed.

Gunz hadn't noticed when he had dozed off and the loud clink of the lock woke him up with a start. He jumped to his feet, expecting to see Mr. Kogan, but to his horror, it was Mrs. Kogan standing in the doorway. She was dressed in a beautiful long robe, which looked like an expensive dress and had a small leather purse thrown over her shoulder.

With the soft movements of a predator, Clarissa sashayed

inside the room accompanied by four guards and gestured for them to close the door. Then she walked to Gunz and halted in front of him, a crooked, arrogant smirk on her face.

"Hello, lover," she purred, her eyes darkened by lust, "finally, we meet again."

"Mrs. Kogan," croaked Gunz and cleared his throat. "What can I do for you? Your husband should be here any minute."

"Oh, sweetie, don't worry about my husband. He knows I'm here and he had no objections." She cackled, patting him on his cheek. "As far as what you can do for me... Well, I think by now it should be quite clear, don't you think?"

"Mrs. Kogan—"

"Mistress."

Gunz choked and fell silent, unable to say the word. She arched her eyebrows at him with an amused smile. "So, what is it going to be, lover?"

"I can't," Gunz cut sharply, his hands clenched into fists. "I can't and I won't. You can't force me to do something like this—"

She interrupted him with her laughter, opened her purse, and pulled out a controller. As she showed the device to him, she cocked her head, placing her finger on the right-most button. "You were saying? And by the way, my husband changed the settings on your controller. You try to step outside this room... Well, you know what will happen then. So, if you are thinking about attacking me and taking this controller away, think again."

Gunz held his breath, his heart pounding somewhere in this throat. "Clarissa, please, don't do it... I can't do what you want, and it has nothing do with your attractiveness. You're a beautiful woman, but I'm still — I can't. Please, have mercy... mistress."

"Oh? Did you just give me the *'it's not you, it's me'* speech?" She cackled coldly. With her finger on the very right button of the controller, Clarissa turned to her guards. "Hold him, boys. I think he needs a little lesson."

Holding his hands up, Gunz backed away from the guards until his back hit the wall. Then he slid down to the floor, cowering in the corner between the wall and the bed. Feeling like a cornered animal, he wrapped his arms around his body and stilled. The guards stood by his side, staring down at him but didn't touch him.

She approached him and squatted down, holding the controller in her hand so he could see it. "You see, Gunz, I can do anything I want with you now. I can even take your life if I want to," she whispered. "But don't worry, lover, I'm not going to do it. Killing you would be a mercy compared to what's coming. And I don't feel merciful today."

She caressed his face, gently wiping the perspiration off his forehead with her fingers. Then she seized his chin and kissed him hard, biting his lip to blood. He grunted and flinched, but there was no space for him to pull away.

Clarissa got up, shaking her head. "Too bad. We could've had so much fun."

She pivoted on her high heels and headed toward the door, followed by her guards. As she opened the door, Gunz saw Mr. Kogan waiting for her outside. He extended his skeletal hand to his wife, greeting her with a warm smile.

"He's all yours, darling," said Clarissa, planting a tender kiss on her husband's sunken cheek, giving him back the controller.

Leaving all the guards outside the door, Mr. Kogan walked inside, followed by the representative of the California House. For a moment, they both stared down at Gunz silently. Then Mr. Kogan reached into the inside pocket of his suit and pulled a folded document out.

"So, Mr. Park, do we have an agreement?" he asked, offering him the document and a pen.

Mr. Park took the document, quickly reviewed it and signed

it. "The Head of the California House authorized me to complete the transaction," said the house representative, handing the document back to Mr. Kogan. "I'm taking him now. In exchange, you will receive what we agreed upon within one month from today."

Mr. Kogan put the document back into his pocket and gave the controller to Mr. Park. Then he lowered down to one knee in front of Gunz. "Sorry, it had to be this way, Gunz. I truly enjoyed your company, but it was never meant to last this long."

"Mr. Kogan, what did you do?" whispered Gunz, the horror of his situation pressing down on him. "Why?"

"I would highly recommend complying with all of Mr. Park's requests. It'll be a lot easier if you went with him willingly," said Mr. Kogan ignoring Gunz's questions. "He can hurt you and not only with that controller. The only reason I'm having this conversation with you right now is because I promised you were not going to be hurt while you were in my house. So, don't make me break my promise. Trust me, you have no choice but to go with him. It was nice knowing you."

He stepped back and Mr. Park took his place. "Get up," he ordered coldly.

Gunz got up, the world spinning around him, his head buzzing with uncontrollable panicked thoughts. He couldn't fight. If he made just one move, the Korean would use the controller, blocking his magic and crippling him. He was surrounded by guards and just like Mr. Kogan said – he had no choice.

"Turn around, hands behind your back," ordered Mr. Park.

Gunz slowly turned around and crossed his arms behind his back. He felt the cold touch of handcuffs on his wrists. One of the guards grabbed his head, tilting it to the side, and he felt a sharp twinge of pain as a needle penetrated the skin of his neck. Gunz gasped and jerked but was held down by the guards. His vision got blurry and his knees buckled. He didn't feel the pain of the fall as his mind plummeted into darkness.

* * *

GUNZ DIDN'T KNOW how long he had been unconscious. When he regained consciousness, he found himself lying down on a cold concrete floor of a small cell. The cell was a tiny box that looked like a cage with a thick iron grid. The handcuffs were gone, but the gray stone jewelry was still in place. Feeling dizzy and weak, he pushed himself up into a sitting position.

He surveyed the cell, noticing that he was either in a dungeon or a basement and there was no one else there besides him. He reached for his magic, but it was blocked and so was his access to the elemental power. He touched the collar on his neck, realizing that his controller, set to the maximum, was blocking his magic and making him weak.

"Mishka, can you get out?" called Gunz and immediately heard the wyvern's response in his head.

"I hate you, Gunz! No, I can't get out. You let them put this awful collar on you and now I'm stuck here without any fire! It's all your fault and I'm going tell Kal everything."

Gunz closed his eyes, clenching his teeth. His last hope was gone. "I'm sorry, Mishka, I should've never gotten you involved. I knew I could end up in a situation like this. I'm sorry, my friend. As soon as I get a chance, I'll set you free."

"Damn right you will," growled Mishka.

Gunz heard loud metallic clinks and opened his eyes. A bulky man stood in front of his cell. He wasn't tall, no more than five-foot-ten, but his whole body was wrapped in a massive set of muscles. His muscles were bulging in places Gunz didn't know muscles existed. He was dressed in tight leather pants and a black tank-top, which hardly covered his oversized pecs. In his hands, he was holding a heavy-duty metal baton and the controller, undoubtedly to Gunz's collar.

The man ran his baton over the grid of the cage with loud clicks and smiled frostily, displaying a set of oversized fangs.

What the hell is he? Not a vampire for sure... A werewolf? Not likely...

"Come on out, little wizard," ordered the man and unlocked the door. Holding the controller in his hands, he wasn't worried about Gunz's retaliation.

"Hey, man, can I ask you a question?" asked Gunz, a derisive twinkle in his eyes. "But please tell me the truth. Have you been working out?"

"A smartass little shit. Aren't yah?" grumbled the man, pushing Gunz forward. "Let's see how fast the master will knock this attitude out of you."

"Sounds promising," murmured Gunz. *Here we go. Dungeons without dragons. Part two.*

CHAPTER 8

~ AIDAN ~

"Sijak!" shouted Aidan, commanding the beginning of the sparring match.

Two seven-year old boys charged at each other, ferociously kicking the air. In their oversized chest gear and shin guards, they looked like two round balls, rolling around the dojang floor. It seemed like their right leg never got tired as they kept kicking with the same leg without care for where the kick would land and if it would land anywhere at all. In most cases, the only opponent who suffered the painful defeat was an invisible one – the air.

"Master McGrath." Aidan felt a soft touch to his elbow and turned around. Angel bowed to him in the traditional Taekwondo bow.

"What's going on, Instructor Angel?" asked Aidan slightly surprised. Normally, no one bothered him when he was working with kids, especially during the sparring lessons.

"I'm sorry to bother you, Master McGrath," said Angel, sounding apologetic, "but you have a call on your personal line, and I think you will want to take it."

Aidan frowned. With everything that had been going on in the city in the last year, he expected bad news by default, allowing himself to feel relieved when his expectation didn't materialize.

"Please take over the lesson, Instructor Angel," said Aidan, heading outside the dojang.

He walked into his office and picked up the phone receiver, pressing the blinking button of his personal line.

"Hello?" he asked, bracing for bad news.

"Aidan." He heard Jim's voice on the other end of the line and slowly lowered himself into the chair. Calls from Agent Jim Andrews were never a good sign. Come to think of it, Jim usually didn't use a phone to call him.

"Agent Andrews," replied Aidan. "You are calling me on the phone as opposed to summoning me?"

After a prolonged silence, Jim cleared his throat. "Well, you're probably forgetting that I'm the only pureblood human among you magic freaks," he said quietly. "And since Angelique is..." His voice faltered and he fell silent again. "Since Angelique is no longer with us and Gunz turned into— since he is gone too, I have no way to summon you. This is why I'm calling you, Aidan. I hope that's not a problem."

"No, of course not. And I didn't forget, Jim, it just... I'm sorry, I probably shouldn't be bringing it up, but you need to hire another witch for your team," he said quietly. "Not to replace Angelique, of course. No one can replace her... But you need someone with magic on your team. Especially since Gunz disappeared."

"Grand idea, Mr. McGrath," taunted Jim, and Aidan could almost see him rolling his eyes. "And how do you propose I do that? I can't really post a job advertising on LinkedIn or Career-Builder, can I? Help Wanted – Witch-slash-Seer. A local FBI office is looking for a witch-slash-seer with minimum of five years field experience. Position requirements... What would you suggest as the position requirements? Witchcraft and wizardry with emphasis on clairvoyance?"

"Jim, I'm sorry. I was just trying to help," said Aidan softly. "I can contact Karma for you and see if she would be interested to work with your team."

"Karma?" huffed Jim. "Aidan, aren't you a fountain of great ideas today. You want me to hire an assassin to work for the FBI?"

"She is a supernatural assassin. She doesn't kill humans," objected Aidan. "You could do with a witch on your team who can also kick some serious ass."

"Yeah, and one who will jump on any high-paid assignment at any time dropping everything she would be working on with me," snapped Jim. "No, thank you very much."

"I doubt she would do such a thing, but it's up to you," replied Aidan, now cursing himself for bringing this subject up.

Jim sighed and fumbled with the phone. "Sorry, I know you are trying to help," he said, notes of awkwardness in his voice. "It's been almost a year since Angie's... death, and I still can't get over it. And with Gunz behaving like an asshole... Ugh. His disappearance didn't help the situation."

"You said it yourself. It's been almost a year and *you* have a hard time getting over it. Imagine how hard it is for Gunz. He was actually in love with Angelique," said Aidan, his fingers crushing the receiver. "Don't you think you should give him some space to grieve and as much time as he needs? Also, I thought he was working undercover on some assignment you gave him."

"It started as an assignment," confirmed Jim. "In hindsight, it was stupid of me to give an assignment like that to him. He was fighting every night, all through the night on the streets and I thought an assignment like that would keep him more in control, you know? I didn't know it would become an obsession. And then he figured out that Akira's son is a captive fighter and dove straight into this mess."

"So, it's true then?" asked Aidan. "Yaroslav was enslaved by one of the Houses?"

"That was the last thing Gunz told me," replied Jim. "But that was a few months ago. I can't believe he could disappear without a trace. Even Mrak Delar doesn't know where he is, and I must tell you – he's pissed."

"I know. I tried to summon him, but he didn't show up. Same with Kal," said Aidan. "I even took a trip to Kendral. I talked to Mrak's wife, Leila, and to Gunz's friend, Oleg Svetlov, and both of them refused to give me any information on Mrak's whereabouts."

"If I ever find Gunz, I am going to kill that son of a bitch myself," growled Jim.

"Jim, you can't find him because he doesn't want to be found," said Aidan with a sigh. "He is not the same boy that walked into your office three years ago. He grew as a person and as a Fire Salamander, and the loss of his love affected him deeper than any of us expected. So, if I ever find him, by some great miracle, the only thing I will do is sit down and listen. And if he needs my help, I'll be there for him, no questions asked."

"I guess you are a better man than I am," muttered Jim.

"I am not a man." Aidan chuckled.

"Well, you are definitely a better god than I am." Jim laughed, but his laughter died out quickly. "Listen, Aidan, there was a reason I called you. I need you to look into something for me. No one in my team is qualified for this kind of research."

"What is it?"

"It's really a two-part story," said Jim. "First, I got a call from FBI Headquarters in DC. They said something abnormal is going on with the supernatural community on the west coast, mostly in California. Even though it's outside my usual territory, they wanted me to take the lead on this case, stating that my team is the best they've got for this kind of assignment.

"Then I decided to call Akira and see if she could shed some light on it. Instead of talking over the phone, she showed up at my office without warning. And you know how Akira is?" He rolled his eyes and sighed. "She can never tell you things straight, and when you try and ask a few extra questions, she sits like a statue, staring at you with those narrow eyes without blinking like you're supposed to know everything without her telling you. Anyway, the only thing I was able to understand was that she is aware of the situation on the west coast, but she cannot help me with the investigation. Maybe you can talk to her and find out what she really knows?"

"So, what's going on the west coast?"

"That's what I need you to find out," said Jim. "The only thing the FBI HQ could tell me was that something is off with the Undead Americans. They do things their kind normally wouldn't, whatever that means."

"Undead Americans?" mumbled Aidan.

"You know, vampires, upirs, demons that wear dead humans' bodies – the undead community. Those creatures of magic that do not have a heartbeat. Do you think zombies are a real thing, by the way? If yes, they could be affected too."

"Yeah, everything is real," muttered Aidan. "Zombies are nothing but corpses, brought back to life by necromancy."

"Shit. I wish you hadn't told me that."

"So, what did they do that's out of character?" asked Aidan.

"For one, a group of vampires or upirs robbed a museum in broad day light. In front of humans," said Jim. "Then a clique of demons infiltrated a pharmaceutical company and stole some chemicals and materials. Anyway, when are your lessons over?"

"At six," replied Aidan, his thoughts already on everything Jim just told him.

"Why don't you stop by my office and I'll give you a file with everything I have so far. You can teleport, if you wish," suggested Jim.

"Sure, I'll see you at six fifteen," replied Aidan and hung up the phone.

CHAPTER 9

~ AIDAN ~

For the rest of the day Aidan walked around in a fog, his thoughts circling back to his conversation with Jim. He couldn't focus on the lessons and by five o'clock he gave up, allowing Angel to finish the day for him.

He quickly shed his Taekwondo uniform, throwing everything on his chair and changed into his normal clothes. Then he practically ran to the small parking lot in the back of the building where his car was parked. He opened it, but didn't get in. Instead, he pulled his cellphone out, quickly scrolled through the list of contact and pressed the dial button. His call was answered right away.

"EverSafe Security. How can I help you?" said a pleasantly-cheerful female voice.

"Ms. Akira Ida, please," he said and added, "This is Aidan McGrath."

"I'm sorry, Mr. McGrath," replied the secretary, her tone quickly slipping into a formal and cold category, "but Ms. Ida isn't accepting calls today."

"She will accept my call, Miss," insisted Aidan. The irritable secretary muttered something and hung up the phone. "What the hell?" Aidan stared at the phone in his hand, his eyebrows slowly climbing up.

He thought for a moment, then locked his car and quickly surveyed the area. He could not see or detect anyone with his second sight – the parking lot was absolutely empty. Aidan decided not to waste any time and snapped his fingers, teleporting to Akira's office.

He materialized in the lobby in front of the desk. The secretary, a youthful-looking vampire, hopped to her feet and hissed, baring her long fangs. Aidan snickered and headed toward Akira's office, completely ignoring the angry secretary.

Akira opened the door of her office before he reached it. She halted in the doorway. Her sharply angled eyes darted from Aidan to her secretary and her thin eyebrows gathered in a frown.

"Mr. McGrath, please come in," she said evenly without taking her eyes off of her secretary.

The vampire shrank under her heavy gaze. "Ms. Ida, you told me you didn't want to take any calls today—," she started but abruptly fell silent. Akira didn't move, didn't say a word. She just kept staring. The secretary squirmed, tears gathering in her eyes.

"Do I have to explain to you that there are exceptions to all rules?" asked Akira, slowly spitting out one word at the time. "When I said I didn't want to talk with anyone, I meant clients and employees. Not the ancient gods!"

"I'm sorry, Your Majesty," mumbled the secretary through tears. "It'll never happen again."

Akira pivoted on her heels and headed back into her office, pulling Aidan in. She slammed the door shut and turned to Aidan, her attentive eyes drenching him with a cold glare.

"Mr. McGrath, I'm sure there is a very good explanation as to why you teleported into my office unannounced. And it had better be something more important than my secretary's oversight," she said frostily.

"There is, ma'am," replied Aidan calmly. Akira seemed to be unusually agitated and the forced coldness was her way to conceal it. "I'm here to talk about what's happening on the west coast. Agent Andrews asked me to assist him with the investigation."

Akira nodded and waved at an empty chair in front of her large desk. Aidan sat down and she took a seat across from him.

"There is not much I can tell you, Mr. McGrath," she started the conversation, her voice low and hollow. "I've heard a few reports that raised my concern. These reports reminded me of the time when your stepmother was roaming this realm, controlling my loyal subjects, turning them into her mindless puppets."

"It's impossible," said Aidan, but a cold wave of doubt rushed through him, making his stomach twist with worry. "Angel locked her inside the void. You know what the void is. There is no way for her to break free from there."

Akira nodded, finally moving her unblinking gaze down. "I know. Mr. Burns told me... I'm not saying that the air demon is running free among the living again. I'm saying everything that's happening on the west coast reminds me of those awful days. Someone has the power to control my kind and they're not shy to use it."

"I understand," replied Aidan. "I'll be leaving for California first thing tomorrow morning. I suggest you stay here. It's not safe for you to be next to a person who can control your kind. We don't want a powerful vampire as yourself to be controlled by someone with unknown intentions. And what I gathered from the little information Jim gave me, I think this person is up to no good."

"Mr. McGrath, my son is there," said Akira, her slim body locked with rage. "Agent Andrews told me about the last report he received from Mr. Burns. Do you think Yaroslav is not a powerful vampire? He is almost three hundred years old and his powers are well developed for his age. I don't believe for a moment, that whoever enslaved him, wants to use him to make a few bucks betting in the underground fighting pits. There has to be more to it."

"That's what I intend to find out, Ms. Ida," said Aidan rising. "I'm going to get to the bottom of this."

"Mr. McGrath, bring my son back," said Akira quietly. "I can't go there to help him. I am well aware that it would be a mistake. So, I trust you and Mr. Burns to take care of Yaroslav for me."

"Yeah, I wish I knew where Mr. Burns was," muttered Aidan, shaking his head. "Last time anyone heard from him was over a month ago."

A tiny smile touched Akira's full lips, hardly lifting the corners of her small mouth, but her narrow eyes remained cold. "You call yourself Zane's friend, but it's amazing how little you know him," she said evenly, a layer of mockery present in her voice now. "I don't need to talk to him to know exactly where he is and what he is doing."

"I don't understand... Do you know something I don't? No one can sense Zane. He became so skilled in shadowing his magical signature, not even the Ancient Master can sense him."

"What don't you understand, Mr. McGrath?" exploded Akira, rising sharply. "No, I haven't heard from Zane and no, I have no news. But if I know anything about Zane Burns, I'm almost certain you'll find him in Los Angeles, California, next to Yaroslav. I'm positive that by now, Zane realized that the only way he could get close to my son was by becoming a captive fighter. That is the only way! So, I can bet you anything – he sold himself to one of the Houses, exchanging his freedom for the challenge to the California House."

"I hope he didn't do it. That would be reckless," said Aidan, a chilly wave of unease spreading through him. "But knowing his current state of mind, I wouldn't be surprised if he did something as stupid and dangerous as that."

"Yes, he is still grieving. Nevertheless, it has nothing to do with his current state of mind, as you put it," objected Akira frostily. "It's his honor and loyalty to his friends and the people he loves that drives him. You find Yaroslav, and you'll find Zane, Mr. McGrath. But as cold as it sounds, before you extract them, I suggest you learn who the person that runs the show is and what he or she truly wants. We might be facing a much bigger problem than just illegal fights and enslaved members of the supernatural community."

AFTER AIDAN LEFT AKIRA's company, he teleported straight into Jim's office who was waiting him, the folder with the FBI logo in his hands. He gave the folder to Aidan, telling him that everything he had so far on the situation in California was in this folder. Aidan opened the folder and quickly read through the reports. Just like Jim said – it wasn't much. With a sigh, he handed the folder back to the agent.

"What's your plan?" asked Jim, putting the folder away.

"I met with Akira before I came here," said Aidan. "She thinks Gunz sold himself to one of the Houses to get closer to Yaroslav. She also thinks that somehow the disappearance of her son and the strange situation on the west coast are connected. So, the first thing I am going to do is find out everything I can about the Head of the California House. After that, I'll buy a ticket to the first available captive event."

"How are you going to get the ticket?" asked Jim, looking at Aidan in awe. "I've heard it's by invitation only and it's practically unaffordable, unless your last name is Rockefeller."

"Getting in is not going to be a problem. I've been receiving invitations from them all the time. I just never bothered with it. Gladiatorial fights were never my thing," replied Aidan with a dismissive wave of his hand. "And as far as the cost of the tickets, money is not an issue either."

"I didn't know owning a martial arts school was such a profitable venture." Jim snickered, giving a quick tap on Aidan's shoulder. "On the serious side, what are you going to do if you see Yaroslav or Gunz during the event? Or both..."

"I have no idea," replied Aidan. "Like I said, I've never been to one of those events before. I don't know where they're held and how they're run. I may need to attend a few events and do some betting first, just to see what's going on. Besides finding Yaroslav and Gunz, I need to understand and investigate the situation in California, so it may take time."

Jim nodded and sighed. "Do me a favor, Aidan. If you manage to pull Gunz out of this mess, first make sure he's okay and then slap him around a few times. For me. The way he behaved in the last few months was—"

"Jim," interrupted Aidan dryly, "if Gunz really sold himself to one of the Houses and is fighting as a captive, don't you think he already got his fair share of being slapped around? Trust me, if that's the case, what he's going through right now is a lot worse than anything you can imagine."

"You're right," said Jim quietly. "I hope that is not the case."

Aidan nodded, then grabbed a sticky note and a pen from the desk and quickly wrote an address on it. "Here," he said offering it to Jim. "I know you don't want to hear about hiring a witch, but I still believe your team needs magical help. Go to *Missi's Kitchen*, Jim. It's a small restaurant in Ft. Lauderdale."

"Yeah, I know where it is," mumbled Jim, twisting the sticky note in his hands. "Gunz's favorite place..."

"That's right," confirmed Aidan. "Talk to Peyton. She's managing the place while Missi is away and she is a witch. I can't tell you how skillful she is, but I'm sure she'll be able to help you with what you need. Just tell her I sent you and see if you can start working together. At least part-time."

"Thanks, but what if Gunz finds a way—"

"If Gunz finds a way to bring Angie back, I'm sure Payton wouldn't mind stepping down. Like I said, I don't know her level of magical expertise, but she's a nice person."

"I'll talk to her," promised Jim, scratching the back of his head, doubt still imprinted on his face.

Aidan's phone shrilled, shattering the uncomfortable silence that enveloped the office. Aidan glanced at the screen and frowned.

"Jim, I must take this call. Is there anything else we need to discuss?" Jim shook his head no. "Okay, then I'll call you as soon as I arrive in LA. I'll keep you posted on every step of my investigation."

Aidan shook Jim's hand and walked out of the office.

* * *

"Hello?" Aidan quickly answered the phone, before the line went dead. The caller ID was showing an unfamiliar Chicago number and he wasn't sure what to expect.

"Aidan, hi!"

He heard Tessa's voice and relaxed for a moment, until he remembered that usually she called him from her cellphone and this number wasn't hers.

"Tessa, is everything okay?" asked Aidan, worry swirling through him. "Where are you calling from? What did you do this time?"

"Ah, Aidan, don't be such a worry worm." Tessa laughed and Aidan finally relaxed. "Everything is fine. Everything is better than fine! I'm calling from the Archmage Allerton's office. He wanted to speak with you."

"Tessa, wait—"

"Mr. McGrath? This is Quinn Allerton," said a deep male voice.

Here you go. Guardians. Aidan sighed. *I wonder if it's one of their powers, to summon me when I have neither time nor desire to deal with them.* "Hello, Mr. Allerton," replied Aidan, his voice tense. "What can I do for you?"

The Archmage laughed, his laughter deep and clear. "Mr. McGrath, please relax. I'm not Ms. Bonneville. I've heard she was treating you poorly, but only now I'm starting to realize the extent of the damage she created to the relationship between you and the Order. Please allow me to apologize again and assure you – it will never happen again."

"Apologies accepted," replied Aidan dryly. "What can I do for you?"

The Archmage sighed. "Mr. McGrath, earlier today we made a serious decision related to Therasia's future and since you're her only—"

"What did she do now?" asked Aidan, feeling the ground slowly melting under his feet.

"Mr. McGrath, no... She didn't do anything wrong. Opposite. In the last nine and a half months, Therasia advanced further in her studies than any other apprentice in our establishment. Her powers and her skills grew significantly, and the Guardians Council made quite an unusual decision.

"Currently Therasia is an Apprentice of the Fifth level. However, we all believe that with her skill level, it would be a waste of time to move her to the next Apprenticeship level. Tessa successfully passed all the tests and tomorrow she will be promoted into a Witch, First level. Like I said, this is quite unusual, but we all believe it's the right thing to do. Anyway, tomorrow, we have a ceremony where a few of our Apprentices will be graduating and I wanted to invite you to share this happy event with us and Therasia. Would you be able to attend, Mr. McGrath?"

"That's quite unexpected," said Aidan and fell silent, thoughts crowding his mind.

The Archmage was right – this kind of promotion wasn't common for the Guardians Order and it was considered a great honor. He recalled the way Tessa sounded – jubilant, elated – and he knew he had to be there.

"I know it's very short notice, but I called you as soon as the decision was made," said the Archmage, sounding apologetic. "We understand if you have a previous engagement that cannot be cancelled."

"No," replied Aidan, "I'll be there. What time is the ceremony?"

"10 AM, Assembly Hall," replied the Archmage. "See you tomorrow."

Aidan hung up and for a moment stared at the dark screen of his phone. *Another few hours are not going to make a difference in the situation on the west coast. I'll teleport from Chicago to LA as soon as the ceremony is over,* he thought, but doubts were ripping his soul apart. He sighed and dialed Jim's number.

"Jim, I have to delay my trip to LA by a few hours," he said as soon as Jim answered his call. "I should be there tomorrow afternoon…"

CHAPTER 10

~ ZANE BURNS, A.K.A. GUNZ ~

Judging by the position of the sun outside the large glass window, it was around noon, but the office was empty. After the dark filthy dungeon cell, the bright light and impersonal cleanliness of the modern business office was almost uncomfortable. Gunz glanced down at his dirty clothes, at his hands with broken nails and skinned knuckles, and his bare feet. He definitely didn't fit in this environment.

The guard stopped him in front of a matted glass door and knocked. After a moment, a deep male voice answered, telling them to come in. The guard opened the door and carelessly pushed Gunz through the doorway. He staggered forward, barely keeping himself from falling.

"My deepest gratitude," said Gunz, turning to the pumped-up asshole. "I have no idea how I would manage to cross the threshold without your assistance."

The guard growled and swung his hand, ready to punch him. Gunz chuckled and stepped back, raising his hands up.

"Theron, stop!"

Gunz spun around and saw a tall man in a dark business suit standing behind a massive desk, his fists planted firmly into its polished wood surface, his electric-blue eyes blazing with fury. Theron shrunk under his heavy gaze and bowed.

"I'm sorry, master, but he—"

"What did I tell you about hurting my captive fighters, Theron?" asked the man in a patronizing tone as if he was talking to a five-year old.

"Not to…" mumbled the guard apologetically.

"That's right. Captive fighters are expensive and it's hard to find good ones. Now, leave us," ordered the man with a dismissive wave of his hand.

The guard mumbled his apologies again and left the room, quietly shutting the door. The man walked around the desk and halted a step away from Gunz, putting his hands in his pockets. He was tall, at least six-feet-four. His long black hair which was slicked down into a low ponytail on the back of his head was falling down below his wide shoulders. His thin lips were partially concealed by his thick black mustache and beard. But what truly stood out on his face were his eyes. Gunz had never seen such a bright blue color. Under his straight black eyebrows, his eyes looked striking and surreal, like they were living a separate life.

"Hello, Gunz," said the man calmly, his strange eyes scanning him. "My name is George Novak and I'm the Head of California House."

"Hello, sir," replied Gunz coolly, meeting his penetrating gaze without blinking. "I wish I could say it's a pleasure meeting you, but I can't."

George Novak smiled, but the smile didn't reach his glacial eyes. "Well, how pleasant this conversation will be is entirely up to you, Gunz." He walked back to his desk and sat down, relaxing in his tall leather chair. "Please, come closer."

Gunz approached the desk, but since the man didn't offer him to sit down, he remained standing. Mr. Novak picked up a manila envelope and pulled a few documents out, quickly reviewing them. Gunz swallowed, recognizing the document Mr. Kogan had signed when he sold him to the California House.

"So, Gunz," continued Mr. Novak, dropping the papers back on his desk, "you used to belong to that dimwit Kogan, but he sold you for thirty pieces of silver... My representative, Mr. Park, said you were shocked. You didn't expect that, did you?"

Gunz didn't reply. There was nothing to say. Yes, he had been betrayed. Yes, he had expected something like this could happen, but he hadn't expected it to happen so quickly.

"I see," muttered Mr. Novak, a cruel smirk hiding beneath his mustache. "Mr. Park warned me that you are not going to be easy to deal with."

"Define easy," said Gunz dryly. "If you expect me to kiss your ass and worship you, then no – it's not going to be easy." He seized the collar with his hand and pulled on it slightly. "Obviously, I'm in the situation where I must obey your command and fight for your House, but that's all you'll get from me."

"Gunz, Gunz, Gunz... You really don't know me. Watch your tongue, my son." Mr. Novak shook his head. He pushed a few papers away and Gunz saw the controller.

"My controller, I assume," said Gunz with an indifferent shrug. "Woof-woof. Oh, please don't hurt me, my kind master. Yeah... I'm extremely terrified."

"You're not afraid of me, are you?" huffed Mr. Novak.

"No, should I be?"

Mr. Novak got up and approached Gunz. Seizing his chin with his long skinny fingers, he forced his face up, his heavy blue eyes drilling into Gunz's. His pupils dilated and then contracted again, and even with his magic completely suppressed, Gunz could feel Mr. Novak's magic invading his head. Soft whispers filled his head, suggesting to give in and stop fighting. The room spun around him and he took in a sharp breath.

"You're fighting me. How is it possible?" hissed Mr. Novak, his fingers digging into Gunz's face. "Your magic and your elemental power are completely blocked. Please explain how you can fight me, Mr. Zane Burns!" He let go of Gunz and folded his arms over his chest.

Gunz stilled, realizing that this man who had complete power over him, knew who he was and most likely knew what he was. Mr. Novak shook his head, observing Gunz's reaction with a cold smirk.

"That's right, Zane. I know who you are," he confirmed. "As skilled as you are in shadowing your energy signature, I know you are a Fire Salamander. Besides Kal, the Fire Elemental, you are the only Fire Salamander in this world. And now you belong to me."

"Temporarily," objected Gunz, slowly regaining his calm.

"Nothing is as permanent as temporary." Mr. Novak cackled. "In the meantime, you may want to know that when Mr. Kogan sold you to me, he added one very unusual clause into the sale contract. And even though I found it a little peculiar, I agreed to it."

"And why would I want to know that?" asked Gunz, sarcasm dripping from his every word. "Obviously Mr. Kogan wants to milk you for all you've got. He's selfless that way, you know."

Mr. Novak ignored his sarcasm. "Actually, he did it for you. Not for himself. The only clause he added – and it was a deal breaker for him, by the way – was that you get to fight my best captive fighter, Alucard." Lost for words, Gunz didn't say anything and Mr. Novak continued, "I promised that I would allow this fight. Having said that, I have to warn you – Alucard will destroy you. You will lose this fight. So, let me ask you, Zane… Or would you prefer me to use your nickname?"

"Whatever… doesn't matter to me," replied Gunz coldly. "I'm not planning to stick around for too much longer."

"Oh, you will stick around for as long as I want you here,"

growled Mr. Novak, cutting the air with his hand. His irritation broke through and Gunz smirked – finally he was able to elicit a human emotion from this man. "And if you are not afraid of me, you need to rethink that. I own you. And it's not a figure of speech. Even though you're an immortal Child of Fire, torturing a Fire Salamander is easy and can be quite entertaining. Besides, you're also a man and you feel pain just like any man would. I can make you wish you were dead."

Gunz laughed bitterly. "I've already heard all of that. It's about time someone came up with a better threat. Yes, you can torture me. Been there, done that, don't care."

"You speak like a man who has nothing to lose," muttered Mr. Novak, narrowing his eyes.

"Look at me? Do I look like I have anything to lose?" Gunz clenched his fists, taking a step closer to his captor. "Just stop threatening me. If you want to torture me, go for it. But don't wave a gun in my face unless you're ready to pull the trigger!"

Mr. Novak cocked his head, staring down at him and shook his head. "We'll see about that. In the meantime, tell me, Gunz, why are you so adamant about fighting Alucard? A glutton for punishment?"

"I'm looking for a challenge. So far no one was able to beat me in the cage. I've heard of Alucard and I thought, why not? I never lost a fight to a vampire yet." He shrugged.

"Do you know that lying is a sin, my son?" asked Mr. Novak severely.

Gunz glanced up, his mouth open. George Novak was completely serious. "Sin? Really?" He chuckled. "Sorry. I'm not religious. But even if I was, I didn't lie."

Novak's eyes got darker, becoming the color of a stormy sea. As he stepped closer to Gunz, his body visibly tensed. Gunz held his breath, expecting some kind of physical punishment, but nothing happened.

"I will allow this fight," hissed Mr. Novak through gritted

teeth. "But know that – you will fight Alucard as a man. No magic, no elemental power. Your controller will be set to maximum, just the way it is set right now."

Yes! Finally. Gunz bowed his head down to hide his true emotions. "That's fine," he said quietly. "I'll fight him as a man. I don't need my magic to deal with a vampire. But you do realize that when the controller is set to maximum, it's not only blocking my magic, it also makes me weaker physically and significantly slower."

"You think?" Mr. Novak snickered coldly. "Of course, I know that. And I'm counting on that. Alucard can't kill you, but I pray he gives you a nice beating and I'll make sure that your controller remains set to maximum even after the fight is over, so you can't heal yourself. Mark my word, I will put the fear of God into you and teach you some respect and humility, my son."

"I'm sure, you will give it a nice try," agreed Gunz, his mouth set in a stubborn straight line. "But whatever you do, don't call me son. You can call me slave, captive, whatever the hell you want, but I'm not your son."

George Novak shoved his hands into his pockets, rocking back and forth on his feet, and stared down at him, his black pupils fluctuating in size. "All God's creations are my children," he said dryly. Then he walked back to the desk and pushed the intercom button, asking Theron to come back in.

The guard entered the room and stopped at the door, shifting from foot to foot uncomfortably. Mr. Novak glanced at him and pursed his lips.

"Theron, please escort Gunz to the captive quarters. I'm done with him for today," he ordered with a light flick of his wrist. "Put him in the room with Alucard. Since he was so adamant on fighting him, I'll give him a chance to get familiar with our champion before he has to face him in the event."

"Yes, master," said Theron. He approached Gunz and seized

his arm, but then let go and halted, a tensed expression on his face. "Master, if I may…"

"What is it, Theron?" Mr. Novak sighed, rolling his eyes.

"I'm sorry, master, but he is a wizard…"

"So?"

"I mean, he has red blood in his veins," continued Theron, his face strained, like he was lifting a hundred-pound dumbbell with every word he said.

"So?"

"Alucard… you know, a vampire… he's always hungry," continued Theron. "You told me I shouldn't hurt your captive fighters."

"Yes, I did."

"But if I put him in a locked room with Alucard, he may, you know…like drain him or something…"

"Oh, I hope he's extremely hungry, Theron." Mr. Novak cackled. "Tell Alucard that he can nibble on him a little. Just make sure he knows not to drain him completely. He can't kill this man. It's an order."

"I understand, master," mumbled Theron. He seized Gunz's arm again and pulled him toward the door. As they were about to exit, Mr. Novak stopped them again.

"And for God's sake, Theron, before you put him in the room with Alucard, send him to the shower room and find him something clean to wear. I can't allow my best fighter to eat junk."

"Don't worry, Mr. Novak, my mom managed to instill at least some manners in me. I'll wash my hands before I let Alucard dine on me," quipped Gunz, snickering and immediately got slapped by Theron.

Nice, now I'm also a chew-toy for a vamp. My status is getting improved by the minute. Let's hope I'm right and Alucard and Yaroslav are one and the same, Gunz thought, as Theron pushed him out of the office.

CHAPTER 11

~ ZANE BURNS, A.K.A. GUNZ ~

Gunz closed his eyes letting the strong jets of hot water wash over him. The cuts and scrapes on his skin prickled, but he didn't care. For the first time in days, he allowed himself to relax. *Well, at least the shower here is good,* he thought, slowly massaging the shampoo into his scalp. He wished he could stay here longer, but he knew that Theron was waiting for him outside the shower stall and the man had the patience of a toddler. Quickly washing the shampoo and soap off his body, he shut the water down and walked outside the stall.

Theron was standing right next to the door, ready to knock again. Gunz noticed a towel in his hands and reached for it, but Theron stepped away, snickering.

"Towel, please," said Gunz with a sigh.

"I think I'll take you to Alucard just like this, naked and afraid."

Gunz tilted his head, narrowing his eyes at the guard. "Remember what your master said? He said you can't hurt captive fighters."

"Yeah..." mumbled Theron warily. "So? I'm not the one who is going to be hurting you. Alucard will do it for me."

"Well, your master didn't say anything about captive fighters hurting overly-pumped ogres like yourself."

Before Theron could react, Gunz covered the distance between them, seized his arm, twisted it behind the guard's back and pulled it up at a painful angle. The man grunted, dropped to his knees and tapped on the floor. Gunz grabbed the towel out of his hand and quickly dried himself, wrapping the towel around his hips. Then he looked down at the guard who was still sitting on the floor, massaging his shoulder, and offered him his hand. Theron gaped at his hand for a moment but took it and got up.

"Fresh clothes for you," he said, offering him a plastic bag, notes of discomfort in his voice.

"Thanks." Gunz took the clothes out of the bag and got dressed.

"Hey, Gunz," said Theron as he directed him toward the captive quarters, "I've heard of you before... You fought in the unattached circles."

"Yeah, so what?" replied Gunz.

"Rumor has it that you've never lost a fight," continued Theron. "Is it true?"

Gunz nodded, not willing to go deeper into this conversation and Theron didn't push for it. They stopped in front of a heavy metal door and Theron unlocked it with a magnetic card, entering a six-digit pin in the key pad.

"Get in," he said, opening the door for Gunz.

Gunz walked into a large room with a tall ceiling. In the center of the room there was a station with security equipment, manned by a few guards. All along the perimeter of the room, he counted at least twenty doors. Each door was locked and had a key pad on the wall next to it. With relief he noticed that there were no one-way mirrors on the walls. Also, he didn't notice video feed from inside the cells on the guards' computer monitors.

"Hey, Theron," Gunz whispered, arching his brow at the guards' station, "do they monitor what's going on inside the cells?"

"Why?" asked Theron with an indifferent shrug. "There are no security cameras in the cells. The doors can't be unlocked from inside. But even if some crazy captive managed to unlock the door and bypass the guards, he won't be able to leave this area because of the gray jewelry radius settings."

Theron pulled him all the way to the far end of the room and stopped in front of the last door.

"Ready?" he asked, reaching for his magnetic card.

What if this vamp is not Yaroslav? A thought flashed through Gunz's mind and chills ran down his spine. "Let's get it over with," he said to Theron, bracing himself for the worst.

The guard unlocked the door and pushed Gunz inside. "Good luck," he said and locked the door behind him.

* * *

Gunz slowly turned around. He saw a man lying on the bed, his long blond hair falling over his face and chest obscuring his features. He appeared to be sleeping, but Gunz wasn't sure he was. The man was a vampire and he could remain completely motionless for hours.

"Alucard?" called Gunz, taking a tentative step forward.

The man jolted up and crouched on the bed ready to pounce. He threw his long hair off his face and Gunz recognized Yaroslav. However, he wasn't sure Yaroslav recognized him. All he could see in front of him was a feral, hungry vampire.

Yaroslav growled, a low rumbling sound, and his eyes shone with a scarlet light. Before Gunz could say anything, he felt Yaroslav's fingers wrapped around his neck, pinning him to the door. He saw the scarlet eyes next to his face and there wasn't a sign of recognition in his eyes or anything at all, except all-consuming hunger.

"Yaroslav..." croaked Gunz, struggling to breathe.

Yaroslav hissed, displaying his long fangs and forced Gunz's head to the side, ready to sink his blade-like fangs into his neck. Gunz pushed against his chest, but it was like pushing against a tank.

"Yaroslav, please..." he whispered, red spots dancing around him. "Slavik... Akira sent me... please..."

Yaroslav's hands shook and he let go. Gunz slid down to the floor coughing, clutching his neck. Yaroslav squatted in front of him and carefully lifted his face. The carnivorous scarlet glow was gone from his eyes and for a moment he looked terrified.

"Gunz?" he whispered. "I almost... What are you doing here? How did you find me?" Then his eyes fell on Gunz's neck and his face became a stone mask. He grabbed Gunz's arms and checked his wrists. "You're a captive? How?"

"It was the only way I could get close to you," replied Gunz.

"You gave up your freedom just to find me?"

"Yeah, but forget about all that," said Gunz. "Now we have a bigger problem. I have to fight you in the cage. I don't know when the event is going to happen, but sooner or later it will."

"Oh, no..." Yaroslav dropped to one knee, his fingers digging into the mane of his golden hair. "No, no, no... That can't happen. If I'm forced to kill you in the cage, all the humans that are present at the event will die."

"Then don't kill me." Gunz chuckled.

"You don't understand," said Yaroslav rising and offered him his hand, "I'm not in control of my actions."

"You mean the controller?" asked Gunz, taking his hand and got up.

"No, the controller is not the problem. It's a lot worse for me," said Yaroslav. He went back to his bed and sat down heavily.

Gunz sat on the second bed, facing him. "Explain, please."

"The gray stone jewelry can control anyone with magic or elemental power," started Yaroslav, "but in your case, it can only control your magic and your physical strength. It doesn't control your mind. But I'm not like you." He lowered his head, hiding his face in his hands.

"Slavik, I don't understand," said Gunz. "What's the difference? I saw vampires and demons controlled by the gray stone jewelry. The effect of the gray stones is a little different on your kind, but it still controls only your body, not your mind."

"Gunz, the collar on my neck is set to none. It's nothing but a décor when it comes to controlling me," said Yaroslav. "George Novak doesn't need the gray stones to control vampires. He can control anything that has no heartbeat and he doesn't need any magical artifacts for that."

"Slavik, is he—"

"George Novak is a necromancer," said Yaroslav, cringing. "He can control my body and my mind. I'm nothing but a mindless weapon in his hands. I've met necromancers before, but never one as powerful as him. If he wishes me to kill you in the cage, I will do it and I won't even know that I'm doing it. When I'm in the cage, I'm completely under his influence. You have no idea..." His voice trailed off and he lowered his face into his hands again.

"Yaroslav... Slavik, don't give up, we'll figure it out," said Gunz quietly. "I went through hell just to find you and I'm not leaving without you."

Yaroslav raised his face and there was so much pain reflected in his eyes that Gunz shuddered inwardly. "You're not leaving at all, my friend," he said, shaking his head. "There is no way to take this collar off. Only your owner can do it. And with this collar on your neck, you have no way out. In case you still didn't figure it out – captive fighters are nothing but supernatural slaves. No way out. No way to send a message to the outside world. No one to ask for help."

"Slavik, now that I found you, I have a way to send a message to the outside world," said Gunz. "All I need is a tiny bit of my fire back."

"What do you mean?"

"My fire and my magic are blocked," explained Gunz. "Novak is keeping my controller set to maximum."

"I think, I can help with that," said Yaroslav rising. "I can convince Novak to give you some access to your magic. Let me talk to him."

"Wait, Slavik," said Gunz. "Before you call him, I need to ask you something."

Yaroslav stopped and turned to him, staring at him quizzically.

"When I just walked in, you looked a bit—um—hungry. What's going on with you? Doesn't Novak feed you?" asked Gunz. "Even right now your eyes are still glowing red a little."

Yaroslav shuddered and bowed his head. "Gunz, I'm sorry. I didn't recognize you. To be honest, I don't think I would recognize anyone in this state. The thirst is driving me crazy."

"This is something I don't understand. Aren't you his best fighter?" asked Gunz, anger slowly building up in him. "He should be taking care of you, not starving you to the point where you're losing your mind."

"What you just said is the point of starving me," explained Yaroslav, stifling a sigh. "He doesn't need my mind clear. When I'm in the cage and he controls me, he subdues my mind to the point that there is nothing left of me but basic instincts. In that cage, I'm a predator – hungry, thoughtless, merciless."

"Slavik, does he get you any blood at all?" Feeling numb inside, Gunz wasn't sure that he was ready to hear his answer.

"Yes, he does," replied Yaroslav, averting his gaze. "After each event. And even then…" His voice disappeared into silence. "I'm not proud of what I'm doing, Gunz... but I'm forced. I have no choice."

"What does he make you do, Yaroslav?" growled Gunz, his fingers grasping at the bed, tearing through the sheets.

For a moment Yaroslav closed his eyes, muscles working in his jaw. "Kill. He makes me kill and drain humans for the entertainment of the crowd," he said quietly. "From what I've heard, these scumbags pay Novak an obscene amount of money to see that. I'm the vampire, but I swear to God, these people who pay to see me kill innocent humans and feed on them... they're the ones who have no soul. This is why Novak keeps me hungry between the events."

"Jesus Christ almighty," whispered Gunz, nausea rising to his throat. "What else does he make you do?"

"You don't want to know," mumbled Yaroslav. "Please don't make me tell you everything. I'm disgusted with myself without you looking at me like I'm some—"

"Slavik, you don't have to tell me anything. And none of it is your fault," said Gunz, shaking his head. "Just one more question. Did Theron tell you anything before he brought me in?"

"Yeah, he told me that I can feed on you as long as I don't kill you," replied Yaroslav. "Of course, I'm not going to do that."

"Yes, you are," objected Gunz calmly. "Can you drink my blood, knowing what I am?"

"Depends on how much fire is in you," mumbled Yaroslav backing away from him, holding his hands up. "I'm not going to do it. Are you nuts?"

"Right now, I have zero fire and yes, you're going to feed on me," said Gunz firmly. "Novak has no idea that we know each other, and I want to keep it that way. I'm sure that as hungry as you are, you would feed on a stranger. Just don't take a lot of my blood. I'm weak as it is."

Yaroslav didn't move, but his eyes lit up with a hungry scarlet light. Nevertheless, he silently shook his head no.

"Do I have to punch you like they do in some stupid movies to provoke you to bite me?" Gunz sighed and tapped on the bed next to him. "Do it, Slavik. We have to make Novak believe we don't know each other."

Hardly moving his feet, Yaroslav approached him and froze, staring down at him, a haunted expression in his eyes. Gunz tilted his head to the side, giving him access to his neck.

"No, not your neck." Yaroslav kneeled before him and took his arm. "It'll hurt but just for a moment."

"Don't worry." Gunz chuckled. "I already forgot when nothing hurt the last time."

Yaroslav pulled his arm to his mouth and his sharp fangs sunk into Gunz's wrist. Gunz groaned as pain radiated through him but didn't fight Yaroslav's grip. Slowly the pain melted away, replaced by a feeling of warmth, bordering on physical pleasure. It took him over, fogging his mind, making him forget where he was and what he was doing. Weak and lightheaded, he closed his eyes, dropping his head to his chest.

Is that how a vampire's bite feels? A thought flashed through his dazed mind. *No wonder their victims don't struggle... I don't think I could fight that even if I wanted...* The scariest thing was that he had no desire to fight it. In fact, his whole body was screaming for more, all his instincts suppressed, nonexistent.

"Slavik..." he whispered faintly, taking shallow breaths. "Please stop... I don't think I can handle it much longer..."

Yaroslav let go immediately and applied pressure on Gunz's wrist with his hand to stop the bleeding. Thin red streams slipped between his fingers. Gunz glanced at his own blood and his stomach clenched. He moaned and eased himself on the bed.

"Your blood," said Yaroslav wiping his lips with the back of his hand, "it's different. Stronger. Are you okay? Did I hurt you?"

"I'm fine. You didn't hurt me. At some point, I wasn't sure if I wanted to fight you or fu— well..." Gunz chuckled.

Yaroslav laughed, throwing his long hair off his face. For a moment, he looked the way Gunz remembered him from a year ago.

"Yeah, the pleasure of a vampire's bite," he said, winking at Gunz. "This is why humans don't fight when we bite them." A dark cloud crossed his face and he sobered up. His expression closed and the haunted look settled back in his blue eyes. "And that's the other service I'm forced to perform. From what I understand, some rich humans pay serious money for that kind of service. But after"—he closed his eyes while pinching the bridge of his nose and exhaled a rugged breath— "every time when Theron escorts me back to this room, I wish I could die, so I don't have to—"

"Call Theron, Yaroslav," hissed Gunz, fury searing through him. "Do whatever you need to do, but I need my fire back."

CHAPTER 12

~ ZANE BURNS, A.K.A. GUNZ ~

A full week passed before George Novak finally got around and summoned Yaroslav to his office. The only thing Gunz remembered from this whole week was endless, brutal training. He left the room early in the morning and came back late at night, hardly able to move, hurting and quite often bleeding.

True to his word, Novak kept his controller set at maximum which made his training even more challenging as the gray stones magic was significantly weakening him physically as well as slowing down his healing process.

Every night when he came back to his room sick with exhaustion, Yaroslav offered to heal him. And every time, Gunz politely refused his offers. He knew Slavik wasn't trying to hurt him or put him under his vampiric control, but he wasn't comfortable with the idea of drinking vampire blood.

They were in the middle of sparring when Theron walked in, interrupting them, and told Yaroslav their master wished to see him in his office after training. Yaroslav lowered his practice sword, waiting for Theron to leave.

"Gunz, listen," he said, a vibe of unease lingering around

him, "I'm going to ask Novak to give you some access to your magic, but we have to put on a show for him. Otherwise, he'll refuse to do it."

"What kind of show?" asked Gunz warily.

"I'm going to play a soulless bloodsucker who doesn't give a damn about what happens to you and you're going to play a beat up, half-dead wizard," replied Slavik, sounding almost apologetic, "and we're going to have to sell it."

"Doesn't sound too hard," muttered Gunz.

"Not for me, but for you – a different story," replied Yaroslav, raising his sword. "We still have some time to waste until the end of the day. Now, attack."

Yaroslav stopped their training ten minutes ahead of time. He took their swords and put them away, then approached Gunz.

"I'm sorry, I have to do this to you," he said, staring down at his clenched hands.

"Just go ahead and do it," replied Gunz, lowering his arms. "I knew what you meant when you said we're gonna have to sell it. So, make it look real."

"I'm truly sorry about this," murmured Yaroslav and punched him in the face.

Yaroslav hardly even pulled his hand back. For him, it was just a light jab, but Gunz felt like he was hit by a sledgehammer. He gasped, clasping his hands to his face as his nose broke with a gut-wrenching crunch. His breath caught and he collapsed, his eyes watering from pain. Yaroslav didn't wait for him to recover. Going down to his knees, he punched him again, driving his fist into the side of his face. Gunz cried out and curved into a ball, covering his face with his arms. The dark bruises spread around his eyes and his left eye swelled to the point where he couldn't open it.

Yaroslav seized Gunz's arm, forcefully pulling it away from his face. Before Gunz recovered enough to object, the vampire sunk his fangs into his arm above the elbow. Gunz flinched and tried to pull away, but Yaroslav held him down. A moment later, the pain melted away into the bliss of the vampire's bite. It was a strange sensation – his face was bleeding and swollen, yet he felt nothing. The only thing he felt was warmth flowing through his body as an overwhelming weakness took him over. He closed his eyes and moaned.

"Gunz, are you okay?" asked Yaroslav, holding down his arm to stop the bleeding. He looked anxious, but his voice sounded strangely distant and thick.

Gunz glanced at him with one eye, still slightly dazed and nodded. "As soon as we're out of this mess, I will take my revenge. You better be ready, because my wrath will be terrible." He tried to smile but winced as the pain in his broken nose and split lips spiked through him.

"Theron is here. Now play your part," whispered Yaroslav. He grabbed Gunz and carelessly threw him over his shoulder.

"Ahh," moaned Gunz. Playing half-dead seemed to come easy in his current state.

Theron glanced at him and his jaw dropped. "Hey, Alucard, what did you do to him? He looks like he's one step away from death."

"None of your business," murmured Yaroslav, heading toward the door. "Take me to our master."

Theron silently escorted them to Mr. Novak's office. Once in a while he carefully touched Gunz's limp arm, muttering something under his breath. Once they reached the office, he opened the door and let them inside.

George Novak was in his office, sitting behind the desk, peering at the computer monitor like it was some mysterious beast. As soon as Yaroslav walked in, he tore his eyes away from the monitor and stared at him. The corners of his mouth quirked up as he took in Gunz's state. Yaroslav kneeled before him, carelessly dumping Gunz on the floor. Gunz moaned, blood slowly trickling from his nose and the corner of his mouth.

Mr. Novak approached him and pushed his arm with the tip of his shoe. "I see you fed on him, Alucard?" he asked indifferently.

"Theron said I could," replied Yaroslav without lifting his head. "Was I wrong to do so?"

"No, my son. You can feed on him, just don't take too much of his blood. I still need him to fight in the next event," replied Mr. Novak, his fingers brushing over Yaroslav's hair.

For a moment, the vampire tensed, and his eyes widened, but he quickly recovered. "This is why I dared to request your attention, master," he said calmly. "I wanted to speak with you about the event where I'm supposed to fight this worthless wizard."

"The event is in five days from now. Please rise, my son, and let's talk," said Novak. He walked back to his desk and sat down, pointing at a chair across from him. "Tell me what bothers you about this event."

Yaroslav got up, leaving Gunz sprawled on the floor, but didn't sit down. "I've been training with this man for a week, master," started Yaroslav. "While I can see that he is a skilled fighter, his controller drains too much of his strength. He is less than a human hunter. Too slow, too weak, and getting hurt too easy. Besides, he's always in pain. The gray stones magic stops him from healing. As a sparring partner, he is useless to me."

"I can assign a different sparring partner to you, Alucard, if that's what you want," suggested Mr. Novak with an indifferent flick of his wrist.

"No, I like him. I want to keep him, if you don't mind, master." Yaroslav laughed icily. "It's like a punching bag and all you can eat buffet in one tiny human body."

"Then what do you want me to do?" asked Mr. Novak, narrowing his eyes at Yaroslav.

"The event," replied Yaroslav. He put his hands on the back of the chair, leaning forward slightly. "You can't let me fight this man with his controller set to maximum."

"And why not? I believe he needs a lesson in humility and serious punishment." Mr. Novak pulled up slightly, leaning over the desk and Gunz met his mocking gaze without blinking.

"He's getting punished enough in training. It's not that," continued Yaroslav, shaking his head. "I'm worried that a match like this will make the guests of the event a little upset. They're coming there to see me fighting a worthy opponent, hoping that the fight will last longer than thirty seconds."

"Oh," muttered Mr. Novak, rubbing his forehead. "You're right. In my desire to punish him, I forgot about it." He opened one of the drawers in his desk and pulled a controller out. Then he got up and approached Gunz, staring down at him with disdain, his lips pursed.

"You have to release his magic at least a little, master," said Yaroslav, approaching him.

"Fine."

Novak pressed a button on the controller and Gunz sucked in a ragged breath, feeling the fire slowly spread through his body. It wasn't strong, but it made him feel better, taking the edge off the pain, slowly restoring his physical strength.

"I gave him some access to his magic. It's not a lot, but it should be sufficient for him to gain some strength and perform better at the event. As far as self-healing, that wouldn't be enough," said Mr. Novak, throwing the controller back on his desk. "Now, Alucard, be a good boy and heal him. He looks like he's about to cross the veil and I can't afford losing captive fighters."

Gunz stiffened, throwing a desperate glance at Yaroslav.

"Master, but I just fed on him. If I give him my blood now, it will—," Yaroslav started to say, but Mr. Novak raised his hand, frowning.

"Are you questioning your master, Alucard? Do as you've been told, or do I need to control you?" he seethed, pushing Yaroslav toward Gunz. "Heal him! I know it will create a psychic link between the two of you and I don't give a damn. I want to see him healed and ready to fight. And if he gets hurt during training, you will heal him again. Am I clear, vampire??"

"Yes, master," whispered Yaroslav. Lowering down to his knees next to Gunz, he bit his wrist. A thick dark liquid trickled down his arm, dropping on Gunz's chest.

"No, please," croaked Gunz, but Yaroslav frowned and shook his head slightly.

"Drink," he ordered, pressing his bleeding wrist to Gunz's lips.

The smell of the vampire's blood invaded his senses and he turned his head away, smearing the dark liquid over his face. Yaroslav seized his hair and jerked his head back. He put his bleeding wrist back to Gunz's lips again and pressed down.

"Drink before my wound heals," he hissed, pulling on Gunz's hair and then quietly mouthed, "Please…"

Gunz cracked his lips open, allowing a few thick drops to slip into his mouth. It wasn't as disgusting as he imagined it would be. On the contrary, it had a sweet flavor to it and as soon as he swallowed the blood, the pain started to fade away. He felt stronger and better than he had in days. He raised his hands and seized Yaroslav's arm, taking more of his blood. The swelling started to go down and he was able to open his left eye again.

After a moment, Yaroslav pulled away from him. Gunz got up, feeling recharged and strangely energized. Nothing hurt, and most importantly, he had at least some of his fire back. George Novak was looking at him, his arms crossed, an arrogant expression on his face.

"So, Gunz, how is your stay so far?" he asked.

"I'm enjoying it immensely," replied Gunz calmly, meeting

his eyes with a deadpan expression. "Wouldn't change it for the world."

"Nothing is a lesson to you, boy," growled Mr. Novak, his pupils dilating, coloring his eyes black. He turned his sinister eyes with fluctuating pupils to Yaroslav and the vampire recoiled under his gaze, wrapping his arms around his head. "Alucard, are you still hungry?"

"No, master," replied Yaroslav, his voice hoarse, and lowered his arms. "I just fed."

"Too bad, I would love to see him squirming while you're draining his blood to the last drop. Oh well. Next time around," exhaled Mr. Novak, his eyes returning to their normal state. "If there is nothing else you wanted to discuss, take him out of my sight. I don't want to see him until the event next week. And when you're in the cage, I'll make sure you don't hold back, Alucard." Mr. Novak walked around the desk and dropped into his chair. "You may leave now."

Yaroslav bowed, then grabbed Gunz by the back of his neck and pushed him out of the office.

* * *

As soon as they walked into their room, Gunz stopped. The stress of this endless day and the severity of everything that had just happened finally caught up with him. He leaned back, resting his back against the door and slowly slid down to the floor, closing his eyes tiredly. Yaroslav sat down by his side, resting his arms atop his bent knees.

"Should I be asking you?"

"No," Gunz cut him off. "Don't ask anything."

"I didn't know that would happen."

"I know. I'm not blaming you."

"I'm sorry—"

"Don't apologize. You have nothing to apologize for."

"I do."

They both fell silent, sitting on the floor, deep in their own thoughts. A few minutes later, Gunz opened his eyes and carefully ran his fingers over the tattoo on his shoulder, sending a tiny amount of his fire magic through it.

"Mishka, can you come out now?" he asked in a soft whisper.

With a light pop the wyvern materialized in front of him. Yaroslav hissed and hopped to his feet.

"Slavik, relax," said Gunz. "This is Mishka, my wyvern."

"You have a pet-wyvern and you carry it with you?" asked Yaroslav, carefully backing away from the wyvern.

"A pet??? Who are you calling a pet, vampire?" squealed Mishka, turning to Slavik, a cloud of fire energy rising around him. Yaroslav raised his arms, taking a few more steps back.

"Mishka, cool down. Sorry, but Yaroslav didn't get a chance to meet you before. Are you okay, my friend?" asked Gunz peacefully, offering him his arm to land on, but the wyvern ignored it.

"Am I okay?" he yelled in a high-pitched voice. "What do you think, firetwat? You left me without any fire for God knows how long!"

"I'm sorry, I had no choice," said Gunz, notes of remorse in his voice. "I couldn't leave Yaroslav without help—"

"That's right. You had to go and get yourself into another mess just to help this blond leech! But you didn't care how it made me feel. It's always about you and what you want and what you need! When are we going to do anything I want or need?"

"Mishka, please, it's not a good time—," Gunz started to say.

"It never is!" shouted Mishka irritably, interrupting him. "Selfish firetwat!"

The wyvern flew up to him and slapped him across his face with his wing. The slap wasn't strong, but Gunz grunted, annoyance flaring through him.

"You two are bickering like an old married couple," said Yaroslav snickering, and sat down on the bed.

Before Gunz could say anything, Mishka landed on his shoulder and wrapped his wings around his neck, pressing his hot head against Gunz's cheek. "I'm sorry, boss, I didn't mean it," he mumbled. "I was a little upset."

"It's okay, Mishka," said Gunz, petting the wyvern's golden wings. "We don't have much time and I need to explain to you what needs to be done."

"I'm ready, boss. No more interruptions."

Yeah, right. Gunz chuckled. "Mishka, I need you to leave this place and deliver two messages for me."

"You want me to leave you here with this leech, completely unprotected?" huffed the wyvern, incredulously.

"Yaroslav is never going to hurt me," replied Gunz, throwing a quick glance at the vampire. *At least not willingly.*

"So, it wasn't your Yaroslav who beat you into a bloody pulp just a few minutes ago?" asked Mishka, blinking furiously at him.

"He had my consent. We had to do it." Gunz sighed. "Mishka, please, let me finish. It's important."

"I swear, your boss is safe with me," promised Yaroslav, struggling to suppress his laughter.

"Fine, then I'm leaving and going straight to Kal. He is the only one who can pull both of you out of this mess," said Mishka, folding his wings on his back.

"No!" exclaimed Gunz. "You are not going to get Kal involved, Mishka. I need you to do everything as I tell you, and the way I tell you to do it. Promise me you will follow my directions."

"Okay, okay, I promise... You're always so touchy. Everything should be the way you want it—"

"Mishka!" yelled Gunz, throwing his hands up. "I need you to deliver two messages. First, you're going to fly to the Celtic

Otherworld and find Gwyn ap Nudd. Once you are done with Gwyn, fly back to Florida and give my second message to Agent Andrews. Do you understand?"

"Yes. First Gwyn, then Jim. Got it," replied Mishka grouchy. "What do you want me to tell them?"

Gunz explained everything to Mishka. The wyvern listened, this time without interruptions, slightly shaking his head. When Gunz was done, he sat quietly on his shoulder.

"Gunz, I don't want to leave you here," he said, finally serious. "This man, Novak, he's evil. I can feel it. Whatever he is doing here, it can't be any good. And he is controlling both of you – an old vampire and a Fire Salamander. It's dangerous, boss. And if I leave now, you'll have no other way to communicate with the outside world."

"I know, Mishka," replied Gunz. "This is why I need to find out what Novak is up to, and then Yaroslav and I can get the hell out of here. Please, my friend, find Gwyn as soon as you can."

Mishka nodded and hugged Gunz one more time. Then he threw a scorching gaze at Yaroslav and with a light pop vanished from the room.

CHAPTER 13

~ AIDAN ~

It had been over two weeks since Aidan left South Florida and traveled first to Chicago and then to Los Angeles. His visit to Chicago was brief. The Guardians award ceremony was short and to the point, and the whole thing took less than an hour.

After the ceremony was over, Archmage Allerton pulled Aidan into his office, thanking him for attending the ceremony. Then in so many words, he told him that he was aware of the situation on the west coast and asked if Aidan would agree to investigate it and report back to the Guardians Order.

By now Aidan knew better – Guardians never asked any favors. It was an order, delivered in a soft and polite way. The Archmage made it very clear that the Guardians wanted him to investigate the situation, and since their order was in line with his original mission, he agreed right away. To his surprise, Archmage Allerton offered his complete support, stating that if during his investigation, Aidan would need help, all Guardians' resources would be at his disposal.

After the meeting with the Archmage, Aidan had spent a couple of hours with Tessa. They had just walked through the gardens and talked. Since the last time when he had seen her, a little less than a year ago, she had changed a lot. Finally, realizing that her powers were no joke, she practically grew up overnight and started taking her magical education seriously.

She was worried about Gunz's disappearance and most of their time together, she spent interrogating Aidan on everything he knew and how he was planning to find him. He couldn't tell her much since his own knowledge was limited, but he promised to keep her updated, as long as she would stay put and didn't break any Guardians rules. She just smiled and reassured him that her days of rule-breaking were over. He probably would have believed her serious voice and stern expression, if mischievous twinkles hadn't been dancing in her brown eyes.

After he said his goodbyes to Tessa, Aidan teleported straight to Los Angeles. He spent almost two weeks investigating everything that was going on in the Los Angeles supernatural community while waiting for the next big event in the captive circles of California. As he suspected, getting an invitation wasn't a problem and finding out who was the new Head of the California House had been easier than he expected.

George Novak wasn't hiding. On the contrary, he was a social butterfly, known and accepted in all the high elite circles of California. Ridiculously wealthy, handsome and mysterious, he was the center of attention in any high society gathering. Women lusted after him and men swallowed everything he was saying, no questions asked.

Aidan made an appearance at a few of these parties, but made sure to stay clear of George Novak, hoping not to draw too much attention to his own persona. He tried to check him with his magical sight but as soon as he touched him, George Novak snapped his head and stared directly at Aidan. His pupils fluctuated in size and a slow smile stretched his thin lips. He gave Aidan a short nod and turned away. The next day, Aidan received his invitation to the next major captive event.

Now Aidan was sitting in his hotel room with his cellphone in his hands, staring at the device like it was about to explode. Nevertheless, when the phone finally rang, he flinched, almost dropping the device. He checked the screen to see that the caller ID was blocked.

"Hello," he said, answering the call.

"Mr. McGrath?" The voice was going through a voice changer.

"Yes," replied Aidan.

"Without sin…" said the voice.

"There is no repentance," Aidan finished the statement. It was the password that was supposed to confirm his identity. *What a ridiculous statement,* he thought, frowning.

"Mr. McGrath, your limo is waiting for you downstairs. Please leave all your weapons, magical or mundane, at home," said the voice and hung up the phone.

Aidan silently smirked at the last statement. Leave all weapons? He *was* the weapon. Can he leave his godly powers at home? He walked out of the hotel and found a black limo waiting for him at the hotel's entrance. The driver opened the back door, bowing to him. He slid inside and the man shut the door.

All the windows were tinted and covered with blinds, so Aidan couldn't see where the driver was taking him. That didn't worry him in the slightest. It wouldn't matter where he was. If he was faced with a dangerous situation, he could always teleport anywhere he wanted.

The entire drive took around thirty minutes, but it didn't really mean the underground fighting arena was within a thirty minutes' drive from the hotel. Possibly, the driver had taken a scenic route or had been circling around for a while to deceive him.

The limo came to a soft stop and the man opened the door for him. Aidan walked out in a semi-dark underground garage. A few limos were already parked there. The driver escorted him toward a door where two large men greeted him with wide smiles and metal detectors. Aidan spread his arms, allowing them to check him for concealed weapons.

While they were searching him, he detected a soft touch of magical energy. One of the guards was a wizard and he was checking him for the presence of magical artifacts. Aidan smirked, carefully shadowing his own energy signature. After a moment, the guards opened the door for him, allowing him to pass. Aidan walked through the doorway and halted, observing the fighting arena in awe.

He was expecting to see a dark musty basement with a rusty cage inside. Instead, he was standing in a large modern arena, lit up with bright electric lights. The guests' sitting area was built around a professional octagon MMA cage that was positioned on a large podium. However, in the sitting area, instead of benches, there were tables with comfortable chairs around them. Everything was breathing luxury and was built for the comfort of the guests.

A man in a black tuxedo met Aidan at the entrance and asked for his invitation. As soon as Aidan gave it to him, the man bent forward in a formal bow, gesturing for him to follow. He escorted Aidan to his table and put a small booklet and a menu in front of him.

Aidan didn't care to order anything, but he reviewed the booklet. It was the schedule of the event. There were ten fights in the Prelims and only one fight was scheduled as the Main Card. Aidan stared at the black page with golden embossed letters and his hands trembled.

"Main Card. Alucard, the Vampire vs. Gunz, the Wizard," he read, staring at the booklet in horror. A cold sweat beaded his forehead. "Alucard?"

"Haven't you seen Alucard fight before?" Aidan heard a pleasant female voice and lifted his face. Two young women were sitting at his table, gazing at him with interest. He glanced around with surprise noticing that most of the tables were filled with guests by now.

The woman who spoke to Aidan looked a little older than her companion. Nevertheless, they looked alike enough to be sisters. Both had long hair shining with the red tint of a dark-cherry dye, oval brown eyes framed by dark eyelashes enhanced by expensive mascara and straight noses which looked slightly long for their faces.

They were dressed in similar elegant gowns that left their chests exposed just enough to arise some curiosity in the male population. A high split in the front of their dresses presented a beautiful view to their long, well-shaped legs. Their high-heel shoes sparkled with small stones reflecting the bright lights of the arena and Aidan wondered if the stones were real diamonds. The women were armed with their undeniable charm and ready for action.

"I'm new to California," replied Aidan with a friendly smile. Both women responded to his smile by shamelessly undressing him with their eyes.

"I've never had the pleasure of seeing you here," said the older woman, extending her hand to him, holding it parallel to the floor. "My name is Nicole, and this is my little sister Olivia."

"Aidan," he introduced himself and took her hand, weighed down by an enormous Harry Winston ring. He gave it a gentle squeeze but didn't kiss it. "It's a pleasure meeting you both."

Slightly disappointed, Nicole pulled her hand back, brushing the palm of his hand with her fingers flirtatiously. He carefully scanned both women with his other sight just to confirm that they were humans, completely magic-free.

"Well, Aidan, you are up for a treat," promised Nicole. A slow seductive smile appeared on her face and her eyes fogged a little as she gazed at him from under her long eyelashes suggestively. Watching this metamorphosis, Aidan wasn't sure which *treat* she had in mind – in the fighting cage or in her bed chambers. Shifting closer to him, she put her hand on his arm and continued in a soft purr, "Alucard, the undefeated vampire of the captive circles verses Gunz, the undefeated wizard of the unattached circles. It's going to be a fight to remember."

"I've heard this Gunz is quite a beast," added Olivia, her eyes sparkling with excitement. "Look at his description. He is short and light, but I've heard he had fought against two opponents twice his size and he put both of them down within one round."

"He stands no chance against Alucard," huffed the older sister, shrugging her shoulders.

"What a strange name – Alucard," said Aidan, searching through the booklet. There was a full description of the fighters, including their supernatural powers, but there were no photos.

"Oh, his nickname makes perfect sense," said Nicole, her hand slowly moving up and down Aidan's arm. "Once you see him, you'll know what I mean. He looks just like Alucard from that Netflix show. And his hair…" She sighed dreamily and continued, "Any woman would die to have hair like his. I'm sure he is a natural blond. His hair looks like a waterfall of gold. And he wears it long, going down all the way to his waist. You would think it would be a disadvantage during a fight, but so far no one was fast enough to grab his hair and use it against him."

"And he's so handsome," purred Olivia. "I would pay anything to spend a few hours with him alone… But I've heard that the waiting list for that is a mile long and the price is enormous."

Yaroslav. It has to be him, thought Aidan, mortified. He didn't know any other vampire who had long blond hair. *What the hell? Gunz has to fight Yaroslav to the death?* The sisters were still talking, but he could hardly hear their words.

"Aidan, are you okay?" asked Nicole, gently massaging his arm with her fingers. "You look like you've seen a ghost."

"I'm fine, thank you." Aidan forced a smile. "Just thinking."

"Thinking who you are going to place your bet on?" asked Olivia.

"Yes, something like that," replied Aidan.

"What's to think about?" Nicole laughed, moving even closer to Aidan, her arm now pressed against his. "Alucard. Bet on him if you don't want to lose your money."

"But they both are undefeated," muttered Aidan, carefully moving away from her. "How can you know Alucard will come out on top?"

"You are new to all this, aren't you?" The sisters exchanged a look and giggled, then Nicole continued, "Let me teach you a little. Look at their descriptions. Alucard is six-foot-four and Gunz is only five-foot-six. Alucard's weight is a hundred ninety pounds, whereas Gunz is only hundred-forty. Physically, they are not equally matched. And magically – even worse. Alucard is a vampire. He has the strength, the speed and some extra powers. Gunz – they didn't even list his powers. They say that he is a wizard, but his magic is insignificant. How do you expect him to beat an old vampire?"

"Good question," muttered Aidan. "If they are so far apart in their qualities, why then did the Head of House match them for the Main Card fight?"

"That's the mystery," said Nicole, winking seductively at Aidan. "Everyone asks this question. Gunz was the champion of the unattached circles in Florida, and no one really knows how he became a captive fighter in California. This is his first event."

"What a shame." Olivia sighed. "It'll be his first and last event. Alucard will destroy him."

"That's what I'm worried about," murmured Aidan. *If Gunz dies a human death, so will every human in the arena and depending on the amount of fire in him, some supernatural guests who sit close to the cage will be obliterated by the fire, too. What the hell is George Novak doing?*

Shortly after, the prelim fights began. With his nerves stretched to the limit, Aidan could hardly focus on what was happening in the cage. He made a few bets, just to keep up the proper appearance, but he didn't even know if he lost or won. With disgust, he was observing everything that was going on in the arena.

The captive fighters were modern day gladiators, killing each other for the amusement of the crowd. The crowd wasn't yelling or chanting for their favorite fighters. They were eating and casually watching the blood and gore show unfolding in the cage, over their wine glasses. They didn't care that in almost every fight, one of the two fighters was doomed to die.

Reluctantly, Aidan watched two werewolves fight in the cage. It was the last fight in the prelims and the closer they were getting to the Main Card fight, the worse he felt. As one of the werewolves finally brought his opponent to his knees, holding a dagger at his throat, the crowd clapped lazily. The fighter looked at the Head of House, waiting for his decision.

George Novak was sitting at his table, surrounded by three beautiful women. He said something and all three of them giggled. Then he got up and casually flipped his fist, thumb down. The fighter's face fell, and he bowed his head, but then slowly moved the dagger across his opponent's neck. Blood gushed from the open wound, coloring the octagon floor scarlet.

Aidan closed his eyes and swallowed, thinking about the fighters that would step into the cage just a few minutes from now. His friends. He felt a touch to his hand and opened his eyes. Nicole was staring at him with a smirk.

"You can't stand the sight of blood?" she asked.

"I can't stand the sight of unnecessary cruelty," he replied through gritted teeth.

"Cruelty?" she parroted, but then tittered, pushing him in the shoulder. "Hardly. It's not like these fighters are humans anyway. They're nothing but ugly monsters. As far as I'm concerned, Mr. Novak does all of us a favor by getting them off the streets and killing them."

"The man who was just killed was a werewolf. And he wasn't a purebred werewolf either. Twenty-eight days of every month, he lived a normal life, possibly had family, kids…" said Aidan quietly.

He didn't know why he bothered explaining anything to these women. Even though they weren't creatures of magic, there was very little humanity in either of them. More than anything he wanted to walk out and never come back to this place again. He sighed, turning away from Nicole.

The lights got brighter over the octagon and the guests got up, clapping. The announcer walked inside the cage with a microphone in his hands. Following the best standards of UFC fighting announcers, the man yelled, "Ladies and Gentlemen, it's time! Introducing first, fighting in the blue corner…"

Aidan's heart skipped a beat as he listened to the announcer presenting Gunz and Yaroslav, recounting their qualifications as fighters and their fights count. Numb inside, he watched Gunz enter the ring, escorted by two massive guards. He was walking slowly with his head bowed down, looking at his feet.

Yaroslav came second, his long blond hair cascading down his back. As he stepped inside the octagon, women screamed his name, waving at him, but he ignored everyone, his eyes fixed on Gunz who was standing in the opposite corner of the cage. There was something so desperate about Yaroslav's expression that it made Aidan's blood run cold.

Carefully, he probed Gunz with his magic and shuddered. He was sure that right before the fight, Gunz wouldn't be wasting his energy to shadow his magical signature, yet Aidan could hardly sense any magic in him. Suddenly, he felt a brush of cold against his skin. He shivered recognizing the presence of dark magical energy. He sharpened his senses and the understanding washed over him like icy rain. George Novak was wielding dark magic.

"He's a goddamn necromancer," hissed Aidan incredulously, slowly rising from his seat. "He is controlling Yaroslav."

"What did you say? Who is Yaroslav?" asked Nicole.

Aidan didn't listen to her, all his attention on the vampire. The fight had begun and the way Yaroslav was fighting confirmed Aidan's suspicions. He had seen Yaroslav fighting before. His weapon of choice was the katana, which wasn't a shock considering who his mother was. His fighting style was always fast and forceful, yet elegant and light at the same time.

The man fighting Gunz was no longer the Yaroslav he knew. It was Alucard, a vampire controlled by a powerful necromancer, a blood-curdling monster who cared for no one and wanted nothing but blood. He moved like a predator, driven by nothing but his primal instincts. With painful clarity, Aidan realized that no matter how good of a fighter Gunz was, without his magic, he couldn't defend himself.

As proof of his words, Alucard punched Gunz in the face with the pommel of his sword, crushing him with his vampire's strength. Gunz tried to avoid the impact, but he was too slow. He fell back and Alucard stepped heavily on his chest, razing his katana above his shoulder.

"No!" screamed Aidan. He forgot where he was and what he was doing. The only thing he saw was his friend, bleeding on the floor of the cage. He channeled his power and his whole body lit up with the brilliant white light. The ground quaked as he walked down toward the cage. The guests screamed in horror, running toward the exit.

Aidan waved his hand, throwing Yaroslav off Gunz's chest. The vampire hissed, quickly recovering and in a heartbeat was back, next to Gunz, his katana at the ready.

George Novak got up, pointing at Aidan and shouted, his voice strangely magnified, "Aidan McGrath, stop at once! You have no right to get involved in the outcome of the fight!"

Aidan's blazing white eyes darted to the Head of House and he sneered. "Neither do you! You're controlling Alucard and blocking Gunz's magic with the gray stone jewelry! This fight is—"

"Not another word, Aodh mac Lir!"

Aidan heard a familiar voice and turned around. Mrak Delar was standing in front of the cage. His eyes were flooded with the darkness of the elemental power and magic he was wielding. He muttered something and waved his hand in a circular motion. A bright white circle erupted around Aidan. The blazing hoop of Mrak's magic got thicker and rose up, wrapping tightly around Aidan's arms and chest.

Aidan fought it, but he couldn't break free. A strange weakness enveloped him, and he moaned, dropping his head to his chest powerlessly. His magic, his power – everything was gone. He couldn't move, he could hardly take a breath.

"Mrak, why?" he whispered.

Mrak Delar gave him a quick once-over and turned to the fighters in the cage. Gunz was back on his feet, facing Alucard.

"Fire Salamander, down," he commanded, pointing in his direction.

Gunz cried out and dropped to his knees. "Mrak, what are you doing?" he screamed, struggling against the control of the Master of Power to no avail.

Mrak Delar didn't reply, hardly even looking at him. "Novak, control your pet vamp!" he shouted. "This fight is over. So, do we have a deal?"

"Alucard, to your knees," ordered George Novak and his pupils dilated as he wielded his magic to control the vampire. Yaroslav slowly lowered down to both knees, placing his katana on the floor.

George Novak ran down to Mrak Delar and extended his hand to him. "We have a deal, Ancient Master," he beamed. "You give me Aodh mac Lir and I will give you the elixir you need."

Mrak Delar shook his hand, a cold smile making his face look dark and sinister. Then he turned to Aidan and twisted his hand, clenching it into a tight fist. The hoop around Aidan's chest got tighter.

"Mrak," he croaked, "what are you doing to me?"

George Novak stopped at Aidan's side and snapped his fingers. One of the guards rushed to him, giving him a small leather bag. He opened the bag and Aidan saw a set of gray stone jewelry inside. Mrak Delar noticed the contents of the bag and chuckled, shaking his head.

"Mr. Novak," he said dryly, "you're not seriously thinking that you can control a god with the gray stones magic, are you?"

George looked askance at him but pulled his hand out of the bag. "Why? Yes, I was going to control him just like anyone else with magic or elemental power."

"These toys are not going to hold a god down for more than a few minutes," replied Mrak Delar. "You see this white light?" He pointed at the magical hoop that was holding Aidan immobilized. "This is the God's snare. This is the only thing that can truly restrain a god. Show me the cell you are planning to hold him in, and I'll place the God's snare over it."

George Novak frowned, staring at Mrak Delar, mistrust written all over his face. "I'm willing to take my chances."

Mrak Delar shrugged. "Well, in that case, I have no choice but to let Aodh mac Lir go. I'm not going to let you torture him for nothing."

Novak cackled, folding his arms over his chest. "Since when are you shying away from torture, Master Mrak Delar. From what I've heard, you were quite skilled at it yourself. And I don't remember anyone saying you were ever tormented by remorse."

A dark shadow crossed Mrak Delar's face, but he smiled coldly displaying the best sample of a poker face.

"If you put the gray stone jewelry on a god, he will be in pain for hours. Maybe days. And when everything is going to be over, he'll shed these useless toys right off," retorted Mrak Delar frostily. "Yes, the torture could be quite effective in getting people to do what you want them to do. And trust me, I have no objections to it, but only when it makes sense. I wouldn't torture anyone for the sake of torture!"

"So, what do you propose?" yelled Mr. Novak throwing his hands in the air.

"Here is what we're going to do," replied Mrak Delar, ignoring Novak's obvious frustration. "Give me a minute and an empty room, and I'll create a prison that will hold a god. In the meantime, you'll continue with whatever your plan was."

"Well, my plan is not going to work, since you're telling me that I can't truly control a god," muttered Mr. Novak. He pulled the zipper over sharply, locking the bag and threw it on the floor. "And if my plan is not going to work, you won't get the elixir you need."

"No, you can't control a god, but you're missing a very important point." Mrak Delar cackled. "Do you see this boy in the cage? Your little captive fighter there." He pointed at Gunz. "I know him well. You can beat him, cut him to shreds, torture him and he'll never give in to you. But you threaten his friends, and he would do anything you want to keep them safe."

Like through a wall, Mrak Delar's words reached Aidan's frazzled mind. *What is Mrak Delar doing? What does Novak have that the Ancient Master of Power is willing to betray his friends to get it?*

"Are you sure? I already tried breaking him. It's impossible. Nothing is a lesson to him," said Novak, staring down at Gunz, who was still kneeling, held down by Mrak Delar's magic.

"Did you hear anything I said? You can't break him because

you don't know how to deal with him." Mrak Delar rolled his eyes. "Let's talk to him together and I'll help you get what you need."

A sinister dark light ignited at the bottom of George Novak's blue eyes. He extended his hand to Mrak Delar again. "In this case, let's make it happen, partner."

"Yeah… partner." Mrak Delar squeezed his hand in a handshake, an ominous smile curving his lips.

CHAPTER 14

~ ZANE BURNS, A.K.A. GUNZ ~

The guards pushed him through the door inside his room and locked it. Gunz fell to his knees and for a few seconds remained down with his arms wrapped around his head, taking ragged breaths. Then he got up slowly and gawked at the blood on the floor. Yaroslav wasn't joking when he said he wasn't behind the wheel when he was fighting in the cage.

As soon as Gunz moved, pain assailed him, reminding him of the short but brutal beating Yaroslav had given him. He couldn't even call it a fight. It was a beating and without his full magic and elemental power, there was nothing he could do to defend himself against an old vampire controlled by a powerful necromancer.

But even worse than the physical pain was the memory of Mrak Delar controlling him, restraining Aidan, betraying all of them by siding with the necromancer. Mrak had been his friend and Gunz had accepted him as such from day one, even though all his friends had told him that Mrak was an irredeemable evil.

His mind had refused to accept Mrak's betrayal, and the dull ache in his soul was far worse than any pain in his aching body. He made it to the bed and collapsed on his stomach. Bright, scarlet splatters spread on the white sheet, but he ignored them. He lay on the bed, silent and motionless until his tormented body won and he blacked out.

The sound of commotion brought him back. Gunz lifted his head and glanced at the door to see what woke him up. In the doorway, four guards were struggling with Yaroslav. That was unusual, since normally no one dared come close to him. But today everything was different.

The four guards were manhandling Yaroslav. One of them wrung his long hair around his arm, forcing the vampire's head down. The strangest thing was that Yaroslav wasn't really fighting them. He was trying to reason with them, struggling to stay on his feet. Finally, either he gave in or the guards were able to subdue him, but Yaroslav ended up flat on the floor, with his arms twisted behind his back. One of the guards kicked him in his side and all of them left, locking the door behind them.

Gunz slowly slid down to the floor and kneeled next to Yaroslav. "Slavik, what happened?" he asked, observing the chains wrapped around Yaroslav's arms. His skin under the chains was raw and bleeding. His back was crisscrossed by angry red welts, which for some reason weren't healing.

"Chains," he whispered, "take them off… please…"

Since there were no manacles or any locks, Gunz gently started unwrapping the chains. Yaroslav's skin was peeling off together with the chains. The vampire moaned and bit his lip, tears of pain gleaming in his eyes.

"What are these chains?" asked Gunz once he was done.

"Silver," whispered Yaroslav. "Don't you know? Can hold any vampire down…"

"You're not healing. Your back and the damage the chains did… Why aren't you healing?"

"Silver…"

Gunz sat down on the floor next to him and carefully lifted his head, pressing his wrist to his lips. "Drink. You said my blood is stronger than normal human blood. It should help you heal."

"I can't." Yaroslav tried to pull away, but Gunz held him down.

"Why? It wouldn't be the first time you fed on me."

"You're also hurt," mumbled Yaroslav closing his eyes, but Gunz caught the scarlet glow under his thick eyelashes. "I hurt you... and Novak ordered me not to heal you anymore."

"You didn't hurt me," objected Gunz. "Novak did."

He lowered Yaroslav down and turned around to his bed. On the side of the bed frame he found a loose screw and pulled it out. With a sharp move, he slashed his wrist with the screw. A thick dark stream of blood gushed down his hand. The heavy metallic scent lingered in the air and Yaroslav lifted his head slightly, his eyes glowing bright red, his long fangs extended.

Gunz placed his bleeding wrist to Yaroslav's lips and felt his fingers wrap around his arm, pulling him closer. He gasped as the vampire's fangs penetrated his skin, but as usual the pain was gone a moment later, replaced by relaxation and temporary oblivion. Gradually, the world around him started to get darker and the weakness became overwhelming.

"Yaroslav, stop..." he whispered faintly and passed out.

When he woke up, he was back on his bed. Yaroslav was sitting on the floor by his bedside. He got up as soon as he noticed that Gunz was awake and smiled tentatively. Then he sat down on the edge of the bed and exposed his own wrist, ready to bite it.

"No, stop," said Gunz, grabbing his wrist. "You shouldn't do it. Let's see why Novak changed his mind first."

Before he finished his statement, the door opened, and Theron walked inside. He stopped in the doorway, shifting from foot to foot and cleared his throat. For a man who looked like a mountain of muscles, he sure knew how to look shy.

"Hey, guys," he said finally and cleared his throat again. "Master wants to see you. He summons both of you."

* * *

As soon as Gunz walked into the office, he saw Aidan. The god of the Otherworld was sitting on the floor, his legs crossed, his arms resting atop his knees, surrounded by the circle of the God's snare. His eyes bored into Gunz and he said something, but Gunz couldn't hear him. Aidan probably realized that too, because he frowned and bowed his head.

Suppressing his anger, Gunz turned away from Aidan and met Mrak Delar's mocking gaze. The Ancient Master of Power was sitting on the edge of the desk, his arms folded over his chest and there was nothing in this man that reminded Gunz of his friend. He was arrogant and cold, and there was a new vicious gleam in his obsidian eyes that Gunz had never seen before.

George Novak was standing next to Mrak Delar, observing both Gunz and Yaroslav with a nasty half-smile on his face. Yaroslav lowered down to his knees. Gunz smirked, staring back at the necromancer, his jaws set, and remained standing. Theron pushed on his shoulder and hissed, "You must kneel before your master."

Dizzy and lightheaded from the blood loss and still in considerable pain, Gunz swayed, but the anger surging through him gave him some strength to retaliate. He grabbed Theron's hand and ripped it off his shoulder. This move opened the wound in his wrist and blood trickled down, sliding from his fingers to the shiny clean floor of the office.

George Novak flicked his eyebrow at the Master of Power. "Just what I expected. I've been the Head of California House for a while now and I broke enough supernatural fighters into submission. Speaking from my experience, I'm telling you,

Mrak, there is nothing you can do to bend this man's will. He'll be a step away from death, but he will still defy you. I ordered Alucard not to heal him. I assumed, that if he was in pain, he would be more agreeable. I have to admit, I was wrong. So, he's all yours, Master Mrak Delar. Do what you must."

Mrak Delar got up and strolled toward Gunz. He halted, staring down at him and then took his wrist into his hand, observing the bleeding cut and the puncture wounds. Then he turned to Yaroslav and grabbed his hair, yanking his head back.

"You fed on him?" he growled, iron notes in his voice. "He was beat up and in pain, but you still fed on him. Fascinating, truly."

Being a vampire and a natural blond, Yaroslav's skin was pearl-white, but at Mrak Delar's words, whatever color he had, drained from his face. Noticing his reaction, Mrak laughed and let go of his hair.

"Stay still and do not fight me, boy," ordered Mrak Delar, turning back to Gunz. He placed one of his hands on Gunz's forehead and the other over his heart. Channeling the healing power of Earth, he mixed some Fire into it and circulated it through Gunz.

Gunz groaned, the healing magic the Master of Power was wielding made him feel weak and lightheaded. His knees buckled and he started to fall. With vampire speed, Yaroslav jumped to his feet and caught Gunz before he hit the floor, returning him into the upright position so Mrak could finish healing him. A few minutes later, Mrak Delar stepped away. He took a piece of Kleenex from the desk and wiped his hands, an expression of disgust on his face.

"Feeling better, Gunz?" he asked, snickering. "You can let go of him—um—Alucard."

Gunz glanced down at his wrist, noticing that the bleeding stopped, and the wound was gone. His body wasn't aching, and he felt stronger. He never experienced the effects of the healing magic of a Master of Power before, but right now he had no time to appreciate it. He raised his eyes at Mrak Delar, searching his face for any signs of his friend but found none. His friend was gone. The man in front of him was the evil former dictator of Kendral.

"Yes, Master Mrak Delar," replied Gunz, lowering his eyes. "Thank you."

"Oh, don't thank me, boy." The Master of Power smirked, shaking his head. "Let's chat. There is something your current owner, Mr. Novak, and I need you to do for us."

"Mrak, I already told him," said Gunz, his voice painfully hoarse. "He wants me to fight for his House? He got that. There is nothing else I'll ever do for this asshole."

George Novak roared, standing next to Gunz in a heartbeat. He raised his arm, ready to strike him, but Mrak Delar seized his wrist, stopping him.

"George, we are partners. Are we not?" he said dryly to the Head of House.

"Yes…" hissed Novak, his voice shaking with fury. "But he is—"

"Disrespectful? Yes, that he is. But you'll survive," Mrak Delar frostily interrupted him. "I don't feel like healing him again just because you can't control your emotions. Let me deal with him, George. I swear, I'll get him to do what we need him to do."

"Fine! You do that, Master." George Novak slipped another scorching look at Gunz, then walked away and sat down behind his desk.

Mrak Delar switched his attention back to Gunz, his lips touched by a light smile. "Gunz, I need you to try and give me your full attention," he said softly. "Can you do that?"

"Why?" asked Gunz, without raising his eyes. He couldn't bear looking at this man who was once his friend and now was… He didn't even know what he was now.

"Did Alucard knock your brains out, boy?" Mrak Delar cackled. "I need you to listen to me because I'm going to tell you what you need to do. And I don't feel like repeating myself twice."

"I'm not doing anything," objected Gunz calmly, finally raising his eyes. "Not as long as you're siding with that dumbass." He jerked his chin toward George Novak, eliciting a low growl out of him.

"I understand. Mr. Novak here has no idea how to motivate his sl—um—fighters properly." Mrak Delar walked to the circle that held Aidan imprisoned and stopped there, half turned to Gunz. "Allow me to demonstrate how it's done."

He raised his arm, gathering his magic in the tips of his fingers and touched the blazing light of the circle, whispering something. The light got considerably brighter, and Aidan cried out, squeezing his head with his hands like he had an unbearable headache.

"Mrak, what are you doing? Why?" yelled Gunz, his hands clenching into fists involuntarily.

"I know you are not going to believe me," said Mrak Delar airily, ignoring his question, "so, I'll allow Aidan to tell you the truth." He turned back to Aidan and continued, "Aodh mac Lir, would you kindly tell our fiery friend what's going to happen to you if I continue applying my magic to the circle of the God's snare."

Aidan didn't reply and Mrak Delar sent more of his magic through the blazing circle. Aidan screamed, raising his hand up, asking him to stop. Mrak Delar stopped, removing his hand from the circle.

"Now speak," ordered Mrak Delar. "He can hear you."

"Gunz, I'm sorry," said Aidan quietly. "I used it on you a while ago, so you know how the God's snare works... He can't kill me, but he can hold me imprisoned forever and put me into perpetual torment."

Mrak Delar waved his hand again and muted Aidan. Then he slowly made his way back to Gunz, moving with the swagger of a man who was confident in his power.

"Mrak, please, let Aidan go. I'll do what you want," pleaded Gunz. He didn't know what he was hoping for, but he had to try.

"I'm a Master of Power, boy," hissed Mrak Delar, towering over him with malice. "I'm not your buddy and you'll do well to remember that. I appreciate when people have good manners. So, next time you address me, remember to use my proper title. Just like I always remember that you're a Great Fire Salamander."

"He is what?" gasped Novak, slowly rising.

Mrak Delar threw a quick glance back at him and chuckled. "You held him captive for all this time and you had no idea how powerful he truly was. You're disappointing me, Mr. Novak," he stated. "But in all fairness to you, the boy got remarkably skilled in shadowing his energy signature."

"I knew that he was a Fire Salamander, but Great?" mumbled Novak, observing Gunz with new interest.

"Yeah, that he is. Not the best of his kind, I must say." Mrak Delar smirked coldly, turning back to Gunz. "Okay, Gunz, let's get back to business. I need you to complete a serious task for me. I believe you are ready to listen now?"

"Yes, Master Mrak Delar," hissed Gunz, his jaw set.

"Wonderful. Just the way I like it." Mrak Delar patted him on his cheek and Gunz cringed from his touch. "You see, your owner and I need to create a little concoction. Elixir, if you will. But we're missing an important ingredient. I need you to travel to the Land of Dreams, find it and bring it back to me."

"What do you want me to find, Master?" asked Gunz.

"Nothing big," replied Mrak Delar. "I need you to travel to the farthest land of the magical nexus, into the thirtieth kingdom and bring me back the Apple of Youth. That'll be it."

"The Apple of Youth," parroted Gunz incredulously. "You're almost three hundred years old, but you don't look a day over thirty and you need the Apple of Youth?"

"Do not question me, boy," growled Mrak Delar. "You'll be leaving tomorrow morning. I'll let you get one good night's rest before I teleport you to the gates of the Land of Dreams. In the meantime, to insure your compliance and swift return, I'll keep your friend Aidan here. If you don't come back… Well, you don't really want to know what I will do to him, should you defy me."

"I will come back," promised Gunz, stiff with anger. "Count on it."

"Was that a threat, boy?" asked Mrak Delar, laughter ringing in his voice.

Gunz didn't get a chance to reply, as George Novak walked up to him with two controllers in his hands. He pressed a button on Gunz's controller, and he felt a wave of fire and magic rush through him. He held his breath as his eyes lit up with fire. Satisfied with his reaction, Novak seized Gunz's collar with one hand, Yaroslav's collar with his other hand and started to chant. Both collars lit up with a dim light and when the light dissipated, he let go.

Mrak Delar frowned and for a moment his face hardened. "Novak, I thought you were going to take the gray stone jewelry off of him," he said through his gritted teeth.

"I changed my mind," replied Novak frostily and ordered. "Alucard, get up. You're going to go with Gunz. I want to make sure he'll come back and do it within the time frame I give him."

"You can't be serious!" yelled Gunz, taking a step forward. "I can't take a vampire with me. He'll slow me down! He's sensitive to the sunlight, remember?"

Novak put his hand in his pocket and produced a ring with a single red stone in it. He seized Yaroslav's hand and forced the ring on his finger.

"I enchanted this ring myself. It'll help Alucard move easily during the daylight," explained Novak and added, addressing Mrak Delar. "I need some additional security."

"You don't trust me, Mr. Novak?" hissed Mrak Delar, his voice infused with danger.

"I trust you, Master Mrak Delar." Novak cackled and pointed at Gunz, switching his attention to him. "I don't trust him. So, here is how it's going work, Gunz. I just placed a connection spell on your gray stone jewelry. From now on, you and Alucard are connected. If one of you dies, so will the other. If the two of you separate by more than hundred yards, you both will die. I know that as a Fire Salamander you're immortal, but Alucard isn't. And I don't know why, but you seem to like him, and I believe you don't want to see him dead.

"And here is the best part of my little spell... You have fifteen days to find the Apple and return here with it. After ten days, the gray stones will start feeding on Alucard's vampiric essence – the essence that sustains him. From that point on, you'll have exactly five days to return. If you are not here within five days, Alucard will die the true death."

Gunz shrugged, staring at him with a crooked smirk. "And what makes you think I care if the vampire lives or dies? I killed hundreds of vampires on the streets of South Florida to protect humans."

"Good question," said Novak, folding his arms. "Before I went through all the trouble of creating this neat connection spell, I tested your loyalty to Alucard. I beat him a little and restrained him with silver before sending him to you. Even though you were a bloody mess yourself, you donated your blood to heal him. So, yeah, I know that you care."

"Dammit," cursed Gunz quietly, exchanging a quick look with Yaroslav. "Fine, we'll be leaving tomorrow morning."

"I think you should know one more thing, Gunz," said Novak, arrogance and aversion in his every word. "While I reset your controller to almost zero, it's still blocking your magic a little. So, you won't be able to revert and use your full Fire Salamander's magic."

"Why?" yelled Gunz, notes of desperation breaking to the surface. "You're sending me to the Land of Dreams, a magical nexus. I don't know what I will run into there. I need my full power and my physical strength to complete this mission. What if I get hurt? If I can't revert, I can't heal myself."

"Well, this is another reason why I am sending Alucard with you," seethed Novak, seizing his collar and forcing his face up. "I believe he has experience healing you, boy!"

Gunz seized Novak's wrist, directing some of his fire toward his hands. Novak yelped, jerking his hand off, red spots of burns decorating his wrist.

"You… you… son of a bitch!" yelled Novak, striking Gunz across his face.

Gunz fell back, wiped his bleeding lips with the back of his hand and laughed mirthlessly. "You shouldn't be touching a Fire Salamander with your bare hands, dumbass."

Shouting curses, George Novak moved closer, ready to kick him, but Mrak Delar stepped between them, holding Novak away from Gunz.

"You can make minced meet out of him when he returns with the Apple, Novak. He's your slave after all," he said coldly, slightly choking on the word *slave*. "But right now, I need him in good shape. Am I clear, Mr. Novak?"

Mrak Delar kneeled next to Gunz, quickly healing his split lips.

"Gunz, Gunz, Gunz," he said with a sigh filled with mockery. "It doesn't matter how much your father and I teach you. Everything we say seems to go into one ear and come out the other. I guess, you're just not that smart, boy. If you were listening to us back in Kendral, you would know that there is no way the gray stones magic could keep a Fire Salamander under control. If Kal was here, he would be out of these restraints in a matter of a few minutes."

"What do you mean, Master?" asked Gunz, his heart thundering against his chest. He searched Mrak Delar's face and found nothing but mockery and loathing in the Ancient Master of Power's expression.

Mrak Delar laughed. Cold and evil, he gawked down at him and shook his head. "I mean that you're probably the worst Fire Salamander I've ever met." He scratched the back of his head and laughed again. "Well, in all fairness, I met only two in my whole life – you and your father, The Great Salamander. You're nothing compared to him, boy. It's like one friend of yours – who you would do well to remember – said, you're just a little Fire Gecko."

"I got it," said Gunz, narrowing his eyes at Mrak Delar. "I'm nothing and you're the big bad. You got me. I'll do what you want. But now I want to go and have that good night's rest that you promised, Master Mrak Delar."

Mrak Delar laughed and shook his head no. "Well, that's not up to me, is it? You have an owner. Beg him, boy."

Gunz didn't say anything to George Novak. Instead he approached the circle of God's snare. He knew that Aidan couldn't hear him, so he just nodded at him silently, hoping that by now Aidan knew him well enough to understand – he would never leave him in this desperate state. Aidan raised his bloodshot eyes at Gunz and returned his nod.

Gunz turned to Novak, pinning him with his igneous gaze. "Alucard and I are leaving now. We both need to get some sleep and get ready for this mission of yours," he said dryly and touched Yaroslav's shoulder. "Let's go, Alucard."

As he headed toward the exit door, he was expecting for Novak to say something, punish him somehow for his disrespectful behavior. But it was Mrak Delar who stopped him.

"And Gunz, one more thing," said the Master of Power and

Gunz felt the fire energy spike around him. He backed away, knowing what was coming, until his back hit the door.

"Fire Salamander, down," commanded Mrak Delar, twisting his hand. The invisible wall crushed Gunz down, forcing him to his knees. He collapsed, breathing hard. "Remember when we talked last time, I told you that when I would see you the next time, I was going to twist you into a pretzel for what you did to Kal."

Mrak Delar turned his fist, applying more pressure. Gunz moaned, endeavoring to fight his control, but it was useless. He lowered his forehead to the floor, clasping his hands behind his head. Mrak Delar pushed him slightly with the tip of his boot.

"That's right, boy," he hissed, so much hatred in his voice that Gunz shuddered inwardly. "Now you know how it feels to be torn inside out and be unable to do anything to help the situation."

Gunz gathered all his remaining strength and lifted his head to see Mrak's face. "But I already knew it, Master. You didn't have to control me for that," he whispered, pain and silent fury making his voice tremble. "You tore my heart right out of my chest and stepped on it with your boot."

Mrak Delar flinched, stepping away from him and dropped his control. Gunz laughed bitterly, getting up to his feet.

"When you see Kal the next time, Master," he said quietly. "Tell him I am truly sorry. I was hurt and grieving, and I didn't think how that was affecting people who cared about me. Tell him he is my Father and I love him."

"Something tells me Kal is not going to be happy to see me any time soon," whispered Mrak Delar barely audible. A pained expression crossed his face and swiftly disappeared. "You may leave now. I'll see you in the morning."

CHAPTER 15

~ ZANE BURNS, A.K.A. GUNZ ~

Gunz hardly slept the rest of the night. He gave it a try, but sleep was eluding him, and he gave up after an hour of tossing and turning. When the door opened up early in the morning, he was sitting on his bed, his back resting against the wall. Yaroslav was sleeping but he woke up from the first noise, sensitive to his surroundings like all vampires.

George Novak strolled into the room, throwing two sets of clothes on the table. "Rise and shine, boys," he announced, his eyes gleaming with an unnatural excitement. "Change. I can't let you into the outside world in these outfits."

"A little privacy," grumbled Gunz, taking the jeans and shirt off the table.

"You'll survive," replied Novak, folding his arms over his chest. "I doubt you have anything I haven't seen before."

"As you wish," replied Gunz.

He waved his hand, manifesting a curtain of cold fire to shield himself and Yaroslav from the observers and quickly changed. After the medical scrubs he wore between the events and his cargo pants designed for the cage fighting, normal jeans and a shirt felt almost uncomfortable.

THE BURNS DEFIANCE

Once they were done, he waved his hand extinguishing the fire. Gunz threw a look filled with defiance at Novak and noticed Mrak Delar behind him. The Master was standing by the door, leaning against the doorframe. For some reason, he didn't look as harsh and cocky as yesterday. He looked almost ill which wasn't possible since Masters of Power couldn't catch viruses. Despite that, his face was drained of life. Dark circles surrounded his obsidian eyes and his pale lips were slightly opened like he had shortness of breath.

For a moment, Novak stared at Gunz with interest. Then he approached him and tugged on his collar. "Before I let the Master of Power transport you to the Land of Dreams, there is something I wanted to show you."

At his words, Mrak Delar got alarmed. "Novak," he said warningly, taking a step forward, "I thought we discussed it and agreed that—"

"Yes, Master Mrak Delar," replied the Head of California House, raking the Master of Power with an arrogant stare, "*we* discussed it and *I* decided that he needs to know. His life belongs to me and I can do with him whatever the hell I want."

"George, please, don't do it," said Mrak Delar softly, but iron notes rang in his voice. "Yes, you own him, but it'll be a giant mistake."

"Master, if you disagree with my actions, you're free to leave any time you wish," stated George Novak coldly and turned back to Gunz. "Like I said, I just wanted to show you something and hopefully, it'll serve as extra motivation for you to complete this mission and bring the Apple to me as soon as possible."

"Show? What and how?" asked Gunz coldly.

"Open your mind," ordered Novak, placing his hand on Gunz's forehead. "Don't worry, I'm not trying to control your mind, I'm just trying to project a vision. I have psychic abilities. I need you to relax and stop fighting me."

Gunz frowned and glanced at Mrak Delar. The Master of

Power looked ashen, every muscle in his body tense, his eyes widened. He shook his head no at Gunz, his gaze almost pleading with him.

"Don't look at anyone else when your master is talking to you," ordered Novak, seizing Gunz's chin and forcing him to look straight at him. "Look into my eyes and open your mind. You're going nowhere until I show you the vision and Alucard's clock is already ticking."

Gunz met Novak's eyes and shivered as if the temperature in the room had dropped a few degrees. His bright blue eyes were glowing with the energy of his magic, but it was his pupils that made chills run down Gunz's spine – they kept changing size, growing bigger and then contracting back into tiny black dots.

"That's right, my son," mumbled Novak, carefully letting go of Gunz's chin and placing his hand on his forehead. "Now, stop fighting me and let the vision in… It's not going to hurt you or control you…"

Gunz felt Novak's magic gently probing his mind, tugging at that invisible barrier he always raised when he was in Novak's presence. Gunz held his breath and dropped the barrier, allowing Novak in. As soon as he did, darkness surrounded him. He felt like he was falling, and his endless fall reminded him of the time when he was pushed through the gates of the Dark Nav. He screamed, fear assailing him, and fought against the man who was holding him.

"Relax, Gunz," he heard a distant voice somewhere on the outskirts of his mind. "I swear I am not going to hurt you."

He felt another pair of hands supporting his shoulders and a different voice sounded in his head – the voice of a man who had once called himself his friend. "Gunz, you must relax. You let him in, now you have to let him show you the vision. You can't stop in the middle."

Gunz took in a deep breath and forced his panicked mind to relax and let go. The darkness slowly dissipated, and he saw

Mount Karasova from a bird's-eye view, like he was flying high in the sky above it.

This place is cursed by pain, suffering and dark magic. Why did you bring me here, Novak? Stop, please! I don't want—

He started to fall. In a fast and uncontrollable downward spiral, he plummeted down to the mountain. Gunz screamed, realizing that if he continued falling, his body would be smashed on the hard rocks of Karasova and shattered into millions of bleeding pieces, each fragment a separate pool of anguish. He felt someone hold his head upright and he fought against their grip.

"Relax, Gunz! It's just a vision. You can't get hurt in a psychic vision." Novak's voice sounded in his mind again.

Gunz squeezed his eyes shut, bracing himself for the pain of the fall, but it didn't happen. When he opened his eyes again, he was inside the cave of Mount Karasova, standing next to the sacrificial stone. The stone slowly shifted from its place and the ground opened up. Inside the deep grave he saw a large wooden coffin wrapped tightly with cold iron chains.

I don't want to be here... I shouldn't be here... "Get me out!" yelled Gunz, thrashing violently in Novak's arms.

"Look. Into. The Coffin!" He heard Novak's icy voice, pronouncing one word at a time. "I'm not getting you out until you do what I say!"

Gunz felt Novak's fingers dig into his face, realizing that unless he did what Novak ordered him to do, it would never be over. Slowly he lowered his eyes and looked at the coffin. The lid of the coffin became transparent and he saw a young beautiful woman lying inside.

She looked like she was sleeping. Her eyes were closed, but her face was tense, a pained expression clouding the familiar features he loved so much. A large serpent was twisting its ugly, scaly body around her. Squeezing her and letting go again, it looked like the snake was feeding on her life energy.

All of a sudden, Angelique opened her eyes. They were a sickening yellow color with the dark red vertical pupils of a serpent. But it wasn't the look of her eyes that stunned Gunz, sending him into an abyss of despair. It was the endless agony that reflected on her face and the haunted expression of her unnatural gaze. For a moment, she stared straight at him and then her mouth opened in a silent scream.

"Angie, no!" Gunz screamed, his whole world exploding around him, hurtling him into a heart-wrenching turmoil. The fresh scars on his soul, that he had been struggling to heal for almost a year, opened up, bleeding and aching. And everything around him became dark again.

"Gunz! Gunz, open your eyes!"

Someone was shaking him. Gunz moaned and cracked his eyelids open. His vision wasn't clear, mental images of the harrowing vision overlapping reality, but he was able to recognize that he was back in his room, sitting on the floor. It was Yaroslav who was shaking him, trying to get his attention, and in his arms, he felt like a limp powerless mass without bones and muscles.

Novak was standing with arms crossed, staring down at him with a contemptuous smirk on his face, and for the first time since he was sold to the Head of California House, Gunz was afraid of him. Mrak Delar looked paler than a ghost. His black eyes widened as he braced himself against the wall with his arm, slightly leaning forward.

A moment later, Gunz freed himself from Yaroslav's hands and huddled into a corner between the bed and the wall, wrapping his arms around his head. In his mind he could still see Angelique's face contorted by unimaginable pain. He could still hear her silent plea for help. His body shuddered in uncontrollable agonizing sobs and he howled in despair.

"I told you!" roared Mrak Delar, slamming his hand on the wall and the floor of the room trembled as his power ran away from his control. "I warned you that if you show him this vision, you'll devastate him so deeply that he'll be useless to us! Look at him, Novak!"

Mrak Delar kneeled before Gunz and gently forced his arms down. Gunz raised his eyes at him, but he couldn't see anything. Silent tears of pure liquid fire were slipping from his eyes.

"What is that?" whispered Novak, pointing at his flaming tears.

Mrak Delar glanced at him over his shoulder and shuddered. "That's his tears, Novak. That's the way the Fire Salamander cries when he's deeply hurt." He switched his attention back to Gunz. "Gunz, look at me, my friend. Listen to my voice. It's me, Mrak. I'm here. Everything is going to be okay."

Gunz slowly focused his vision on Mrak Delar's face. He saw his dark eyes gazing at him with his usual sympathy and understanding. It was his friend. He was back. And for a moment Gunz forgot where he was.

"Mrak, why?" he whispered, his voice torturously hoarse. "What the hell was that? Was it real?"

"I don't know," replied Mrak Delar honestly. "It was just a vision and it's over now. Can you stand up?"

Gunz nodded and slowly got up, supported by Mrak Delar. His eyes stopped on Novak's face and abruptly, with agonizing clarity he remembered everything. His eyes darted back to Mrak Delar and he jerked his arm out of his hands.

"Stay away from me, you evil bastard," he hissed, anger drying out his fiery tears and igniting furious flames on the bottom of his eyes.

"He's ba-a-ack," sung Mrak Delar, chuckling. He raised his arms up and retreated back to the exit door. Gunz sat down on his bed, rubbing his face with his hands and then looked up at Novak.

"Was it true?" he demanded quietly. "Why did you show this vision to me?"

"Yes, the vision was real," replied Novak coldly, "and here is why I showed it to you. A slightly modified version of the same elixir that I'm going to create for myself, may allow me to separate the essence of your witch from the essence of the Skiper-Zmey."

"What?" hissed Gunz. "If you're messing with me, I swear I'm going to rip you apart with my bare hands!"

"Why would I mess with you," replied Novak arrogantly. "Yes, I believe I can make an elixir like that, but besides the Apple, I would need one more ingredient. In the Thirtieth Kingdom, there is a sacred garden. In this garden, the Apples of Youth are growing. Under the Apple Tree, you'll find a well. I need you to bring me some water from this well. It's the Water of Life. You get me the Apple and the Water of Life and I'll make the elixir that may free your witch."

"May?" asked Gunz.

"In a situation like this, I can't guarantee the outcome," explained George Novak dryly. "However, I can promise that I'll do everything I can to bring your lover back to life. Now, let me ask you, Gunz. What would you do to have this elixir in your hands? What would you do to embrace the woman you love again?"

Gunz dropped his head but didn't say anything. Instead he turned to Mrak Delar who was still standing by the door. "Master Mrak Delar," he said evenly, "I believe we are ready. Can you teleport Alucard and me to the Land of Dreams?"

Mrak Delar nodded, gesturing for him to come closer, but before Gunz made a move, George Novak stopped him.

"I have something for you," he said. He pulled a small Swiss army knife out of his pants pocket and offered it to Gunz. "Your previous owner gave it to Mr. Park when they signed the sale contract. I believe he said this toy was your weapon of choice."

Gunz took the knife from Novak and put it in the pocket of

his jeans. It felt good to have his trusty sword back. "Did he give you my bag, by any chance?"

"No," replied Novak. "This knife was the only thing he gave me."

"Low-life bastard," muttered Gunz, shaking his head. He didn't care about anything in this bag except for the watch that was Angelique's last gift and the fire bracelet.

Novak cackled. "Maybe he's a low-life bastard. Maybe not. He actually liked you in his own perverted way. Nonetheless, I made him an offer that no one in his position would refuse. I offered him his life in exchange for yours."

"Whatever," said Gunz with an indifferent shrug. "I'll deal with him right after I'm done with you."

"Are you trying to scare me?" Novak laughed. "That's cute."

"Why would I do that? I'm just stating a fact." Gunz smirked and turned to Yaroslav. "Alucard, ready to go?"

Yaroslav nodded but halted in front of Novak on his way out. "I will need my katana, master," he said with a light bow. Novak gestured to the guard who was standing outside the room. Before the guard walked inside, Mrak Delar intercepted him, taking the sword and sheath from his hand. He handed everything to the vampire and put his hands on Gunz's and Yaroslav's shoulders.

"Onward and upward. See you in a jiffy, Georgie," he said with a sly wink in Novak's direction and vanished from the room, taking Gunz and Yaroslav with him.

CHAPTER 16

~ ZANE BURNS, A.K.A. GUNZ ~

Mrak Delar summoned three light orbs and threw them up in the air. The blue shimmering light illuminated the dark narrow corridor, its walls supported by rough brickwork. The low ceiling and the musty smell left no doubt that they were underground. The Master of Power didn't stop, silently gesturing at Gunz and Yaroslav to follow him.

He placed his hand on the wall of the underground passage and whispered a spell. A soft golden glow erupted from his hand and quickly spread around the surface. He lowered his hands and walked through the shimmering wall, like it wasn't solid. Gunz and Yaroslav exchanged a look and followed him.

As soon as they emerged on the other side, Gunz halted, observing his surroundings in awe. He was standing in a large room that looked like a treasure cave from a fairy tale or at least an art museum. Priceless pieces of art with jewels and gold encrusted weapons and religious artifacts, chests topped with precious stones, jewelry and gold, filled most of the room. All this treasure gleamed dimly in the blue light of the magical orbs.

Mrak Delar seized Gunz's arm above his elbow and pulled him farther toward the other end of the room.

"I trust you recognize where you are, Gunz," he whispered without slowing down.

"I've never been in this room before, but I suspect I'm somewhere close to my home," said Gunz, a touch of nostalgia tightening his throat. "I recognized the underground passage and the brickwork supporting it. I was here when I was younger. We're under my city, Gomel, and this is one of the catacombs that runs under the river."

"Right you are," confirmed Mrak Delar, stopping in front of a door. The entire surface of the door was spinning, shimmering with the bright blue light of a portal.

"This is the entrance into the Land of Dreams," said Mrak Delar, pointing at the portal. "I didn't want to teleport you directly into the magical nexus because I believe you need to talk to the Gatekeeper. I don't think you can find the Apple of Youth and leave the nexus with it without her assistance."

"Thanks," said Gunz dryly, "we'll take it from here."

He was just about to walk through the portal, when Mrak Delar put his hand on his shoulder. Gunz stilled, his gaze slowly fell on Mrak's hand and the Master of Power took it off.

"Gunz, I believe that except for the short time you spent on the Isle Buyan last year, you've never traveled through the magical nexus before," said Mrak Delar, and his heavy gaze bored into him. "I just wanted to give you a small tip – remember, anything is possible. Expect the unexpected and be careful."

"You sound almost like you care what will happen to me, Master Mrak Delar," said Gunz dryly, raking Mrak Delar with a frosty stare.

Mrak Delar blanched and rubbed his temples with his elegant fingers. "Old habits die hard, I guess," he whispered and chuckled. "Of course, I care. I need Novak to make the elixir for me and without the Apple of Youth, it won't be possible. So, while I couldn't care less about either of you, I do care about you surviving this trip so you can complete your mission."

Gunz smirked and shook his head. "Please, don't allow me to detain you any longer, my lord," said Gunz bowing low to him, the way Kal had taught him. But no matter how hard he tried, his every move exuded an unhealthy amount of scorn. He pivoted on his heel and stepped through the portal.

* * *

IT WAS EARLY MORNING, but the sun was blasting mercilessly, showering a wide-open field with its smoldering rays. Gunz stopped and closed his eyes, enjoying the warmth and the feeling of the elemental powers that were flowing freely in this place. It was his second time in the magical nexus and he still hadn't gotten used to the effect of the concentrated magical energy of this place.

"The sunlight doesn't bother me," said Yaroslav, his voice unusually soft and elated.

Gunz glanced at him and a lighthearted smile appeared on his face. "At least something good came out from meeting Novak. You can get a tan now."

"So, in which direction do we go from here?" asked Yaroslav, stretching his arms, visibly enjoying the sunlight.

Gunz surveyed the area. They were standing in the middle of a wide field, covered in tall lush grass. The swirling light of the portal was shimmering right next to them and it seemed that the door to the Land of Dreams was opened permanently. A tall dark forest rose far on the horizon, surrounding the field from all directions.

"I'm not sure," mumbled Gunz, sharpening his senses. "I think there is a house right there, at the edge of the forest. Didn't Mrak Delar say that we need to talk to the Gatekeeper first?"

"Yeah, I wish you asked him for directions before you killed him with your everlasting sarcasm," muttered Yaroslav. "Let's go."

"Asking for directions was never my strong suit." Gunz chuckled, heading toward the house at the edge of the field. They didn't get a chance to walk far when a stern elderly voice stopped them.

"Zane Burns and Yaroslav Potemkin. What an unlikely companionship. Where do you think you're going, boys?"

Gunz spun around and saw an elderly lady. She was dressed in a white shirt and a long dark skirt. A large kerchief with a traditional Russian pattern was thrown over her shoulders and chest. Her hair was braided into a single thick braid that was slithering down her chest like a silver snake. She wasn't tall, but the way she was talking and holding herself made him feel like he was a first grader standing in front of his teacher. But what shocked Gunz the most was the old woman's eyes. She had her eyes closed, yet he had a strong suspicion that she was staring directly at them.

"My lady, the Gatekeeper," Yaroslav said, taking a knee, bowing his head respectfully. Gunz bowed to her, wondering if he should kneel too.

"Get up, Yaroslav, you don't have time for all that," she said waving at him impatiently. She opened her eyes and Gunz suppressed a gasp. She was blind and her eyes were porcelain-white.

"My lady—," Gunz started to say, but she frowned pursing her lips.

"Call me Baba Maria. Your friends in Kendral do," the Gatekeeper said in a no-nonsense tone. "And right now, I would deeply appreciate it if you both shut up and listen. The time the necromancer gave you is not going to be enough to complete the mission."

"How did you know—," gasped Gunz just to get raked with another furious blind stare.

"What did I say about keeping your mouth shut, young man?" she asked sternly, her bushy silvery eyebrows gathering above her unnerving eyes.

"Sorry…"

"Like I said, fifteen days is not going to be enough to complete your mission and come back if you walk. Teleporting or opening your Fire Salamander portals is not going to be an option for you either since you don't know where you are going. I can't help you with that, since I don't know where the sacred garden is located," she continued.

Gunz threw a quick glance at Yaroslav, biting his lip. "But Mrak Delar said that you could help us—"

"I know what the Ancient Master said, and he was right. I will help you as much as I can," said Baba Maria, "but I can't tell you how to find the Thirtieth Kingdom and the garden. There is only one person who can help you – the old witch, Yaginya."

"Yaginya?" asked Gunz incredulously. "Are you sending us to Baba Yaga? The old witch who munches on kids and travelers?"

"Ugh." Baba Maria stomped her foot, irritably. "These latest Russian fairy tales didn't do her any favors. Never mind. You have no time for long explanations. Considering that one of you is full of fire and the other one has been dead for centuries, I don't think either of you can be a part of her well-balanced diet. Just trust me, you'll be fine. So, let me give you an Apple, so you don't get lost in the Land of Dreams."

"An Apple and a silver platter?" asked Yaroslav.

"Why does everyone always ask this question?" muttered Baba Maria reaching into the pocket of her skirt. She produced a device that looked like an iPhone, but instead of the company logo on the back of the phone, there was a large shining green apple. "This is Apple in a silver case. All you need to do is ask the guiding spirit, Darling Lily, for directions and she'll show you where to go. And also, if the logo on the back of the device shines red – you're in trouble. Any questions?"

"No, ma'am. Thank you," said Gunz, taking the device with caution. "I've heard a lot about Darling Lily. It'll be interesting to finally meet her."

Baba Maria smiled, a sad smile that brought up a net of small wrinkles around her eyes. She gently touched the collar on his neck and sighed. "It's been a while since I saw this horrible torture device used on a person. Unfortunately, I can't help you take it off. I don't have that kind of magic. So, you need to rush and if you can, find yourselves horses. I hope to see you here before the dark spell the necromancer placed on your collars will kick in."

"Baba Maria, do you know anything about the necromancer?" asked Gunz. "Something tells me George Novak is not his real name. Do you know who he is?"

The old woman closed her blind eyes and frowned. "He veils himself well. Even my sight can't penetrate the wall of his magic. I don't know for sure, but I have some suspicions."

"Well, in that case, we'll be on our way," said Gunz with a light bow. "Thank you for your help."

"Godspeed, both of you," replied Baba Maria with a sigh. "And be careful. Remember where you are. Anything is possible in the magical nexus. Be ready…"

Baba Maria snapped her fingers and vanished from the field.

CHAPTER 17

~ ZANE BURNS, A.K.A. GUNZ ~

Gunz pressed on the home button of the device and immediately the screen lit up with a bright pink light. "Hello Darling Lily," he said cautiously, remembering all the stories his friends told him about the little guiding spirit of the magical device.

The screen lit up brighter, showing an animated picture of a young girl, stretching. "Well, hello, handsome," sung Darling Lily. "Okay, who do we have here? I do like what I see... Fire and Ice. Life and Death. How the two of you can get along, I have no idea. You are polar opposites."

Gunz and Yaroslav exchanged a surprised look. "I'm Gunz," said Gunz, "and this is Yaroslav—"

"Gunz, right... You're Zane Burns and your coldblooded friend is Yaroslav Potemkin," interrupted Darling Lily. "Yum. Can you two get any cuter?"

"Darling Lily, can you please show us how to find Yaginya?" asked Gunz, ignoring Lily's last remark.

"I see, straight to business then," grumbled Darling Lily, displaying a frown on her screen. "All work and no play. Fine. Please follow the highlighted route."

The screen blanked out for a moment and then a standard GPS map appeared. A bright pink line cut through the field and went into the forest. At the bottom of the screen, Gunz read, "Time to destination: 10 days."

"Ten days?" gasped Yaroslav, horrorstricken. "And this is just to reach Yaginya. When are we going to have time to find the sacred garden and come back to LA?"

"Well, at the pace you are moving right now, you're never going to get anywhere, are you?" pointed out Darling Lily not without mockery in her voice.

"She's right, Slavik, let's go," said Gunz, offering Yaroslav the Darling Lily device as he started to walk toward the forest. "I think it would be better if you kept the device. If I need to use my magic, the phone will get fried."

"Hey, hey, hey!" squealed Darling Lily, her girlish voice trembling with fear, displaying a picture of a bar-b-que grill on the screen. "I don't like to be fried!" Yaroslav took the phone and put it in the chest pocket of his shirt. Darling Lily sighed with relief. "Aw, this is so much better. Your skin is so cold, and I love being so close to your silent heart."

* * *

Two days had passed since Gunz and Yaroslav entered the forest following Darling Lily's directions. The forest was incredibly thick, and the heavy crowns of the ancient trees hardly allowed any sunlight to break in, keeping it dark and cool. The trail they followed was covered in a soft layer of foliage and a mild scent of fresh greenery lingered in the air.

The darkness wasn't a problem neither for Gunz nor Yaroslav as they could easily see in the dark with their heightened senses. But the heavy thickets that blocked the hardly visible trail here and there were severely slowing them down. They walked as fast as they could, but even without discussing it, Gunz knew they weren't moving fast enough.

Even though they hardly took any breaks and didn't stop at night, Darling Lily still insisted they were moving too slow – her words being, like two overgrown snails. She stubbornly kept showing that they still had eight days to go at the current pace.

As the night slowly descended upon the dark forest, Gunz started noticing that Yaroslav was displaying symptoms of fatigue. It wasn't normal as vampires could go for days without rest. But the facts were staring him in the face – the vampire started to slow down, and his face showed signs of weariness. Feeling worn out himself, he suggested to take a few hours rest, eat and get some sleep.

Yaroslav didn't argue and as soon as they came across a small clearing, they made camp. While Gunz conjured a fire, Yaroslav silently disappeared into the woods. Every time Yaroslav was hunting, Gunz was praying that the vampire wouldn't go farther than a hundred yards distance. But somehow, he managed to religiously keep the proper boundaries and still bring back something to eat.

Yaroslav returned thirty minutes later, carrying a dead rabbit. He sat down on the ground, a safe distance from the flames, and quickly skinned the animal. He passed it to Gunz and wiped his bloodied hands with grass.

Slowly frying the game over the fire, Gunz carefully observed his companion. Yaroslav was lying on the ground, his arm folded under his head and there was something about his face that gave Gunz an unpleasant jolt. His skin, normally marble-white, had a sickening gray tint to it. Dark shadows were etched beneath his eyes and under his high cheek bones, making his face look almost skeletal. His long golden hair had lost its normal shine and was falling limply around his face.

His eyes were closed, but Gunz knew he wasn't sleeping.

"Slavik," he called softly and watched Yaroslav open his eyes. "Are you okay? You don't look well."

A faint smile touched Yaroslav's lips. "I'm just tired..."

"Slavik, may I remind you that you're an old vampire. Vampires don't get tired. So, let me ask you again, are you okay?"

Yaroslav sat down, pulling his knees to his chest and wrapped his arms around his knees. For a moment he remained silent, staring into the darkness of the forest. Then he sighed and said, "No, I'm not okay. And I don't know what's wrong with me. I feel like I'm sick... And you don't need to remind me that vampires can't get sick. I know that and this is why I have no idea what's going on with me."

Gunz frowned, quickly scanning him with his magical sight. A dark shadow was lingering around Yaroslav's collar. It wasn't news to him that the necromancer had placed a dark spell on both of their gray stone collars, but the cloud surrounding Yaroslav somehow seemed to be heavier. Sinister and malignant, it was pressing on his neck, squeezing it in its deadly grip.

"What do you see?" asked Yaroslav, his fingers fidgeting with a small twig absentmindedly.

"I'm not sure, but it seems your gray stone jewelry is active," replied Gunz quietly. "When you said you felt sick, what exactly did you mean by that?"

"I am slower and weaker," replied Yaroslav looking away. "My vampire speed... It's gone. I'm still faster than you are without your full Salamander's power, but I'm a lot slower than I used to be. I feel it when I hunt. And I get tired." He shook his head frowning. "Like right now. I can hardly move." He raised his eyes and Gunz noticed a dim scarlet glow.

"I think Novak did something and now your collar is affecting you," said Gunz. "When I was fighting in Florida's captive circles, I saw vampires with active collars. They were slower and weaker, just like you said. I think this is one reason.

And the second reason – you're hungry. I don't think rabbit's blood can sustain you."

"Why would Novak do that?" whispered Yaroslav. "He needs us to bring the Apple of Youth to him, so why would he make me weaker. It makes no sense."

Gunz shrugged. "There is nothing we can do about that. But there is something I can do about your hunger." He got up, suppressing his elemental fire. Then he sat down next to the vampire, extending his arm to him. "Go ahead, feed. You need your strength."

Yaroslav peered down at his arm and exhaled a ragged breath. His eyes lit up brighter, shining red in the darkness, and his lips parted, exposing his blade-like fangs. But he turned away, shaking his head.

"Let's don't do it, Slavik," said Gunz firmly. "We both know that without blood and with an active collar, you won't be able to go on for much longer. So, spare me the drama and feed."

Yaroslav snapped around, an angry low growl rumbling in his chest. He seized Gunz's arm and his fangs pierced his skin. Feeling dizzy, Gunz lay down and closed his eyes. A few seconds later, Yaroslav let go.

"Did you take enough?" asked Gunz, pressing his hand over the bleeding wound on his arm without opening his eyes.

"Enough not to kill you," hissed Yaroslav, aggravation in his voice.

"Do you think, there is a pharmacy somewhere in the Land of Dreams? If we continue like this, I will need something for anemia..."

"Why don't you get some sleep, and I'll take the first shift," suggested Yaroslav, sounding as guilty as he looked. "I'll wake you up in a couple of hours."

Gunz nodded and turned to his side. Weak from the blood loss and two days of walking, he was asleep a moment later.

* * *

Gunz woke up with a start and sat upright. He saw Yaroslav crouching next to him with his katana in his hand, ready to spring into action. He probed the area with his senses and carefully reached for his Swiss army knife. The magical energy of the nexus seemed to spike up a short distance from them as a low throaty growl rolled through the woods.

"What is it?" asked Gunz, turning his knife into the sword.

Yaroslav reached into his pocket and pulled out the Darling Lily device, showing the bright red apple shining on the back of it.

"Wild beasts. Many of them," he replied, staring unblinkingly in the direction of the sound. "But I don't think they're after us…" His voice trailed into a whisper and he fell silent, listening intently to what was going on somewhere far in the forest.

"Wolves?"

Another loud growl rumbled through the woods and a multi-vocal howl followed it, sending chills down Gunz's spine. The howl became louder and then suddenly disappeared, replaced by another deep growl of a different animal.

"Not sure." Yaroslav got up, putting the device back in his pocket and gestured at Gunz to follow him. "Let's check it out," he whispered.

They walked into the forest heading toward the sound. The howl rose above the trees again. Hungry and dangerous, it spread through the area, accompanied by roars and growls that didn't sound like typical wolves. Abruptly a new sound broke through the cacophony of animal voices.

"A horse?" whispered Yaroslav, stopping in his tracks.

"I'll be damned," hissed Gunz, his fingers wrapping tighter around the hilt of his sword. "Sounds like a horse neighing. If there is a horse, there is possibly a person there too. Let's go."

Silently they ran through the woods, avoiding making any

sounds, until they reached a small open space surrounded by low hills. They stopped at the edge of the forest, keeping behind the trees and looked down. An enormous pack of wolves spread around the clearing. They were barking and howling at something at the opposite side of it, but neither Gunz nor Yaroslav could make out what it was.

But it wasn't the pack that drew their attention. Standing on their hind legs, stretched up to their full height, five giant brown bears were leading the wolves. With their mighty roars combined in one earth-shattering rumble, the animals were slowly advancing toward the edge of the clearing. The wolves were shifting from side to side, hiding behind the massive bears.

Through the discord of their voices, Gunz kept isolating a different sound – something that sounded like the neighing of a horse. The neighing became deeper and louder, but it didn't sound fearful. It mostly sounded infuriated and a little annoyed. Wondering if the horse and its rider were in trouble, Gunz turned to Yaroslav, pointing at the other end of the clearing.

Yaroslav shrugged. "Well, I had enough rest for the night," he whispered. In the blink of an eye, Yaroslav was gone. Moving almost at full vampire speed, he ran around the perimeter of the clearing and a moment later, Gunz saw him appear at the other end with his katana at his shoulder.

"Gunz, there is a horse here, but I've never seen—"

Gunz heard Yaroslav's voice in his mind and flinched. "What the hell?"

"You forgot, we have a psychic connection," reminded Yaroslav. *"Just think, and I'll hear you. Anyway, there is no rider, but we can't leave this horse here. It's not your regular animal."*

At this moment, the bears noticed the new threat. They stopped what they were doing, all of them turning in Yaroslav's direction at once. Their roar became deeper and more sinister as they gaped at him. The wolves stopped shifting and came to a silent alert.

"Oh, shit..."

A heartbeat later Yaroslav became a blur of a slicing and stabbing blade as he attacked the wolves closest to him. The dead animals as well as their severed heads and paws fell around him in a terrifying bloody mess. The angry howls rose in the air and the pack came into motion, advancing at the vampire from every direction. Gunz decided not to wait any longer and ran downhill. Igniting his sword, he attacked the animals from the rear.

He didn't move as fast as Yaroslav, but his fire magic gave him an extra advantage. *"Ignius,"* he hissed setting the ground in front of him on fire, hoping to scare the pack into a quick retreat. To his surprise, the animals didn't shy away from the flames. If anything, they got angrier. A few wolves jumped over the fire, attacking him. He met them with his flaming sword, cutting their bodies and setting their fur into scorching flames.

Gunz wasn't sure how many beasts he destroyed when he heard a mighty roar and Yaroslav's desperate call in his mind. Gunz swung his sword, clearing a path in front of him, so he could focus on what his friend was doing. Yaroslav was surrounded by bears, getting pushed from every direction. As fast as he was, the mere size and ferociousness of the beasts was dominating him.

"Gunz, I'm losing my strength and speed. The collar..." Gunz heard his desperate voice in his mind.

"Hang in there, Slavik!" Gunz shouted, gathering as much of the fire power as the gray stone jewelry would allow him.

He knew that he couldn't revert into the natural state of the Fire Salamander, but despite the controller's settings, he was able to tap into the pure flow of the elemental powers of the magical nexus. He didn't know what prompted it – the advancement of his own power as a Fire Salamander, or the fear for the life of his friend – but in a split-second, his whole body was ablaze with smoldering flames.

"Slavik, when you see me approaching, take cover!"

Gunz dropped his sword, expanding his arms wide. The grass went up in flames on either side of him and the blazing trail ran all the way to the edge of the forest, setting the nearby bushes and small trees on fire. The heavy clouds of smoke veiled the dark sky, rising up in dark swirls. The sparks and burning embers twirled around him, as he moved forward, allowing the hungry flames to devour everything in his path. The wolves didn't have a chance to run. The fire didn't just burn them but instantly obliterated their bodies into piles of hot ash.

The animals realized the danger and squealed in terror, trying to get away from imminent death. Gunz walked forward, the mighty wave of death and destruction spreading around him. In the meantime, Yaroslav was still struggling alone against four massive beasts. One of the bears was lying on the ground in a motionless heap of bloodied fur.

"Yaroslav, run!" Gunz yelled, raising his arms up above his head, accumulating more of the fire energy between his arms. Yaroslav made one last effort, piercing one of the bears with his sword and rolled on his shoulder, escaping the deadly circle of the beasts. Quickly he climbed up the hill and disappeared into the darkness of the woods.

"Fire Salamander, go!"

Gunz heard Yaroslav's command and brought his hands together. As soon as his palms touched, a powerful blast expanded around him. He wasn't sure how he was doing it with his partially suppressed magic, but it wasn't the energy of his elemental power. It was a blast of unadulterated flames. It swept through the clearing, killing everything in its path, starting a raging forest fire.

A moment later everything was over. Gunz waved his hand, ordering the fire to cease. The land was blackened, all the grass gone, and the trees around the clearing stood naked, marred by hungry flames. All the animals were gone too, devoured by the fire.

"Slavik, are you okay?" Gunz asked, heading toward the hill. The vampire didn't reply, and worry gnawed at him. He sped up, running as fast as he could in his current state. He wasn't hurt, but such a significant use of his magic drained him physically. As he reached the foot of the hill, he noticed a large hole in the ground. He peeked inside and his mouth fell open.

A large stallion was chained inside the hole with iron chains, each chain as thick as his forearm. The stallion had the most amazing coloring. His body was dark-gray bordering on black, which slowly transitioned into a dark-chestnut shade toward his legs. But it was his long mane and tail that drew Gunz's attention. In the surrounding darkness, they shone like pure gold. He lifted his head, staring at Gunz with his deep slightly purple eyes.

"I'll be right back," said Gunz, as if the horse could understand him.

"Sure, I count on it," replied the stallion and Gunz almost jumped, gaping at the horse, flabbergasted. The stallion snickered, displaying a healthy set of large choppers and asked, "What? Never saw a talking horse before?"

"I can't say that I have," Gunz managed to reply. "I'll be right back. I need to check on my friend."

He ran up the hill and quickly searched the area. He found Yaroslav a few feet away from the edge of the clearing, behind the thick trunk of a fallen tree. He was lying on his back, his katana on the ground next to him. Gunz kneeled by his side and carefully touched his hand. It was cold.

Of course, it's cold, he thought frowning, *he's a goddamn vampire. No pulse, no checking for vital signs.*

"Slavik." He shook him gently, noticing a few cuts and deep claw marks on his skin that weren't healing. *Why is he not healing? He's a vampire, he is supposed to heal almost right away.* Gunz opened his magical sight and quickly scanned him. The dark magic of the collar was a lot heavier than it was just a few hours ago. *Dammit, Novak, what the hell are you doing?*

"Slavik, open your eyes," he demanded, shaking him stronger.

Yaroslav cracked his eyelids open and gradually focused his eyes on Gunz. "Gunz," he whispered, hardly moving his dry lips. "What's wrong with me? I feel like…"

"Like a human?" asked Gunz, giving him an arched stare. "I think Novak set your controller to maximum. From now on, no more fighting for you. No more speeding or lifting heavy weights. Until we get back to LA, except for your diet, you need to behave like a human."

"I don't think I remember how to do it," whispered the vampire, closing his eyes.

"Can you walk?" asked Gunz, wondering if he could donate some of his blood but then decided against it. He was too weak as it was.

"Give me a few minutes and I'll be fine," promised Yaroslav, closing his eyes.

"I'll be right back," said Gunz and headed downhill. As fast as he could, he crossed the clearing and found his sword. With the sword in his hand, he went to the stallion and jumped inside the hole.

"Finally," muttered the stallion, dancing impatiently. "Now, break these chains and set me free."

"Easy for you to say…" mumbled Gunz surveying the thickness of the iron. The chains had no visible locks either. After a moment of thinking, he ignited his sword, sending some fire energy through its blade.

"Whoa!" The Stallion neighed warningly, backing away from the smoldering flames.

"Do not move!" ordered Gunz. He swung his sword, channeling more fire through it and with all his remaining strength, crashed the blade on the chains. The sword slid through the iron, melting it like it was butter. He swung it again and the second chain was gone.

"Yassss!" The stallion danced around Gunz, who slowly went down to his knees, feeling too tired to stand. "You're one scary man! The fire and all. Wow!"

The stallion pushed off the ground and easily jumped out of the hole. Then he bent his knees, carefully lowering the remains of his chains down. Gunz seized the chain and the horse pulled him out. He dropped to all fours, breathing laboriously. This last bit of his magic seemed to drain whatever strength he had left after the fight with the pack.

The horse lowered next to him, gently nudging him on his shoulder. "Climb up," he suggested. "I'll give you a ride to wherever you're going."

Gunz raised his hand up, taking a few deep breaths and finally managed to say, "Not me... my friend..."

"Your friend?" repeated the stallion. "Are you talking about the tall man with golden mane almost as long as mine?"

"Yeah, him..."

"Don't you know that he is a vampire? Vampires don't get tired and they can heal almost instantaneously."

"Yeah, no," exhaled Gunz, "not this vampire."

"Do you have yourself a defective vamp for a friend?"

"He's not defective," objected Gunz irritably, slowly rising. "He is — never mind. Can you help him or not?"

"Sure, I'll help him," agreed the stallion right away. "But don't expect me to carry both of you. Nah-uh, sir. I'm not doing that."

"No problem," said Gunz, slowly moving up the hill. "Do you know where we can find one more horse?"

"That I can help you with," announced the stallion proudly. "I'm not sure it's a good idea for me to go back to this place, but I'm willing to take a chance for you."

They found Yaroslav, and with a twinge of worry, Gunz

noticed that the vampire hadn't changed his position since he left him here. Tiredly, he kneeled next to him and gently shook his shoulder.

"Slavik, wake up."

Yaroslav opened his eyes and smiled tiredly. "I'm a little better now. If you help me a little, I can get up."

The stallion lowered down next to Yaroslav, pushing him slightly on his side. "Golden-maned vampire, I'll carry you. Climb up."

Gunz helped Yaroslav to climb up on the horse. Yaroslav still couldn't hold the upright position and had to lean forward, wrapping his arms around the horse's neck.

"Ugh, cold," muttered the stallion, starting on his way downhill.

They returned to their camp and Gunz reignited the fire. Even though the stallion didn't appreciate the idea of spending a few more hours in the wilderness, both Yaroslav and Gunz needed some rest and he had to agree.

As Gunz lay down, he checked the stallion with his sight, noticing an enormous amount of magical energy around him.

"Hey, horse, how should we call you?" asked Gunz, turning to his side.

The stallion stared at him for a moment, his round eyes filled with amusement. "You don't know?"

"Should I?" replied Gunz, suppressing the rising annoyance.

"Siv," said the horse, shaking his head disapprovingly.

"Siv?" repeated Gunz, slowly rising up on his elbow as understanding washed over him. "Siv? As in Sivka-Burka?"

"Sivka-Burka? Yes, but don't call me that," said the stallion irritably. "The name is Siv now. Jeez, man, are you as ancient as your undead friend here? No one has called me that for years."

"Fine. Siv, the magic horse," muttered Gunz, his eyes slowly closing.

CHAPTER 18

~ ZANE BURNS, A.K.A. GUNZ ~

Gunz woke up a few hours later and found Yaroslav still asleep. Sprawled on the ground, he seemed to be relaxed. His face had lost its gray shade and the dark shadows beneath his eyes had disappeared. Siv was sitting on his butt, supporting himself with his front legs, staring at the last flickering flames with his purple eyes.

He can't even sit like a normal horse, thought Gunz, suppressing an overwhelming desire to laugh.

Gunz touched Yaroslav's shoulder, waking him up. The vampire was in much better shape than after the fight, but as soon as they started walking, Gunz could see that he wasn't his usual self. He didn't complain but his movements were slow and heavy. After a few minutes, Siv offered to give him a ride and Yaroslav didn't refuse, which was an additional indication of his poor physical state.

Once Yaroslav mounted the horse, they were able to move a lot faster. After about an hour of walking, they approached the border of a small town. The town was surrounded by a tall wall, but the gates were wide open. As soon as they approached the gates, Siv stopped, doubt reflected in his every move.

"Siv, what's the problem?" asked Gunz, stopping by his side.

"Well... you know..." mumbled the stallion, a guilty smile stretching his muzzle. "I kind of tried to steal something from the Lord of this town..."

"You tried to steal something," repeated Gunz, incredulously.

"Yeah... How do you think I ended up in that hole in the forest? The town's wizard cursed me..." Siv shifted from hoof to hoof, neighing uncomfortably. "Anyway, long story short, if you want a good horse that can stay up with me, the Lord of this town has it."

"I guess we'll have to deal with the consequences of your petty theft," muttered Gunz. "Lead the way."

"What petty theft? I just wanted to have a little fun," snorted Siv.

They walked through the gates, following Siv, who suddenly lost his cockiness and happy disposition. The town was larger than Gunz expected, the main street branching out to the left and to the right. Despite the early hour, the streets were full of life. As they passed by, people stopped what they were doing to gape at the strangers with curiosity.

The main street ran into another hefty brick wall. Behind the wall, Gunz could see the roof of a large house. Siv halted in front of the gates, but then took a deep breath and knocked on the door with his hoof.

After a few minutes, the door opened up with a painful screech. An old man in shabby clothes stopped in the doorway, his pale eyes burning with fury. He ignored Gunz and Yaroslav, and stepped closer to Siv, his bony hands clinched in tight fists.

"You!" he hissed, stamping his foot. "How dare you show up here, thief?"

"Whoa, old-timer," neighed Siv, raising his hoof up. "I'm not here because I want to be. Look, just call Lord Miller. I brought him some help. These two can help him get rid of that little problem he has."

The old man's eyes darted to Gunz, measuring him with his heavy gaze and then to Yaroslav who looked half-dead, hardly holding himself in an upright position. He shook his head and tapped his foot irritably, planting his fists on his hips.

"These two?" he asked, notes of mockery in his voice. "One looks like he is a step away from crossing the veil and the other one is not much better. What kind of scam are you running now, Siv?"

"No scams. I swear, everything is legit." Siv shook his head, his golden mane swiping over Yaroslav, blending in with his hair. "Call your master, old man."

"Fine. Stay here," ordered the old man and headed back to the house.

Gunz grabbed Siv's long mane pulling down on it. "What the hell were you talking about, huh?" he hissed, forcing the horse's head lower. "You brought us here? To do what exactly?"

"Take it easy, little man," neighed Siv, shaking his head to get rid of Gunz's hold. "Did you seriously think that the Lord of the town would give you a horse for free?"

"You don't get to call me 'little man', got it?" growled Gunz, sending some of his fire toward his eyes, making them glow red. "What kind of problem does this man have? Spill it!"

"How would I know," replied Siv, taking a step away, his purple eyes widened. "No matter what he does, his house and his yard are a hot mess. Everything goes down the drain in his household. If it'll continue this way, soon he'll lose everything he has, including his famous stable. And he has some beautiful mares there. Hubbu-hubbu!" Siv winked, wagging his eyebrows.

"Siv!" yelled Gunz, throwing his hands in the air. "Stay on topic. I want to know what kind of bullshit you got us into before I talk to the Lord."

"Right, right," muttered Siv, getting back to the story. "Anyway, the wizard of this hole-in-the-wall said that his misfortune is of the supernatural kind, but he couldn't help him. Not powerful enough, you know? But you and your defective vamp might have what it takes to help him."

"Damnit, Gunz," said Yaroslav, frustration in him almost palpable. "We don't have time to waste here…"

"Where are you going?" asked Siv, turning his head to the side to glance at Yaroslav.

Yaroslav pulled out the Darling Lily device and pressed the home button, showing the map to the horse. "Here."

"Lily, darling!" purred Siv, smiling seductively. "How are you doing, sweetheart?"

The screen of the device lit up with a bouncing red heart. "Aw, Siv, how nice to see you again. You didn't change a bit. Still the same heartthrob."

"Lily, honey, you're too kind… So, where are these two going?" asked the horse, staring at the screen.

"Yaginya's land," replied Lily nonchalantly. "But they're moving so slow that it'll take them another eight days to get there."

"Got it, thanks," said Siv, nodding at Yaroslav to take the device back and turned to Gunz. "Well, how about I make you a deal, fire-wizard. You convince the Lord to give you the horse of my choice from his stable and I'll take you to Yaginya in two days."

"Two days?" asked Gunz, narrowing his eyes at the stallion. "No gimmicks?"

"Two days. I swear, no gimmicks of any kind," promised Siv, stamping his hoof into the dusty ground. "Cross my heart, hope to—"

Abruptly, Siv fell silent, his ears up, his eyes two purple plates, as he noticed Lord Miller approaching the gates. The Lord of the town was a small, scrawny man in his late seventies. His balding head, surrounded by a soft cloud of gray hair, resembled a fluffy dandelion. An old robe that was patched many times over, hung off his narrow shoulders and the front of his shoes which looked even older than his robe, were torn, allowing a set of dirty toes to peek through.

His dark-amber eyes drilled into Siv and his bushy silver eyebrows went down in a frown.

"I came in peace," neighed Siv, "I promise."

The old lord pursed his lips, shaking his head. "My servant said that you brought two wizards who can take care of my little problem," said the Lord, his elderly voice cracking at high notes. "Is that true?" His eyes flashed from Siv and his rider to Gunz and back to the stallion.

Gunz stepped forward and bowed. "My lord, we would love to help with your problem," he said as respectfully as he could muster, "but do you mind telling us first what is it that troubles you?"

"Oh," mumbled the old lord, scratching the back of his head, making his flyaway hair spike up. "Why don't you come in, so you can see it with your own eyes."

Following Lord Miller, they walked through the front yard that was giving a vibe of abandonment. Tall, windblown grass covered the land in front of a two-story house. The roof with missing tiles was broken here and there and the holes were mended with pieces of wood to prevent leaks during rains. The paint, bleached out by the sunlight, was peeling, bubbling up in places, and the dark patches of uncolored wood showed through. The window shutters hung unevenly, partially torn off their hinges.

The appearance of the property and the desperate state of the old lord gave Gunz an unpleasant jolt in the pit of his stomach. He glanced at the stallion, wondering what kind of trouble he was about to face, but Siv rounded his eyes, blinking at him with an innocent expression.

They approached the three steps leading to the entry door and Lord Miller halted, turning his head back. "Okay, just be careful, don't get him angry."

"Who?" asked Gunz, helping Yaroslav to dismount off the horse.

"I don't know." The Lord shrugged. "I was hoping you could tell me what I've been dealing with for the last few years." He walked up the steps and opened the door, gesturing for them to come in, but then turned to Siv and wagged his finger. "You're staying here, four-legged thief."

Gunz walked inside, followed by Yaroslav, and they both halted observing the large dark room in shock. A putrid odor with a hardly noticeable trace of Sulphur lingered in the air. It wasn't heavy, but it was enough to make Gunz's stomach clench for a moment.

Every piece of furniture was either demolished completely or damaged to the point where it could hardly be used. The slivers of glass and litter were scattered around the room, concealing the dirty floor beneath it. The windows were covered in a layer of grime so thick that the light from outside couldn't reach through it. The only place that remained relatively untouched was a large cold fireplace.

"What the hell happened here?" asked Gunz, turning to Lord Miller. "The war of the worlds?"

"You tell me," said the Lord. "Can you cleanse my house from this evil or not?"

As soon as he said the word "cleanse", a gust of cold wind rushed through the house. Something lifted a piece of wood in the air and forcefully propelled it at Lord Miller. The old man yelped and hopped aside with amazing speed and agility for a man his age.

Gunz couldn't see anything, but his Salamander senses were on the highest alert. Yaroslav peeked at the Darling Lily device and pointed at the bright red apple on the back of it. Gunz opened his magical sight and took in a sharp breath.

"Holy mother of pearls," he exhaled. Then he pointed at the entrance door and shouted, "Everybody, out! Now!"

Pieces of furniture and debris rose up, flying like spears through the air. Avoiding a piece of chair, Gunz rushed to the exit door and held it open, allowing everyone to exit. As Yaroslav was nearing the doorway, something invisible hit him in his back. The impact wasn't strong, but the vampire coughed, clutching his chest and staggered over the threshold almost falling. Gunz slammed the door shut and leaned his back against it, breathing hard.

"Did you see what it was?" Yaroslav's voice sounded in his mind.

Gunz gave him a tiny nod and turned to the Lord of the town. "Lord Miller, would you mind giving my partner and me a moment?"

The Lord frowned but didn't object. He leaned heavily on the hand of his servant for support and walked off, halting a few feet away. Siv decided not to get involved, keeping an equal distance from the house and the owner.

"What was it?" ask Yaroslav quietly.

"Hell if I know," replied Gunz. "It looked like an oversized dog, all covered in long fur. But unlike dogs, this thing was walking on its hind legs, wearing boots and hurtling heavy objects at us like they were feathers." He scratched his head. "Oh, yeah, it was also hunching. A hunchback dog in boots. Have you ever seen anything like that?"

For a moment Yaroslav stared at him without blinking and then burst out laughing. "I'm sorry," he managed to say through the laughter. "It's really not funny. I'm probably having a nervous breakdown and this laugh is hysterical." He pressed his hand over his mouth, trying to suppress his laughter.

"Come on, Slavik," muttered Gunz. "The Lord is watching us. What the hell is this thing and how can we get rid of it?"

"It's a Zlydzen," explained Yaroslav, finally serious. "Someone must really hate this old man to curse him with an evil house spirit, especially this one."

"Oh," mumbled Gunz lamely. "I have heard of Zlydzens before, but I never imagined they were real."

"Why not?" asked Yaroslav, his eyebrows rising. "You are real and I'm real, and this annoying talkative horse, Sivka-Burka, is real. Why can't an evil house spirit be real?"

"Remember, anything is possible. Expect the unexpected and be careful," Mrak Delar's parting words sounded in Gunz's mind and he bit his lip. "You're right," he agreed. "So, how can we get rid of it?"

"That's not going to be easy," started Yaroslav with a sigh. "Nothing can kill it. You can shoot it or cut its head off – it'll survive. Even if you burn it to ashes with your Salamander's fire, it'll still rise. There are only two ways to rid a household of a Zlydzen. You either capture it and drown it in a swamp, or you lock it in a box and bury it in the crossroads."

Gunz thought for a moment and a slow smile transformed his face as an idea flashed through his mind. "Slavik, I think we can do it. The only thing I would need is about an hour to place a fireproofing spell on this house and your help. Do you think you can handle it?" He quickly explained his plan and Yaroslav nodded to him.

"Worth trying," he agreed.

"My lord, I think we can help you," said Gunz approaching the Lord and his servant. "The monster that has been destroying your life is a Zlydzen and my partner and I can help you get rid of it for a small price."

"Name it and it's yours," promised the Lord, hope gleaming in his amber eyes.

"We just need one horse from your stable," said Gunz. "You give us a horse of our choice and we cleanse your property."

"After you are done, I'll walk you to the stable myself. Any horse you pick is yours," said the Lord of the town, extending his hand, crossed by bumpy blue veins.

Gunz shook his hand and asked, "Is there anyone in the house besides you and your servant?"

"No," replied the Lord with a heavy sigh. "Since that Zlydzen showed up, all my servants, my wife, my kids – everyone left me... It just the two of us here now."

"Okay, I need you and your servant to stay away from the house for about two hours, to be safe. Can you do it for me, my lord?"

"Yes, of course, anything you ask... We'll go to the stable. It's on the other side of the property."

"And one more thing, my lord," added Gunz. "Do you have a strong box with a tight lid? Doesn't have to be big."

The Lord waved at his servant and ordered him to bring a box. A few minutes later, the servant showed up with a sturdy iron box. It had a lid that was closed and locked with a small hook. Gunz carefully examined the box, making sure there were no holes or cracks. It was perfect. He thanked the Lord and waited for both of them to leave the area. Then he asked Siv to leave too. He wasn't sure what to expect and he didn't want to see the stallion getting hurt in the crossfire. Nevertheless, he wasn't surprised when the horse eagerly agreed and disappeared behind the corner of the house in a quick gallop.

When they were gone, Gunz carefully opened the door, letting Yaroslav in first. Then he locked the door from the inside and conjured a few light orbs, sending them up in the air. He opened his magical sight and scanned the house. Zlydzen was sitting on top of the fireplace with his legs crossed, observing everything he was doing with a cocky smirk on its dog face.

"It's here, on top of the fireplace. Ready?" Gunz asked Yaroslav, communicating using their psychic connection.

"Let's get it over with," replied Yaroslav, turning toward the fireplace. He unsheathed his katana and bent his knees slightly, ready to spring into action.

Gunz channeled his magic and started to weave the spell, slowly and carefully making sure that everything inside the house – the left-over furniture, walls, ceiling and even windows – was resistant to the fire and his elemental energy. As he did that, he kept his Salamander senses sharp and vigilant, expecting an attack.

As soon as he said the first words of the spell, Zlydzen got agitated. It hopped off the fireplace and slowly shuffled toward Gunz, dragging his feet in the massive boots. A wave of dark energy swept around him as the evil spirit grew angrier with every passing second.

"Slavik, get ready," muttered Gunz without stopping what he was doing. "It's right behind me and it's angry."

Just as he finished talking, he heard a loud crack and felt something move through the air with considerable speed. He didn't turn to see what was going on, confident that Yaroslav would take care of whatever it was.

A soft breeze touched the back of his neck as Yaroslav's katana whistled through the air, deflecting the flying object. Zlydzen squealed, his voice unexpectantly loud, and the walls of the house trembled. Dust fell from the ceiling and a heavy wind rushed through the room, lifting the dirt and litter off the floor. For some reason, the stench of burnt hair spread around even though nothing was burning. The air swirled in a wild merry-go-round, and a dusty tornado filled with debris originated in the middle of the room. The wind howled, or maybe it was Zlydzen's cry, as the dark funnel moved toward Gunz.

"I got it," Yaroslav shouted over the noise of the twisting air, rising high to the ceiling. He dove inside the twisting funnel and a moment later, the tornado dissipated.

Completely trusting Yaroslav to protect him, Gunz continued his work. All hell broke loose behind his back, but he ignored it – the howling of the wind, banging and whistling of projectiles thrown by Zlydzen, wild squeals of the angry spirit and Yaroslav's diabolical laughter as he wielded his katana to deflect whatever the spirit was throwing at him.

"*Slavik, slow down,*" Gunz warned him, thinking that Yaroslav's collar was feeding on his vampiric essence, making him weak and vulnerable. "*You'll drain yourself. You could hardly walk on the way here.*"

"*I feel strangely recharged,*" replied Yaroslav. "*Almost like I have an adrenalin rush. And we both know, I can't experience that anymore. But whatever Zlydzen hit me with earlier, gave me an energy burst.*"

"Just be careful. I'm almost done," Gunz said aloud and immediately regretted his mistake.

"You're almost done, little wizard?" screeched Zlydzen and cackled. "We'll see about that."

The wind in the house died down and a low rumbling noise invaded his senses. It wasn't just a sound. He could feel the vibration with his skin. It seemed like every brick in the walls of this house was moving, grinding against each other and dancing a crazy jig, threatening to fall apart at any moment, burying them all under rocks and debris.

Gunz glanced to the right, noticing the soft glow of the magical energy in the walls. Just one more foot and the circle of protective magic would be complete. Something fell with a loud jingle and he heard Yaroslav's strangled gasp. Gunz threw a quick look over his shoulder and saw the vampire levitating a few inches above the floor, his arms pinned to his body by a shadowy hoop of dark energy. The hoop was squeezing tighter despite Yaroslav's vigorous struggle.

"*Slavik, I need to finish it, give me a moment,*" thought Gunz, returning to his spell.

He turned back to what he was doing, slowly completing the circle of the fireproofing magic. When he could see the red glow of his spell covering the entire surface of all walls in the house, he touched it with his fingers and whispered, "*Circula Archni.*"

For a heartbeat, the house lit up with a bright scarlet glow, confirming that his enchantment was complete.

Gunz turned around and smirked at Zlydzen who was holding Yaroslav in the deadly grip of his malignant magic. Zlydzen screeched and howled, the earsplitting sounds crushing Gunz's eardrums. He growled, anger igniting the fire within him.

"Silenties," he hissed pointing at the evil house spirit and Zlydzen fell silent, his dog-like face contorted by fear. Gunz didn't wait for the spirit to recover and hit him with the second spell. *"Ventius!"*

A well-targeted hurricane-force blast rushed through the house, slamming the spirit in its barrel chest. The spirit opened its mouth to scream, but no sound came out. Zlydzen flew through the air, phased through the fireplace, and disappeared on the other side. The hoop of his dark magic dissipated, releasing Yaroslav.

"Now, out of here," commanded Gunz quietly and started channeling the energy of the Fire. Yaroslav opened the box and pushed it next to Gunz's feet. Then he left the house and Gunz heard the click of the lock.

With regret, Gunz wished he could use his full Salamander's power and revert into his natural state. That would make everything so much faster and easier, but he knew that it wasn't possible. He channeled as much magical energy of the nexus as he could, connecting with the Fire. Just like he did in the forest, he raised his arms up, but this time, an enormous fireball was twirling between his hands, crackling with sparks. The fireball grew bigger and bigger, as Gunz channeled more fire energy into it.

When he felt he had as much energy as he could gather, he brought his hands together. The fireball exploded with a thunderous bang and a wall of fire swept through the house, filling every corner with smoldering flames. Gunz stilled, noticing with delight that his protection spell was working perfectly well. Although the house inside looked like a raging inferno, the building itself and the left-over furniture weren't burning.

Zlydzen left his hidey-hole behind the fireplace and levitated in the air attempting to avoid the flames. Gunz raised his hand up, pointing at the evil spirit and a ray of purifying fire hit it straight in its chest, setting the fur ablaze. A moment later, Zlydzen was gone, devoured by the merciless flames. A small pile of ash with boots in the middle of it, was all that remained of the wicked creature.

Gunz ordered the fire to cease, staring at the ash and the boots with curiosity. But he knew that the Zlydzen couldn't be killed by fire and he had a very limited window of opportunity before it would rise again.

Swiftly, he swept all the ashes into the box, threw the boots on top of the ashes and closed the lid, locking it with the hook. Holding the box in his hands, he ran to the door, breaking through the half-rotten wood with one kick of his leg. Yaroslav and Siv were already waiting for him by the steps.

Gunz shoved the box into Yaroslav's hands and flew up on top of Siv's back, grabbing the stallion's golden mane. "Siv, can you keep up with Yaroslav?" he asked. "Him and I cannot be separated by more than a hundred feet."

"What are you? Lovers?" asked Siv mockingly, rolling his eyes. "You can't be separated... Let's see if your defective vamp can keep up with me."

"I'm not defective," growled Yaroslav, for the first time showing his true annoyance with the cocky horse. "You will—"

"Stop it! Both of you!" roared Gunz. "This is not a race between you two. Siv, Yaroslav and I cannot be separated. Period! Slavik, no games. We need to bury this box and we need to do it swiftly. So, Siv will lead us to the nearest crossroads and you will stay by his side. Am I clear?"

"Fine," replied Yaroslav, throwing a furious gaze at the horse.

"Fine!" neighed Siv, starting to walk toward the gates, pushing Yaroslav with his shoulder as he passed him by.

Gunz had learned how to ride a horse when he was just a five-year old boy. He had also had enough practice in horseback riding when he lived in Kendral. But none of his previous experiences prepared him to how it felt riding the legendary Sivka-Burka. The magical stallion moved with incredible speed, hardly touching the ground with his massive hooves. The wind whistled as he rushed forward, silent like a shadow.

He leaned forward, almost lying atop the stallion's neck, his fingers frantically grasping at the silky mane. Gunz wasn't scared. On the contrary, he wanted to let go and spread his arms as the smooth movement of the stallion made him feel like he was flying.

Gunz looked to the side and saw Yaroslav moving along his side, clutching the box in his hands. He didn't want to call his fluid, soundless motion a run. It was so much more than that. He wasn't even sure if the vampire was touching the road with his feet or if he was airborne – graceful and weightless, yet dangerous like any predator.

Yaroslav caught his gaze and smiled a joyful smile. He was fast and he was strong, just the way Gunz remembered him. Whatever Zlydzen hit him with had counteracted the effects of the gray stone jewelry, at least for a short while.

Siv stopped in the middle of an intersection. Two narrow byroads crossed here, surrounded by dark woods. Gunz slid off the horse's back and surveyed the area. There was no one here. Yaroslav kneeled, putting the box next to him, and quickly made a deep hole in the ground.

Carefully, they lowered the box inside the hole and covered it with a layer of dirt. Siv watched them with curiosity and when they were done, he approached the place where they buried the box and hit it with his hoof a few times, making sure the ground was well packed.

"Are you sure, it'll keep this whatchamacallit down?" Siv asked, a layer of doubt in his words.

"I'm sure," replied Yaroslav dryly, shaking the road dust off his pants. "Zlydzen is not coming back."

"I wasn't asking you, glitchy vamp," snapped Siv, baring his massive teeth.

"You—," started Yaroslav but cut himself off, shaking his head and turned to Gunz. "Let's go, Gunz. Time is working against us."

"Wait," said Gunz, raising his hand. "I need you both to shake hands and make up. If we're planning to travel together, I can't have you two constantly at each other's throat."

"He started it," neighed Siv pouting, turning his head away.

Gunz turned to Yaroslav, frowning. "If you're going to tell me that he started it, I swear, I'm going to kick your undead ass."

"You could never kick my ass," said Yaroslav, a boyish grin splitting his face. "Even when you were in your full power. Too slow, too small and too weak, little lizard."

"Ugh," muttered Gunz, admitting to himself that Yaroslav was right. Even though he fought and killed enough vamps, when it came to fighting, Yaroslav was in a league of his own. "Never mind that. Shake hands and make up. We need to get moving."

Yaroslav pursed his lips but extended his hand to the stallion. Siv pressed his ears down and stared at his hand, narrowing his eyes. Then he snorted and touched Yaroslav's hand with his hoof, quickly pulling it back. Gunz mounted the horse and a few minutes later, they walked inside the gates of Lord Miller's house.

CHAPTER 19

~ ZANE BURNS, A.K.A. GUNZ ~

Siv galloped through the gates and didn't stop until he reached the stable. He danced impatiently as Gunz dismounted and Gunz found his eagerness worrisome. With everything he had seen so far from the magical stallion, he wasn't sure what kind of trouble he was going to walk into next. Yaroslav was standing by the door of the stable, leaning against a pole, his arms folded over his chest. The expression on his face was a perfect reflection of Gunz's thoughts.

"Siv," said Gunz, grabbing the horse's mane, stopping him, "what are you not telling us? You better tell us everything before we walk into your next con."

"Why? What did I do?" The stallion turned his head to Gunz exuding purity and blissful unawareness. "I just want to be away from this town already. That's all…"

"Are you sure?"

"Cross my heart—," started Siv, but Yaroslav interrupted him.

"And die you will, if you're lying to us," he promised in a low growl, baring his blade-like fangs. "After all the fighting and running, I feel a bit peckish, and horse's blood would do perfectly well."

Siv winced and backed away, his ears down. "Well, maybe there is a little something," he mumbled, his oversized eyes glued to Yaroslav. "But I swear, it's not going to affect you or your mission in any way."

"I told you," said Yaroslav with a half-shrug. Gunz glanced at him and couldn't help but chuckle – the terrifying vampire's fangs didn't work well with a very much human, boyish grin on Yaroslav's face.

"Spit it out, Siv," said Gunz with a sigh. "What is it this time?"

"Wizard, you're not going to let your vamp feed on me, are you?" asked the stallion carefully, stepping from hoof to hoof.

"I don't know." Gunz shrugged, suppressing laughter. "Yaroslav is my friend and I don't want to see him starve, you know? So, it depends on what you're going to say next."

"I swear, it's not going to affect you," Siv reassured them again. "But have you ever been in love? The kind of love that doesn't let you sleep, eat, or think clearly? And you would do anything just to be with her again, to be able to run by her side one more time, to see her mane flowing freely in the wind… You know?"

Gunz blanched but suppressed the agonizing memories Siv's question brought forth. "Let's assume for the sake of this conversation that we know what you mean," he said dryly. "What does it have to do with us?"

"Well, the beautiful Mariella, the mare I love, is in this stable," explained Siv, inching his way closer to Gunz. "All I want you to do is pick her as your price. She's strong and powerful and almost as fast as I am. If anyone can keep up with my pace, it's Mariella. Please, fire-wizard, pick her…"

"Is she as talkative as you are?" asked Yaroslav snickering.

"Um… no," replied Siv, looking away from Yaroslav's fangs.

"Oh, good." Yaroslav sighed in fake relief. "So, how do we know which horse to pick?"

Siv neighed happily, his normal upbeat disposition coming back to him. "It's easy. She's the only white mare in this stable."

Gunz shook his head and walked inside the stable. Yaroslav and Siv followed him. The stable was light and clean. Unlike the house, everything here was in perfect order. For some reason Zlydzen's vile presence hadn't affected it. There were at least fifteen horses housed in the stable – all pure bred, long-legged beauties.

Lord Miller was sitting on a bench at the far end of the stable. With his hands folded on his lap and his head bowed down to his chest, he appeared to be sleeping. However, as soon as Gunz walked in, he lifted his head and a hopeful gleam lit up his eyes.

"My lord." Gunz greeted him with a light bow. "Your house and your property have been cleansed. You can safely return to your life, sir."

"I can't believe it," whispered the old man, tears gathering in his eyes. "Are you sure it's gone?"

"Yes, my lord," replied Gunz with a light smile. "You can send your servant to check."

"No, no." Lord Miller shook his head. "I would not disrespect you by not trusting your word, young wizard. What can I do to repay you and your friend?"

"All we need is one horse from your stable," said Gunz.

"Pick any horse and it's yours." Lord Miller waved his hand around.

Yaroslav headed toward the white mare. Tall and elegant, with her long silvery tale and mane, she stood out among the other horses in the stable. Her smart brown eyes were staring longingly past Yaroslav, at Siv.

"We'll take her," said Yaroslav, throwing a quick look at Siv, an uneven smirk on his lips.

"I was expecting that," said Lord Miller, pursing his lips. "I knew that this sneaky thief would find a way to get her. All the same, I'm a man of my word. Mariella is yours."

He waved his hand at his servant, ordering him to get Mariella ready for the ride. The old lord also offered them a saddle and bridle for Siv, suggesting that Gunz would be more comfortable riding the magical stallion with a saddle.

Needless to say, Siv wasn't thrilled with this idea, but in the end he agreed and picked the best saddle and bridle the old lord owned. Lord Miller was so happy that the evil house spirit was gone, he didn't object to that either.

Thirty minutes later, Gunz and Yaroslav left town, directing their horses toward the "highlighted route" as Darling Lily put it.

* * *

WHEN SIV PROMISED that he could get them to Yaginya's land in two days, he hadn't been kidding. Both Siv and Mariella were galloping at such speed that the only thing Gunz could see was a continuous blurry wall of trees. They rode through the endless dark forest, with hardly any stops to get food and water.

Despite all the training in horseback riding Gunz had received in Kendral, by the end of the second day, only the power of his will was holding him upright in the saddle. His back was aching mercilessly, and he could hardly feel his legs. He kept readjusting his position, quietly cursing the endless ride and absence of proper transportation in the magical nexus.

Once in a while, he threw a quick glance at Yaroslav. Unlike him, the vampire looked like he was born in the saddle. Slightly leaning forward, with his wrists soft and flexible, he didn't show any signs of tiredness, seemingly relaxed and comfortable. The only thing Gunz was concerned with was how long the energy boost that Zlydzen gave Yaroslav would last.

By the end of the second day, as the sun gradually lowered down toward the horizon, the horses slowed down to a soft trot. The forest was still just as gloomy and thick as ever and with the sun gone, the darkness became overwhelming.

"Siv, why are we slowing down?" asked Gunz, readjusting his position to straighten his aching back.

"We're almost there," replied Siv in hushed voice. "You'll see soon."

Just to be sure, Yaroslav pulled out the Darling Lily device. He pressed the home button and the screen lit up, displaying the map. The checkered flag that marked the final destination was visible at the end of the bright pink line.

"Darling Lily," called the vampire, and the corners of his mouth quirked up in anticipation of Lily's antics.

"Hell-ooo, kitty. Mmmmm, my processor is on fire…" purred Lily, the screen displaying a large winking eye. "What can I do for you, golden handsomeness?"

"Can you please tell me how much farther to Yaginya's land?" asked Yaroslav, stifling laughter.

"I can tell you anything you want to hear, my cold hotness," purred Lily, arrows with red hearts flying across her screen. "Your final destination is only a hundred feet ahead."

"Thanks," said Yaroslav, putting the device away.

"You're actually enjoying this." Gunz snickered, shaking his head. "For a few-centuries old vamp, you're a bit on the vain side, aren't you?"

Yaroslav chuckled, wild twinkles dancing in his eyes, but didn't object to his friend's snide remark.

A few minutes later, the forest opened up into a small clearing. Gunz stopped Siv at the edge, carefully surveying it. The space was perfectly round, like someone drew it using a compass. The dark sky above the clearing was punctured with little dots of stars and the bright disk of the full moon was showering it with its cold light.

A small hut with a tall gable roof covered with straw was positioned right in the center of the clearing. The edges of the roof and the window frames were decorated with lacy wooden designs, and a wind vane in the shape of a rooster topped the tip of the roof. But it wasn't the roof that drew Gunz's attention. The whole contraption was sitting on thick chicken legs.

"A hut on chicken legs," mumbled Gunz, exchanging a quick look with Yaroslav. "Really?"

"Should we try?" asked Yaroslav, his hand slowly traveling to his sword.

Gunz rolled his eyes. Did he really have to repeat the words from Russian fairy tales to make this hut turn around? That felt absolutely ridiculous. He sighed, riding forward and halted in front of the hut.

"Hut, hut," said Gunz throwing a warning gaze at Yaroslav, whose eyes started to spark with laughter, "turn your back to the forest and your face to me."

For a moment he held his breath, wondering if the fairy tales his mother read him when he was a child were just that – fairy tales. But when the hut on chicken legs screeched mournfully and slowly started turning around, stepping carefully on the tall grass with its chicken legs, he almost gasped.

"It worked," muttered Gunz, staring at the rotating hut in awe.

"Gunz, forget about the hut. We're not alone," hissed Yaroslav. He was off his horse, holding his katana at the ready.

Gunz scanned the area with his senses, realizing that Yaroslav was right. A presence of strong magical energy somewhere next to them was undeniable, and the old vampire with his constantly heightened senses had registered it right away. Gunz manifested his sword, but besides feeling the magic somewhere nearby, he couldn't see anything or anyone.

"Slavik," he said quietly, channeling the energy of the Fire, "come here and stay as close to me as you can." Then he turned to the stallion. "Siv, I need you to keep an eye on Mariella. I don't want her to get scared and run when she sees the fire."

He waved his hand, conjuring a flaming circle around them. The wall of fire surrounded them from every direction, shredding the darkness with its fiery presence. To his relief, both horses didn't react to the fire, standing calmly inside the circle.

"Whatever it is, it's here..." He heard Yaroslav's voice in his mind. The vampire was standing back to back with him with his sword in his hands.

Through the wall of fire, he noticed that the hut had finished its rotation and there was someone standing in front of it. The swirls of hot air made the figure shimmer and its silhouette appeared to be distorted and blurry. The veil of white smoke rising above the circle didn't help the situation.

At first, the person was just standing there, silently staring at the bright light of the fire. After a moment he or she slowly moved forward, toward the fire circle. Even through the veil of smoldering flames, Gunz could feel this person's magical signature and it was incredibly powerful, too powerful for a witch or a wizard.

"Aw, boys, you picked the wrong element to fight me," said the stranger whose voice unmistakably belonged to a woman, "I love fire. My favorite toy." She put her hand into the flames and the fire slowly subsided. "Now that I can see all of you, I would love to say I smell humans, but neither of you are. At least not entirely."

"Baba-Yaga?" asked Gunz flabbergasted.

He was expecting to see an old, ugly crone with matted gray hair and warts on her face, riding in a mortar with a broomstick in her bony hands. The woman standing before him was no more than thirty years old. She had a pleasant oval face with a clear complexion, surrounded by wavy strands of long deep-brown hair. The outside corners of her honey-colored eyes were turned down slightly, giving her a sad appearance. Dressed in black leather pants, leather jacket and tall boots, she stood almost as tall as Yaroslav.

"I would prefer if you called me Yaginya, boys," Baba-Yaga said, a slight smirk touching her coral lips. "The image of Baba Yaga was severely damaged by some of the Russian fairy tales and I don't feel like doing damage control."

"Yes, ma'am," mumbled Gunz, but a split-second later, he got over his initial shock and bowed to her respectfully. "My lady, we were looking for you."

"Zane Burns and Yaroslav Potemkin. I was expecting you," she said calmly, pivoting on her heels and headed toward the house. After a few steps, she halted and glanced back at them, her eyebrows raised. "Do you need a special invitation? Sheath your swords, boys, and follow me." Then she waved at the stallion and continued, "Siv, you and your lady-friend can stay in my barn, behind my house. You'll be safe there and there is enough hay for the both of you."

CHAPTER 20

~ ZANE BURNS, A.K.A. GUNZ ~

As Yaginya approached the hut on chicken legs, the air around her shimmered like a mirage on a hot summer day, and it seemed like she passed through an invisible power field. As she emerged on the other side, her appearance began to change. The leather pants and jacket got replaced with a beautiful silk robe that fell in rich folds down to her elegant high heels. Her long hair got styled into a thick braid and wrapped around the back of her head.

She glanced at them with a challenging smirk on her face and gestured at them to come closer. Gunz motioned Yaroslav to wait and walked up to the invisible field. As he reached forward and carefully touched it, his hand slid through it without any problems. He wasn't sure why he did it, but he inhaled like before a dive and stepped through the field. In a way it did feel like walking through a thin layer of water.

"Your dead friend can safely walk through my shield," said Yaginya dryly. "It's not going to burn him. I promise. It's just an illusion to keep some unwanted visitors away." She waited a moment until Yaroslav joined them and then gestured toward her house. "My home is your home. Please, come in."

Gunz turned toward the hut and his jaw dropped. The hut on chicken legs was gone. Instead, he was standing in front of a modern contemporary home, built of glass and concrete. The front door was opened, and soft music was drifting through the doorway.

"Please come inside. I believe your undead friend needs a special invitation," said Yaginya, addressing Gunz. "Make yourself at home while I take care of your wonderful horses."

Gunz walked inside the house and halted indecisively. The marble floor was polished to perfection and everything inside the house was perfectly clean and in order. He glanced down at his shoes, covered in a thick layer of road dust and dirt and then at his clothes which weren't exactly clean either.

"That's as far as I go," said Yaroslav shaking his head. "I don't want to anger the ancient sorceress by messing up her floors. Something tells me, she dislikes me already."

"I'm not a sorceress and a few footprints on my spotless floors are not enough to set me off." Yaginya walked into the house and took in their less than immaculate appearance. "Let's do this, boys. First, I'll let you clean up a bit and once you're ready, you can join me for dinner here. There is a lot we need to discuss."

Yaginya escorted them to the second floor of her house and showed them to separate bedrooms, mentioning in passing that in their bedroom closet they would find something that should fit their size and taste in attire.

* * *

GUNZ TOOK A QUICK SHOWER, dried his hair and body and walked back into the bedroom. After the shower, he started to feel how truly tired he was, his every muscle buzzing with exhaustion from the endless ride. Nevertheless, he didn't want to waste any time. They had been on the road nearly five days already. It meant that out of the fifteen days Novak had given them, they already used almost a third, and he still didn't know how long it would take them to find the sacred garden.

Besides that, he wasn't sure what kind of game Novak was playing. The necromancer wasn't an idiot. He knew the gray stones couldn't kill a Fire Salamander. The magical stones could hurt him, make him as weak as any human, but they couldn't kill an immortal being. However, they could kill a vampire, no matter how powerful or ancient he was. It was obvious that George Novak wanted them to bring the Apple of Youth and the Water of Life, so why would he make both of them weaker, diminishing their chances to succeed in this mission?

Gunz opened the closet and found a plain black t-shirt, jeans and a light leather jacket that fit his size perfectly. He threw everything on the bed and quickly placed a fireproofing spell on all the clothes. Leaving the jacket on the bed, he put the pants and shirt on, and grabbed a pair of motorcycle boots out of the closet. After that, he moved his Swiss army knife from his old jeans into the new ones and headed downstairs.

Yaroslav was there already. He was sitting next to a dining room table that was set for a king. His long hair was still a little wet after the shower. His head was bowed down and the golden strands fell over his chest, leaving damp spots on his white shirt. His long legs, clothed in black leather pants and tall riding boots, were stretched out and his arms were folded over his chest. He looked like he was sleeping, but as soon as Gunz walked inside the room, he lifted his head and a tiny smile warmed his features.

"How are you?" Gunz asked, registering a hardly noticeable red glow in the vampire's eyes. "Are you starting to feel the effect of the gray stones again?"

"A little," replied Yaroslav, "but it's not bad. Not yet—"

"Aw, you both look scrumptious," said Yaginya as she walked into the dining room. "Good enough to eat."

"I hope we're not on your menu," said Yaroslav, smirking.

"Ha-ha," muttered Yaginya, rolling her eyes. "Coming from a freak of nature who lives on a liquid diet of human blood."

Gunz turned to Yaroslav, giving him a warning stare. Then he smiled at Yaginya. "My lady, the Gatekeeper sent us here. We need your help."

Yaginya sat down, placing some salad on her plate. "Please, help yourself first. We'll talk later."

Gunz was so worn out that he didn't feel the hunger, but out of respect to their hostess, he filled his plate and started eating. So did Yaroslav, and Gunz just had to wonder if vampires could eat human food. Whether they could or they couldn't, Yaroslav had perfect table manners so Gunz couldn't tell if the vampire enjoyed the meal.

Once they finished eating, Yaginya touched the table cloth. It shimmered with bright sparks and everything disappeared from the table, leaving it spotlessly clean.

"I'm not big on cooking," she said with a guilty smile. "So, the magical tablecloth works perfectly well for me. So, how can I help the two famous, undefeated fighters?"

Gunz frowned. "Undefeated fighters?"

"Yes, undefeated fighters – Gunz and Alucard." Yaginya shrugged, an innocent expression on her face making her look young and carefree. "Well, I'm guilty as charged... Sometimes, I travel to the mundane world for some light gambling. A bad habit of mine."

"Never mind." Gunz rubbed his face tiredly. *So, she is a gambler, betting on underground fights. Big friggin' deal!* He sighed and continued, "It's very late, so if you don't mind, let's just get straight to business. Yaroslav and I need to retrieve the Apple of Youth from the sacred garden, but no one seems to know where the garden is located. Can you please point us in the right direction?"

"Are you sure you want to do it?" asked Yaginya, a deep vertical crease etched between her dark eyebrows.

"Yes, I am sure," replied Gunz meeting her narrowed eyes. "We have no choice but to do as ordered."

Yaginya reached forward and touched the collar on his neck, shaking her head. "I see," she muttered, and he felt the touch of her magic probing his gray stone jewelry.

The gray stones reacted to the magical invasion by sending a jolt of electricity through his body. He grunted, his fingers frantically grasping at the edge of the table.

"Stop, please," he hissed through clenched teeth.

Yaginya let go right away and pursed her lips. "We always have a choice, Fire Salamander. Sometimes the choices we have are not ideal, but they are still valid choices," she said dryly, throwing a frosty gaze at Yaroslav. "You chose to bow down and obey. This is why you are here with this dead leech."

"No," snapped Gunz, his hands curling into fists. "I chose to save my friend's life and stop a delusional maniac from torturing another person who is important to me."

"But let me ask you, oh brainless one," said Yaginya snidely. "Why does the delusional maniac need the Apple of Youth in the first place, eh? Did you think what would happen when he gets it?"

Gunz averted his gaze, swallowing hard. "He wants to make an elixir of immortality."

"Nice!" hissed Yaginya, slamming her hand on the table. "So, your choice is to save a worthless walking corpse by giving the gift of immortality to a dangerous dark wizard. Is that right, Fire Salamander?"

"Let me repeat," growled Gunz, fire slowly rising in him as his exhausted mind could no longer control his emotions, "Yaroslav is my friend. He stood by my side and fought to protect a city full of humans. I don't care if he is dead or alive,

I'm proud to call him my friend! And I would do anything to save him and stop George Novak from torturing Aidan McGrath!"

Gunz got up, spreading his flaming arms, no longer able to control his power and headed outside. He halted by the door, thinking that insulting the only person who could help them wasn't a good move and turned around with a sigh. "My lady, I apologize for my behavior and I'm begging your forgiveness," he said with a bow. "I need a few minutes to get in control. I'll be right back."

He walked outside closing the door and sat down on the steps. The cold night air engulfed him, and he leaned forward, wrapping his arms around his head to suppress the desire to scream. Yaginya made perfect sense – making a dangerous maniac like Novak immortal would have unpredictable consequences. Possibly, deadly consequences.

At the same time, somewhere in the back of his mind, he knew that killing Yaroslav to break himself free would be a mistake. A mistake more dangerous than giving the elixir of immortality to the necromancer. He had no idea how he knew it, he just did, and he was sure that the decision he made was the right one.

I'm just tired, I'm just extremely tired, he thought, his fingers digging into his scalp. *I need a few minutes to calm down and think.*

He felt a light touch to his shoulder and slowly raised his head. Yaroslav was sitting next to him. The vampire was staring straight ahead, his arms powerlessly resting on his knees.

"Gunz, Yaginya was right," he said quietly. "We can't allow this dangerous necromancer to become immortal."

"Slavik, please, not you too," whispered Gunz, lowering his eyes.

"She is right, Gunz. You have to let me die."

"No," objected Gunz flatly. "I'm not going to give up on you or on Aidan for that matter. Plus, even if I let you die, I still have the collar on my neck, and Novak is the only one who can take it off. With the controller in his hands, he can bring me down to my knees even if I'm in a different world."

"That's not entirely true, Gunz. And I'm sure you know it," said Yaroslav. "During our last conversation, Mrak Delar said something that made me think. He said if Kal was in your place, he would be out of these restraints in a matter of a few minutes. If Kal can do it, you can do it too."

"I heard that evil son of a bitch," muttered Gunz. "And he probably said it just to hurt me. He succeeded. Nevertheless, I'm not going to let you die, Slavik. So, let's drop this conversation." He raised his eyes, meeting Yaroslav's scarlet gaze and shook his head. "How long has it been since you had something to eat?"

He reached into his pocket and pulled his knife out, but Yaroslav seized his wrist, stopping him.

"You're too tired and I don't want you to deal with blood loss on top of it," he objected quietly. "I know, I sound like a broken record every time when you offer me your blood. And every time I feed on you anyway... But you have no idea how horrible it makes me feel."

"You're right, Slavik. You do sound like a broken record. I need you alive. I swore to your mother that I would bring you home to her." He took a few deep breaths, suppressing his fire and slashed his wrist with his knife. Dark streams of blood trickled down his hand, dropping on the soft dirt under his feet. "Drink. Don't make me kick your undead ass."

Yaroslav sucked in a sharp breath and seized Gunz's bleeding wrist, his icy fingers trembling. He pressed it to his mouth, carefully piercing his skin with his fangs. Gunz turned away, feeling slightly nauseous and weak as the wave of warmth spread through his body. The vampire let go a few seconds later, squeezing his wrist to stop the bleeding.

"Thank you," he said, wiping his lips with his hand, his voice sounding hollow, void of emotions. "But to be honest, you couldn't kick my ass even if your life depended on it."

"What are you saying?" asked Gunz drowsily. "We sparred before… in training. And I killed enough of your kind—"

"Those other vampires you killed, they were nothing like me. And in sparring, you fought me, but I didn't really fight you back."

"What are you saying, Slavik?"

"Why do you think Akira chose to turn me? She had never done it before and has never done it again. Have you ever asked her about it?"

"No and I don't care—"

"You should," roared Yaroslav rising. Levitating a few inches above the ground, he spread his arms throwing his head back. His vampiric energy lingered around him like a stormy cloud and his hair fanned, surrounding his face and shoulders. "I have some powers unlike any other vampires you've met before. I'm a monster, Gunz. I killed more humans than you've met in your life."

Yaroslav spun in the air and a moment later, a giant golden wolf was standing in his place. He snarled, a low growl rumbling in his throat and charged Gunz. Gunz didn't move a muscle, not even when the wolf pushed him back and placed his thick paw on his chest, his terrible fangs less than an inch from his face. The wolf growled, his eyes burning with a bright scarlet light.

"Are you done with your shenanigans?" asked Gunz unimpressed. "Enough with theatrics, Yaroslav. I'm not going to let you die."

The wolf yelped, backing away and a split-second later, Yaroslav assumed his human form. He sighed, lowering down on the step next to Gunz.

"I move faster than any average vampire and I'm stronger than any average vampire. I can shapeshift into a wolf or a large bird, and I can glamour humans and kill them before they know what's happened to them," he said quietly. "I haven't killed in years, but before that…" His voice disappeared into the silence of the night forest. "Gunz, you must kill me. Aidan is a god. He'll find a way to get himself out of this situation. Your loyalty to me and Akira is the only thing that keeps you on this destructive mission. You kill me and you're a free man to stop Novak from achieving his goal, whatever that might be."

"So, why did Akira choose you as her only son?" asked Gunz, unfazed by Yaroslav's heated speech. "I'm sure when you were a human boy, you didn't have all these wonderful powers."

"No, I didn't have any powers, except the power to suffer and die a miserable death," he whispered, dropping his head. "I was a twenty-year old boy, dying of consumption… It was my blood that Akira sensed. I wish she let me die!" He punched the marble steps he was sitting on with his fist, leaving a tiny crack in the stone.

Yaroslav fell silent and Gunz didn't dare to say anything, horrified by the anguish in the vampire's voice. After a few minutes, he finally asked, "Yaroslav, what was so special about your blood? The blood of a Russian royalty, Prince Potemkin?"

"No, of course not." Yaroslav threw a quick glance at Gunz, a bitter smirk on his ashen face. "I was nothing but another *bajstryuk* – bastard. My biological father didn't know about my existence. And I doubt he would care about me even if he knew. It was the blood of my poor, destitute mother that drew Akira. The bloodline of Vlad Tepes… You know him as Vlad the Impaler."

"Dracula… He was real?"

Yaroslav laughed humorlessly. "When are you going to put it through your thick skull, Gunz? Everything is real." He sighed. "So, I'm the last of Dracula's bloodline and I'm a vampire… Life made a full circle. This is why I can do some things other vampires can't. This is why Akira chose me, Gunz… And this is why you should kill me. I'm dangerous and what we're planning to do makes me even more dangerous. Think about it – a vampire with extreme abilities controlled by a powerful immortal necromancer."

Yaroslav got up and unsheathed his katana. Then he lowered down to both knees, offering his sword to Gunz, holding it with both hands in the Japanese manner.

"Set me free, Gunz," he said quietly. "I'm not going to be a weapon in the hands of evil. Never again…"

Gunz got up and took the sword from Yaroslav's hands. He stared at the blade, slightly tilting it back and forth to let the bright light of the full moon play on the polished steel. Yaroslav gathered his long hair and moved it to the side, exposing his neck.

"Do it, Gunz," he said, without raising his eyes. "Just the way my mother taught you. Make it quick."

Gunz sighed and sat down on the ground in front of Yaroslav, placing the katana between them. "I'm not going to kill you," he said dryly. "This is bullshit, Slavik."

"What is?" Yaroslav lifted his face and there was so much pain reflected in his eyes that Gunz shuddered.

"Everything you just said is," replied Gunz, anger slowly rising up in him. "Of course, I know you're dangerous. I always knew it. But I also knew that you didn't kill in years. Maybe a century, maybe even longer. I went through hell, Slavik, just to find you. The amount of pain and humiliation I had to suffer to get closer to you… And after all that, you want me to kill you? If you want to die, all you have to do is run faster than me. And from what I understand, you're a lot faster than I am. You put more than hundred yards between us and you're as good as dead."

"There is no honor in that kind of death," said Yaroslav quietly. "I refuse to take my own life."

For a moment Gunz stared at him, his eyes widened, his

anger quickly melting away. Then he pressed his hand to his mouth and turned away. Possibly it was his exhaustion that was playing with his frazzled mind, but at the moment, this whole situation seemed to amuse him. He stifled the laughter and picked the katana off the ground, slowly rising to his feet.

He stood over Yaroslav, biting his lip, as the vampire bowed his head, moving his hair away to expose his neck, again. Gunz raised the katana and gently lowered it to the vampire's neck, drawing a few drops of blood. Yaroslav didn't move, remaining still like a statute.

"I would rather die than take the life of my friend," said Gunz coldly, lowering the sword and extending his hand to Yaroslav. "We'll figure it out, Slavik. We always do. We'll get the Apple and we'll find a way to stop the necromancer before he becomes indestructible. And if Yaginya doesn't want to help us, we'll find some other way."

Yaroslav looked up at Gunz, shaking his head but accepted his hand and got up. He took his sword and sheathed it. "When it comes to your friends, you have a blind spot, Gunz, and one day it will be your undoing," he said, his voice hoarse.

"I second that."

Both Gunz and Yaroslav spun around to find Yaginya standing right behind them.

"Yaginya," said Gunz, raking his fingers through his hair, "how long have you been standing here?"

"Long enough," she replied frostily. "Long enough to see that a vampire has more common sense than a Fire Salamander. I should have a word with Kalidus first chance I get. Nevertheless, what I witnessed, made me change my mind."

"You are going to help us?" asked Gunz, a spark of hope warming him from inside.

"I am," replied Yaginya dryly, raising her hand up to stop him from talking, "and don't thank me, because by helping you, I am going against everything I believe in. So, both of you – off to your rooms and get at least some sleep. You're leaving early in the morning and your trip is not going to be easy. And do it without speaking. Don't give me a reason to change my goddamn mind!"

Silently, Gunz bowed to her and walked back into the house.

CHAPTER 21

~ ZANE BURNS, A.K.A. GUNZ ~

Early in the morning, Yaginya softly knocked once on his bedroom door, but it was enough to wake Gunz up. He opened his eyes, noticing the yellowish-pink flares of early sunrise on the walls of his room. He got up and stretched, his muscles still sore and aching from two days of riding. Between his restless mind and worn out body, he barely got any sleep. Nevertheless, he felt a little better than last night.

By the time he had cleaned up and made it downstairs, Yaroslav was already waiting for him. The table in the dining room was set up for breakfast but served only for two. Yaginya showed up a moment later sporting a glass filled with blood. She put it in front of Yaroslav, expression of disgust prominent on her face.

"Pig's blood," she said, wrinkling her nose. "I know that while you can eat regular human food, you neither enjoy it nor does it give you the nourishment you need to sustain your strength. And I don't want you feeding on the Fire Salamander. At least not in my house."

Yaroslav accepted the glass, silently inclining his head. Even though he appeared to be as calm as ever, his eyes betrayed the burning shame he felt. While Gunz was eating, Yaginya took the Darling Lily device from Yaroslav and quietly conversed with the guiding spirit.

She gave all the instructions to Darling Lily and explained to them that finding the sacred garden was not going to be easy, because it kept moving within the boundaries of the nexus, vanishing from one place and immediately manifesting in another, every seven days. Their only hope was that the magical horses like Siv and Mariella could take them there before the garden switched its location.

Instructed by Yaginya, Darling Lily searched the Land of Dreams for the current location of the garden and a few seconds later she announced that with Siv's speed in mind and if they would ride without stops, they could reach the garden in approximately two days. Gunz wasn't looking forward to two more days in saddle, but it was better than the original ten days that Lily projected in the beginning of their journey.

By the time they walked outside, Siv and Mariella were saddled and ready to ride. A bag with food and water was attached to Siv's saddle. Yaginya bid her farewell, wishing them good luck with their mission and they took off in a speedy gallop.

* * *

ALL DAY they rode through the endless forest. The ancient woods, a mix of leafy trees and pine trees, surrounded them in every direction. At first, a hardly visible trail was slithering through the thorny thickets and bushes, but after a few hours it disappeared completely.

Yaroslav kept the Darling Lily device out and she was giving the directions to their horses, commanding them where to go in her usual bossy manner better than any modern GPS. Nevertheless, it slowed them down significantly and Lily kept complaining that even magical horses couldn't keep up with their schedules and deadlines, comparing them to the construction companies who never delivered anything on time. Siv didn't bother replying to her. Breathing hard, he focused on the road ahead or rather the absence thereof.

Another hour passed and the sun disappeared completely, leaving them in the eerie darkness of the forest. Darling Lily activated the flashlight on her device, but it wasn't nearly bright enough to illuminate the path ahead. The horses slowed down to a soft run, carefully choosing their every step. Gunz conjured five light orbs, sending them flying up and ahead of them.

After a while, Yaroslav sped up and came closer to Gunz. Pointing up, he asked, "Did you amplify your light orb spell?"

Gunz glanced up and his mouth fell open. Seemingly, his light spell was magnified significantly without him doing anything and now they were riding surrounded by hundreds of tiny lights. He could still recognize five of his original light orbs as they were shimmering with a brilliant blue glow.

The new orbs gleamed with a soft green light, fading in and out of darkness, flickering brighter before subsiding into a hardly visible green glow. He stared mesmerized at the new lights, his mind enthralled by their nonstop motion and their hypnotic radiance.

A loud buzzing brought him out of his trance, and he looked in the direction of the sound. The Darling Lily device was vibrating, emitting a bright red light and Lily was screaming the same word over and over, at the top of her speakers. "STOP!"

"Siv! Stop!" yelled Gunz, pulling on the reins.

The stallion neighed, shaking his head, and skidded to a screeching halt. Mariella stopped right next to him, neighing softly. Gunz dismounted. As he hit the ground, he realized that the land under his feet wasn't firm and stable. Carefully he walked around the stallion closer to Yaroslav, who was observing his surroundings with wide-open eyes.

"Do you see anything?" asked Gunz in a soft whisper. But as softly as he spoke, a light night breeze picked up his words, bouncing them from tree to tree in a hollow echo.

Yaroslav shook his head, frowning. Gunz sharpened his eyes but at first couldn't see anything either. He probed the area with his magical sight and drew in a short breath. They were surrounded by a powerful magical energy. While the energy signature felt familiar, he failed to identify it with any magical creature he knew.

"There is someone here," he said quietly. "Someone is messing with us…"

As an answer to his words, the forest exploded in a discord of sounds. Somewhere ahead of them, a bubble blew up with a loud pop and a cold wind picked up, playing with the tree branches, their rustling fusing into a continuous background noise. Farther, somewhere in the depth of the woods, an even beat of something sounding like a woodsman's axe broke through the overall pandemonium.

The green lights shone brighter, their movement becoming faster and more chaotic. Siv neighed nervously, ready to take off, but Gunz grabbed his bridle, stopping him. He petted the stallion's mane, raking his fingers through it.

"Hush, Siv," he whispered, looking around. "You and Mariella can't move. You understand me? Do you feel how soft the ground under us is? We are surrounded by a marshland and I don't know where the deadly swamp starts. So, stay still and wait until I tell you what to do."

Gunz found a large branch under his feet and carefully took a couple of steps forward, probing the ground with the branch. He took another step and stopped. The branch fell through the thin surface covered with grass and foliage, swallowed by the muddy soil. Dropping the branch, he backed away from the swamp and ran into Yaroslav.

"I don't understand how it happened," said the vampire,

cleaning his muddy hands. "We're standing on a small isle of a relatively hard land, surrounded by swamp. How the hell did we get here in the first place?"

"Nothing like this ever happened to me," said Siv, exchanging a bewildered look with his girlfriend. "I'm good with directions. I swear."

"I don't think it has anything to do with you, Siv. I can feel the presence of some magical energy," said Gunz. "It's oddly familiar, but I just can't remember what it is."

He stopped talking, staring into the woods. The wind calmed down a little and most of the sounds slowly melted away. Only the even beat of an axe was loud and clear in the midnight forest.

"What if we go in the direction of that sound?" suggested Siv. "Sounds like an axe. Where there is an axe, usually there is a woodsman. Maybe they can help us find our way back to the road." At his words, the green lights got agitated, zooming in and out of the darkness, like they were inviting them to proceed.

"We are surrounded by a swamp," said Yaroslav. "Where exactly do you want to go?"

"We could probe the ground—," started Siv but suddenly fell silent, staring in the direction of the sound.

Gunz turned around and froze. A few yards away from them, he saw a large deer. The animal was standing motionlessly, staring at them with its round dark eyes. Its head was decorated with large antlers that were glowing with a bright golden light, prominent in the dark forest.

"What the hell?" muttered Gunz.

The deer caught his gaze and nodded at him. Then the animal turned around and took a few steps deeper into the woods. Since Gunz didn't move, the deer stopped and turned his head as if inviting him to follow.

"I think he wants us to follow him," said Yaroslav. "I don't think we should…"

"Agreed," muttered Gunz, demonstratively folding his arms over his chest to show the deer that he wasn't going to move.

The deer got upset, shaking its massive glowing antlers and digging the ground with its hoof. The green lights started to spin faster, and the wind gained some strength. Gunz narrowed his eyes, noticing something behind the animal. However, no matter how hard he stared, he couldn't make out what it was.

"Slavik, do you see a shadow lingering behind that deer?" he asked using their psychic connection.

"Yeah… there is something out there, but even though I have twenty-twenty vision in the dark, I can't see it clearly…" Yaroslav frowned, squinting his eyes at the dark silhouette behind the animal.

Gunz explored the deer and the shape behind it with his magical sight. Both were glowing with the energy of magic so powerful that he held his breath for a moment.

"Fire Almighty," he whispered Mishka's favorite expression. "This thing, whatever it is, is exuding magic. Its magical signature is beyond—"

Gunz stopped talking as a wild thought flashed through his mind, but before he could say anything to Yaroslav, all hell broke loose. The wind picked up with renewed ferocity and he had to brace himself to keep on his feet, covering his eyes with his arms, as a cloud of dry leaves, broken branches and debris rose in the air, swirling around them, hitting them with the full might of the wind.

A piece of branch whistled an inch away from him like a spear, almost catching the side of his face. Through the wild howls of the wind, Gunz heard Yaroslav's cry of pain and a dull thud a moment later. He snapped around and found Yaroslav sprawled on the ground, a piece of wood stuck in his chest. The vampire was clasping the branch with both hands, blood sipping through his fingers.

Fighting the pressure of the wind, Gunz made it to Yaroslav and kneeled next to him, only one terrifying question on his mind.

"It missed my heart..." He heard Yaroslav's voice in his head and sighed with relief. He seized the branch and pulled it out in one sharp move. The vampire gasped, dark liquid spilling out of the gaping hole in his chest and dripping down the corner of his mouth. Gunz pressed his hands to the wound to stop the bleeding.

"I think I know what we're dealing with!" he shouted, forgetting for a moment that they could communicate telepathically.

The forest replied to his words with an outburst of wild laughter. Something clapped right next to him and the soft ground wobbled beneath him. Gunz hopped to his feet, channeling the fire. His body got enfolded in bright flames, illuminating the area.

"Turosik!" he yelled, extending his blazing arm toward the deer. "I know what you are, and you can't scare me, forest deity!"

The laughter got louder, and the deer rose on its hind legs, its golden antlers shining brighter. The dark shape moved forward and now Gunz could see an old man with a long green beard and hair. He was as tall as the tallest tree and his clothes were covered in dark patches of moss.

"How about me? Are you not afraid of me either, little wizard?" boomed the giant. "I do not appreciate the fire in the midst of my forest."

"Leshy... Oh, shit," gasped Yaroslav.

"Leshy?" mumbled Gunz and laughed as Mrak Delar's words surfaced in his memory. *It's like one friend of yours – who you would do well to remember – said, you're just a little Fire Gecko...* "You were right, you evil bastard, I would do well to remember this friend of mine. And thank you, Aidan, for forcing me to memorize all the summoning runes!"

He strained against the wind and got up, turning to face Turosik and Leshy. Using his fire energy, he drew a complex rune in the air and slammed his palm over it. "Sven!" he roared, his voice carrying far through the forest. "Svyatobor! Get your trickster's ass down here! Now!"

The air shimmered with green sparks and a giant brown bear with an axe materialized in front of him. The bear roared angrily, but as his furious gaze stopped on Gunz, he stopped roaring and morphed into his human form.

"Zane," said Svyatobor, his eyebrows rising as he took a step closer to Gunz, "what's going on here? Why are you in the Land of Dreams?" His eyes fell on Yaroslav who managed to get up to his knees, pressing his hand to the bleeding wound. "And you are here with a vampire… who is not healing. What the hell is going on here?"

"Those two idiots – are they friends of yours?" asked Gunz, shouting over the howls of the wind, ignoring Svyatobor's questions. "Can you do something about all this mayhem?"

Svyatobor turned toward the deer and Leshy and his large eyes lit up with bright phosphoric light. "Leshy, Turosik!" he roared waving his hand. The winds seized and the noise gradually melted into the soft whispering of the night forest. "Stop what you're doing at once! These men are my friends. Anything happens to them while they are traveling through the Land of Dreams, and I'll hold you responsible. Do I make myself clear?"

"Apologies, my lord," mumbled Leshy, reducing himself to normal human size. He put his hand on the deer's antlers and both vanished, leaving a trail of green sparks behind.

Svyatobor shook his head and turned back to Gunz. "Okay, Fire Gecko, care to explain why you are here when everyone is worried sick about you back home? And why is this old vamp not healing?"

"It's a long story, Sven," said Gunz. "And this old vamp is Yaroslav, Akira's son."

"I have time." Svyatobor shrugged, staring at Yaroslav with interest in his phosphoric eyes.

"But we don't," objected Gunz. In a few words, he told Svyatobor the gist of his mission and explained why Yaroslav wasn't healing.

The god of Nature frowned, carefully observing the bracelets on Gunz's wrists and the collar on his neck.

Then he sighed and shook his head. "I can't help you, my friend. It's my duty to protect the sacred garden from outside intruders. Both the Apple of Youth and the Water of Life should never end up in the hands of evil. Besides, I'm not the only one who protects the garden. I'm sorry, but your mission is doomed."

"I understand," said Gunz, bowing his head. "Then Yaroslav will be dead in a few days and Aidan—"

"Aidan? What about him?" asked Svyatobor, narrowing his eyes.

"Novak and Mrak Delar are holding him, Sven. Didn't you know? They are holding Aidan hostage, imprisoned by the God's snare until I come back with the Apple of Youth and the Water of Life."

"Whoa! Hold it right there," said Svyatobor, raising his both hands. "Novak and Mrak Delar? What does the Ancient Master have to do with the Head of California House? Something doesn't sound right."

"Mrak Delar betrayed us," growled Gunz, everything inside him twisted with pain and anger. "He sided with Novak. He was the one who captured Aidan."

"It's impossible. He would never—"

"Sven! Listen to me!" yelled Gunz, anger boiling up in him, raising the furious flames at the bottom of his eyes. "Mrak Delar is back to his old ways! Novak tortured Aidan. He held him locked up within the God's snare and Mrak let him do it. He was the one who conjured the God's snare in the first place. I need you to go back to Florida and tell everything I just told you to Angel and Uri. They must find a way to set Aidan free. In the meantime, I have no choice but to break into the sacred garden and steal that goddamn Apple. I can't let Yaroslav die."

"Damnit," muttered Svyatobor, rubbing his face with his hands.

"Sven, I'm not asking you to help me break into the sacred garden. I understand – you're bound to protect it," said Gunz, his anger slowly morphing into despair. "But I am asking you to help Aidan. If I know that Aidan is safe, I'll be free to deal with Novak." He threw a quick glance at Yaroslav and added, "Well, almost free."

"Zane, I hope you know what you're doing. You could be delivering two powerful magical artifacts into the hands of a dangerous dark wizard," said Svyatobor, a shimmering green light surrounding his body as he channeled his power and kneeled next to Yaroslav.

He ripped the shirt on the vampire's chest and carefully placed his glowing hand over the bleeding wound. Yaroslav eyes flew open and he groaned, his hands grasping at the grass. A moment later, Svyatobor let go, wiping the blood off his hand with a bunch of leaves. The bleeding stopped and the wound closed.

Svyatobor got up, offering his hand to Yaroslav. "You should feel better now," he said. "Stronger."

"I do, my lord," replied Yaroslav, bowing to Svyatobor. "Thank you."

"My lord? That would be my father and I believe, he'll send me to Chernobog's dungeons if he ever finds out what I'm about to do," muttered Svyatobor, shaking his head. He turned to Gunz. "I healed your vampire and gave him an energy boost, but the effect of my magic is temporary. Soon the gray stones will start feeding on him again. Hopefully, it'll be enough for you to make it to the garden and back."

"Thank you, Sven—," started Gunz, but Svyatobor shook his head, a mirthless smirk on his face.

"Don't thank me, Zane," he objected, "as I'm not doing a great favor to you. Even if you make it into the garden, I don't think you can get out."

"Why?" asked Gunz.

"I'm not the only one who protects the sacred garden," replied Svyatobor. "I don't know who will be on duty at the time you arrive. Besides wyverns and dragons, there is an army of wizards skilled in combat magic whose duty is to make sure no one can get in or out of the garden alive. And a powerful sorceress who runs this whole show… Ugh…" Svyatobor shuddered. "She gives me the hibbie jibbies and I'm a god!"

"So, what's new?" replied Gunz with a bitter smirk. "You take care of Aidan and that will be the biggest help you can give me."

"Wait, let me at least try to get rid of the gray stones for you," offered Svyatobor.

He placed his hands around the collar on Gunz's neck and carefully applied some pressure. Gunz gasped as pain surged through him and grabbed Svyatobor's wrists. At the same time Yaroslav cried out and dropped to his knees, his hand at his heck.

"Stop! Sven, no more," shouted Gunz. "Whatever you're doing is killing Yaroslav and crippling me."

"Holy shit!" muttered Svyatobor, exploring the gray stone jewelry with his magical sight. "I've never seen a dark spell so elaborate in its cruelty and so unbelievably powerful. I don't know how to break it without killing him and doing some serious damage to you, Zane."

"Maybe it's for the best," mumbled Gunz, watching Yaroslav slowly getting up, his skin around the collar marred by red blemishes and blisters. "I think if you took the gray stone jewelry off, Novak would know and who knows how it will affect Aidan's situation. We'll be fine, Sven. Thank you for trying."

Sven nodded and approached Siv. Softly threading his fingers through the stallion's golden mane, the Slavic deity whispered something into his ear. The horse neighed and shook his head. Sven laughed, patting the horse on its elegant neck and went back to Yaroslav.

"Yaroslav, I wish I could say that we'll meet again, but as long as you're next to this man, no one can guarantee your safety," he said, smirking. "He is a magnet for trouble."

The vampire smiled, shaking his head. "I beg to differ, my lord," he replied calmly. "I begged him to let me die so he could free himself from Novak's control, but he refused to give up on me."

Svyatobor squatted down and placed his hands on the ground. A wave of soft green light spread around his hands like ripples on water. Then he rose and extended his hand to Gunz.

"Take care of yourself, Fire Gecko," he said with a sad smile, squeezing his hand in a tight handshake. "I paved the road through the marshlands for you. Siv will take you all the way to the garden. He knows what to do."

Svyatobor snapped his fingers and vanished.

CHAPTER 22

~ ZANE BURNS, A.K.A. GUNZ ~

Svyatobor had meant it when he said he paved the road through the marshland for them. Siv and Mariella were running in a smooth gallop, their hooves drumming on the firm ground. The thorny thickets and bushes that were blocking their path parted before them as soon as they approached, allowing them to pass. But when Gunz glanced back, he noticed that the path behind them was obscured by thick greenery again.

By the morning of the second day, their path ran into a tall wall, built out of large marble blocks. It looked unexpectedly modern for its wild surroundings. As Gunz looked to the left and to the right, he could see the edge of the wall on either side. Despite that, when they tried to ride around it, the wall just kept extending farther and farther. In the end they gave up and returned back to where they started.

Gunz probed the wall with his magical sight and noticed the soft glow of magical energy around it. It didn't strike him as something dangerous, so he dismounted and approached it, placing his hands against the cold marble. As soon as he touched it, something clicked, and a thin square piece of rock slid to the side.

"What the hell?" mumbled Gunz, staring flabbergasted at the window in the wall.

Embedded into the rock, was a modern display screen. He probed it with his Salamander's senses but again didn't notice anything alarming. Seemingly, it was just a normal computer monitor, most likely a touchscreen since the message on the screen read, "Touch the screen to begin." He glanced at Yaroslav, who looked just as shocked as he felt, and carefully touched the screen. The screen lit up and displayed a new message.

"To proceed, please select one of the options," read Gunz. "A. He who goes to the left will save himself but will lose his horse. B. He who goes to the right will save his horse but will lose his life. C. He who goes straight will become a married man."

"Wow. Is that a *'Bylinny'* stone on the crossroads?" asked Yaroslav approaching Gunz. "We're living a friggin' Russian fairy tale."

"Yeah, and the further we go, the scarier it becomes," mumbled Gunz, tracing the edge of the screen with his finger. "So, multiple choice test here. Option A – we live, Siv and Mariella die. Option B – we die, but the horses will live. Option C – we are all gonna die." Gunz smirked, rubbing his forehead.

"He-e-e-y," neighed Siv indignantly, coming closer to the stone. "Don't you think Mariella and I should have our own vote on which option we select?"

"Not a democracy, Siv," said Gunz dryly. "If you're afraid for your life, both you and Mariella are free to leave now."

"I wish we could," snapped Siv, pushing Gunz with his hoof irritably. "Svyatobor is our god and he ordered us to assist you all the way until you are ready to leave the Land of Dreams. We can't disobey our god."

"You're free to leave, Siv, at any time," said Gunz with a light smile, petting the stallion's neck. "I'll talk to Svyatobor when I see him. It's your choice whether to stay with us or to leave, but the choice of the path belongs to Yaroslav and me. Sorry."

Siv glanced back at Mariella and the white mare inclined her head. "Fine," grumbled Siv irritably. "We're staying. At least until you're ready to leave the Land of Dreams."

"I appreciate it," said Gunz and turned to Yaroslav. "So, Slavik, the way I see it, options A and C are out of the question. At least for me. And from what Svyatobor explained, option B sounds like the kind of place where the garden would be."

Yaroslav chuckled. "Agreed. We're going to the right. You're immortal and I am... Well, I'm already dead."

"You're not dead. You're undead and let's try and keep it that way," objected Gunz and pressed the large letter B on the display.

As soon as he made his choice, the screen lit up with a bright light, displaying words "Thank You!" and the stone plate slid back in place covering the display. The wall shimmered with green light and slowly opened, allowing them to pass through.

The scenery that unfolded before their eyes was entirely different than the land they had been traveling through for the last few days. Gone was the darkness and gloominess. A wide-open valley was showered by sunlight and the air was infused with freshness, and the scent of flowers and grass. The rays of sunlight created playful bright flares all over the grass, reflecting in the morning dew. It was peaceful and quiet.

Yaroslav inhaled deeply, closing his eyes for a moment. Gunz observed him with a light smirk. One good thing that had come out from all this mess was the ring Novak gave Yaroslav. Despite common belief, vampires could walk in the daylight, but they were extremely sensitive to sunlight and preferred to stay indoors during the day. Whatever spell Novak put on the ring allowed Yaroslav to walk freely in the open sun without any side-effects.

"Too peaceful," said Yaroslav, pulling the Darling Lily device out. The apple on the back was nice and green.

"I was just going to say the same thing," replied Gunz, staring at the device in Yaroslav's hand. Even though the guiding spirit wasn't predicting any trouble, a feeling of unease spread through him.

"If we ride at full speed, we should reach the garden by sunset," said Yaroslav, exploring the GPS map.

"We should get going. We already lost too much time dealing with Leshy. We can't afford losing more. Siv, ready?" asked Gunz, patting the stallion's neck.

* * *

THE LAST RAYS of the setting sun touched the rough stones of a tall wall, adding inappropriately cheerful pink shades to the gloomy rocks. The chilly evening breeze touched Gunz's skin and he shivered. The cold didn't bother him. It was that same dreadful feeling of upcoming trouble that kept gnawing at his soul since they had left the forest. It didn't leave him for a moment, getting heavier as they approached the wall.

Gunz craned his neck, assessing the height of the wall. It was so tall that the top of it disappeared into the dark sky and there was no way to say how tall it was. As far as he could see, there were no gates or any other way to enter the garden. On the other hand, he didn't notice anyone guarding the area either.

The horses halted a few feet away from the wall. Gunz opened his magical sight, carefully examining the wall and the area before it. Every brick was infused with protective magic – wards, protection spells and enchantments the likes of which he had never seen before.

"I'm not surprised I don't see any guards," muttered Gunz, shaking his head.

"The wall is breathing with magic," said Yaroslav. "I can

sense it with my skin. And not only the wall. It seems that the wards spread above it too. It's like a giant dome built of magic."

"Any ideas on how we can get inside?" asked Gunz.

"I wish we weren't limited by this damn spell," said Yaroslav, dismounting. "I could easily shift into a bird and fly over the wall. Would be nice to know what's going on inside the garden."

"I could jump over the wall," suggested Siv.

"Wouldn't do any good. First of all, you said you couldn't carry more than one rider. Yaroslav and I cannot be separated by more than hundred feet and this wall is taller than that. And besides the fact that you don't know where you would be landing on the other side, we will trigger the wards —," Gunz started to say, but cut himself off. He stared at Yaroslav for a moment, then said, "Slavik, we're going to trigger the wards. This is the only way we can get the guards to open the gateway in this wall. We'll have to fight."

"Let's do it." Yaroslav smirked, his fangs slowly expanding and unsheathed his katana.

Gunz conjured a high-voltage energy orb. For a moment, he stared at the twirling, crackling ball of energy, then he pulled his hand back and sent the ball flying. The ball hit the wall and exploded into a bunch of tiny lightning bolts and a shower of bluish sparks. The wards lit up, displaying a web of thin glowing white lines. *Yaroslav was right,* thought Gunz observing an enormous shiny dome that encapsulated the wall and the garden within.

He didn't wait and conjured another energy orb. Propelling one orb after another at the wall, he didn't stop until the wards and protection spells started to vibrate, filling his ears with a menacing low-pitch buzz. The protective dome around the garden glowed brighter, illuminating the area, sending light beams into the dark sky.

A heavy wave of raw elemental energy of Fire touched his senses and Gunz stopped. He craned his neck, looking into the sky and a slow smile stretched his lips. He touched Yaroslav's shoulder, pointing up. Dark silhouettes of strange creatures with massive wings and long, spear-shaped tails emerged from behind the wall and were moving steadily toward them. He squinted his eyes, realizing that the creatures were possibly dragons or wyverns with riders on their back.

"Dragons?" asked Yaroslav, echoing Gunz's thought.

Gunz shook his head no. "Not dragons, my friend. Wyverns! I can't believe I am actually going to say it out loud – I wish Mishka were here." He smirked, channeling his power. "Either way. They chose the wrong magical creature to fight me. Stand back and take the horses with you, Slavik. It's about to get hot here."

Yaroslav took both horses by their bridles and walked them a few yards back, giving Gunz some space. "Are you sure you can handle all this alone?" He pointed up as the sky grew darker with the approaching wyverns. "You're not the Fire Elemental."

"I know that, Mr. Obvious." Gunz snickered, throwing a quick glance back at the vampire. "But I learned a few tricks while I was hanging around the real Fire Elemental."

He channeled as much power energy as the gray stone jewelry allowed him. The surge of elemental power rushed through his body and the fire ignited at the bottom of his eyes, his arms engulfed in scorching flames. Yaroslav gasped and staggered a few more steps back, away from the smoldering heat.

"Stay clear, Slavik," said Gunz, hardly recognizing his own voice.

He turned toward the slowly approaching wyverns and reached with his Salamander's power to the nearest one. As he stared at the wyvern, he saw this magical creature the way he had never seen it before. The wyvern was glowing with the energy of Fire, the orange-red streams of the elemental power flowing through its body like blood vessels. In the center of the wyvern's chest, Gunz saw his beating heart that looked like a pulsing fire orb.

Gunz reached for that beating heart and wrapped his elemental power around it, squeezing tightly. For a moment he felt like his own essence merged with that of the wyvern, and at that moment, he knew he could make the wyvern do anything he wanted. He was in control. The wyvern stalled for a moment, its igneous eyes fixed on Gunz.

Is that what Kal feels when he controls me? A thought flashed through his mind, but he had no time to dwell on it.

"Wyvern, down!" he commanded, extending his hand toward the creature. The wyvern obediently lowered himself to the ground, folding its wings and bowed to him.

One down, twenty more to go.

He could see the rider, pulling on the Wyvern's wing, struggling to bring him back up in the air, but the beast wouldn't obey him, still under Gunz's control.

"Gunz, it was only one. Can you do the same with the rest?"

Gunz heard Yaroslav's voice but didn't reply. He pulled in more of the elemental power, channeling the unlimited supply the nexus provided. The collar on his neck started to heat up, pulsing angrily, but he ignored it gathering more fire. His body got engulfed into smoldering flames and he rose in the air, supported by the flow of the elemental energy.

For the past few years, since he had discovered the Fire, he had never felt like this. He wasn't channeling the elemental Fire or using it. He was it. He was the Fire in its purest form. He heard Yaroslav scream something to Siv and Mariella, but he ignored them, focusing on the approaching wyverns.

In one move, Gunz connected with every single beast at the same time. He reached forward with his arms, feeling like he was holding their fiery beating hearts in his hands and he knew he didn't have to say anything. He just thought that he wanted all the wyverns to land and his will was enough to make every single beast go down, ignoring their riders' commands.

Gunz peered down at the riders who were dismounting from the motionless wyverns. They gathered their magic and he could see the flow of magical energy surrounding them. In a heartbeat, the air was filled with flying energy orbs, fireballs and energy strikes.

"*Praecidio Amnia,*" shouted Gunz, erecting a protection shield around Yaroslav. His shield was strong enough to protect the vampire from a rogue fireball, but it wasn't restraining his movement or slowing him down.

A moment later, he glanced down, but Yaroslav was gone. He searched the field and suddenly realized he could see him. Yet the way he saw him was completely different since he wasn't using his eyes. Through the prism of his elemental power, he saw the dark outline of vampiric energy moving with unbelievable speed between the riders and he knew it was Yaroslav. His katana was cutting and slashing through the air like a silvery blur and with each strike of his blade another rider fell on the ground, dead.

A few minutes later, everything was over. Yaroslav kneeled. With his head bowed down, he leaned heavily on his sword, surrounded by a pile of bloodied bodies and dismembered body parts. His golden hair fell down his face in blood-smeared strands. After a moment he lifted his face and stared at Gunz tiredly, his long fangs showing between his parted lips. His drained face was covered in scarlet stains and the bright glow was slowly vanishing from his sad eyes.

"*We killed the guards, but the wards are still armed, and I didn't notice any entrance,*" he said to Gunz, using their connection. "*Now what?*"

"*Now, we're going to bring down the wards,*" replied Gunz flatly and shuddered inwardly from the emptiness of his own voice. He stared at the dead men – the guards of the sacred garden, wizards, warriors – and felt hollow inside. They did what they had to do. It was a kill or be killed situation. Either him and Yaroslav or these people who attacked them. Then why did he feel so awful? Why did Yaroslav look so demolished?

Gunz sighed and switched his attention to the wyverns whom he was still holding under his control. "Wyverns, you're my brothers in element and I wish you no harm. You are free to leave," he said. "But before you go, I want you to remember me. My name is Zane Burns and I am the Great Fire Salamander. Next time you dare to attack me or one of my friends, I will not be as merciful as I am today."

He released his control and the wyverns bowed to him of their own volition. Then soundlessly, they rose in the air and disappeared into the dark sky.

For a moment, Gunz stilled in midair, checking the wards. As the elemental power flowed freely through him, he could see the glowing lines of wards and sense the movement of the magical energy along them. Slowly, he drifted through the air and carefully lowered himself to the ground a step away from the wall. Then he glanced back and raised his hand up, asking Yaroslav and both horses to stay away.

Gunz placed his hand on the wall and sent his fire energy through it. At first the wards and protection spells resisted his intrusion. Buzzing angrily, they retaliated back at him. As the pain of an electric shock surged through his body, Gunz grunted but didn't stop what he was doing. The red glow of his elemental power slowly started spreading through the wards, replacing their white light with red.

The wards emitted an ear-splitting howl and the wall trembled. Despite the resistance of the spells, Gunz increased the flow of his power. The collar on his neck squeezed tighter as its dark magic endeavored to prevent Gunz from gathering more elemental and magical energy. Struggling to breathe, he didn't let go, sending more fire through the wards. A split-second later, with a loud bang the wards crashed, leaving the wall to the sacred garden unprotected.

Slowly, Gunz released his elemental power and turned around. Leaning his back against the wall, he slid down on the ground. He felt drained magically and beyond tired physically. Yaroslav walked to the wall and sat down on the ground next to him, resting his arms atop his bent knees.

"You were terrifying," said the vampire quietly, without meeting his eyes.

"Look who's talking," muttered Gunz, his eyes half-closed. "You just dismembered at least twenty men if not more in less than a minute."

"That's not what I meant," objected Yaroslav. "I meant, you reminded me of Kal, and it was terrifying."

"Like father, like son…"

Yaroslav chuckled, shaking his head. "So, the guards are gone, the wards are down. Now, where is that goddamn door? How are we going to get in? Any bright ideas?"

"Let's see what I can do."

Gunz forced himself to his feet, ignoring the debilitating exhaustion, and turned around, placing both his hands on the wall. He connected with the nexus, gathering some magic in his hands.

"*Rilekti Amnia,*" he whispered the words in Dragon tongue and the shimmering golden glow spread around his hands.

He waited until a large area of the wall was consumed by the glow of his spell before removing his hands. But when he pushed on the wall, it remained as hard and solid as ever. The spell that was supposed to help him walk through any solid object didn't work. He waved his hand, removing the glowing effect of the spell and braced himself against the wall as weakness assailed him.

"Wow! You seriously thought that a basic spell would work on a wall like this?"

Gunz heard Siv's laughing voice and slowly turned around. The stallion was standing in front of him, his large teeth bared in the semblance of smile.

"Do you have any better idea?" challenged Gunz.

"Always," replied Siv, nodding. "Hop on."

"Whoa, hold it," said Gunz, realizing what the stallion was about to do. "You said you can't carry two riders and I can't be separated from Yaroslav by more than a hundred yards. So, your bright idea is not going to work."

"Well, I guess I'll have to make an exception," replied Siv snidely, derisive twinkles in his purple eyes and added with severity in his voice, "Just this one time. Both of you, get on."

Gunz mounted the stallion, his every move coming with serious effort, and offered his hand to Yaroslav. The vampire got up, took his hand, and flew on top of the horse. Siv walked to the white mare and gently rubbed against her elegant neck.

"Wait for me back in the forest, sweetheart," he said, stepping away. "I'll be with you as soon as these two jokers are done."

The mare neighed affectionately and galloped toward the forest. Siv waited until she was gone and turned toward the wall.

"Now, hold on, boys," the stallion said and pushed off the ground.

CHAPTER 23

~ ZANE BURNS, A.K.A. GUNZ ~

Siv pushed back from the ground and flew high up, leaving a deep dent in the dirt as a thick cloud of dust rose in the air in his wake. He soared effortlessly, moving higher and higher, like the two grown men on his back didn't weigh anything. The wall ended up being a lot taller than Gunz had thought, but Siv had no problem clearing it.

Gunz clutched the horse's golden mane with both hands to make sure he wasn't going to fall, but he enjoyed every moment of this flight and the short-lived sensation of absolute freedom. The magical stallion landed softly on the other side of the wall.

Before dismounting, Gunz quickly surveyed the area. They were standing at the edge of a green paradise. A wide flowerbed with a rainbow of unusual flowers circled around the area that looked like an enormous park. Despite the night hour, the flowers weren't closed. Their petals were wide open and fresh with glistening dew like it was early morning. Their tender aroma mixed with a light scent of freshly-cut grass drifted through the air.

A few paths paved with light pebbles ran into the park and melted into its velvety darkness, forking in different directions.

Tall trees of unknown origin raised their branches into the midnight sky. Everything was empty and the silence of the park was disturbed only by an occasional cry of a night bird and the high-pitch shrills of cicadas.

Yaroslav dismounted first, soundlessly stepping on the pebbles and pulled out his katana, but since he couldn't sense any danger, he lowered his sword. Gunz carefully slid off the horse and stopped next to the vampire, turning his knife into the sword.

"I can't believe he was able to carry both of us over this wall," said Yaroslav, his eyes sliding up and down the wall. "Wow, Siv, what a jump!"

"Oh, that's the way, uhh huh, uhh huh, I do it," sung Siv rephrasing the popular song as he did a running man dance move with all four of his legs.

"So, Siv," Gunz said, seizing his mane, "seems like you had no problem clearing this exceptionally tall wall with two riders on your back."

Siv stopped dancing, his eyes two round purple plates, and tried to back away. "Yeah, why?" he neighed nervously.

"So, why did you tell us that you couldn't carry two riders?" hissed Gunz, pulling the stallion's head down, his flaming eyes staring directly into the horse's. "What kind of con were you running, you magical jackass, huh? You forced us to go out of our path, fight Zlydzen and request Mariella as a price for our services. But worst of all, you made us lose time!"

"Let it go, Gunz," said Yaroslav peacefully. "Let's get what we came for and get out of here. Even though we got rid of the guards, we don't know if there is anyone else protecting the garden."

"We'll get back to this conversation later, Siv," promised Gunz but let go of the stallion's mane.

He switched his attention to the park and closed his eyes, probing the area with his Salamander's senses. He couldn't detect the presence of anyone else, but straight ahead he could feel a large accumulation of magical energy. It didn't feel like it belonged to anyone but was rather like a concentrated pool of pure magic.

"There is something there," he said pointing toward the path leading straight ahead, into the depth of the park.

Even though it was past midnight, as soon as they walked into the park, against all odds, it got lighter. Small insects that looked like fireflies were zooming above their heads, their tiny bodies shining with bright blue light. The pebbles of the path were also gleaming dimly with a soft white light and every tree seemed to produce a slight green glow.

Gunz didn't know how long they were walking as their surroundings remained the same. No one tried to stop them, and nothing got in their way. Maybe it was the serenity of this place or possibly he was just too tired, but a sense of safety and content enveloped him, and he turned his sword back into the Swiss army knife, hiding it in his pocket.

After a while, the path led them to a wide meadow located in the heart of the park. A large apple tree grew in the center of the meadow, its branches bending down under the weight of leaves and fruits. In front of the apple tree was a well.

Gunz approached the well and peeked inside. It was deep and dark, and he couldn't see the bottom. A wave of powerful magical energy hit him and for a moment everything around him spun. He leaned forward, supporting himself on the edge of the well and closed his eyes to get over the dizziness. When he opened his eyes, he saw Yaroslav standing next to him, looking just as disoriented as he was.

"This is it," said Gunz breathlessly.

He headed to the tree and reached for one of the apples. He touched the fruit, feeling the raw energy of its magic gently surrounding him like a weightless warm cloud. He pulled down slightly and the apple separated from the branch. Gunz turned around, holding it in the palm of his hand, a light golden glow surrounding the magical fruit.

Nothing happened.

The apple tree stood motionless, and even the cicadas didn't stop their endless chorus. He didn't know what he expected. For a magical alarm to go off? To be struck by lightning? But nothing happened – nothing at all, and it was more shocking than any magical alarm or lightning strike.

Yaroslav opened a small travel bag that he wore attached to his hip and brought up a small box. Gunz placed the apple inside and Yaroslav put the box back into his bag. Then he pulled out a small vial that Novak had given them before they left Los Angeles and approached the well.

There was nothing around the well that would suggest how to get the Water of Life – no ropes, no buckets. Nothing. Gunz looked down, straining his senses but he couldn't see the bottom.

"The Water of Life," said Yaroslav, sounding hollow. "Its magical energy is a pure energy of life. I can feel its touch." He slowly moved his hand over the opening of the well.

"I'm going to go down," suggested Gunz.

"How?" asked Yaroslav, shaking his head. "We don't have rope, so I can't lower you down. And even if we had it, you're not the right person for this job. Even though it's the Water of Life, it's still water. Fire and Water don't get along well. You'll get hurt. I'll go."

Yaroslav put the small glass vial back into his bag and before Gunz could object, he twirled in place shifting into a large white raven. The bird made a circle over the well and then dove inside. Gunz leaned over the side but could see nothing as the bird gradually melted into the darkness.

After a short while Gunz still didn't hear anything and he started to worry. He didn't want to call Yaroslav or make any noise and he wasn't sure that their psychic connection was working after the vampire shifted. He remembered Svyatobor's warning that besides wizards and dragons, there were other magical beings guarding this place and if they still didn't realize they were here, he didn't want to attract their attention by screaming.

Finally, he heard a hardly audible splash of water and then Yaroslav's constrained gasp. Gunz strained his ears but that was it. He slammed his hand on the edge of the well, worry and frustration boiling over.

"Slavik!" he hissed into the echoing emptiness of the well but heard nothing back.

A moment later, a large white bird erupted from the well, twirled in the air and turned into Yaroslav. The vampire dropped to his knees, bending forward, clutching his chest with his hand. Gunz squatted in front of him and moved his hair to see his face, but still couldn't find anything wrong with him.

"Slavik, are you okay?" he asked softly. The vampire lifted his face and Gunz saw thin streams of blood running from his eyes. "Are these... tears? I saw your tears before, they were never red..."

"I'm okay. It's just tears. Sometimes, when I am—" He cut himself off and then repeated, "It's just tears." Yaroslav reached into his bag. He found the glass vial filled with the Water of Life and showed it to him.

"What happened?"

"Nothing," replied Yaroslav unwillingly. "When I was filling the vial, I accidentally touched the Water of Life with my fingers... It restarted my heart, Gunz. And it hurt like hell when it happened. But then..." His voice faded and he dropped his head.

"Is your heart still beating?" asked Gunz.

Yaroslav just shook his head no without looking at him and then froze abruptly in that disturbing way only vampires could do.

"Do you hear that?" he whispered slowly rising to his feet, his eyes searching the surroundings.

"Hear what?" asked Gunz, but he caught what Yaroslav was talking about before he finished his question.

Someone was walking toward them. Not really walking – hop-skip-and-jumping along the pebbled path while murmuring a song in a high-pitched girlish voice.

"The itsy-bitsy spider
Climbed up the water spout.
Down came the rain
And washed the spider out..."

The steps and the hops were getting closer and the song sounded louder and clearer. Gunz stared at the dark woods in the direction of the sound, thousands of thoughts crowding his mind, but none of them were making any sense. He reached in his pocket and brought his Swiss army knife out, ready to turn it into a sword.

The song came closer, and finally a tiny figure materialized at the edge of the woods. Gunz's jaw dropped as he watched a little girl hop, skip, and jump toward them, singing the same song. By the looks of her, she was no older than ten years old. Her blond hair was styled into two short ponytails on either side of her head. Her checkered skirt hardly reached her knees and was bouncing up and down with her every step.

The girl hopped along the path, singing, without giving them as much as a second look. Only at the time when she reached the place they were standing at, she halted and cocked her head, staring at them with curiosity. She approached them without any sign of fear and smiled, her bright pink lips remaining closed.

Gunz observed her face. It was a normal face of a ten-year old girl. Small orange freckles were splattered all over her nose and cheeks, and her tight-lipped smile brought up two dimples to her round cheeks. But it was her eyes that drew his attention.

They were large and blue. The kind of shocking electric-blue color that he had seen only once in his life – that was the color of George Novak's eyes.

"Fire and ice," she said, pointing at Gunz and then at Yaroslav. "Life and death. What are you two doing in my garden?"

Yaroslav and Gunz exchanged a bewildered look. They had expected pretty much anything, but not a child. The girl pursed her lips and put her hands on her hips, tapping with her tiny shoe on the pebbles. Then without any warning she waved her hand, sending a wave of magic toward Yaroslav. At the touch of her magic, his bag vanished and immediately manifested in her hands. As fast as the vampire was, he wasn't fast enough to catch it.

She opened the bag, absolutely unconcerned with the fact that two grown men were standing next to her and it was their bag she was going through. The girl pulled out the Apple and the vial with the Water of Life.

"So, you two are nothing but common thieves," she said raising her blazing blue eyes at them. "How dare you steal from my garden."

Somehow the night became darker and stormy clouds gathered over their heads. A moment later, the first drops of water hit the dry ground and the scent of ozone invaded Gunz's senses, predicting a quickly approaching thunderstorm. In a heartbeat, the rain got heavier, and the lightning split the night sky.

Gunz grunted, wrapping his arms around himself as every drop of water that landed on his skin caused a surge of pain through his body. The girl observed him with interest in her blazing eyes.

"Are you afraid of the rain?" she asked him, twirling her ponytail around her finger. "That's funny. Are you going to melt like the Wicked Witch of the West?" Notes of hungry childish curiosity sounded in her voice.

"No, my lady," replied Gunz. "I'm not going to melt, but I don't enjoy the touch of water on my skin."

"Does it hurt you?" she continued the interrogation.

"Yes, my lady," replied Gunz, trying to sound as respectful as he could in the face of a ten-year old child.

The girl stepped closer and unceremoniously grabbed his hand. A wave of her magic scanned him and for a moment, he felt like she was turning him inside out. He endeavored to pull his hand back, but for a little girl, she had an extremely firm grip.

"Aw, would yah look at that?" she sung, pinning him down with her bright eyes. "You're a Child of Fire. And quite a skilled one to boot. I didn't recognize the Fire Salamander in you until I touched you. Where did you learn to shadow your magical signature so well?"

"My lady, we mean no harm to you—," started to say Gunz, but she shook her head, narrowing her eyes at him.

"So, you were the one who sent away all my wyverns," she stated.

"Yes, my lady," replied Gunz calmly.

The girl grabbed Yaroslav's hand and her lips stretched into a frosty smirk. "In that case, I guess we need to get comfortable and have a nice long chat."

Gunz didn't notice her doing anything, but the garden spun around him like a crazy carousel and then everything went dark.

CHAPTER 24

~ ZANE BURNS, A.K.A. GUNZ ~

Gunz woke up with a start and sat upright on a bed. Bright rays of sunshine reflected off white walls and the white tiles of a floor, blinding him for a moment. He looked around, not recognizing his surroundings. The place was mostly empty. Besides the bed he was sitting on, there was only an open coffin made out of redwood at the far end of the room, which seemed to be out of place in the surrounding whiteness.

He didn't know what time it was, but judging by the position of the sun, it was somewhere around noon. The question that was burning in the back of his mind was, how long he had been unconscious. A few hours? A few days? He cringed, wondering how much of their precious time they had lost.

Where is Yaroslav? he thought as his eyes halted on the coffin. *A vampire in a coffin? Nice! One can never get tired of this timeworn cliché.* He got up and headed toward the other end of the room. He didn't make it all the way as he ran into an invisible barrier. An electric shock threw him back, making his muscles spasm. He hit the floor hard, sliding back on the tiled floor all the way to the bed.

He rubbed his forehead, staring at the invisible barrier. It was still shining with a brilliant white light. The way the barrier reacted to his touch and the white light it was emitting, was all too familiar.

"Goddamnit!" Gunz swore and slammed his fist on the floor. "This little bitch locked me inside the God's snare!"

"OMG! How rude! Watch your language around children and ladies," a girlish voice squealed behind him.

She actually said "OMG". The thought flashed through Gunz's mind as he jumped to his feet and spun around. The same little girl that he had met in the garden was standing by the bed, her arms folded, disapproval written all over her face.

"I don't see neither a child nor a lady here," countered Gunz, fighting a losing battle with his rising irritation.

The little girl pouted for a moment, but then flicked her eyebrow at him and snapped her fingers. In a split-second, the white room disappeared, replaced by a dark musty dungeon and Gunz found himself attached to the wall with his arms pinned to his chest, held by multiple thick chains crisscrossing his body. The only thing that remained constant was the coffin.

He glanced at the girl ready to express everything he thought of her in the most creative way, but once he laid his eyes on her, the words stuck in his throat and he coughed, averting his gaze. She transformed herself into a grown woman but forgot to reimagine her attire.

She was tall and slender, her golden hair still tied up in two wavy ponytails on either side of her head. Her face was a perfect oval and while undeniably beautiful, it had the hardness of a person who went through one too many battles in her life. The school-girl skirt was so short now that he could see her white lacy underwear and her white shirt lost a few buttons at the top, giving him an unobstructed view of her perky round breasts.

She probably caught his reaction because she giggled and snapped her fingers again. Immediately, the checkered skirt got replaced by ancient Russian armor, complete with chainmail and a silk red cloak that ran from her shoulders down to the tips of her leather boots. A sword in a jewel-encrusted scabbard was attached to her belt. Her new outfit seemed a lot more appropriate for her face, like she was born to wield the sword and fight the battles.

"Oops," she said with a shameless smirk on her face, "sometimes when I transform myself, I forget to change my clothes. I hope you enjoyed the view."

"I can never unsee that," grumbled Gunz rolling his eyes.

"Ugh." She stomped her foot, and her metal spurs jingled. "Do you have to be so rude? I was trying to be nice to you. I thought that as a modern man you weren't used to the dungeons and chains, so I gave you a nice clean room and no physical restraints except for the God's snare spell, that is."

"You are holding me here against my will and you want me to be nice?" shouted Gunz, pushing against the chains. "What did you do with my friend and with my horse?"

"You and you friend stole from me!" the young woman yelled back, her blue eyes burning with uprising anger. "What did you expect I was going to do? Make out with you?"

"No! How about you try and talk to me first? Ask why I did what I did?"

"And why should I care? I'm the sorceress of this garden and the only thing I care about is protecting my domain from the likes of you, jackass! I'm doing my job! Be grateful, I didn't kill you on the spot!"

"You—," started to say Gunz, but she snapped her fingers and one more chain materialized across his neck, strangling him. He choked and fell silent.

"I think I like you silent a lot more," she stated, heading toward him. "So, what is it going to be, Child of Fire? I'll get you your nice white room back and we'll talk like civilized individuals or you're going to continue with your shenanigans decked out in chains?"

Gunz jerked in his restrains, anger setting his body ablaze, and since he couldn't talk, he flipped his middle finger at her. All of a sudden, the air behind the woman shimmered and a large black raven materialized in the dungeon. At first, Gunz thought it was Yaroslav, but he quickly realized that it couldn't have been him. Yaroslav transformed into a white bird, but this raven was jet-black. The raven spun and Voron manifested in its place.

"Voron," croaked Gunz.

The woman spun around and threw her hands in the air. "Father," she said reproachfully. "What are you doing here?"

Chernobog's righthand man ignored her and headed toward Gunz. He touched the chains and shook his head, scolding his daughter with the scorching gaze of his dark eyes, and snapped his fingers. The chains vanished and the dark dungeon got replaced with the white sunlit room.

Gunz slid down on the floor, clutching his throat, struggling to fill his lungs with oxygen. Voron chuckled, offering him his hand.

"Zane Burns," he said, "it's nice to see you again, old friend."

"You have no idea," muttered Gunz, taking his hand and rising.

The woman stomped her foot and grabbed Gunz's arm, her sharp fingernails digging into his skin, leaving tiny half-moon imprints.

"Your so-called old friend is a petty thief," she seethed, squeezing Gunz's arm tighter. "And you no longer hold any privileges here, Father."

"Vasilisa, calm down," said Voron with a sigh. "Chernobog sent me here. We need to talk."

Vasilisa gawked at him, blinking furiously, but then released Gunz's arm and removed the God's snare with a dramatic wave of her hand. "Fine," she said snidely, manifesting a few chairs.

"Let's see what's so important that the mighty god of Destruction decided to part with his righthand man."

Both Voron and Vasilisa sat down and she motioned at the empty chair, offering Gunz to take it. He just shook his head slightly, remaining standing.

"First, I need to know what happened to Yaroslav and Siv," he said, working to suppress the aggravation that seemed to be permanently embedded in him since the moment he met Vasilisa.

She rolled her eyes, blowing her cheeks. "Don't worry. Your cute vamp is perfectly undead and well. I just put him into a temporary coma. And as far as Siv, I sent him behind the wall, back to his girlfriend. What were you thinking, bringing this four-legged swindler into the garden full of magical apples?"

"Coma?" yelled Gunz, throwing his hands in the air. "How long has he been in this temporary coma of yours? And come to think of it, how long was I out?"

"Umm… About seventy-two hours. Give or take… Probably give…" she replied, innocently batting her eyelashes at him.

"Seventy-two hours?" parroted Gunz, fury rising in him with all-consuming strength. "Three full days??"

He froze, breathing hard, with his arms down at his sides, hands clenched into tight fists. Then he took a deep breath and turned to Voron.

"Voron, we need to leave at once," he said through gritted teeth. "Novak placed a spell on our gray stone jewelry. We have only fifteen days to complete the quest and go back to him. After ten days, the spell will start feeding on Yaroslav's vampiric essence, slowly killing him, and by the end of day fifteen, he'll be dead."

"He is already dead," noted Vasilisa with a dismissive wave of her hand. "Why do you have your panties in a bunch over it, I don't understand. He's a vampire, for God's sake."

"He'll die the true death, you dumb bitch—," hissed Gunz, turning to her, fireballs forming on the palms of his hands.

"Whoa, whoa!" yelled Voron stepping between him and his daughter. "Let's not get personal. Zane, you need to tell me what is going on. This is why I am here." Then he turned to his daughter, frowning. "Vasilisa, where is the vampire?"

She shrugged with a wide grin, pointing at the other side of the room. "In the coffin, of course. Isn't it how vampires sleep? In their coffins?"

Gunz passed her, ignoring her last statement. But when he reached the coffin and peeked inside, his anger ignited with new strength bringing his fire energy to the surface.

"What the hell is that?" he yelled, pointing at the coffin.

Yaroslav was lying inside the coffin on top of a blanket made of wild flowers. His hair was artistically fanned out around his face, and bright red flowers and silk ribbons were weaved into his long golden strands. His sword was lying inside the coffin by his side. With his colorless skin and unmoving chest, the vampire looked deader than ever. But at the same time, his slightly parted lips and relaxed face made him look like a sleeping boy, young and vulnerable.

Voron came closer and slapped his hand over his mouth to stop himself from laughing. "Vasilisa," he said after a moment, trying to sound stern, but laughter was coming through in his voice. "Is that the way to treat the old Russian prince? Wake him up."

"But why?" she whined, tittering. "He looks so cute like this. Almost like a real boy. And you know, Daddy, you never bought me a doll when I was little, so I'm compensating…"

Gunz swallowed his anger, bringing his hands up in a peaceful gesture. "Vasilisa, please don't waste our time. Thanks to you, we lost three days and today is the eleventh day since we left. The goddamn gray stones are already slowly killing him.

Please, wake him up." He wasn't shouting anymore. His anger slowly subsided, leaving him tired and resigned.

"Daughter!" growled Voron.

Vasilisa sighed but leaned over the coffin and observed Yaroslav's face for a moment. "He does look like a porcelain doll. Rather stunning for a soulless vamp." She touched Yaroslav's forehead, whispering something and then stepped back, away from the coffin.

A few seconds later, Yaroslav was awake. He didn't move, but his eyes opened wide, his dark pupils dilated. He stared straight up at the ceiling and Gunz wasn't sure if he could see anything. He carefully tugged at the vampire's shoulder to attract his attention. Yaroslav slowly turned his head in Gunz's direction, fixing his eyes on him.

"Zane," he exhaled. His Adam's apple moved like he was swallowing, and he closed his eyes for a short moment. "Zane, what's going on? Where are we?"

"Remember that little dipshit that knocked us out?" asked Gunz, unease settling in the pit of his stomach. "Well, we're in her… um… holding cell, I guess. She is the sorceress of the sacred garden."

Yaroslav grabbed the sides of the coffin and endeavored to get up but powerlessly fell back into the bed of flowers.

"Why am I so weak?" he mumbled, a demolished look shadowing his features. "And my neck…" He lifted his hand and placed it over his collar.

Guns leaned down, moving his hand away, and carefully shifted his collar up. Yaroslav grunted and his whole body stiffened. Under the collar, his skin was raw and blistered like from a second degree burn. Gunz let go of the collar and bit his lip.

"Okay," said Yaroslav, his forehead creasing, "spill it, Zane. I see you biting your lip. Usually it means nothing good."

Gunz rubbed the stubble on his cheeks and sighed. "Slavik, you slept for three days. Today is the eleventh day of our journey and Novak's spell kicked in. You're so weak because his dark magic is feeding on your vampiric essence, slowly killing you. And your neck hurts because the collar seems to be burning your skin." He took the vampire's arm and carefully moved the bracelet, showing him the burns on his wrist.

"I have only four days left," whispered Yaroslav, averting his gaze. "We're never going to make it back in time."

"We'll make it," promised Gunz, quietly cursing at how unconvincing he sounded. He cleared his throat and repeated, this time sounding more assertive, "We'll make it. This time I know our exact destination points, so teleporting is an option. As soon as we leave the garden, I will teleport us to the gates of the Land of Dreams. And once we walk out of the magical nexus, I can teleport us straight into Novak's office."

"May I remind you that you are not very good at teleporting yet. And teleporting with a passenger is even harder," objected Yaroslav. "I'm afraid you won't be able to pull it off."

Gunz had no choice but to agree with Yaroslav. Of course, he could open his Fire Salamander's portal, but the fire would kill Yaroslav instantly if he attempted to pass through it on his own. He carried humans through his portals before without conjuring the protective shield. But Yaroslav was a vampire and he wasn't sure how the touch of the purifying energy of fire would affect him.

It meant Gunz would have to conjure a protective shield around Yaroslav and then carry a two-hundred-pounds man through the portal. And he would have to repeat it twice – once inside the magical nexus and once in the outside world. Doing it in the outside world, where magical energy doesn't flow freely like in the nexus, would be a lot harder and would require a significant effort on his part.

"Damnit," he whispered, frowning. "You're right. I'll have to carry you through the Fire Salamander portal."

He turned to Voron and Vasilisa who were standing a few

feet away from them. He noticed that contempt and mockery in Vasilisa's eyes were replaced with a semblance of curiosity and surprise.

"Vasilisa, I'm sorry to ask for something so... well, do you have any blood here? I mean something like pig's blood, of course, not human," said Gunz, quickly correcting himself. "Yaroslav was sleeping for three days and he is getting drained by a dark spell. He needs some kind of nourishment to restore his strength at least partially."

Vasilisa's eyes grew wider and her eyebrows climbed up as she stared at Gunz. "Blood? Animal blood? Are you crazy? This is the sacred garden!" she shouted, waving her hand around. "I would not harm an animal here to feed your vamp."

"So, you were willing to kill me or Yaroslav, but you wouldn't harm a fly in your garden," said Gunz, turning back to the coffin. "That's just great..."

"You were stealing from the garden!" yelled Vasilisa, but her voice lost its confidence. "I was just doing my job..."

Gunz didn't reply. He leaned on the coffin and pulled out his Swiss army knife. With one sharp move, he cut his arm above the wrist. "If you say one goddamn word, Yaroslav, I will end you myself," he hissed, pressing his bleeding arm to the vampire's mouth.

The vampire growled, anger and pain and hunger jammed into a single sound as he sunk his fangs deep into Gunz's arm, using more force than usual. Gunz braced himself with his free arm against the edge of the coffin and turned away. He met Voron's eyes, noticing shock imprinted on the old warrior's face. Slowly the room started to spin around him as weakness settled somewhere in his knees.

Yaroslav let go almost immediately and Gunz slid down to the floor, resting his back against the coffin and pressed his hand over the bleeding wound on his other arm. The vampire tried to get up again and with Voron's help, he was finally out of his flower bed. He sat down on the floor next to Gunz, raking his fingers through his hair to get rid of the petals and ribbons and silently nodded at him.

"I guess, we'll talk here then," said Voron. He flicked his wrist, moving the two chairs closer, one for himself and one for his daughter. "So, Zane, now that this — whatever this was — is over, do you mind filling me in on what the hell is wrong with you!" He finished his statement shouting.

Gunz smirked. "You don't see?" he asked quietly. "I'm a goddamn slave and I must do what my owner bids me to do."

"Oh, give this horseshit to someone else, Zane," roared Voron, slamming his hand on his thigh. "You're the goddamn Great Fire Salamander. Get out of this collar and be done with this nonsense."

"I can't!" yelled Gunz, jumping to his feet, his fists clenched, his chest rising with angry breaths. "Not without killing Yaroslav. Damnit, Voron! If you are here to help me then stop wasting my time with nonsense."

"Screw this!" growled Voron.

He got up and seized Gunz's collar with one hand and Yaroslav's with the other. His black wings opened up behind his back and the heavy energy of his magic streamed through the collars. The dark spell that Novak placed, retaliated instantly, sending Gunz into an abyss of pain. He seized Voron's wrist with both hands, struggling to remove his hand, but the ancient warrior was too strong. Gunz glanced at Yaroslav, realizing that the vampire was on the verge of fainting.

"Voron, stop, you are killing him," croaked Gunz, fighting his grip.

Voron let go and for a moment he just stood silent, his eyes darting from Gunz to Yaroslav and back. Then he turned to his daughter, throwing his hands in the air.

"Check it out," he said, jerking his thumb toward Gunz. "I've seen enough of dark magic in my time, but I've never seen a spell like this. I don't even know where to begin."

Vasilisa approached him and carefully touched Gunz's collar, sending a smidge of her magic through it.

"I'm not a goddamn lab rat! Please, stop with your experiments." Gunz pushed her hand away. "Voron, I'm begging you, I just need one Apple and a little bit of Water of Life. That's all I need. Please! I need to go back to LA as soon as possible."

"Both, the Apple and the Water of Life are powerful magical artifacts," said Voron, pulling his daughter back, "and this dark wizard, Novak, doesn't strike me as a person you want to call for dinner. How can you be so nonchalant about delivering all that to someone like him, Zane? And how could you let yourself get enslaved by a master of Dark Arts in the first place?"

"Out of all people, I thought you knew," said Gunz tiredly.

"What am I supposed to know?"

"I don't know who Novak was in his previous life," Gunz started his explanation, "but I'm almost positive that he was one of the souls Morena let out of the Dark Nav last year. You're the Chernobog's righthand man. How can you not know that?"

"Why would you think so?"

"He came into the picture shortly after the fight for Mount Karasova," continued Gunz. "Almost immediately, he imbedded himself into the underground fighting circles. At that time, I just started my search for Yaroslav and was fighting in Florida's unattached circles. By gathering information from other fighters and from the Head of Florida House, I realized that even though Novak was an extremely powerful dark wizard, no one heard of him before he surfaced in LA.

"I can't explain why or how I put two and two together. It was more intuition than anything else, I think. And I know what you think"—he raised his hand to stop Voron from speaking— "intuition is not enough to draw this kind of conclusion and act upon it. It's neither here nor there, but I also knew that Novak had Yaroslav and the only way I could get anywhere close to either of them was by fighting in the captive circles. So, I took a chance and let this dumbass, Kogan, enslave me.

"Anyway, saving Yaroslav was just one of my goals. I wanted to know why Novak was here, in the realm of the living. Morena let a bunch of phantoms out, but only a handful of souls. I was sure she or the Lord of Chaos had some kind of plan in mind and I needed to know what it was.

"And the first time I came in close contact with him, I knew I was right – Novak was one of those twisted dark souls that escaped the Dark Nav that day. I wasn't guessing and it was no longer on the level of intuition. He was exuding the energy of the Dark Nav. It was dripping from his every friggin' pore."

Gunz shuddered, wiping the cold sweat off his forehead with the back of his hand.

"So, yeah... I let myself get enslaved and I am going to deliver the Apple and the Water of Life to Novak. Voron, you know me... I swear, I'll find a way to stop him before something unthinkable happens, but we all need to know what he is up to. Since Morena was the one who released him, whatever he is doing now could be related to the Lord of Chaos. This world can't afford another battle like we had last year... I can't..." His voice faded off and he swallowed hard. "Anyway, this was the only way I could find out what he was up to. And if I have to suffer in slavery a few more days or even months, so be it."

Voron glanced at his daughter and she gave him a curt nod. "I do know you, young Salamander," said Voron. "Vasilisa, give him what he needs."

Vasilisa got up and snapped her fingers, vanishing from the room.

"Zane, you are right about Novak," continued Voron. "Chernobog did a lot of work cleaning up the mess Morena created last year. He captured all the phantoms that escaped that night and a few dark souls. But at least three are still missing."

"So, what do I need to do to send him back to the Dark Nav?"

"I'm not sure," replied Voron with a sigh. "Different dark souls have different curses placed upon them. It's like a fail-safe switch. In case they escape, the curse attached to them would let Chernobog claim them and return them where they belong. But to activate the switch, we need to know whose soul it is."

"Can Chernobog come over and take a peek?" suggested Gunz with a lopsided smirk. "He's a god, right? How hard could it be?"

Voron stared at him for a moment before he started laughing. "Very hard, Zane. There are rules and even the gods must follow them. Chernobog can't claim a dark soul while it is in a living body. To separate the soul from its body, you cannot just kill him like you would kill a mundane. You must activate the curse I told you about and then summon Chernobog."

Gunz rubbed his forehead, shaking his head. "Sometimes I hate magic and all these stupid rules. Why can't it be easy? I kill the evil dude – the dark soul is separated from the body – Chernobog claims the soul. One, two and three – done."

"Oh, boy," mumbled Voron. "Come here, Child of Fire, and raise your shirt. I'm going to place a rune on you that will help Chernobog identify the dark soul we're dealing with."

Gunz cringed, remembering the last time someone placed a rune on him. It wasn't pleasant. Still, he raised his shirt, exposing his midriff. Voron placed the palm of his hand on his side over his ribs and muttered a short spell. It wasn't as bad as when Valeria Demidova had forced a rune on him, but all the same, it felt like Voron pressed a hot iron against his ribs. He sucked in a sharp breath, stifling a scream.

Voron removed his hand and Gunz glanced down expecting to see a glowing red rune, but there was nothing there. The old warrior noticed his bewildered look and smiled.

"I didn't think you wanted more scars on your body, so I

made it invisible," he explained. "When you are close enough to touch Novak, you will need to activate it by sending a tiny amount of your fire energy through it. Once the rune is activated, it will register the magical signature of the dark soul and send it to Chernobog."

"And then what?" asked Gunz and Yaroslav at the same time. Until now, the vampire had sat silently, listening to the conversation between Voron and Gunz, but the last statement raised a question and he couldn't help but ask.

"Once Chernobog identifies the dark soul we are dealing with, he will know how to trigger the curse," explained Voron. "In the meantime, do everything you can to learn what Novak's true purpose is. I do not believe that brewing an elixir of immortality is his main goal. Like you said before, there has to be more to all this craziness."

Gunz nodded, agreeing with Voron. At least now he had some way to find out who George Novak truly was. And with Chernobog and Voron on his side, he had at least some fighting chance against the necromancer and the Ancient Master of Power who betrayed him. He sighed, thinking of Mrak Delar.

With a light pop, Vasilisa materialized next to her father. In her hands, she was holding Yaroslav's bag. She threw it on his lap. The vampire opened the bag, checking its contents and nodded to Gunz. Then he got up and attached the bag to his hip.

"Thank you," said Gunz with a light bow in Vasilisa's direction and turned to Voron. "We must go. Yaroslav's clock is ticking and I can't take the chance of being late. Thank you for your help, my friend." He offered his hand to Voron and the old warrior squeezed it in his.

"Farewell, Zane. Hope to hear from you soon." Voron put his hand on his daughter's shoulder and they both vanished from the room, leaving Gunz and Yaroslav alone.

Gunz turned to Yaroslav, connecting with the magical energy of the nexus. He cast a spell, conjuring a protective shield around Yaroslav. The vampire bowed his head, shame reflected in his every move.

"Slavik, I believe you would do the same for me," said Gunz with a sigh. "Let's just get through all this silently. What I'm about to do requires a lot of my strength and magic, so don't make it harder on me. Don't fight me and don't argue with me."

He waved his hand, opening the fire curtain of the portal and turned to the vampire. With effort, he lifted Yaroslav, carefully placing him over his shoulder and walked through the fire.

CHAPTER 25

~ AIDAN ~

What is your worst enemy when you're imprisoned without any means of communication with the outside world? For Aidan it was the endless time he had on his hands. The time he couldn't accurately measure because in the dark basement of a Los Angeles high-rise there were no windows.

It was like sitting in a black, hollow void, where he could hardly see anything past the shiny metal bars and every sound was bouncing of the tiled walls and ceiling, repeated a few times until it finally melted into darkness. Someone was keeping this place clean and the light scent of cleaning chemicals lingered in the air.

The same man delivered his food once a day, but Aidan could never get him involved into a conversation. The man would push the tray with food and a glass of water between the bars and leave. An hour later, he would return, pick up the empty tray and leave until the next day. By counting his visits, Aidan approximated that it had been about thirteen days since he was captured and imprisoned by George Novak.

The only thing he could do was think and thinking was throwing him into a labyrinth of unexplainable mysteries. What was George Novak up to and who was he? Why would Mrak Delar betray them? Aidan hadn't seen it coming. No one had. He remembered the pained expression on Zane's face and cringed.

No matter what he tried, he couldn't break through the God's snare. There was a reason why this spell was called *the God's snare* after all. Even the most powerful gods couldn't break through it. Only a very powerful wizard could cast or remove this spell. Well aware of how it worked, he didn't think he could breach it with his magic and power disabled, but with all the free time on his hands, why not give it a try one more time?

Aidan sat down on the floor and closed his eyes, focusing on channeling his power. He didn't want to think about how many times he had already tried and failed. The result was always the same – he couldn't do it. He couldn't even get in touch with the magical energy that was within him.

The God's Snare that Mark Delar had conjured was by far the most powerful one he had ever experienced. The Ancient Master wasn't a god, but he was an extremely gifted Master of Power and Wizard, and with his knowledge and skills in wielding magic, he was more powerful than some gods.

Aidan sighed and lay back down, folding his arms under his head. The other thing his captors didn't care to provide him with was a bed or at least a mattress. He had to sleep on the cold, hard tiled floor. And after thirteen days, he felt sore all over.

"Hello, Aidan."

He heard a cold voice and sat up, wondering what brought Mrak Delar to his cell for the first time in almost two weeks. The Master of Power was standing on the other side of the bars. With his left arm in the pocket of his stylish modern pants, he looked elegant and slightly bored. His face, however, was bearing an arrogant expression bordering with disdain.

"Master Mrak Delar," replied Aidan frostily without getting up. "What can I do for you?"

The corners of Mrak's lips quirked up a little as he gave Aidan a quick once-over. "Yes, there is something you can do for me," he confirmed. "But you don't really need to *do* anything, per se. I'll take care of everything. Please, remain seated."

Mrak Delar squatted down in front of the bars and touched the floor, channeling his power. The God's snare lit up with a blinding white light. The Master of Power whispered something in Dragon tongue, combining the God's snare with a new spell.

Once he was done, he straightened up and raised his arm, pointing at the ceiling. Muttering another spell, he made a complicated move with his fingers and a rune, glowing with a deep red light, materialized above his head. A moment later, it dissipated.

As his chest tightened with worry, Aidan observed what Mrak was doing but couldn't recognize any of his spells. For the first time in his very long life, he felt the icy fingers of fear wrapping around his heart.

He had no idea what Mrak Delar's intentions were and within the circle of the God's snare, he was nothing but a powerless human. Almost. He still couldn't be killed. But his magic and power were blocked, and he was in a vulnerable position.

"What are you doing, Mrak?" asked Aidan, his voice hoarse. "What do you want from me?"

Mrak Delar laughed – a frosty sound that sent chills down Aidan's spine.

"Not much, god of the Otherworld," he replied with a crooked smirk. "I just want you to scream."

Mrak Delar slashed his hand through the air and Aidan bent

forward, clutching his chest with his hand. He gasped, staring down with shock at the dark red liquid streaming between his fingers, staining his white shirt. He raised his eyes at the man he used to consider his friend, breathing hard.

"Mrak, why?"

A dark, pained expression crossed Mrak Delar's face, but as fast as it was gone, Aidan noticed it.

"Why, Mrak..."

"Because I need you to scream," answered the Master of Power dryly. Mrak pointed at Aidan again whispering another spell and Aidan braced for pain. The soft glow of Mrak's power reached through the God's snare and wrapped around Aidan. As the Master of Power continued chanting, the glow formed into a bright hoop, squeezing Aidan in its menacing embrace.

As Aidan struggled against the hold of Mrak's magic, he felt a light warmth within, realizing that at least some of his own magic was available to him. In one desperate move, he connected with whatever scraps of magic he could gather, and his eyes lit up with a dim white light.

Mrak Delar noticed it and his lips drew back in a snarl.

"Thank you, Aidan. This is exactly what I needed," he hissed and hit him with another spell, creating a tiny opening in the God's snare at the same time.

An excruciating pain twisted Aidan's body and he dropped to his knees, screaming. Driven by agony that tormented him, the energy of his magic exploded, surrounding him with a protective shield. In a heartbeat, the Master of Power gathered it and redirected it toward the ceiling, quickly closing the opening in the God's snare and dropping his spell.

When both the pain and his magic were gone, Aidan collapsed on the floor, drained and agonizingly sore. The wound on his chest was bleeding and the room around him was nauseatingly shaky. With horror, he felt the floor under his back tremble. Somehow, the darkness in the basement got thicker and heavier.

"Oh, no..." he exhaled as realization dawned on him.

"Oh, yes." Mrak Delar laughed, rubbing his hands.

The ceiling melted into the darkness as a giant black portal opened up, consuming all light. A man in a black trench coat with large black wings behind his back slowly descended from the void. He stepped softly on the floor and waved his hand, closing the void.

"Angel, run..." moaned Aidan.

"He can't," objected Mrak Delar. "There aren't too many options when it comes to capturing Death. I believe, even the God's snare can't control him. But I happened to know a very effective trap."

Angel took a step forward and ran into an invisible wall. Mrak Delar pointed at the ceiling and both Angel and Aidan looked up. The rune, which the Master of Power had created earlier, was glowing in the air above Angel's head.

"Do you know what that is, Angel?" asked Mrak Delar with a malicious smirk.

Angel nodded and bowed his head. "I'm sorry, Aidan," he said quietly, looking at Aidan over Mrak Delar's shoulder. "I couldn't help you."

"You evil bastard. You're back to your old Kendral antics," hissed Aidan, trying to get up. But as soon as he moved, the wound on his chest started bleeding heavier and he fell back.

"Evil bastard?" repeated Mrak Delar with a dismissive wave of his hand. "That I am. And I'll take it as a compliment... Don't you think the word 'evil' should be directly associated with the words 'smart' and 'resourceful'? You, good guys, are so predictable. It's ridiculous."

"What do you mean by predictable?" asked Angel exchanging a bewildered look with Aidan.

"Do you think I didn't expect that Zane Burns would

summon Svyatobor as soon as he crossed into the Land of Dreams?" asked Mrak Delar with a light shrug. "I was the one who reminded him that he could do it. So, I expected him to summon Svyatobor and tell him about Aidan's situation. As you can see, he didn't disappoint me. Like I said – predictable."

"But how could you know that I would come?" asked Angel. "It could have been Uri or Svyatobor or all three of us."

"Yes, of course," agreed Mrak Delar. "I expected it. This is why yesterday, I made this whole building inaccessible to anyone with magic or elemental powers, except you, Angel. Even gods can't get in. Trust me, it wasn't easy."

"It's true," confirmed Angel shaking his head. "Neither Svyatobor nor Uri could get in. Only I could."

"And you didn't think it was a trap?" Aidan yelled and coughed, choking on the pain.

"Of course I did," growled Angel. "But how many traps do you know that can hold Death? I knew only one and it was a well-hidden knowledge. I have no idea how this wicked jackass learned about it!"

"I know many things. You'll be amazed at what I can do," noted Mrak Delar dryly.

He approached Angel, holding his arm parallel to the floor and a set of manacles materialized in the palm of his hand. He touched the iron, chanting softly and a few of the same runes appeared on the surface of the manacles in a glowing red circle. Angel winced, involuntarily taking a step back.

"Now, now," muttered Mrak Delar, his black eyes fixed on Angel, "I do not believe for a moment that Death is scared of a Master of Power." He stopped, lowering his arms and shook his head. "Your hands, please. Your choice is simple. You comply with my demands and no one will get hurt." He jerked his thumb in Aidan's direction and the manacles in his hands jingled.

Aidan caught Angel's tortured gaze and shook his head no.

As quick as this silent communication was, Mrak Delar noticed it. He didn't say anything, but the magical energy around him spiked up as he slashed his arm through the air. Aidan cried out, pressing his hand to his shoulder, a dark red spot quickly spreading on his white shirt.

"Stop," shouted Angel, stretching both arms forward, his fists clenched, "don't do it, Mrak. I'll go with you."

Mrak Delar approached Angel and shackled him. As the iron touched his skin, Angel sucked air in and swayed.

"Dizzy?" asked Mrak Delar, sounding concerned. "It should go away in a moment. It's the rune's magic."

"Don't you think I know it," hissed Angel. "Stop pretending that you care."

Mrak Delar flinched, his black eyebrows lowering over his blazing eyes. Then an uneven smirk twisted his lips and he waved his hand, removing the rune from the ceiling.

"You're right, Grim Horseman, I don't care." He seized Angel's shoulder and pushed him toward the exit. "Now, move it."

"The day will come, Ancient Master, when I come for you," growled Angel, darkness gathering around him. "You are *not* immortal."

"And that's exactly what I'm trying to fix."

The Master of Power laughed, as he unlocked the door and pushed Angel out. But before leaving, he lingered in the doorway for a moment and then turned to Aidan.

"Aidan," he said so quietly that Aidan could barely make out his words. "It's going to be over soon. I'll let you leave as soon as it's all over." Without waiting for Aidan's response, he walked out and locked the door.

As soon as Mrak Delar was out, Aidan sighed and eased himself on the floor. He felt weak and the wounds on his chest and shoulder were still bleeding. But it was Mrak's betrayal that tormented him more than any physical pain could.

What the hell was that all about? What is Mrak doing and why? Immortality? I can't believe it...

With no way to heal his tortured body, he gave in to the weakness and let the darkness swallow him.

CHAPTER 26

~ ZANE BURNS, A.K.A. GUNZ ~

Gunz walked out on the wide empty field right next to the portal leading out of the nexus. He lowered Yaroslav to the ground and sat down next to him breathing laboriously. He had expected that walking through the Fire Salamander portal while holding a protective shield over the vampire wouldn't be easy, but he had no idea how much energy it would take from him.

It was possibly not only the magical exhaustion but physical as well. In the last few days, he had lost a lot of blood, and decent food and rest had been scarce. And right now, he felt weaker than ever. He sighed, thinking that the world around him was a little too shaky and blurry for his liking, but got up, offering his hand to Yaroslav.

"Zane, wait," said Yaroslav, taking his hand and rising. "You look like you're at the end of your rope. Maybe we should wait a little and give you a chance to rest."

Gunz glanced at Yaroslav's neck and noticed that the redness had spread wider around the collar and looked angrier with burgundy tentacles reaching down to his chest. He carefully moved his collar up. The burns on Yaroslav's skin were significantly deeper now, even though less than an hour had passed since he checked it the last time.

"I don't think we can spare any time for rest," he said quietly. "We must go at once. I'm afraid you don't have four days. The way your skin looks around the collar, you have just a few hours at the most. Let's go…"

THEY PASSED through the portal and walked out into the underground room where Mrak Delar left them eleven days ago. Gunz's heart stalled for a moment as it occurred to him that he was standing under the city he grew up in. It was the city he loved and missed so much, and he would give anything just to walk these streets one more time…

He sighed and waved his hand unfolding the fire curtain of his portal. Then he channeled his magic, but it didn't come easy to him. The energy of magic here, in his world, wasn't as readily available as it had been in the nexus and he was so worn out that he could hardly keep a vertical position.

He whispered a spell conjuring the protective shield around Yaroslav and lifted him, placing him over his shoulder. As he did, his legs gave way and he dropped to one knee but didn't let go of Yaroslav. Grateful the vampire didn't say anything, he forced himself to his feet and stumbled through the portal.

HIS CALCULATIONS WERE PERFECT. He didn't walk out but rather fell through the portal and landed on his knees in the middle of Novak's office. Carefully he lowered Yaroslav on the floor and leaned forward, supporting himself with his arms. Breathing heavily, he glanced at Yaroslav and his heart fell.

The vampire was sprawled on the floor in the same position

he placed him. His eyes were opened, blindly staring into space. The redness around his collar consumed all visible area of his neck and chest. Even though he had a protective shield around him, passing through the Fire Salamander's portal took whatever strength the vampire had left in him.

"Alucard… Please, say something," whispered Gunz, switching to their underground fighting names and gently touched the vampire's icy hand. Yaroslav didn't respond.

"He's dying… He has but a few minutes left… Say your goodbyes, Gunz. He can hear you."

Gunz lifted his head and saw Mrak Delar. The Master of Power was standing a few steps away. He wasn't gloating over Yaroslav's desperate situation, but his face showed no emotions at all.

"But it's been only eleven days. I came back in time." He looked over Mrak Delar's shoulder at Novak who stood with his arms crossed next to his desk. "Mr. Novak, we brought you the Apple of Youth and the Water of Life. Please, sir, remove the curse… Save him."

George Novak didn't move. He stared at Gunz without blinking. His pupils fluctuated in size, flooding his eyes with blackness and then narrowed down into hardly visible dots. His mouth started to stretch into the semblance of a smile, growing wider and wider until his face distorted into a terrifying mask.

Gunz gasped, involuntarily raising his arm to shield his face as fear chilled his insides. But a split-second later, the mask of horror was gone, replaced by Novak's human face, like it had never been there, and Gunz wasn't sure if it really happened or it had been his overtired mind conjuring the horrific vision.

"Give everything to the Master of Power," ordered Novak coldly.

With shaking hands, Gunz unlocked Yaroslav's bag and brought the Apple and the vial with the Water of Life out, offering it to Mrak Delar. The Master of Power bent down and took both magical artifacts from Gunz's hands.

"Now, Mr. Novak, you have what you asked for," said Gunz, sitting back on his heels. "Save Alucard. Please."

"No," replied Novak flatly. "And I want you to know that his death is on your conscious."

"Why?" whispered Gunz, his words felt like a knife to his heart.

"What were you thinking taking a vampire through the Fire Salamander's portal?" asked Novak, disgust curving his lips. "Vampires are unclean creatures. They're nothing but reanimated corpses, held together by the magic of vampiric essence. And you carried him through the purifying fire of the Fire Salamander's portal. Idiot! Did you seriously think that your meek attempt at a protective shield would keep him safe?"

"Your dark magic was killing him!" yelled Gunz, his anger giving him strength he didn't expect he still had. "I had no choice. He was dying either way!"

"Your stupidity is only rivaled by your hubris, boy!" Novak jeered, folding his arms over his chest. "I gave you fifteen days. Today was only day eleven. You had absolutely no reason to rush. So, it was you who killed Alucard, costing me my best fighter. His death is on your hands."

Gunz howled, jumping to his feet, his internal anguish and rage bringing forth his fire. A giant fireball formed in the palm of his hand and he threw it at Novak. Connecting with the power of Fire, Mrak Delar jumped between them and caught the fireball, making it dissipate.

"Fire Salamander, down!" the Ancient Master shouted, moving his arms forward.

Gunz growled fighting his control, feeling his body obeying the command of the Master of Power against his will. An image flashed in his mind and with painful clarity he recalled that moment when he controlled the wyvern by the walls of the sacred garden. He remembered the wyvern's fiery heart beating inside the grip of his magic, his will dominating that of the wyvern. And he wondered, if that was what the Master of Power was doing to him now.

Through the prism of his fire power, he looked down at his chest and he saw his own flaming heart beating desperately, surrounded by a foreign energy. Gunz channeled more fire power, fighting to burn the intruding magic out of his body. Battling Mrak Delar's control, he screamed strenuously, slowly rising back to his feet.

For a moment, Mrak's eyes widened in shock. He channeled more power, connecting to all four elements and increased the flow of his magic. His dark eyes swirled with all four colors of the elemental powers and his magical energy doubled. Gunz retaliated, fighting the mighty control the Master of Power with everything he had left in him.

Novak ran around the desk and found the controller for Gunz's collar, setting it to maximum strength. The electric shock of the gray stones magic shattered him and Gunz screamed, falling to his knees. But despite the fact that his magic was blocked now, somehow, he was still connected with the elemental Fire. Smoldering flames engulfed his body, burning the magic of the Master of Power into nothing.

"How is it possible?" muttered Mrak Delar. He made an intricate motion with both his hands and a ray of his magical energy hit Gunz, wrapping around him in a tight hoop. The hoop was shimmering with the colors of the four elemental powers, squeezing him tighter in its grip. Something cracked, and Gunz cried out, his fire slowly starting to die down. Mrak Delar didn't wait for him to give in and splashed him with a stream of icy water.

Gunz grunted, realizing that he couldn't fight the magic of the gray stones and the Ancient Master of Power at the same time. As the pain intensified, he stopped fighting and hung his head, seemingly giving in, but his mind was racing a hundred miles per hour, thinking how he could get closer to Novak so he could activate Voron's rune.

"Master Mrak Delar," he moaned, allowing the pain he felt to surface in his voice. "Please release me. I'm done fighting..." He raised his eyes at Novak, meeting his unblinking stare. "Mr. Novak... My lord... please, save Alucard and I'll be yours to do as you please. I will obey your every word."

Novak nodded at Mrak Delar and the hoop that was crushing Gunz disappeared. He moaned and fell to his knees, bowing his head to his chest. Novak came closer but still wasn't close enough for Gunz to touch him.

"So, Salamander, am I your lord and master then?" hissed Novak, snidely.

"Yes, my lord," replied Gunz without raising his eyes. "You are, sir."

"Look into my eyes," ordered Novak, taking another step closer.

One more step... just one more... Gunz raised his face, meeting Novak's eyes. "As you wish, my lord. Please, remove your curse and save your best fighter."

Novak shrieked with laughter, putting his hands on his hips. "And here I was wondering how to break you into submission, boy," he managed to say through laughter. "Mrak Delar was right after all. You're so predictable."

"My lord, please," pleaded Gunz, lowering his eyes again.

To his relief, Novak took one more step forward and seized Gunz's hair, yanking his head up.

"Fine," he said, a mocking sneer on his face. "Promise me that from now on, you'll do as I command and kiss my hand. You do that, and I'll give life back to Alucard."

"Yes, master, I'll do as you wish," replied Gunz, his voice void of emotions. He took Novak's hand and brought it to his lips, feeling hollow inside. While doing it, he pressed his other hand to his ribs and sent a tiny spark of his fire energy through the rune, activating it.

Novak snickered, staring down at Gunz. Then he patted him on his cheek and kneeled next to Yaroslav. He took Yaroslav's collar with one hand and Gunz's with the other and started chanting. Gunz felt his dark magical energy washing over him like a poisonous cloud and his stomach twisted. Fighting nausea, he took a deep breath and closed his eyes for a brief moment.

A few seconds later, it was all over. Novak removed the curse that was connecting their life forces. Then he got up and headed back to his desk. He picked up the receiver of the phone and pressed an intercom button.

"Please send Theron in and tell him to bring a bag of A-negative," he ordered and hung up the phone.

While they were waiting, Novak found Yaroslav's controller and reset it to minimum. By the time Theron walked into the office with a medical bag of blood, the redness on Yaroslav's chest slowly started to give up its position, retreating closer to the collar.

"Theron, give the blood bag to Gunz," said Novak.

Gunz took the bag and quickly ripped it open with his teeth. Then he lifted Yaroslav's head, placing it on his lap and opened his lips slightly. He pressed the bag to his lips, forcing a few drops of blood into his mouth.

At first the vampire didn't react, but a moment later he swallowed, his eyes lit up with a scarlet glow, and he seized the bag with shaking hands, drinking hungrily. A thin red stream trickled down the corner of his mouth, dripping on Gunz's leg. The bag was empty within a few seconds and Yaroslav wiped his mouth with the back of his hand.

"Hello, Alucard," said Novak, once the vampire was done. "Welcome back. Can you get up now?"

Yaroslav stiffened at the sound of Novak's voice. He pushed

off the floor and got up into a kneeling position. "Yes, master," he said quietly, "I can."

Novak nodded to him. "Theron, please take these two to clean up first and give them some fresh clothes. Then escort them to their room."

"Yes, master," said Theron, approaching Gunz and Yaroslav and easily jerking them both up to their feet.

"And Theron. A couple more things," added Novak, gesturing at his servant to wait. "Alucard will need more blood to restore his strength. Give him as many blood bags as he asks for. And this one"—he jerked his chin in Gunz's direction—"will need a nice hot meal. And... hmm... perhaps some vodka. Make sure he gets it."

"As you wish, master," replied Theron with a bow.

"After you take care of that," continued Novak, "I want you to stay outside their door and guard it until I call them in tomorrow night. No one... You hear me? No one is to bother them. If they ask for more food or blood, give it to them. They need to be completely rested and their strength must be restored. Do you understand me, Theron?"

"Yes, master," replied Theron obediently, "I'll do as you command."

"You may leave now," said Novak, waving his hand dismissively.

Both Gunz and Yaroslav bowed to him and headed toward the exit, escorted by Theron.

CHAPTER 27

~ ZANE BURNS, A.K.A. GUNZ ~

It was past midnight, but Gunz was in his bed, sleepless. He was lying on his back, his arms wrapped around his chest, afraid to take a breath since every move he made resonated with a sharp pain. When he was fighting Mrak Delar, the Ancient Master of Power hadn't held back. Infuriated by his resistance, Mrak had squeezed his power-hoop too tight and had broken at least a few ribs.

Gunz wasn't sure if there was any other damage. He could hardly breathe – his chest seemed to be compressed and every breath was taking an effort. Something wheezed and squeaked every time he inhaled, and his chest sounded like an old accordion.

With his controller set to maximum he couldn't heal himself. So, he had no choice but to lie still on top of his bed, afraid to make a move. After a while, Yaroslav got up and soundlessly approached him. He took a knee next to his bed and bit his wrist. Pulling on Gunz's hair, he forced his head back slightly and pressed his bleeding wrist to his lips.

"If you say one word, Gunz, I'll end you myself," he said, the hint of a warm smile in his eyes. "Isn't that what you told me in the Land of Dreams?"

Gunz cringed inwardly at the smell and taste of the vampire's blood, but he knew it was the only way to heal. His choice was simple – it was either that or keep suffering. He held Yaroslav's bleeding wrist tighter and kept drinking until the vampire pulled away.

"I will never get rid of you from my head, will I?" he asked, enjoying the fact that nothing hurt, and he could finally relax.

"Count your blessings, little Salamander." Yaroslav chuckled and returned to his bed.

Gunz closed his eyes and fell asleep almost immediately. Unfortunately, his peaceful slumber was short-lived. He felt a touch to his shoulder and stiffened, not sure he wanted to open his eyes and see who it was. Someone tapped on his shoulder persistently.

"Slavik, come on..." mumbled Gunz.

"Zane, wake up," said a deep, slightly raspy voice and Gunz recognized Voron.

Gunz opened his eyes and in the darkness of the room, he saw Voron and Yaroslav standing at his bedside. He sat up, lowering his bare feet on the cold floor.

"I'm awake, Voron. Barely but awake," he said, scratching the back of his head. "I guess it's not written in the stars that I would get one good night's rest."

"You can rest when all this is over," replied Voron in a low whisper. "You have a guard sleeping by your door. A bulky fellow... So, let's not wake him up."

"Theron. He is..." Yaroslav chuckled softly. "Let's put it this way – the muscle bulk compensates for the shortage in other departments. Don't worry about him."

"Okay," agreed Voron, shaking his head and continued, "the rune worked, Zane. We know which dark soul we're dealing with. Now I understand why he sent Yaroslav with you to the

Land of Dreams, connecting your life forces with a deadly dark spell."

"Well, I'm glad one of us understands…" mumbled Yaroslav. "I thought—"

"Anything you thought, Yaroslav Potemkin, was wrong," Voron cut him off. "He sent you to the Land of Dreams, hoping that you would perish there. He wanted you dead. He didn't think the young Salamander would go through so much trouble to keep you alive. He underestimated Zane's loyalty to his friends."

"It doesn't make any sense. I am his goddamn slave, Voron," hissed Yaroslav, his eyes lighting up with a furious scarlet glow. "He holds my life in his hands in more ways than one. He's a powerful necromancer and I'm a vampire. He could have made me commit suicide. He could have killed me at any time he wished. All he had to do was swing his sword or wield his dark magic."

"No, Prince Potemkin, he couldn't," Voron objected quietly, sadness clouding his features. "And he knew that he couldn't. Not without activating the curse Chernobog placed on his soul. Why do you think he abducted and enslaved you in the first place, huh? He wanted to keep the only person who could kill him and send him back to the Dark Nav under his control. You *are* the trigger, Yaroslav."

Voron extended his arm and a white light surrounded his hand. When the light dimmed down, Gunz saw an old-style revolver and a single bullet in the palm of Voron's hand. The bullet had engravings that were glowing with a soft blue light.

"Do you recognize this weapon, Yaroslav?" asked Voron quietly.

The vampire raised his hands, backing away. His face became so white that it was glowing in the dark and his eyes widened in shock.

"No," he gulped, shaking his head. "It can't… not him…"

"Yes, Yaroslav," replied Voron with a sigh. "It's him and you are the only person in all the worlds who can put an end to him. Again."

"How did I not recognize him before?" he whispered. "George Novak..."

"Also known as Grigory Novih," confirmed Voron. "That is his real name. But most commonly, he's known as Grigory Rasputin, and it is his dark soul we are dealing with."

Yaroslav dropped on his bed, hiding his face in his hands. He whispered something into his hands and his shoulders tensed. Gunz approached him and carefully touched his arm.

"Slavik, what's going on?" he asked, throwing a quick look at Voron.

The vampire raised his colorless face and just now Gunz noticed that his long fangs were extended and the nails on his fingers were elongated into claws. He looked like he was ready to fight.

"I killed this man," growled Yaroslav. "It was more than a century ago. I killed him and now he came back to haunt me."

Gunz frowned. "Allow me to remind you that you are a few centuries old vampire," he said dryly. "Over the course of your life as vampire, you killed hundreds if not thousands of people."

"Yes, I did," agreed Yaroslav. "And I'm not proud of it. But Rasputin was the only man I killed for a reason other than the vampire's thirst. And a hundred years later, I still can't forget it."

"Yaroslav Potemkin," growled Voron, pushing the vampire on his shoulder, "snap out of it. You did the right thing then and you are going to do it again! Rasputin is a powerful master of the Dark Arts! There is a reason Morena and Skiper-Zmey chose his soul to be released from the Dark Nav. So, you two boys, have an assignment. Before you kill Rasputin and summon Chernobog, you must find out what his purpose is, and why Morena released him and not someone else. You cannot kill him until you know that. Am I clear?"

Gunz put his hand on Voron's shoulder. "Give me the revolver, Voron," he offered peacefully. "A gun is my type of weapon. I can do it. I'll kill this monster and my hand is not going to tremble when I press that trigger."

"No, you can't," objected Voron. "You still don't get it. Yaroslav killed Rasputin in 1916 with this revolver and an enchanted bullet. To trigger the curse, history must repeat itself. It must be him."

Yaroslav got up, throwing his long hair off his face and squared his shoulders, his face calm and composed once again. He took the revolver from Voron's hands and put the bullet inside the cylinder.

"How do I hide it?" asked Yaroslav, his voice wintry-cold.

Voron touched it, turning it invisible. "No one can see it now, except the three of us. Are you sure you can do it, vampire?"

Yaroslav laughed. Cold and dangerous, for a split-second he reminded Gunz of his mother, Akira.

"Like you said – I did it once, I can do it again," said Yaroslav. "I think the news that the man who tortured and abused me for months was Rasputin got me a little shaken. But it's over now. Trust me, Voron, when the time comes, I'll plant this enchanted bullet right between his eyes. After everything he's done to me, it would be a kindness to end him so quickly and easily…" His voice dissolved into a low hiss as his eyes lit up with a dangerous glow.

"Just don't forget, you must learn of his true intentions before you kill him," reminded Voron.

"We'll do our best," promised Gunz. He had no idea how they could find out what Rasputin was planning. It wasn't like they were on his confidant's list. "Let's just hope Mrak Delar is not going to interfere. He may present a problem."

"It's up to you and the vampire to deal with the situation. I still can't believe the Ancient Master of Power turned back to his old ways," said Voron shaking his head. "Anyway, once Rasputin is dead, summon Chernobog. He'll take care of everything else. Do you know how to summon him?"

"Yes, sir," said Gunz.

"Then I'll see you once it's all over. Farewell, my friends." Voron bowed and vanished from the room.

* * *

AFTER VORON HAD GONE, Gunz went back to bed. He lay with his eyes closed for a while, but sleep eluded him. Yaroslav wasn't sleeping either. As soundless as the vampire was, he could hear him pacing at the other end of the room.

"Hundred yards," Gunz said bitterly and sat up on the bed.

Yaroslav stopped pacing and stared at him. "What are you talking about?"

"Now I'm starting to understand why Novak put such a short leash between us – just one hundred yards," explained Gunz.

"Wasn't it obvious before?" asked Yaroslav with a shrug.

"No, not entirely," replied Gunz. "He didn't underestimate my loyalty to my friends, the way Voron put it. He showed me a vision of Angelique, even though Mrak Delar told him not to…" Gunz bit his lip and rubbed his temples with his fingers. "All this time I kept wondering why he did it. I thought that your life and Aidan's life were enough of an incentive for me to come back here and bring him everything he asked for. Why did he have to show me the vision and then tell me that he could make a potion that would separate Angelique from Zmey?"

"You're right," said Yaroslav. "He was hoping that your love for Angelique would be stronger than your loyalty to me. This is why he activated my controller shortly after we crossed into the Land of Dreams."

"He was hoping that when you started slowing me down, I

would kill you to free myself from the burden," said Gunz shaking his head. "And you were asking me to do it too."

They both fell silent for a moment and then Gunz asked, "Slavik, do you think there is such a potion? You know, to separate Angie's essence from Zmey's?"

For a moment Yaroslav stared at him, a deep wrinkle crossing his forehead. Then he sighed and sat down next to Gunz on the bed.

"You're not seriously considering it, Gunz, are you?" he asked.

"I don't know…"

"Gunz, you know you can't… Even if this potion existed, you can't use it…"

"Don't you think I know that?" asked Gunz, pain shredding his insides. "But if you had seen that vision—"

"This is what he does, Gunz!" exclaimed Yaroslav throwing his hands in the air. "He manipulates people into doing what he wants. He is using your pain against you."

"I know, Slavik, but it feels like I'm killing her again… I pray to all the gods that he was just talking out of his ass and a potion like this doesn't exist."

"Take it out of your head, Gunz," said Yaroslav rising. "Even if it exists, no matter what, you can't use it. Now go to sleep, my friend. In a few hours, we'll have to face Morena's evil flunky again."

"Yes, of course," replied Gunz, lying back down, folding his hands over his stomach. "It was just a thought… I would never use this potion at the risk of freeing the Skiper-Zmey again."

Would I?

CHAPTER 28

~ MASTER OF POWER, MRAK DELAR ~

It was past midnight, but Mrak Delar was lying on his bed fully dressed. He wasn't sleeping and the tiny spike of magical energy inside the building didn't escape his attention. Even though it was skillfully suppressed, the Master of Power could still sense it. Someone had teleported inside the building. Someone who wasn't invited. Yet somehow, their magical signature felt familiar.

He got up and tiptoed his way to the door. For a moment he stood with his hand on the door handle, thinking if he should walk or teleport. Teleporting was a safer option – he didn't have to worry about meeting anyone or attracting the attention of the guards. It was also a lot faster.

On the other hand, teleporting required a serious amount of magical energy and it would create an energy spike around him, and in case Novak was keeping an eye on him, it would betray his location. Mrak Delar sighed. After everything he had done, Novak still didn't quite trust him. The necromancer was constantly watching him, questioning his every word and arrogantly turning down his every suggestion.

Mrak Delar rested his forehead against the door and closed

his eyes. "Screw it!" he said, pushing away from the door. "I can't do it anymore." He snapped his fingers and vanished from the room.

* * *

He manifested in the basement a few feet away from Aidan's holding cell. The basement was dark, and from this distance he could see only the vague outline of a man on the floor. He approached the bars and peeked inside. Now he could see Aidan clearly. The wounds on his chest and shoulder were still slightly bleeding, and his ashen-gray face wore a tortured expression.

Mrak observed his handiwork and shuddered, remorse tormenting him. This picture painfully reminded him of his past – the distant past he was working so hard to put behind. He pressed his hands to his eyes, swallowing his guilt and the angry tears that were burning somewhere deep behind his tightly-shut eyelids.

He had no time to deal with the shadows of his past. He had to suppress his emotions so he could focus on his magic. The Master of Power squatted down and touched the circle of the God's snare, removing the spell. Once he was done, he snapped his fingers and teleported to the other side of the bars.

Aidan woke up as soon as he appeared next to him. He jolted up, but the pain and weakness from the blood loss didn't let him get up. He cried out and fell back, shielding his head with his arms.

"Aidan… Aidan, hush," whispered Mrak Delar, holding his finger to his lips. "Please… no one should know that I am here."

Aidan slowly lowered his arms and gaped at him. "What… are you… ahh…" he panted, pressing his hand to his chest. "Why?"

"Oh, Aidan, I'm so sorry for what I did to you." Mrak lowered to his knees by Aidan's side and placed his hands on his chest and forehead, carefully channeling the healing power of Earth.

"Do... not... touch me!" hissed Aidan and jerked away from him.

"Aidan, please," pleaded Mrak Delar, "let me heal you. We need to talk. Please, just give me a few minutes of your attention and you'll understand."

"I can... heal myself... if you remove the God's snare... you evil..." growled Aidan.

"Aidan, I already removed the God's snare, but you are so drained that you can't sense it." Mrak Delar sighed. "Just relax and let me help you."

Aidan sighed and closed his eyes, looking like he was fighting nausea. "Do it," he said so quietly that Mrak practically had to read his lips.

"Thank you," mumbled Mrak, placing his hands on his chest and forehead and focused on the healing process. A few minutes later, he stopped the healing but didn't remove his hands, holding Aidan down. "Stay still, Aidan. I healed your wounds but let me give you an energy boost. You're going to need your full strength of a god back."

Aidan grunted but didn't object. Mrak manifested a low-voltage energy ball in the palm of his hand and showed it to Aidan. "Ready?"

Aidan nodded, and Mrak thrust the energy ball through his chest. Aidan gasped and for a split-second his body arched as his wide-open eyes lit up with the blazing white light of his restored magic.

Mrak Delar got up and offered his hand to him. The god of the Otherworld measured him with his blazing eyes and got up without taking his hand. As soon as he was up on his feet, he swung his arm and his massive fist plunged into Mrak's jaw. The Master of Power fell back, pressing his hand to his jaw. For a moment, a bright white light exploded in his head blinding him.

"I deserved it," he said, raising his eyes up at Aidan. "What I had to do to you—"

"What you had to do to me?" growled Aidan, his fingers clenched into fists. "How about what you have done to Gunz and to Angel!"

"This is why I'm here now, Aidan," started Mrak Delar. "Gunz's life is in danger—"

"He's an immortal Fire Salamander. He can't die! We trusted you and you betrayed us all! How can I believe anything you are saying?"

"Yes, he can die — and you know it — by dissolving into his own element. The Black Fire," objected Mrak Delar quietly, keeping his arm up in case Aidan decided to punch him again. "And I didn't betray you. I did what your mentor ordered me to do… Against my will. And against my better judgment."

"No! Gwyn ap Nudd would never ask something like this of you. Or anyone else for that matter!" shouted Aidan as the brilliant light enveloped him.

Mrak Delar sighed and got into a kneeling position. Even though the god of the Otherworld looked terrifying in his anger and in his full power could smite him with one move of his hand, he wasn't afraid. All he could feel was endless despair and exhaustion. He extended both his arms forward, whispering a spell. A long black sword materialized in his hands.

"As the Master of Power, I swear that every word I am telling you now is the truth," he said, calmly meeting Aidan's blazing eyes and offered his sword to him. "Take this sword, Aidan, and give me a few minutes to explain everything. By the end of my explanation, if you still believe that I betrayed my friends, kill me."

Aidan took the sword and placed its sharp point at Mrak

Delar's throat, under his jaw. He pressed on it a little, drawing a few drops of blood and smirked.

"Or I can just run this blade through your throat right now and free both worlds, Earth and Kendral, from the unspeakable evil that you are," he said coldly.

"Yes, you could do it," agreed Mrak Delar, thinking how tired he was of all this, "but then the young Fire Salamander will die and with his death, the master of the Dark Arts will come in possession of a deadly substance called the Living-Dead Flame. Do you know what that is, Aodh mac Lir, and what it can do?"

Aidan's hand trembled and he lowered the sword. "It can't be…" he said quietly, shaking his head. "It takes a lot to create the Living-Dead Flame. I don't believe you."

"Sit down, Aidan. Please," said Mrak Delar gesturing at the floor before him. "I swear on my power – again – that everything I'm about to tell you is nothing but the truth. So, please, let me explain."

Aidan slowly lowered himself on the cold floor, placing the black sword between them. "Fine, go ahead, explain. I'll listen. You got five minutes to convince me."

"That is all I need," replied Mrak Delar, slightly relieved, and started his explanation. "It happened about two and a half weeks ago…"

CHAPTER 29

~ MASTER OF POWER, MRAK DELAR ~

About two and a half weeks ago

It was late evening and the sun was long gone. A bright moon was bathing in the silence of the dark sky, gazing down at its reflection in the ocean. Mrak Delar stared at the ocean from the balcony of Kal's penthouse in South Florida. Leaning heavily on the rail, he had been standing like this for at least an hour, thinking about his last and only conversation with Gunz.

What is this boy doing? He alienated everyone and now he's on his own, doing god knows what. Why? He's not an idiot. There has to be a reason to his madness...

He raked his fingers through his hair as the late-night breeze threw a few strands into his face.

And Kal... Here is another one that locked himself away in the tower... well... in his smithy in Kendral. He doesn't want to see anyone, and he doesn't want to speak with anyone. Even the dragons and his Phoenix are staying away from him... What the hell is going on with the Fire Salamanders these days?

The Master of Power missed his wife. He didn't like to be

away from her for too long, but the situation with the young Fire Salamander was troubling him. And as much as he wanted to be in Kendral, at home with his beloved Leila, he couldn't leave this world. Not until he knew that Gunz was safe.

He felt a light headache coming up and rubbed his temples with his fingers. The headache got stronger, quickly becoming a pounding nightmare. It was an urgent, persistent summoning call threatening to become a consistent torture if he didn't respond immediately. Gwyn ap Nudd was summoning him and he made it clear that he wasn't in the mood to wait.

Mrak Delar snapped his fingers and teleported into the underground labyrinth of Glastonbury Tor. It was the only place where Gwyn ap Nudd could open a door into the Otherworld where he resided most of the year. As soon as Mrak arrived, he saw the door. Lit with the bright white light of Gwyn's magic, it was ready for him.

The Master of Power walked through the light and found himself inside Gwyn ap Nudd's living room. Gwyn loved white color and everything inside his spacious glass-and-concrete house was either white or some shade of light gray. Despite the location of the house and the age of the owner, everything inside was modern, including the big screen TV on the wall and an Xbox gaming console.

Gwyn was pacing in his living room, and the energy of his magic was flowing around him like a heavy cloud. Usually the Lord of the Otherworld was in control of his emotions and his magic, but not today. Mishka, the wyvern, was following Gwyn's every turn, hovering in the air above him. As soon as Mrak Delar walked in, the wyvern hissed something into Gwyn's ear and vanished.

"What took you so long, Master!" asked Gwyn ap Nudd, throwing his hands in the air, his unnerving white eyes scanning his insides.

"Ugh, Gwyn, stop scanning me!" yelled Mrak Delar. "I came

here as soon as I heard your call. It's enough that your summoning call gave me a mighty migraine, now you're doing the soul check?"

"I need to be sure," replied Gwyn, averting his eyes. "Anyway, we have a problem."

"I figured," said Mrak Delar sitting down. "Since I saw the wyvern here, let me guess – the young Fire Salamander needs your help."

"No, Mrak," said Gwyn, lowering himself in the armchair across from Mrak Delar. "He sent me a message with the wyvern, but he wasn't asking for help for himself. From what I understand he's holding his own just fine. The reason he sent me a message was because he went as far as he could. The rest is up to us."

"Gwyn," said Mrak Delar, worry clawing through him, "can you speak plainly for once? What's going on? No riddles! Where is Gunz and what is he doing?"

"Gunz is in Los Angeles. He is fighting as a captive for the California House," said Gwyn quietly. "He is a slave, Mrak."

Mrak stiffened, staring heavily at Gwyn ap Nudd as the word "slave" resonated through him with pain. He shook his head, words stuck somewhere in his throat.

"I know, Mrak, slavery is a painful subject for you," said Gwyn ap Nudd, sympathy warming up his cat-like eyes. "But Gunz did it for a reason. Actually, for a couple of reasons. He found Yaroslav, Akira's son. Novak, the Head of California House, abducted him. But the main reason Gunz went through all the troubles was because he suspected Novak was not who he said he was. And from what I understand – he is right."

"Who is this Novak?" growled Mrak Delar and the glass walls of Gwyn's house trembled. "I'll kill him myself."

"You can't, Mrak," continued Gwyn ap Nudd, throwing a worrisome glance at the glass ceiling of his house. "Gunz suspects Novak is one of the dark souls Morena released from the Dark Nav last year. He was able to get close enough to him to confirm his suspicion. It means that no mortal weapon can kill him. Only the curse that Chernobog placed on his soul can send him back."

"Okay, I understand," said Mrak, slowly getting in control of his power. "So, what can I do to help?"

"What Gunz couldn't do was find out Novak's true intentions," continued Gwyn ap Nudd. "As a captive fighter, he is not close enough to Novak to learn the truth. This is where you come into play, Mrak. I need you to get close to Novak. Get him to trust you. We must know what he is planning and stop him before he does something unspeakable."

"And how do you propose I do it, Gwyn?" asked Mrak, leaning back in the couch. "Novak has never met me. He doesn't know me. Why would he trust me?"

Gwyn ap Nudd got up and walked around the coffee table, stopping in front of him.

"He will trust you, because you are going to give him my son," he said quietly.

"What?" asked Mrak Delar rising. He was standing in front of Gwyn ap Nudd, staring up at him in horror.

"You heard me," said the Lord of the Otherworld dryly. "You will give Novak my son Aidan. You will help him enslave a god. And Aidan is not going to know that it's an act. He will put up a fight. So, be ready. And after that, you will keep playing your part, and if it means that you have to betray Gunz and Yaroslav too, so be it. You do whatever it takes, and you don't stop until you know what Novak's up to. Am I clear, Ancient Master?"

"No. Gwyn, I can't do it," said Mrak Delar, backing away from Gwyn ap Nudd until he fell on the couch. "You're asking me to betray people I care about. I can't—"

"Ancient Master," said Gwyn ap Nudd, putting his hand on his shoulder. "I'm not asking you. I'm ordering you, and you will do as you are told."

"No, Gwyn, please," moaned Mrak Delar, his fingers digging into the thick mane of his obsidian hair. "I'm begging you, don't ask me to do it... I can't..."

"Mrak, I'm sorry, but it has to be you," said Gwyn ap Nudd, lowering himself on the couch next to Mrak Delar. "I can't do it, and neither can Kal. No one would believe us. But you are a different story. You have a colorful past and it's not a secret. If Novak decides to check your background, he'll find out that you tortured the Young Master of Power in your dungeon for a year and you were known as the worst dictator who ever reigned over Kendral—"

"And I have to live with it for the rest of my life!" barked Mrak Delar, anguish shredding his heart. "And you know that it wasn't me. I was controlled!"

"I know that, Mrak," replied Gwyn ap Nudd calmly. "Of course, I know that you're not that man. But outside our small circle, not too many people know about it. Novak certainly doesn't know, so you are the only person among us who can do it. You give him a god and help him tame the young Fire Salamander. He will trust you."

For a few minutes, Mrak Delar sat silently, hiding his face in his hands, slowly rocking back and forth. He wasn't really thinking – his thoughts were scrambled. He understood that Gwyn ap Nudd was right. Nonetheless, the thought of bringing the evil dictator of Kendral back to life was killing him inside.

Gwyn ap Nudd went to his kitchen and came back with a bottle of wine and two glasses. He filled the glasses with a dark-red liquid and offered one to Mrak.

"Gunz didn't want you involved," said Gwyn ap Nudd, taking a sip of his wine. "His wyvern made it very clear that he didn't want you or Kal anywhere next to Novak. This is why he asked me for help and not the two of you."

Mrak Delar took the glass and drank everything at once. He

put the glass back on the table and Gwyn filled it to the brim again.

"Why?" asked Mrak Delar, taking the glass.

"He didn't want you to see a collar on his neck or get exposed to slavery again," explained Gwyn with a sigh. "The young Salamander cares about you, Master. He said that he already hurt you and Kal enough."

"Okay. When?"

"Soon," replied Gwyn ap Nudd. "You'll spend the night in my house. Take any room upstairs. Tomorrow is a big captive event where Gunz is going to face Yaroslav in the cage. I'm sure Aidan is going to be there to stop the fight. It's your only chance to get in."

Silently, Mrak Delar got up and headed upstairs, grateful that the Lord of the Otherworld didn't try to stop him.

Inside he was numb.

He was dead.

The only thought that was still alive in his mind was that in a few hours, he would have to become the man he once was. The man he loathed and despised. Many years ago, he was controlled and compelled to be that evil despicable thing... He brought Kendall to the verge of poverty and famine. He killed, tortured and enslaved with no remorse.

And now he would have to become that evil thing again.

Against his will...

Against his better judgment...

CHAPTER 30

~ MASTER OF POWER, MRAK DELAR ~

Back to present time

"Well, Aidan, you know the rest," finished Mrak Delar. "Gwyn ap Nudd opened a portal for me before the event started and I had a few minutes to make a deal with Novak. Then I teleported right into the middle of the mess you created in that captive event, and I did exactly what your mentor ordered me to do. I captured you and helped Novak break Gunz. So, if you still wish to kill me – go ahead. I deserve it."

For a while Aidan remained silent, his fingers playing mindlessly with the pommel of the black sword. Then he sighed and pushed the sword back to him.

"No, Mrak, you don't deserve it. I hope Gwyn knew what he was doing," he said quietly, shaking his head. "I'll be honest with you. It's a little hard for me to look at you after everything you've done, but I'll get over it… And Gunz will, too. Eventually. He said himself that with understanding, forgiveness comes easier."

Mrak Delar got up and turned away from Aidan. Remorse

was twisting him on the inside, and he didn't want Aidan to see it. It took him a moment to compose himself and turn back.

"Everything I've done has been for nothing," he said flatly. "I don't know what Novak is up to. Not entirely. And I can't continue, because if I will, Gunz will die. And this is where I draw the line. I was willing to sacrifice my soul, but I'm not willing to let my friend die."

"How can you be sure Novak is planning to create the Living-Dead Flame?" asked Aidan. "The spell itself requires an enormous amount of magical energy and I don't think any of the masters of the Dark Arts have what it takes to create it. Besides, to extract the essence of Death, he will need a specific ceremonial athame that is one of a kind and as far as I know, it was lost centuries ago."

"He found the athame," replied Mrak Delar. "I saw it with my own eyes. All this time, the athame was in some museum here, in California. He compelled demons to steal it for him. As you're well aware, there is only one use for this athame – extracting the essence of Death."

"Damnit!" Aidan cursed, slamming his fist on the wall.

"Also, I saw a set of chemicals in his lab that is needed to conjure the Living-Dead Flame," continued Mrak Delar. "So, now he has everything he needs. He has the ingredients and the athame. He has Death imprisoned and he has the Fire Salamander to bring the Living-Dead Flame to life. And since he is one of the dark souls, then we might have to consider the fact that Morena infused his soul with the energy of Chaos before releasing it. If that's the case, then he has more than enough dark magical energy to sustain and complete the conjuring spell."

"Any idea what he is planning to do with the Flame?"

"No. He wouldn't let me anywhere close to all that," said Mrak Delar. "I don't think Novak trusts me." He chuckled darkly. "I guess I didn't do enough damage to the people around me to earn his complete trust. I also have no idea why he needed the Apple of Youth and the Water of Life. He sent Yaroslav and Gunz to the Land of Dreams to bring all that to him, but neither of these artifacts are needed to conjure the Living-Dead Flame."

"Didn't he say something about making an elixir of immortality?" asked Aidan.

"He did," replied Mrak with a tired smirk, "but I don't think he needs it. He is already immortal. Unless Chernobog finds a way to trigger the curse he placed on his soul, of course. That's the only thing that can kill him."

"We need to know what his plans are," said Aidan. "He wasn't the only dark soul Morena released. What if everything he's doing now is just a small part of a bigger picture? So, what are we going to do?"

"Why is it even a question?" asked Mrak Delar. "We fight. We fight for our friends. We save the young Fire Salamander and we deal with Novak to stop him from conjuring the Flame."

"But Gwyn ap Nudd was right. We need to know Novak's plans. We must do whatever it takes—"

"To what end, Aidan?" growled Mrak Delar, desperation and anger breaking to the surface. "How far are you willing to take it? Is the life of your friend worth nothing to you?"

"Of course it is! But if we don't learn the bigger picture, the consequences could be horrific. We need to think about the greater good—"

"Yeah… greater good… Every single life is precious, Aidan," said Mrak Delar quietly. "The lives of those we love even more so to us. I can see that you think it would be the right choice for me to stay undercover and learn more about Novak's plans. For the so called greater good. But did you consider the price we are going to pay and the risks of doing that? I already risked enough by letting Novak capture Death. Did it help me gain his trust? No! He still doesn't share his plans with me.

"So, how much further do you want me to take it? Think

about it, Aidan. If we let Novak go through with his plan, he will kill the Fire Salamander to conjure the Living-Dead Flame. Not only will we lose our friend, but we will give our enemy a terrible weapon. How is that going to benefit your greater good?"

"But is there any other way to stop him without blowing your cover?" asked Aidan. "Steal the athame. Without it, he can't go through with the spell."

"Already tried," replied Mrak Delar tiredly. "Don't bother, Aidan. Anything you suggest, I already tried. Novak is careful. He has human guards as well as supernatural – demons and vampires whom he can control with his necromancer's magic."

"Since when are vampires and demons a problem for you, Master?" asked Aidan, sarcasm layering his voice.

"They're not a problem, Aidan, but you do realize that I can't slip by them unnoticed, don't you? Besides that, Novak placed powerful protection spells and wards on his lab. Even if I somehow pass the guards without them noticing me, I can't break the wards without creating mayhem that would be heard in Kendral. There is no way for me to break in without a fight. So, if I have to fight, let's do it right and for the right reasons."

"I was just looking for a way to…" Aidan's voice trailed away, and he shook his head. "I have no idea what I was thinking…"

"You were trying to find a way to keep the sheep safe and the wolves fed." Mrak Delar chuckled, exhaustion settling somewhere in his knees. He sighed and leaned against the wall, folding his arms across his chest. "Sometimes there is no such way and we have to do a seemingly wrong thing for the right reasons. So, let's take care of our friends and then we'll see what we can do about the greater good."

"When?" asked Aidan.

"My guess, in a few hours," replied Mrak Delar. "By midnight."

"So, what's your plan?"

"Plan? We don't need no stinking plan. We come. We see. We conquer." Mrak Delar chuckled humorlessly, shoving his hands in the pockets of his pants. "A half-baked god of the Otherworld and an evil Master of Power against an indestructible master of the Dark Arts, infused with the energy of Chaos. What could possibly go wrong?"

"A half-baked god of the Otherworld?" repeated Aidan, his eyebrows rising. "Have you been watching local TV?"

"Yeah. We don't have TV in Kendral," he replied with a half-shrug. "I had nothing better to do. I couldn't go home until I knew what was going on with Gunz and he made it impossible to find him. So, I stayed in Kal's apartment, hoping... I have no idea what I was hoping for." He sighed.

A sad smile crossed Aidan's face. "I know the feeling. He completely isolated himself after Angie's death. Wouldn't let anyone in. And then he was gone. Just like that. Not a word to anyone. Even Jim and Akira were puzzled."

"I feel responsible for him, Aidan," said Mrak Delar, suddenly serious. "When I met him, he was just a normal young man. Human. I didn't know he was a Fire Salamander, but I knew he was a Child of Fire the very first time I laid my eyes on him. I should have kept my mouth shut. He could have lived a normal human life. Now, he is—"

"No, Mrak," objected Aidan. "You know that sooner or later the Fire Salamander in him would have found its way out. You just pushed it a little by showing him how to channel the fire. Anyway, how are we going to handle the situation with Novak?"

"Later tonight, I am meeting with Novak in his lab," said Mrak Delar. "If I'm right, he'll attempt to conjure the Living-Dead Flame then. When the time comes, I'll summon you. I'll need Aodh mac Lir in his full godly power, not Aidan. Be ready."

"I'll be ready, Mrak," replied Aidan. "But wait a moment. There is something, I believe, I need to do."

He touched the Guardian's pendant, sending some of his

magic through it and his eyes shone with the light of his power. For a few minutes he sat silently, his unnerving white eyes staring at the ceiling. Then his eyes returned to his normal blue color and he lowered his head with a tired smile.

"It's done," he said, rising.

"What's done?" asked Mrak Delar, observing him with interest.

"I contacted the Archmage of the Guardians Order and asked for his assistance. This evening they'll be ready," explained Aidan. "We don't know what to expect and I don't want humans to get hurt in the magical crossfire. The Guardians will do what they do best – guard. They will create a protective shield over this whole building, driving humans away from this area."

"I suppose it's a good idea. I'll see you soon," said Mrak Delar and vanished from the basement.

CHAPTER 31

~ ZANE BURNS, A.K.A. GUNZ ~

Theron stopped in front of a tall door and knocked.

"Wait there! I'll call you when I'm ready!" Novak boomed from behind the closed door, notes of irritation in his voice.

The guard turned around, his eyes shifting from Gunz to Yaroslav and back. Gunz surveyed the area, realizing he had never been in this part of the building before.

"Where are we?" he asked.

"Lab," replied Theron flatly. "The master ordered me to escort the two of you here."

"Lab?" Gunz frowned. The word didn't give him a warm and fuzzy feeling. "Do you know why he wants us here? What is he planning to do?"

"It's not my place to question my master," growled Theron, exposing his fangs. "Neither is yours. When your master orders, you quietly bow and do what you've been told."

Since the morning, Gunz had been trying to suppress his nervousness and irritation, and Theron's words, like a catalyst, sent him over the edge.

"What's wrong with you, Theron?" he hissed. Quick like a

strike of a snake, his arm shot forward, seizing Theron's collar. "You're just another slave here, wearing a collar on your neck. Not even a fighter. Novak will kill you for his amusement without giving it a second thought. Why are you pushing me and Alucard around, like we're your enemies? We're on the same side. Don't you get it?"

Theron snarled, a real animal-like growl escaping his lips and his eyes lit up with a furious orange glow as he started to transform. His fingers wrapped around Gunz's arm, hooked yellowish claws puncturing his skin. Gunz let go and backed away.

"What are you, Theron?" he asked, staring at him with curiosity. He wasn't scared. Just curious. Theron in his human form was strong and muscled, but as he started to transform, his muscles seemed to get bigger and bulkier and his eyes changed, resembling the eyes of a wild cat.

Theron caught his calm gaze and exhaled, his anger quickly deflating. "I'm a weretiger," he replied. "Why?"

"Weretiger? I've never seen one before," said Gunz observing him with interest. "Werewolves are strong. I can just imagine how strong and fast you must be! Why are you letting Novak push you around and treat you the way he does?"

"Yeah, really?" Theron folded his massive arms resentfully. "How about the two of you? Ancient vamp and a Fire Salamander, huh? Well, I can understand Alucard – he is dead, so Novak can make him do whatever he wants. But you, Gunz. You are a goddamn Fire Salamander. I didn't even know your kind still existed!"

"And did you know Santa also exists?" asked Yaroslav stepping between them, his blue eyes sparkling with laughter.

Gunz tore his eyes off Theron and stared at Yaroslav for a moment, before bursting out laughing. Perhaps it was his overly stretched nerves, but he found all this amusing, ridiculous even.

Theron's yellow eyes darted from Yaroslav to Gunz and he joined them laughing.

The sound of slow clapping bounced through the empty dark hall, and Gunz flinched and spun around. George Novak was standing in the doorway, glowering at them with annoyance.

"I hate to interrupt your... whatever that was," he said frostily and Gunz felt goosebumps rising on his skin. "But it's time you remember who you are and why you are here. I can understand these two, but you, Theron! Your job was to keep them restrained, not entertained. And do I see any restraints? No!"

He approached Theron and slapped him across his face. The weretiger gasped, pressing his hand to his cheek and dropped his head.

"I'm sorry, master," he said quietly, keeping his eyes down.

"I'll deal with you later," hissed Novak. "Now, bring these two inside. It's time to get it over with." He pivoted on his heels and headed inside the lab.

"Let's go," said Theron, his voice dull. He pointed at the door and let Gunz and Yaroslav pass through first.

As soon as Gunz crossed the threshold, his breath caught. The walls of the room were infused with dark magic. *This room is a deathtrap*, thought Gunz miserably. *If I go any farther, I won't be able to leave unless Novak lets me out.* He probed the walls with his Salamander's senses just to confirm that the wards Novak placed on the lab were considerably above his level of magical expertise.

As he proceeded inside the lab, the word "deathtrap" took on a completely new meaning for him. He saw Angel. Gunz froze in place, holding his breath, unable to take another step. With his arms twisted behind his back, Angel was suspended lifelessly, supported by chains that seemingly weren't attached to anything, yet they were holding him restrained in midair.

He was in his true form and his dark hair hung in limp

strands over his face. His trench coat lay on the chair next to a table and his shirt was ripped on his chest. Dark red runes were dimly glowing on the chains holding him, and thick drops of blood were trickling down from under the manacles.

"Angel," whispered Gunz, his body filled with lead.

Ignoring everything around him, he approached his friend and gently lifted his hair. Angel was conscious. He raised his eyes and Gunz shuddered. His eyes were completely black, and it was like staring into the void itself – nothing but infinite emptiness. Gunz held Angel's gaze, his heart twisting with sadness, and death stared back at him from the void of his eyes. Angel opened his mouth, but no sound came out and his face contorted in pain.

Gunz felt someone's hand squeezing his shoulder, roughly pulling him away. He stepped back, slowly gaining a grasp on reality and looked around. The lab was an empty room with light gray walls. At least a few thousand square feet, it was as large as any warehouse. Gunz had expected to see some equipment, vials with chemicals, syringes, microscopes or anything that would validate the word "lab", but there was nothing like that in the room.

The windows were tightly closed with heavy window shutters, even though it was dark outside. The electric lights were off, and the room was filled with the shimmering light of candles. The candles were everywhere – on the table, chairs, and on the floor along the walls. A slight burnt smell lingered in the air and long shadows, thrown by unsteady candlelight, were shifting on the floor and walls.

Except for a few empty jars, there was only an office multi-line phone on the table. Mrak Delar was sitting in one of the chairs, slightly leaning forward with his hands crossed on his lap. With his long hair in disarray and deep dark circles under his eyes, the Master of Power looked drained. Novak stood next to him, observing Gunz with a crooked smirk.

"Alucard," he said with a light wave of his hand, but Gunz sensed the dark energy of his malignant magic spiking around him. "Why don't you take a knee, my son. Our mutual friend Gunz and I have business to attend to. I'll deal with you after I'm done with him."

Gunz glanced at Yaroslav and cold sweat beaded his forehead. The vampire's eyes were almost as empty as Angel's. His face relaxed and he slowly lowered down to one knee, bowing his head. Gunz carefully checked him with his Salamander's senses, just to confirm that the necromancer was controlling him.

He glanced back at Angel's desperate situation and a sudden wave of fury rushed through him, igniting his fire. Despite his controller set to maximum, the fire energy enveloped him, and the collar responded with an intense electric shock that almost brought him down to his knees. He grunted, his hands locking and unlocking at his sides as the flames broke through, wrapping around his arms.

Novak's eyes widened in shock and he pulled the controller out, checking its settings. Then he threw the controller back on the table and turned to Mrak Delar.

"Control him, Master of Power," he hissed, anger making his voice shake. "I don't understand how it's possible, but he is able to channel his elemental power through the gray stones magic. I'm about to begin and I can't afford a rebellion or any kind of interruptions from him. Control him or I will squash him like a bug!"

Mrak Delar got up and slowly walked toward Gunz, his every step making the floor quake. Gunz raised his eyes at him, realizing with shock that maybe for the first time in his life, the Ancient Master wasn't in complete control of his power. Mrak Delar stopped a few feet away and took a deep breath.

"Gunz, do not fight. Let go," he ordered, channeling the

elemental power of Fire. His eyes lit up with red light and he extended his arm forward, ready to strike.

Do not fight? Let go? That's a new one. Ignoring the pain, Gunz channeled more of his power, focusing on his own heart, getting ready to fight the Master of Power's control. Mrak Delar slammed him with his power, but Gunz didn't feel the intent to control him. Instead, Mrak's power wrapped around him like a dense fire-shield.

What kind of game is this evil bastard playing now? Gunz thought. In a split-second decision, he focused his fire energy on the Master of Power's heart. He felt it beating within the hold of his power, just like he felt the heart of a wyvern. He squeezed a little, commanding the Master of Power to let go.

Mrak Delar grunted, fighting his control. "No, you can't. It's not possible," he whispered. "Stop... Gunz, no!" He doubled the flow of his power and with overwhelming clarity, Gunz realized the Ancient Master wasn't trying to control him.

He raised his eyes, meeting Mrak's igneous gaze and with shock saw that there was no anger, or mockery, or disdain in his eyes. The Master was silently pleading with him. Gunz's jaw dropped, but he let go.

"Fire Salamander, down!" Mrak Delar commanded, extending his hand forward.

Gunz felt Mrak's power surrounding him with the warm embrace of the fire energy, giving him an extra boost of strength. Still not able to wrap his mind around everything that was happening, he slowly went down to his knees.

"All the way down. Or I swear to God, I'll crush every single bone in your body, boy!" shouted Mrak Delar, increasing the flow of his power. A glowing red hoop materialized around Gunz's body, gently squeezing him.

Gunz moaned, bending forward, his forehead almost touching the floor, and clasped his hands behind his head, like he would be forced to do if Mrak Delar was fully controlling him.

"That's right." Mrak Delar chuckled. "Stay down, until I tell you that you can get up. Am I clear, Salamander?"

"Yes, Master," replied Gunz, doubts tearing him apart. *What the hell is he doing now?*

Mrak Delar sauntered back to Novak. "He's not going to be a problem, Novak," he said coldly. "Now, before you jump into action, care to share with me what we are doing and why? I thought you were planning to make an elixir of immortality, but all these preparations make me think that there is more to it than just a vanilla elixir."

Novak walked around the table and pulled two small jars containing a bright red liquid out of one of the drawers.

"Your elixir of immortality, Master. I always keep my word," he said dryly, offering him both jars. "One for your wife, as we agreed, and as an extra bonus for all your hard work, one for you. After all, you helped me capture Death. And since there are no known ways of killing Death, he may keep a grudge against you." Novak cackled derisively. "So, you may need some help to avoid his wrath."

Mrak Delar glanced at Angel and visibly cringed. He took both jars and put them in his pocket, avoiding Novak's mocking stare.

"Thanks," he said dryly, "but I still would like to know what you're planning to do and why."

"I'm sure you would," replied Novak arrogantly, "but it's on a need-to-know basis only. I'm sorry, partner, but I don't think you fall into that category. Nevertheless, I don't mind if you stay and assist me. In case our young flaming friend decides to give me a hard time."

Novak turned his back to Mrak Delar, completely ignoring him and headed to Angel. Channeling his dark magic, he kneeled under him and drew a glowing circle on the floor. He started his chant, drawing something in the air with his fingers. As a dark red rune materialized within the circle, Novak stepped out, wiping his hands on his pants.

Angel's eyes flew wide-open as he stared at the rune gleaming right under him. The dark void of his eyes lit up with a black light as his gaze darted to Gunz and he jerked in his restraints. Gunz observed his reaction and his heart pounded against his chest as fear swirled through him. It was unmistakable – whatever Novak was doing scared Death himself.

Novak went back to the table and reached for the drawers, but Mrak Delar blocked his way.

"You need to stop what you're doing, Novak," he said coldly. "I recognized the rune and I can't allow you go through with your plan. To create a Living-Dead Flame you need to kill the Fire Salamander and I can't let you do it."

"Why is that, Master?" asked Novak snidely. "Did you have a change of heart and suddenly you care about the life of this cocky little lizard?"

"No, I don't," replied Mrak Delar, taking a step closer to Novak. "But if Kal finds out what you did to his child, he'll find a way to kill an indestructible dark sorcerer and I can guarantee that your death isn't going to be easy."

Novak cackled. "I'm not afraid of you or Kal. He's nothing but another puny lizard. None of you stand a chance against me!"

He wielded his magic, gathering it in his hands so fast that Mrak Delar didn't get a chance to react. A dark stream of undiluted magical energy slammed him in the chest, and he flew across the room, hitting a wall with his back. He fell on the floor, struggling for breath.

"Stay down, Master of Power, if you ever want to see your lovely wife again," he hissed, staring down at the Ancient Master.

Gunz jerked, ready to spring into action, but caught the

warning gaze of Mrak Delar and remained on his knees. In the meantime, Novak went back to his desk and produced a long dagger. The weapon glistened in his hands with the reflected light of the candles. Angel gasped and thrashed in his restraints.

Mrak Delar got back to his feet and covered the space between them in a few jumps, seizing Novak's wrist. Gunz watched the black eyes of the Master of Power lock with the sinister eyes of the necromancer and held his breath, nauseating fear rising to his throat.

Novak's eyes didn't look human anymore. The glowing yellow eyes with dark-red vertical pupils of the Lord of Chaos were staring back at the Ancient Master. Gunz froze staring at the necromancer in horror. *Voron was right... Morena infused his soul with the energy of Chaos.*

"Did you seriously think you've got what it takes to stand up to me?" Novak hissed, and a dark hoop of his magical energy wrapped around Mrak Delar's neck, raising him up in the air.

Novak twisted his fist, wrapping Mrak tighter in his deadly magic. The Master of Power groaned, fighting him but unable to break free. The necromancer moved his hand up, lifting Mrak Delar higher and turned back to Angel.

"Now, where were we?" He pulled Angel's torn shirt apart and slashed his chest with the dagger.

A soul-crushing howl erupted from Angel's lips as steel cut through his flesh. A long gash opened up on his chest but there was no blood. A thick clear liquid, shimmering with silvery light, slowly trickled out of the gruesome wound, falling one drop at a time. The drops didn't reach the floor, accumulating into a silver orb a few inches above it. Novak watched as the silvery orb grew bigger, his eyes gleaming with a maniacal yellow glow.

Distracted, the necromancer didn't notice Mrak Delar escaping the restraints of his magic. The Ancient Master drew another rune in the air and infused it with his power. Slamming his hand against it, he whispered a summoning spell.

As he did, the whole building trembled, the windows jingled and the empty jars that were sitting on the table fell and rolled to the floor, shattering into small pieces. The energy of magic seemed to quadruple within a second and a few candles went out as a gust of cold wind rushed through the room. Gunz raised his head, recognizing the magical signature and a slow smile stretched his lips.

Novak spun around and met Mrak's cold gaze. "You didn't think that I came alone, did you, necromancer?" growled the Master of Power.

"Who did you summon?" hissed Novak, his eyes looking more serpent-like than before. Since Mrak Delar ignored his question, he yelled again, "Who! Did! You! Summon!"

The walls of the room trembled again, and the windows imploded, showering everyone with shattered glass. An ear-splitting racket filled the room as the attacker started breaking through the wards, fighting the dark magic that blocking the entrance. Novak muttered a spell and a large hidden door, which wasn't visible before, materialized in the opposite wall.

"I never trusted you, Mrak Delar! And I was right!" he bellowed. Snake-like fangs extended in his mouth, a foul green poison dripping down his chin. "A man who betrays his friends can never be trusted. But you underestimated me, too. I came prepared!"

He snapped his fingers and dark smoke rolled into the lab through the open door. As the smoke settled down, Gunz saw a small army of demons flooding the lab, polluting the air with its suffocating demonic energy. Some of the demons were possessing human bodies, but most of them were pureblood demons like the ones he saw in the Dark Nav. A stench of sulphur invaded his senses, making his stomach twist with nausea.

The demons possessing the human bodies weren't a problem neither for him nor for the Master of Power. However, the pure-blood demons were the spawns of hell and they weren't easy to get rid of. He was ready to get up when the main door flew from its hinges with a thunderous bang and a brilliant white light enveloped the room.

"Aidan," whispered Gunz, feeling surprised and relieved at the same time.

"Aodh mac Lir!" hissed Novak, staggering backward toward his army of demons.

"A god," noted Mrak Delar matter-of-factly, gently lowering himself down to the floor. "You see? I'm answering your question, Novak. I summoned a god of the Otherworld to send you back to the dark hole you clawed your way out of."

"I don't think your so called god can," replied Novak smugly, a crooked smirk cracking his arrogant face. "I don't think any of you have what it takes."

The white light slowly dimmed down, and Aidan stepped through the threshold. He was in his full godly form, dressed like an ancient hunter with a bow and quiver on his back. In his hand he was holding his sword that was glistening like ice. His eyes burned with the energy of his magic, and the walls trembled slightly responding to his every move.

"Give it up!" roared Aidan, pointing his sword at Novak.

Novak just cackled. He threw a challenging stare at Aidan and focused on Yaroslav. A dark magical energy struck the vampire, surrounding him in a tight cocoon, and he slowly got up to his feet, unsheathing his katana.

"Master, I'm yours to command," said Yaroslav with a bow, his empty eyes glued to Novak.

"Destroy the Salamander!" yelled Novak at Yaroslav. Then he turned to his demonic army. "Attack! Kill the Master of Power and keep the half-breed busy!"

In a split-second, all hell broke loose. The demons charged

all at once. Aidan stepped forward and met their attack with a mighty blast of his godly power. The blinding white light rushed forward, devouring the demons possessing the human bodies, evaporating their hosts and their demonic essence in place. But the pure-blood demons withstood the attack. Their furious battle cry rose as they charged at Aidan and Mrak Delar.

Yaroslav turned to Gunz and moved forward into a frontal attack with his katana at his shoulder. Gunz sprung to his feet, manifesting his sword just in time to deflect Yaroslav's attack. He connected with the elemental Fire, powering his way through the resistance of the gray stones magic. Now, using his Fire Salamander's senses, he could detect Yaroslav's movement, despite his vampire's speed. And as fast as the vampire moved, Gunz was able to avoid his every attack.

"Yaroslav, wake up!" he yelled, stepping aside to avoid his next strike. "Slavik, stop!"

There was no way of reasoning with him. His dead-empty eyes set on Gunz, Yaroslav moved with one deadly purpose – to destroy the Fire Salamander.

"Ignius!" shouted Gunz raising a smoldering circle of fire around Yaroslav and turned around, searching the lab for Mrak Delar.

Between the dark swirling smoke of the demons and blinding brilliance of Aidan's godly power-strikes, it was hard to find him. Finally, he spotted the Ancient Master. He was standing not far from Aidan with his black sword in his hands.

Gunz sent a small amount of his power energy toward him to attract his attention. Mrak Delar snapped around, a silent question in his eyes, swirling with the colors of power.

"Master, can you break the necromancer's control over Yaroslav?" yelled Gunz.

"Yes, but—," started to say Mrak Delar, but was interrupted by Aidan.

The god of the Otherworld grabbed three arrows from his

quiver and positioned them on his bow. "Mrak, help Gunz!" he yelled over the noise of the howling demons. "I'll be fine here. Almost done anyway!"

He infused the arrows with his power and let them fly. Blazing with the white light, the arrows cut through the suffocating smoke of the demonic energy, finding their targets. Three more demons fell on the floor, slowly disintegrating, leaving a puddle of disgusting goo behind.

Mrak Delar rushed back to Gunz and halted before the flaming circle. Within the circle, Yaroslav was pouncing like a wild tiger in a cage. He couldn't go through the fire without killing himself, yet the necromancer's magic was demanding that he do it and kill his target.

"Mrak," yelled Gunz into Mrak Delar's ear, "we need to get Yaroslav back to normal! He is the only one who can kill Novak. He's the trigger, and Novak knows it."

"Keep his attention on you," said Mrak Delar and circled around the fire.

"Slavik," yelled Gunz, "come get me, dimwit!" He walked through the fire and stopped at the edge, waving his hand at the vampire.

Yaroslav snarled, exposing his blade-like fangs but didn't get a chance for another attack. Mrak Delar's arm wrapped around his neck, squeezing it. Applying his magic and his physical strength, the Master of Power brought the vampire down to his knees and started to chant softly. Yaroslav groaned, dropping his katana and leaned back powerlessly. Mrak Delar kept chanting until Yaroslav passed out. The Master of Power gently lowered him on the floor and waved his hand, ordering the fire to cease.

"He is clean," said Mrak Delar, looking up at Gunz. "Now what?"

"Now we're going to kill Novak—"

A loud scream interrupted him. The howl of anguish mixed

with horror was rising over the noise of Aidan finishing up the remaining demons. Gunz spun around and fear locked him in place, breathless. Angel was screaming, but it wasn't only the pain that forced this terrible sound out of him. With his eyes fixed on Novak, he appeared to be scared and furious and desperate at the same time.

The necromancer stood next to Angel, a carnivorous smirk distorting his face that hardly looked human. His eyes, the eyes of a serpent, shone with a malevolent gleam and large fangs that would put Yaroslav's vampire fangs to shame, protruded from his mouth.

He was holding his hand out, parallel to the ground, and a silvery orb made of pure essence of death hovered an inch above his opened palm. Novak touched the orb, muttering something under his breath and set it on fire. But it wasn't a regular fire. The black flames rose ominously over the orb.

Gunz stared at the black fire knowing perfectly well what it meant for him. Mrak Delar put his hand on his shoulder and he flinched, tearing his eyes off the magical flames that were his imminent death. Aidan, finally done with the demons, stepped between Gunz and Novak, shielding him with his body.

"Do not move, Gunz," Aidan said, holding his arm back.

"But he has to," hissed Novak mockingly, his disturbing smile getting wider. "The Black Flames fueled by the essence of death. Master Mrak Delar, I've heard you were one of the most knowledgeable Masters of Power in the history of Kendral. Please enlighten your friends on the meaning of it."

Mrak Delar visibly shuddered, throwing a haunted gaze at Gunz. "The Black Fire sustained by the essence of death and touched by a Fire Salamander," said Mrak Delar, his voice thick and hoarse, "creates the Living-Dead Flame – the most powerful magical weapon, capable of destroying anything it touches, mundane or magical, tangible or immaterial, dead or alive."

"Very good, my dear partner," jeered Novak, strolling toward them. He halted a step away from Aidan and smirked. "Now, Master, I have a feeling, your young friend thinks he has a choice in the matter. Why don't you explain to him and all of us here, why he has no choice but to touch the Black Fire, sacrificing his young life."

Mrak Delar bowed his head and sighed. "If a Fire Salamander doesn't complete the process, the burning orb will continue growing, expending exponentially and consuming everything in its way until…" His voice faded into silence and he turned to Gunz, true tears glistening in his black eyes. "I'm sorry, Gunz…"

"No!" shouted Aidan. "We'll find some other—"

Gunz put his hand on his friend's shoulder and smiled sadly. "It's okay, Aidan. I don't think there is any other way," he said quietly. "You know how it is. The needs of many… the greater good… and so forth and so on."

"The greater good?" echoed Aidan, his eyes shifting to Mrak Delar. "Every life has a meaning… every life counts… The lives of those we love even more so."

Gunz walked around Aidan and approached Novak. The Black Flames were crackling over the silvery orb. Gunz moved his hand over the fire without touching it. The flames stretched up, trying to lick his skin and he pulled his hand away. It was his death… What happens when a Fire Salamander dies? Where will he end up? In which realm of Death? He glanced up over Novak's shoulder, looking for Angel and froze, astounded.

Angel was gone. The broken chains were lying on the floor and the rune that was holding him in place had been partially destroyed. Gunz spun around, searching the lab, but he was nowhere to be found. Novak also twirled around, and his mouth dropped open. He looked from left to right, fear twisting his face.

"Who?" mumbled Novak, the hand that was supporting the

deadly orb trembled. "How? None of you could... You were all busy..."

Abruptly, a muscled arm wrapped around Novak's neck, squeezing him in a deadly choke. "You forgot about me, master," growled Theron. "I'm not going to wait for you to deal with me later. I am going to deal with you now. On my terms."

Novak wheezed something incoherent as Theron started to transform, his figure growing taller and burlier. A cold breeze rushed through the lab, extinguishing every single candle and only the Black Fire kept burning, providing neither heat nor light. The silence became absolute and it seemed like the darkness swallowed every sound.

Slowly and soundlessly, Angel descended from the ceiling, the magic of Death surrounding him with a blackness darker than the darkness of the room. He glided on the floor and walked toward Novak. His long black hair and his torn shirt were flowing as if in the wind, even though the air was absolutely still.

Novak twitched, but couldn't get away from the bearhug of the weretiger. Angel carefully took the flaming orb, supporting it in the palm of his hand, just the way Novak had been doing just a moment ago.

"Gunz, please step away," he whispered and in the silence of the room his hushed whisper sounded louder than any shouting would and scarier than an explosion. "It is not your time to die yet, young Salamander."

His other hand slid over the orb, his long fingers moving slowly, drawing complicated shapes. As his fingers moved, a small dark portal opened up under his hand. He brought his hands together, pushing the orb through the portal and when he lowered his hands, the orb and the Black Fire were gone.

Angel turned his deadly gaze at Novak, his face darkened by rage. Novak met his eyes with a cold smirk.

"You can't kill me, Death. You no longer have a say so over

my destiny," he hissed, pushing against Theron's hold. He laughed maniacally, his serpent eyes glowing brighter.

"You're right – he can't… But I can…"

Gunz heard Yaroslav's voice and shuddered at how deadly the vampire sounded. He glanced at him over his shoulder and saw Yaroslav levitating a few inches above the floor. In his right hand, he was holding the old revolver, aiming it at Novak.

"Prince Yaroslav Potemkin," hissed Novak, venom dripping down his chin.

"Grigory Rasputin. I pray this time the Dark Nav will keep your soul from rising," responded Yaroslav coldly and slowly pressed the trigger.

CHAPTER 32

~ ZANE BURNS, A.K.A. GUNZ ~

The sound of the gunshot tore the silence to shreds. Time slowed down, and Gunz held his breath, following the fiery trail the enchanted bullet was leaving in the air. The bullet reached its target and burned through Rasputin's skull right between his eyebrows.

Time stopped.

Just for a heartbeat, everything stilled.

The deafening silence was louder than the gunshot.

Then an ear-piercing shriek broke through the silence, restarting the flow of time. The necromancer screamed, the sound of his voice bouncing off the walls, repeating over and over. As the bullet exited the back of his head, he pressed his hands to his forehead and dropped to his knees, leaning backward. His snake-like eyes bulged, threatening to explode out of his skull, blood streaming from his ears, nose and eyes.

For a moment, Gunz thought Rasputin's head was going to blow up, but it didn't happen. Slowly, his body started to melt away, dripping down into a disgusting puddle of slime. In a manner, it reminded him of the way pureblood demons disintegrated when they were killed in this world.

No one said a word, watching with horror the slow demise of George Novak. Yaroslav landed on the floor. Still holding the revolver in his hand, he stared at his disintegrating enemy with so much loathing that if Chernobog's curse didn't kill him, the vampire would do it with his own hands.

A few minutes later, it was all over. George Novak was no more, just a puddle of gunk left on the floor. The dark spirit of Grigory Rasputin levitated ominously above the revolting remains of his body.

"Gunz, summon Chernobog. Now!" barked Yaroslav, his whole body locked by rage.

"Allow me," whispered Angel and his eerie whisper was louder and scarier than Yaroslav's shouting.

He expanded his arms wide, throwing his head back. The wind picked up inside the lab, fanning Angel's black hair around his face. The dark vortex of a portal opened up in front of him. Angel threw one look at Rasputin and the evil spirit visibly shrunk under his deadly stare.

Angel touched the blackness of the portal, slowly drawing an invisible shape with his long fingers and whispered, "Chernobog… I summon thee…"

The whole building shook like during an earthquake. The vortex of the portal swirled faster, and the Slavic god of Destruction materialized in the room accompanied by Voron. He surveyed the room, his heavy dark eyes stopping on each person present and waved his hand, igniting every single candle at once.

Without saying a word, the Lord of the Dark Nav approached the spirit of Rasputin. The spirit wailed, a chilling horrifying sound escaping the gaping hole of its mouth. Its outline got blurry and he shimmered in and out of focus.

"Nothing that's dead should be in the realm of the living," said Chernobog, glowering at the malignant spirit. The spirit shrieked, struggling to get away, but he couldn't move.

Chernobog opened his hand and a wooden box materialized in his palm in a puff of dark smoke. It was made out of dark oak and sealed with strips of iron. The ancient god touched the box and it slowly opened up. As it gradually sucked the spirit inside, the box lit up with the magical energy of the Dark Nav.

Chernobog closed the box and sealed it. He turned to Yaroslav and nodded to him. "For now, it's over, Yaroslav Potemkin," he said with a sigh. "But for as long as you walk the realm of the living, you are the trigger of the curse I placed on Rasputin's soul. It'll never change."

"I understand, my lord, and I'll keep it in mind," replied the vampire coldly, "but I pray, I will never have to come face to face with Grigory Rasputin again."

The god of Destruction smiled, the corners of his mouth lifting just a little. "Fire Salamander," he said turning to Gunz. "Did you find out what Rasputin's purpose was? Why did my wife release him from the Dark Nav and infuse him with the energy of Chaos?"

"No, my lord," Gunz said quietly, bowing his head. "The only thing I know is that he was trying to conjure the Living-Dead Flame. But why and how he was planning to use it, I don't know."

Chernobog frowned and turned to Mrak Delar. Under his reproachful stare, the Master of Power shrunk. "You failed, Ancient Master," said Chernobog. While his voice was heavy, he didn't sound angry. Just tired. "You had one mission and you failed it."

"I did, my lord," replied Mrak Delar without meeting the ancient deity's eyes. "There are no excuses for that, and I accept the consequences of my failure."

Aidan stepped in, raising his hand. "That's not true," he said calmly. "Mrak Delar didn't fail his mission, but he couldn't proceed any further. It was too risky. Rasputin didn't trust him entirely and to allow this dangerous maniac to conjure the Living-Dead Flame was too dangerous."

Chernobog nodded. "Be that as it may, Aodh mac Lir, the Ancient Master failed his mission. I'm not here to judge him or reprimand him in any way. Don't get me wrong, while I understand his reasons, now we are all going to pay the consequences of his failure and they will be severe.

"Rasputin wasn't the only dark soul that was released that night from the Dark Nav. I believe they were all infused with the energy of Chaos and each of them had their own purpose. We had one piece of this puzzle in our hands and we failed to discover its purpose... What a shame."

"Maybe we failed but not entirely," said Gunz. "We know he was planning to conjure the Living-Dead Flame. We just need to puzzle out what he planned to do with it."

Both Chernobog and Voron exchanged a quick look and laughed.

"That can take a while," said Voron, patting Gunz on his shoulder. "You can destroy anything with this weapon. I mean – anything at all. No exception."

"Let me ask," mused Gunz. "He could rip the veil with it. Couldn't he?"

"Yes," replied Voron.

"From what Mrak Delar explained, the Living-Dead Flame can destroy even non-tangible things, like ancient curses. Am I right?"

"Yes," replied Voron and swallowed hard as understanding transformed his expression.

The silence became eerie. Gunz observed everyone in the room. It seemed everyone had the same horrifying thought on their mind.

"Perhaps, I should talk to Veles about keeping an eye on Mount Karasova," said Chernobog, shaking his head.

"Sounds like a good idea," agreed Gunz quietly.

"It's time for me to go. I can't leave the Dark Nav unattended for long," said Chernobog with a light bow. "If something new comes up, do let me know."

He took Voron's elbow and both went through the portal. As soon as they were gone, Angel closed it and turned to Mrak Delar. The Ancient Master withheld his furious gaze, but his body stiffened.

"It's time we had a little chat, backstabber," hissed Angel.

Slowly covering the distance between them, he stopped in front of the Master of Power and raised his hand. A dark energy of death swirled in his open palm, blue electrical discharges flashing within it. Mrak Delar's eyes darted to Angel's hand and he smirked mirthlessly.

Unbuttoning his shirt, he kneeled before Death. "Do it," he said calmly, exposing his chest.

"No!" shouted Aidan, grabbing Angel's arm. "No, Angel. You know it's not his time. And there is a reason for that."

"There had better be," hissed Angel, lowering his hand, dissolving the energy of his magic.

"I'll tell you all the details when we get back home," promised Aidan, pulling the Master of Power up, back to his feet. "For now, you all need to know one thing – Mrak Delar never betrayed any of us."

"It had better be a good explanation," muttered Angel, irritation breaking through in his voice. He extended his hand toward the table and his trench coat flew to his hand. He put it on and vanished from the room.

Gunz looked at Mrak Delar, pain ripping his soul apart. The Master of Power caught his gaze and a haunted expression shadowed his features.

"Gunz, let me explain…"

Gunz came closer to him, shaking his head. "I understand. If Aidan said you didn't betray us, I believe him… But how could you? How could you do it to me and—" He swallowed and bit his lip. Fueled by pain, anger rose in him. He swung his arm, infused with his magic, and punched Mrak Delar in his jaw.

The Master of Power dropped to the floor and blacked out for a moment. Gunz stood, staring down at him, not sure how he felt. Mrak Delar opened his eyes and carefully probed his jaw with his fingers. He remained on the floor, holding his arm up as if he was afraid that Gunz would punch him again. Gunz knew better. Mrak Delar could disable him with his magic in a heartbeat and seeing the Master of Power so defeated at his feet on the floor, made him feel even worse.

"Get up, Master Jackass," he said flatly. "I have some unfinished business and you're going to help me."

Mrak Delar got up and stood silently, not raising his eyes.

"Gunz, can I trust you not to disfigure him if I leave?" asked Aidan with doubt in his voice. "I need to go downstairs and relieve the Guardians. They don't need to shadow the building anymore. And then I need to go home and have a talk with Angel."

"Yeah, you can go, Aidan." Gunz chuckled. "I think you should worry more about what Angel would do to him instead of what I would do." Aidan gave him an arched stare, and Gunz rolled his eyes. "Go already. I'm not going to touch him. Cross my heart." He drew a flaming cross over his chest with his finger.

"Firetwat." Aidan rolled his eyes and vanished from the room.

As soon as Aidan was gone, Mrak Delar raised his eyes and cleared his throat.

"How can I help you?" he asked calmly like Gunz didn't just send his ass flying to the floor.

"You can start by removing the gray stone jewelry from all of us," replied Gunz, waving in Yaroslav's and Theron's direction. "I've heard you have some experience in doing it without a key."

"I can do it," said Mrak Delar, but Gunz sensed unease in his voice.

"You're not sure," stated Gunz, frowning. "Why?"

"The last time I took the gray stone jewelry off without a key, my hands were burnt to the bone," he explained with a sigh. "And I had to free just one person. Here I have to do it for three people. But I'll try…"

Mrak stepped closer to Gunz and took his hand, carefully probing the bracelet on his left wrist. Gunz sucked in a sharp breath as the gray stones magic retaliated against the intrusion. He jerked his hand away when Theron approached them and halted in front of Mrak Delar, shifting from foot to foot uncomfortably.

"Master Mrak Delar," he said with a respectful bow, "if I may?"

"What is it, Theron?"

"I know where the key is," said Theron simply. "You don't need to hurt yourself."

The weretiger ran to the table and opened the drawer. For a while he was fumbling with the contents until he finally found the key. He brought it over and offered it to Mrak Delar. The key didn't look like a key. It was just a thin silver stick, about two inches long. Mrak took the key from Theron, thanking him and turned to Gunz.

"Gunz, you're first. Lie down."

"Why?" asked Gunz, taking a step back.

"Taking the gray stone jewelry off is almost as bad as putting it on," he explained with a sigh. "I have to put you to sleep before I do it."

"Hold on," objected Gunz, raising his hand up. "No one said anything about you knocking me out. It's not like I don't trust you, but I really don't trust you."

"Yaroslav," called Mrak Delar dryly. As soon as the vampire came closer, he unsheathed his black sword and gave it to him.

"Put this sword to my neck. If you just suspect that I'm planning to harm Gunz, kill me. Am I clear?"

An icy smile twisted the vampire's lips. "It would be my pleasure, Master," he said, placing the sword to Mrak's neck. "So, tread lightly."

* * *

GUNZ WOKE up a few hours later and before opening his eyes, reached to his neck and explored it with his fingers. The gray stone jewelry was gone. He smiled with relief, then he opened his eyes and saw Mrak Delar sitting on the floor next to him, talking with Yaroslav and Theron in a hushed voice.

I'm finally free... Ugh, never again...

He sat up and called Yaroslav. All three of them turned around, but only Theron got up. The weretiger walked to the table and brought back a small box. It was beautifully gift-wrapped and had a name tag attached to it. Theron gave the box to Gunz and he took it from his hands cautiously, like he was expecting a snake to spring out and bite him.

"What is it?" asked Gunz, turning the box in his hands. Inside, something fell and rolled from side to side. He glanced at Yaroslav and Mrak Delar, but they both shrugged.

"Novak left this box for you," explained Yaroslav. "I recognized his handwriting. Look at the name tag."

Gunz read his name on the tag and started to tear the wrapping paper.

"Are you sure you want to open it?" asked Mrak Delar. "There can't be anything good in there."

"Unless I open this box and take a look, we'll never know," objected Gunz dryly, throwing the leftover of the wrapping paper on the floor, and opened the box.

Inside there was a small glass vial and a piece of paper, folded in two. Gunz picked up the vial and looked through it at the candlelight. It was filled with clear liquid that appeared to be slightly thicker than water. He carefully unfolded the paper and started to read aloud.

"Mr. Zane Burns.

I am writing this letter to thank you for your ever-flaming bleeding heart.

Mrak Delar was right. You good folks are all so predictable. It is your desire to always do the right thing that makes you predictable in the first place. It makes you weak and vulnerable to those who are willing to go the extra mile and explore other opportunities, outside the boundaries of the so called "good and evil".

Having said that, here is my parting gift to you, boy. In your hands you're holding the life of the woman you're madly in love with. Your first owner, Kogan, told me how deeply you were grieving. I always keep my promises. So, I used whatever I had left from the Apple of Youth and the Water of Life to create this elixir for you.

So, here you go. Inside this tiny vial, there is the only elixir in all the worlds that can separate her essence and life force from that of the Lord of Chaos. All you need to do is go back to Mount Karasova and spill this elixir over the sacrificial stone. You do it and she will be free to love and to cherish... and do whatever else the two of you are doing when you are alone together.

You can save her and bring her back to life.

Or you can kill her.

Again.

The decision is yours.

Grigory Rasputin."

Gunz's hands shook and he dropped the letter on the floor. Mrak Delar picked it up and quickly re-read it.

"Gunz—"

"Shut up," whispered Gunz, backing away from him. He squeezed his head, his fingers digging into his hair. "Shut up! Don't say one goddamn word!"

For a moment he stood like this, breathing hard, thoughts

crowding his mind, and no one dared to say anything. Then he lowered his hands, putting the vial into the pocket of his pants.

"There is something I need to do," he said, his voice painfully hoarse. "It's time I paid my debts."

He walked to the table and picked up the phone. Pressing the receiver to his ear, he dialed Jim's phone number. It was the middle of the night and Gunz was counting the beeps, hoping that Jim would answer the call. When he did, Gunz sighed with relief.

"Jim, hi," he said, "sorry for the late-night call—"

Jim interrupted him. The agent wasn't upset with the late call. He was furious with Gunz for his disrespectful behavior and all his "shenanigans". In so many quite colorful words, Jim expressed how he felt about all that, without holding anything back.

"I know, Jim. I'm a goddamn asshole and I deserve everything you just told me," said Gunz peacefully. "But I'm also the asshole who just destroyed the Head of California House and about to deliver you the key to the Florida underground fighting circles. Did Mishka talk to you?"

Jim confirmed that the wyvern delivered the message and that he was ready for Gunz's call.

"Perfect," said Gunz. "Meet me at the address Mishka gave you by 8 PM. Bring your friends."

He chuckled darkly and hung up the phone.

CHAPTER 33

~ ZANE BURNS, A.K.A. GUNZ ~

At 8 PM sharp, Gunz stood at the gate that was blocking his way to Mr. Kogan's mansion. Mrak Delar, Yaroslav and Theron were standing by his side. Even though Mrak Delar had offered Yaroslav and Theron to take them anywhere they wanted to go, both decided to stay with Gunz and make sure his mission went as planned.

Gunz probed the gate, confirming that the Head of Florida House had wards and protection spells placed on it and on the wall surrounding the property. His gaze followed the road leading from the gate to the mansion, and all the painful memories rose to the surface, making him cringe inwardly.

He pulled out a cheap prepaid mobile phone he had bought before coming here and dialed Jim's number.

"Jim, are you in position?" he asked.

"Yes, everyone is in position," replied Jim. "All teams, all over the state."

"We're about to start," warned Gunz, slowly gathering his elemental power in his hands.

"Gunz, no matter what. I need him alive," said Jim quietly. "I can't imagine how you feel, but I must have him alive and well. You understand me?"

"You have no idea what you're asking of me —," Gunz started to say, muscles tense in his jaw, but cut himself off and added, "Stand by."

He hung up the phone and put it in his pocket. "Mrak, do you see what I see?" he asked, pointing at the gate.

Mrak Delar nodded, a cold smirk curving his lips. "I see it. I don't see a problem though."

He approached the gate and placed his hands on it, directing his magic at the wards. Gunz opened his magical sight, watching the Master of Power at work with awe. He still had a hard time getting over everything Mrak Delar had done while pretending to side with his enemy. Since he had met the Ancient Master, that was the first time he had to witness his dark side.

Nevertheless, love or hate, he had to admit that as a Master of Power and a wizard, Mrak Delar was in a league of his own. It wasn't only that he was knowledgeable and extremely gifted magically, but he had a natural finesse and class that was showing in anything he was doing, no matter how trivial his task was. Gunz thought that even if this man was tasked with cleaning toilets, with a dirty mop in his hands, he would look just as regal and noble as any knight of King Arthur's court.

The wards that Kogan's wizard placed on his gate were child's play for the Ancient Master. After a few minutes, all the wards and protection spells were gone, leaving the entrance into Kogan's property wide open. Mrak Delar touched the lock on the gate and whispered, *"Recludius".* Then he pushed the heavy gate open and bowed elegantly, pointing inside.

"After you, my lords."

They crossed inside and walked through the park toward the mansion. They made it all the way to the building without acquiring any unwanted attention. Even if the Head of Florida

House realized that he had uninvited guests, he didn't make his presence known yet.

Gunz ran up the steps and placed his hand on the door handle. *"Recludius,"* he said the spell in Dragon tongue and pushed the door. The door opened up quietly, but as much as he wanted to charge in guns blazing, he suppressed his anger and halted in the doorway.

He sharpened his Salamander's senses, probing the lobby of the mansion and smirked, giving an arched stare to Mrak Delar. He recognized the magical signature of Kogan's captive fighters, tainted by the magic of gray stones.

Gunz turned to Yaroslav. "One more captive event, Alucard?" he asked, chuckling darkly. "Let's give my old owner a show he'll never forget." He pulled his Swiss army knife out of his pocket and transformed it into a medieval sword.

"Any time," said the vampire, unsheathing his katana, his devilish grin displaying his sharp fangs.

Gunz turned to Theron, but the man was gone, replaced by a giant Siberian tiger, his orange fur shining in the electric lights of the mansion. The tiger growled, softly rubbing his shoulder against Gunz's side.

"I guess, it's a yes from Theron," said Gunz with a smirk.

"I don't think you'll need your toy," said Mrak Delar, jerking his thumb toward Gunz's sword. "You want a show? We'll give this friggin' slaver a show he'll remember for the rest of his useless life."

Laughing ominously, the Master of Power rose a few feet in the air and spread his arms, throwing his head back. Dark stormy clouds quickly gathered above the mansion. The electric lights went off and the house got submerged into darkness. Lightning forked through the dark sky, for a split-second illuminating the mansion, and thunder rolled above their heads.

The ground quaked and the walls of the mansion swayed as if the building was nothing but a flimsy house of cards. Mrak

Delar roared, striking forward with his hand and the thunder echoed his mighty battle cry. The walls of the house trembled under the pressure of his magic and a large part of the façade fell through, exploding inside the lobby in a shower of dust and debris.

Mrak lowered himself softly to the ground and gathered the power of Air, sending a hurricane force wind through the gaping hole that once was an entrance door. Terror-filled screams carried through the howling of the winds. Mrak Delar twisted his fist and glanced at Gunz over his shoulder.

"I believe these captive fighters of yours are ready now for a peaceful negotiation," he said, a boyish grin splitting his face. "You can sheath your swords, guys. Something tells me they won't be necessary."

As the winds died out, Gunz followed Mrak Delar through the hole into the lobby, or whatever was left of it. Theron, who chose to remain in his tiger form, fell into step with him and Yaroslav with his katana at the ready, closed the procession.

Gunz walked inside and halted with his jaw dropped. All ten of Kogan's captive fighters and Sensei himself were in the room, pinned to the wall by an invisible force. They struggled to get free to no avail.

The Sensei's furious eyes landed on Gunz and he pushed with his massive chest against the restraints of Mrak's magic. His eyes lit up with a yellow light as he tried to transform. After a moment, he realized that he couldn't do it and stopped his fruitless attempts.

"Gunz," he said, sounding almost pleading, "please tell your friend to let go. I swear, if I knew it was you, I wouldn't fight you anyway. None of us would."

"Like I said…" Mrak Delar waved his hand at the immobilized fighters.

"Where are Kogan and his bitch?" asked Gunz coldly. "Tell me, and I'll let all of you go."

Sensei laughed bitterly. "Do you seriously think I want to protect that dumbass after everything he has done to us? I wish I could rip his heart out with my own hands." His eyes lit up brighter with a furious glow. "But I think I'll leave it up to you. You'll find him on the second floor. In his bedroom, behind the curtain, there is a hidden door. Him and his wife are in their panic room."

"Panic room, eh?" asked Gunz, chuckling. "I think right now is a good time for him to panic." He turned to Mrak Delar and asked, "Mrak, do you still have the key for the gray stone jewelry?"

Mrak Delar nodded, reaching in his pocket and offered the key to Gunz. He took the key and approached the werewolf.

"Sensei," he said calmly, "this silver stick is the key that will unlock your collar and bracelets. I must warn you that unlocking the gray stone jewelry is almost as painful as installing them."

"I don't care," growled Sensei. "I want... No, I need my freedom. I don't care about the pain."

"Fine."

Gunz flicked his eyebrow at Mrak Delar, asking him to remove the power field that was holding the captive fighters immobilized. As they fell on the floor, breathing hard, Gunz approached the werewolf and gave him the key.

"If I catch any of you on the streets engaged in any kind of questionable activities, I'll kill you without hesitation," he said icily. "Consider yourselves warned."

"I swear, you will never see or hear of any of us again," replied Sensei, offering his hand. "Thank you for what you did for us today."

Gunz shook his hand and turned to his friends. "It's time for me to say hello to my owner and his lovely wife."

* * *

GUNZ STOOD in front of a heavily armored door, staring at it with loathing as if he could see the faces of Robert and Clarissa Kogan already. He put his hands on the door, resting his forehead on the cold metal and took a deep breath. All he had to do was to say the spell to unlock it, but his internal turmoil was making his elemental power unmanageable and he needed to be in control.

"I can open it for you," offered Mrak Delar, gently touching his shoulder.

Gunz flinched and turned around, his igneous eyes burning through Mrak Delar. "Blow it up," he said through his clenched teeth. "Don't open it. I want a loud bang."

Sadness clouded the Ancient Master's features for a moment as he nodded to Gunz. "Stay back," he commanded and channeled his power, redirecting it at the door. A loud bang rattled the silence of the mansion and the armed door exploded inward, warped into a shapeless chunk of metal by the magical impact.

Mrak Delar stepped aside, allowing Gunz to pass through first. He walked in and stopped. As the dust settled, he saw Mr. and Mrs. Kogan cowering in the corner, his arms wrapped around her protectively. An unwanted memory flashed through Gunz's mind – that moment before Kogan sold him to the California House, when Mrs. Kogan visited him in his cell. With painful clarity he remembered himself sitting on the floor, covering his face with his arms, cornered and vulnerable. Just like they were sitting now. He stared down at them and felt nothing but resentment.

Mrak Delar and Yaroslav stood on either side of him as Theron lay down next to his feet, his orange eyes of a predator hungrily watching Mr. and Mrs. Kogan's every move. Mr. Kogan raised his eyes, meeting Gunz's deadly gaze. He shuddered and quickly averted his eyes.

"Gunz," he said finally, his voice shaking with fear.

"Hello, master. And mistress," said Gunz coldly, with a mocking bow. He glanced at Mr. Kogan's wife and smiled, the kind of smile that left Clarissa Kogan whimpering into her husband's sunken chest. "I think it's about time we had a little chat."

"Of course, Gunz, of course," mumbled Mr. Kogan, unlocking his wife's hands and rising, pressing his back against the wall. "Anything you wish… just name it."

Theron sprung up with a low growl and bared his terrifying fangs at Kogan, his long tail swiping from left to right.

Mr. Kogan gasped, his eyes wide, his hands shaking. "And your friends too… What can I do for you all?"

"My friends?" asked Gunz with an uneven smirk. "Oh yes, of course. Allow me to introduce my friends."

He waved at Mrak Delar.

"Ancient Master of Power Mrak Delar," he introduced. Mrak Delar crossed his arms over his chest, an ominous smile lingering on his lips. Gunz glanced at the expression on Mrak's face, mirroring his smile. "I'll let you in on a secret, Mr. Kogan. The Ancient Master hates slavers and the idea of people wearing collars makes his powers run wild." As proof of his words, Mrak Delar connected with the power of Earth, and small tremors rattled the house.

Mr. Kogan raised his hands up, covering his face, but he had nowhere to back away. Gunz waved at Yaroslav and proceeded with introductions.

"Allow me to introduce the undefeated fighter of the captive circles, Alucard. But to his friends, he's known as Prince Yaroslav Potemkin." Gunz threw a hate-infused gaze at Mrs. Kogan. "I believe you wanted to see him, Clarissa? There you go. Take a look. You can try and touch him, if you want to take your life in your hands… mistress."

Yaroslav raised his katana, pointing the blade in her direction. His lips curved in a snarl and his eyes lit up with a hungry scarlet glow.

"Prince Yaroslav Potemkin?" moaned Mr. Kogan. "The Scarlet Queen's son?"

"One and the same," replied Yaroslav, giving him a smirk to show off his fangs.

Gunz petted the tiger, receiving a small snap from Theron in response and introduced him. "And this is Theron, the weretiger." Theron growled, lowering his massive head and took a step closer to Kogan.

If Mr. Kogan could shrink any smaller, he probably would. Tears were gleaming in his eyes and his ashen face was contorted in terror.

"I recall, during one of our friendly chats, you said you wanted to know my real name. I guess, being a slave, I can't say no to my kind owner and master," continued Gunz snidely. "So, allow me to introduce myself – FBI consultant Zane Burns. But in the World of Magic, I'm better known as the Fire Salamander."

"The Fire Salamander…" echoed Mr. Kogan horrified, pressing his hand to his chest like he was about to have a cardiac arrest. "But I thought you were just a wizard… with fire magic…"

Mrak Delar chuckled darkly. "He is a wizard, you idiot. An extremely powerful and skilled wizard," he growled, making the house shake again. "And that makes him the Great Fire Salamander. He doesn't need the fire magic. He is the fire itself!"

Gunz extended his hand toward Mr. Kogan, forming a smoldering fireball in the palm of his hand.

"Gunz… um… Mr. Burns, please!" yelped Mr. Kogan. "I've never meant for all this to happen. I swear—"

"All you had to do was set up a fight, so I could meet Alucard!" yelled Gunz, bright orange flames running up and down his arms. "Why did you sell me to Novak?"

"I had no choice," cried Mr. Kogan, clasping his hands together like in a prayer. "I swear! Novak had something I desperately needed and the only way he would give it to me was if I delivered you to him."

"And what might that be?" roared Gunz. "What could be so goddamn important that you betrayed a person who trusted you with his life and his freedom?"

"My life! He promised me my goddamn life!" shouted Mr. Kogan, but then shook his head, averting his pained gaze. "I'm dying, Mr. Burns. Stage four pancreatic cancer. I have only a few months to live. Novak promised me an elixir that would heal me and make me immortal in exchange for you. I'm sorry, but I couldn't say no to that. And come on, Gunz. You trusted me?"

"Of course I didn't trust you," yelled Gunz, punching the air. "But I was hoping you had at least some decency to warn me—"

"Warn you?" squealed Mr. Kogan, throwing his hands in the air. "So you could fight me and escape? No, thank you very much. I'm not that stupid!"

"I wouldn't fight you, asshole!" Gunz took a step closer, his body set in rage. "I thought I made it abundantly clear that I needed to see Alucard and that I would do anything to make it happen! You knew that you were my only way in. Why would I fight you?"

"Why would anyone give up their freedom to save a vampire!" Mr. Kogan forgot about his fear for a moment, throwing an arrogant stare at Yaroslav. "For God's sake, Gunz. He's nothing but a low life vamp. Why would you risk everything to free him?"

Gunz stared at Mr. Kogan, his rage slowly simmering down. "Because, vampire or human, he is my friend. True friends are a rare commodity. And if you were lucky enough to meet people like this, you should be there for them, no matter what… I would give my freedom, my life... I would do anything to make sure that the people I love are safe."

He fell silent, looking at Mr. Kogan, feeling nothing but pity for this man. His wife slowly got up, cowering closer to her husband.

Gunz sighed and shook his head. "But what would scum like you know about things like that. The words honor and loyalty don't exist in your vocabulary. I wish I could kill you... smash you like a cockroach under my foot... but I can't. I don't kill humans, even though I can hardly call you that," said Gunz, waving dismissively at his former owner. "Well, now you get to spend the rest of your miserable existence in prison."

"Prison? I think not." Kogan chuckled. "I have two-three months to live. What kind of court is going to send me to prison? By the time the trial is over, I'll be dead."

"Aw, don't worry about that." Gunz smirked, flicking his eyebrow at Mrak Delar. "After the Master of Power heals your cancer, you'll have a very long and full life in a very special FBI prison ahead of you. You'll spend the rest of your life surrounded by monsters you used to torture and kill in the fighting pits."

Mrak Delar approached the Head of the Florida House, his eyes flooded with darkness. "You have no idea how much I want to destroy you, worthless slaver, so if you know what's best for you, don't make a move," he growled, hate distorting his face.

He placed his hands on Mr. Kogan's forehead and chest and started the healing process. A few minutes later, he took his hands off, wiping them on his pants with an expression of disgust and nodded at Gunz.

Gunz pulled out his phone and dialed Jim's number. "Jim," he said, "they're all yours. You can come in now."

A few minutes later, Jim and his team walked inside the room. The FBI agents stared at them with curiosity, cautiously walking around Theron. As they took away Mr. and Mrs. Kogan in handcuffs, Mrak Delar grabbed Mr. Kogan's arm stopping him.

"One more thing, slaver," he said calmly. "From now on, I'll keep an eye on you. If I find out that you did anything… unseemly, this very cancer that I just healed will get back to you with a vengeance. I'll make sure that you die screaming. Am I clear, scumbag?"

Kogan's eyes bulged and he stared at the Master of Power with his mouth agape as the FBI agents pushed him out the door.

After they were gone, Gunz turned to Mrak Delar. "You can do that?"

Mrak Delar shrugged, grinning at him. "No, of course not. But he doesn't know that."

CHAPTER 34

~ ZANE BURNS, A.K.A. GUNZ ~

Gunz walked through the portal and stopped in the center of his living room. It had been months since he had left his house in the middle of the night and dove into the muddy waters of the supernatural underground fighting. Nothing had changed since. Everything was still just the way he left it.

He was finally home... He was safe and he didn't have to be on the constant look out, waiting for the other shoe to drop. Without thinking, his hand moved up to his neck. No more collars and abusive owners. No more need to bow before anyone. He was finally free.

Gunz sighed, feeling relieved and headed upstairs. Drained physically and magically, he was at the end of his rope and the only thing he wanted, was to get into his bed and sleep. Despite that, he went into the shower first. He had to get rid of the dirt and stench of slavery. Even though he couldn't wash it off of his mind, at least he could scrub it off his skin.

He remembered coming out of the shower and collapsing on his bed. He was probably asleep before he closed his eyes because the next thing he remembered was waking up to a bright, sunlit room. But until he picked up his phone and looked at the date, he didn't realize that he had slept almost thirty-six hours.

He sat up, lowering his feet to the floor and smiled sadly, gazing down at his wrist with Angie's watch back on it. Before he left Kogan's house, he had found his bag. Everything had been in place. He didn't care about the money that was there. The only things he had wanted were his watch and the bracelet that Mrak Delar had made for him.

Gunz went to the bathroom and quickly cleaned up before heading to the kitchen. He needed coffee. Just a plain cup of hot coffee. A simple thing which he had been deprived of for months.

As he walked out of his bedroom, the bitter aroma of coffee invaded his senses and he stopped, wondering how that was possible if he was home alone. He checked the wards and protection spells – everything was intact. He probed the house and relaxed, recognizing the powerful fire energy signature of the Great Salamander.

He rushed downstairs to the kitchen and halted in the doorway. Kal wasn't alone. Mrak Delar was sitting across the table from the Great Salamander, and they were conversing in hushed tones. As soon as they saw him, they stopped talking. Mrak Delar blanched and got up. Kal turned around and a slight smile touched his thin lips.

"Gunz," he said, happiness igniting his eyes, "my boy..."

Guilt swirled through him and he stepped closer, lowering himself to one knee before the Great Salamander. "I'm sorry, Father," he said quietly, meaning every word he said.

Kal ran his fingers through Gunz's hair in a very fatherly manner and patted his shoulder. "Get up, Gunz. We need to talk."

Uh-oh, thought Gunz, rising. *Kal wants to talk to me? And he brought the Master of Power with him. Can't be anything good.*

Gunz sat down at the table, turning to Kal. "What is it,

Father?" he asked. Noticing that his nervousness was obvious in his voice, he cleared his throat.

"Mrak told me everything that happened in California," continued Kal. He leaned slightly over the table and asked, "Did you attempt to control a Master of Power, my child?"

Gunz thought back to that day in Novak's lab when he felt Mrak Delar's heart beating within the grip of his power. "I was hurt, Father, and I was furious with him. So, I remembered the way I controlled wyverns in the Land of Dreams and I just went for it."

Kal's eyebrows climbed up as he exchanged a quick look with Mrak Delar. "You controlled a fully-grown wyvern?" asked Kal, disbelief prominent in his voice.

Gunz shrugged. "Not one, maybe twenty or twenty-five of them. Why?"

Kal exchanged another look with the Master of Power and that got Gunz truly nervous.

"I never taught you that. I want to see how you do it," said Kal, gesturing at Mrak Delar to come closer. "Mrak, could you please assist him."

Mrak Delar walked around the table and stopped a few feet away from Gunz. The sight of the Master of Power brought back unwanted memories, and angry fire ignited on the bottom of his eyes. He grunted, fighting his internal battle with bitterness and frustration. Without thinking about what he was doing, he connected with his elemental power and reached for Mrak's heart.

He felt it beating desperately, surrounded by the fierce flow of his fire power. His own heart thundered in his chest as all the unspoken emotions boiled up within him into one explosive concoction. His hand clenched into a fist and he twisted it, squeezing Mrak's heart tighter. The Master didn't fight him, but small beads of sweat glistened on his strained face.

"Gunz, please," he whispered, "let go…"

Gunz didn't hear him. For a moment he forgot where he was and who he was with. His body dissolved into flames as he stepped closer to Mrak Delar.

"Kneel, you evil bastard," he hissed, and the fire energy magnified his voice, making it stronger and deeper.

Mrak Delar raised his hands in the air and slowly lowered down to his knees. "I'm sorry, my friend. I truly am," he said, breathing laboriously, now fighting the grip of Gunz's power. "I had to do it. It wasn't my choice. And it was killing me every minute of the day! What I had to do to you… If you can, please forgive me, because God knows, I can't forgive myself."

Gunz's arm shook with strain, but he didn't let go, unable to unlock his fingers. He felt a soft touch on his shoulder and glanced back. Kal was standing next to him, sympathy in his flaming eyes.

"He's telling you the truth, my boy. Let it go," the Great Salamander said softly. "Cease."

Gunz felt the flow of his Fire power being interrupted and he finally lowered his arm. Mrak Delar sat back on his heels, wiping the sweat off his forehead with the back of his hand. Gunz stared down at him for a moment, but then sighed and offered his hand to him.

"I forgive you," he said quietly.

The Ancient Master raised his eyes and stared at him for a moment. His lips slightly parted as he inhaled, relieved. Then he took his hand and got up.

"I told you, Kal," he said, arching his eyebrow at the Fire Elemental. "Did you see it?"

Kal nodded and turned to Gunz. "It takes an incredible amount of power to control another Child of Fire, like a wyvern. And you're telling me that you controlled over twenty of them at once. Are you aware that we, as Fire Salamanders, cannot control a Master of Power?" Kal paused, gazing down at him as his hard face warmed up and mischievous twinkles danced in his eyes. "We wield only one elemental power. He controls all four."

'Then why did he obey my command? Why did he kneel?" asked Gunz. As his eyes traveled to Mrak, he caught a sad smile on his face.

"Because I chose to do so," explained the Ancient Master. "Because I believed that I owed you my apologies. But you gave me a hard time, Junior. Kal is right – you can't control me, but you could slow me down and give me a hard time, which not too many people can do. In the short few years that I've known you, you grew to be extremely powerful, young Salamander."

"Having said that," continued Kal, "this is not the only reason why we're here, son." He reached under the kitchen table and brought up a Publix plastic bag. "We need to teach you another very important lesson and you're not going to like it."

"Neither Kogan nor Novak should be able to control you with the gray stones magic," said Mrak Delar taking the plastic bag from Kal's hands. "In reality – no one can. And I told you that when I met you for the first time in Novak's office. I tried to help you, but you didn't recognize it as advice. So, now we're going to show you how you could have escaped the restraints, so no one can ever do it to you again."

He opened the bag, spilling its contents on the table. The gray stone jewelry, a controller and the key fell on the tabletop with a cold metallic jingle. Gunz gawked at the tools of torture that he had had to endure for the last few months and backed away, holding his hands up.

"No," he said with a shudder. "You can't be serious."

"I'm dead serious," confirmed Kal. "No one will ever control my son. Never again. And I'm not going to stop until I see you escaping the magic of the gray stones." He turned to Mrak Delar, pointing at Gunz. "Do it, Master."

Gunz backed away, hitting the wall with his back and raised his arms defensively. The last thing he remembered was the Ancient Master touching his forehead and everything went dark.

* * *

When he woke up, he found himself lying on top of the kitchen table. The lights were off, and the full moon was staring at him through the kitchen window. Mrak and Kal were sitting next to the table. He raised his hands, staring at the bracelets on his wrists and touched his collar with a shudder. *Déjà vu.*

"How long?" he asked, his voice painfully hoarse.

"Six hours all together," said Kal, "give or take."

"I need to place new wards on my house. The kind that wouldn't let stray Masters of Power or Fire Elementals cross my threshold without my invitation," grumbled Gunz.

He sat up on the table, feeling dizzy and weak, and moved his shoulders. His muscles responded with overwhelming soreness. Mrak Delar waved his hand, muttering something under his breath, his eyes swirling with all the colors of power.

"All your wards and protective spells are up and reinforced," he said. "Kal is going to tell you what you need to do to shed these useless toys off. Don't worry. You can safely use your full Fire Salamander power."

Kal showed him a controller. It was set to maximum. "Gunz, you feel weak because your magic is suppressed by the gray stones," started Kal. "What you failed to understand was that while the gray stones magic can suppress your magic, it cannot destroy the Fire Salamander in you. Your element is always with you. No matter what. All you need to do is call upon it and let it take you over. Do you understand me, my child?"

Gunz scratched the back of his head. "I'm not sure. I tried to revert when I was in Novak's care. I couldn't. The pain was more than I could handle."

Kal chuckled. "I didn't ask you to revert. You have everything you need at your fingertips, my boy. You have the power. Just like Mrak said, you've become more powerful than I could ever imagine. Now open your mind... sense that fire that is not only within you... but the fire that you are. As cliché as it sounds – allow yourself to be free. Be yourself and burn these goddamn restraints off your body."

Feeling lost, Gunz slid down from the table, opening himself to the flow of the elemental power. Nothing came. The gray stones suppressed every scrap of magic or Fire power he had. It seemed like the jewelry Kal used was a lot stronger than the one Kogan used. He touched the collar on his neck and felt something wet under his fingers. He glanced at his fingertips stained with his blood and raised his eyes at the Master of Power.

"This jewelry is a lot stronger than the one the low life slavers used on you," explained Mrak Delar. "I built these myself. And I can guarantee – you can burn them out. Now, stop trying to channel the Fire. Be the Fire."

"When I get out of these restraints, remind me to kill you, Mrak Delar," said Gunz miserably.

"Sure I will, but only after you become the Fire." Mrak Delar laughed, giving him a quick tap on the shoulder and walked back to Kal to give him some space.

Gunz closed his eyes and took a few deep breaths, clearing his mind. *Be the fire... Easy to say. What the hell is that supposed to mean?*

He thought for a moment and then instead of channeling the elemental Fire, he connected with the small flame that always burned in his heart. He lowered his head and through the prism of his power, looked at his chest. He could see the fire flowing through him.

Gunz focused on his flaming heart and let go of his control, allowing the Fire to take him over. In a way it felt similar to the way he felt when he reverted into the natural state of the Fire Salamander and yet it was different. There was no elemental energy blast. There was only the Fire – the most powerful element in its full glory. Burning bright like thousands of suns, he spread his arms wide, enjoying the overwhelming feeling of his own strength, power, and absolute freedom.

From the corner of his eye, he saw Mrak Delar surrounding him with a power shield to contain his fire and he laughed. He didn't know why he found it amusing. The way he felt at the moment was beyond comprehension. Then he remembered the gray stone jewelry and in his current state, it seemed like an unimportant, insignificant nuisance. He redirected fire toward his neck, wrists and ankles and a heartbeat later, the gray stone jewelry was gone, evaporated, destroyed by the Fire.

Kal walked through the shield and gently touched his shoulder. Gunz turned his igneous gaze at him and smiled.

"Father... it's incredible."

Kal chuckled softly. "Yes, it is. But you shouldn't stay in this state too long. Now, control your Fire and come back to me, my boy."

It was harder than he thought it would be. It wasn't hard for him to get the Fire under control. It was hard to part with the feeling of power and freedom. Nonetheless, he suppressed the Fire, returning back to his human form. The gray stone jewelry was gone and the weakness, dizziness and soreness were gone with it.

He stood, breathing hard, staring at Kal and Mrak Delar. They exchanged a look and hooted with laughter.

"You should see your face right now," Mrak Delar finally managed to say. "If you're ready, you can try and kill me now."

Gunz chuckled, shaking his head no. "I think I want to keep you around for the next few hundred years, Mrak."

Kal smiled, listening to them joking. "I'm just glad to have you back," he said finally, his voice sounding deeper than usual. "No one can ever enslave my children and live to see another day. Do you understand me, my boy? Never again!"

Gunz ran his fingers over his neck and smiled. "Never again."

EPILOGUE

* * *

Two weeks later
~ Aidan ~

THE SHRILLING ring of his cell phone rudely ripped Aidan out of his dream. He jolted up, wildly searching the dark room for the source of the sound. The phone was ringing and vibrating angrily on top of the coffee table and just now Aidan realized that he had fallen asleep in his living room.

The last two weeks since his return from California had been nonstop work. Even though Uri had done his best taking care of his school, there was a lot that needed to be done and Angel's state of mind wasn't doing Aidan any favors. Even though he explained everything to him, Angel wasn't in a forgiving mood, constantly getting back to the subject of Mrak Delar and his so-called betrayal. And as soon as Chernobog had arrived and asked for Angel's help to search for other dark souls that Morena let out of the Dark Nav, Angel jumped on this task and disappeared.

Theron had decided to stay in South Florida and Aidan offered him work in his school. He was a sweet guy and loved kids, but he needed a lot of training in everything, including how to keep his true nature under control and well-hidden at all times.

On top of all that, he had to help Jim and Zane. With both of them gone for a while, the city was in a state of supernatural turmoil. Every night, he came home exhausted and last night, apparently, he hadn't made it to his bed but fell asleep on his couch.

He grabbed the phone, almost dropping it, and swiped the screen from left to right, answering the call.

"Hello?" His voice was sleepy and hoarse.

"Mr. McGrath?"

Aidan recognized the voice of the Guardians' Archmage and a feeling of unease spread through him. Archmage Allerton was calling him, not summoning him.

"Yes," he replied, pressing the phone tighter to his ear as if he was afraid to drop it.

"Mr. McGrath, sorry for the late call, but we have an urgent situation," he said, his voice gruff and tired. "I could have summoned you, of course, but I prefer not to do it. The headache it gives is a bitch. Especially in the middle of the night."

"Yes, thank you for that, Mr. Allerton," replied Aidan, rubbing his forehead with his fingers. "What's your emergency and how can I help?"

"Well, Mr. McGrath, I'm sorry I have to do this to you, but I need you here, in the Guardians HQ as soon as possible," he said, a vibe of discomfort in his voice. "It's important."

"Fine," replied Aidan, rising off the couch. "Give me thirty minutes and send Jamie Coldwell to meet me at the gates."

* * *

THIRTY MINUTES LATER, Aidan was at the gates of the Guardians HQ. Jamie stood outside the gate with his car. As soon as Aidan materialized, he opened the backdoor of the car, offering to Aidan to get in.

"I'll ride with you, upfront," objected Aidan, getting into the front passenger seat.

Jamie opened the gate and got into the car, slowly driving through the property.

"Is there anything I should know, Jamie?" Aidan asked, staring at the approaching building of the Guardians HQ. "Anything you can tell me."

"Mr. McGrath," started Jamie and choked, falling silent.

The sound of his voice and the look of sympathy on his face made Aidan want to run and to be as far away as possible from this place that brought nothing but pain to him.

"Jamie, what happened?"

"I don't know," replied the young man. "I'm just a guard. But I believe it's about your Tessa. I haven't seen her in lessons for the last couple of weeks and yesterday there was a closed assembly of the Guardians Council."

"Dammit," muttered Aidan, slightly lightheaded as the world around him crashed.

Jamie stopped the car in front of the Guardians HQ building and rushed around to open the door for Aidan. He walked out of the car and followed the guard inside, hardly registering anything around him. He was expecting to be escorted to the Assembly Hall, but Jamie walked him through the long corridor and knocked on the door of the Archmage Allerton's personal study.

The guard opened the door for him, and Aidan walked inside. Quinn Allerton got up greeting him and waved at an empty chair, offering him to sit down.

"Mr. McGrath, I called you here in the middle of the night because Tessa is missing," said the Archmage without any preamble. "She left the Guardians HQ without notifying anyone and as such she broke a few major rules. Nevertheless, it's not her rule breaking that worries me. The real problem is that we don't know where she is. Even her friend Missi has no idea. We can't sense her magical signature or presence anywhere within this realm."

Aidan got up, opening himself up to the full flow of his power, illuminating the room with a brilliant light. He rose up and for a few seconds silence lingered in the air. Then he lowered himself on the floor and fell into the chair.

"I can't sense her neither in this realm nor in the Otherworld," said Aidan. *What the hell did she do now? Why didn't she call me?* "When did you say she disappeared?"

"Two and a half weeks ago," said the Archmage. "Why?"

"She didn't call me," said Aidan, shaking his head. "And now I know why. She probably tried, but I was unavailable – locked within the God's snare in Novak's facility. Dammit!" He slammed his hand on the desk, breaking it in two.

The desk collapsed and all the paperwork spilled on the floor, followed by the stationary office phone. Luckily, the Archmage didn't have a computer on his desk. Quinn Allerton hopped to his feet, knocking his chair on the floor.

"Jeez, the way you look, Mr. McGrath, I forget that you're an ancient god with the strength and powers of an ancient god," he exhaled, staring down at the two pieces of his demolished desk.

"I'm sorry, sir," mumbled Aidan uncomfortably. "I'll pay for the damage."

"That won't be necessary," objected the Archmage dryly. "I called you here because I need you to find Tessa. She's grown extremely powerful, yet she's not in control of her power. And we're talking about the power of a god. The god of Thunder to boot! The consequences could be disastrous should she lose control of her power."

"Any idea on why she left and where she could have gone?"

"No. We asked everyone she was friendly with and no one knew anything." Quinn Allerton shook his head. "Mr. McGrath, I don't need to remind you—"

"You don't need to remind me of anything," Aidan interrupted him, rising. "I'll find her. Can I count on the Guardians' help, in case I need it?"

"Of course, Mr. McGrath," replied the Archmage with a sugary smile. He approached Aidan and tapped with his finger on the silver pendant on his chest. "As a loyal member of the Guardian Order you can always count on our support. And judging by the situation with Tessa, you'll be a member of our Order for quite some time."

Aidan held his breath, counting in his mind to ten and back and then smiled icily. "It's late, Mr. Allerton, and as much as I enjoyed our little chat, it's time for me to go. I will notify you as soon as I hear anything about Tessa's whereabouts."

Without waiting for Allerton's approval, he inclined his head slightly and left the office.

***

Same night
~ Zane Burns, a.k.a. Gunz ~

TWO SWORDS COLLIDED with a loud metallic clang and steel sung as blades slid against each other all the way to their guards. A few sparks emerged from under the blades, shining brightly in the surrounding night.

The vampire's eyes, glowing with a dim scarlet light, were just a few inches away from Gunz's face. Yaroslav applied some pressure on his blade, pushing Gunz back and quickly switched his position, making him lose his balance and fall to one knee.

Yaroslav laughed and pulled away, allowing Gunz to regroup. Gunz chuckled, wiping perspiration off his forehead and got up, heavily leaning on his sword.

"You're getting better, Zane," noted Yaroslav, sheathing his sword.

"Thanks, Slavik, it's nice of you to say that," he replied, shaking his head. "I don't think I'll ever get to your level. You're the only person besides your mother who can give a hard time to Mrak Delar and his black sword."

"You're not as bad as you think," objected Yaroslav with a half-shrug.

"I didn't say I was bad. I said you were better." Gunz laughed, heading toward the house. "*Po malenkoj?*" he asked, tapping on his neck in a Russian drinking gesture and motioned at Yaroslav to follow him.

"*Po malenkoj?*" repeated the vampire, grinning. "Sure, I'll take a shot."

They walked into the kitchen and Yaroslav sat down, tapping his long fingers on top of the table. Gunz brought two shot glasses and filled them with vodka to the brim. The harsh smell of alcohol reached the vampire's sensitive nose and he grimaced, picking up his shot glass.

"It's been a while," he said wrinkling his nose. "I always hated the smell though."

Gunz lifted his shot glass, clinking it with Yaroslav's.

"*Nu, poehali,*" he said, downing the vodka in one gulp.

"Let's go," agreed Yaroslav, repeating the same statement in English and emptied the shot glass.

"Can you still speak Russian?" asked Gunz, playing with his empty shot glass.

"I can understand, but I've been told that I speak funny," replied Yaroslav, brushing his long hair off his face. "I was just twenty when Akira turned me and took me away from my home. I think I speak Japanese a lot better than I speak Russian."

Gunz nodded and leaned back in his chair relaxing.

"Where is Aidan?" asked Yaroslav, also reclining in his chair, stretching his long legs.

"Probably with his crew, patrolling the city," replied Gunz absentmindedly. "I'm usually out there with them, but today I took some time off to practice my sword skills with you."

"I wish I could join you and Aidan," mused Yaroslav. "But I'm not sure if Aidan and his crew would approve."

"Why wouldn't they? You're fast and strong, and your fighting skills are superior to most fighters I know."

"Vampire, remember? He's a god. He may not like working alongside with someone like me."

"Aidan?" Gunz smirked, shaking his head. "He's not that kind of a god. He doesn't discriminate. Trust me. He'd love to have you by his side. Plus if he has someone new to torment during his martial arts lessons, maybe he'll get off my case."

Yaroslav nodded and his eyes slowly drifted from him to the dark square of the window where a small vial filled with a thick clear liquid sat on the counter. Gunz followed the direction of his friend's gaze and tensed.

"I thought you disposed of it," said Yaroslav quietly.

"I was going to…" Gunz bit his lip, avoiding the vampire's eyes. "I couldn't."

"You have to, Zane. This is the kind of temptation you don't need," said Yaroslav, frowning. "You know that you can't even think about using it."

"I know," replied Gunz miserably. "I wasn't planning to. Just—"

"Zane, listen to me," said Yaroslav leaning forward, his voice a low growl. "Even the slightest thoughts of using it are dangerous. If you separate Angie's essence from Zmey's, you'll free not only her but also the Lord of Chaos. And to get her out, you'll have to open the coffin. I know you're hurt and grieving, but consider the consequences, my friend."

"Don't you think I know that?" Gunz slammed his hand on the table, everything inside him twisting with pain. Then he took a deep breath. Yaroslav was his friend and he was just trying to help. "I know that, Slavik, and I'm not going to do anything to jeopardize the safety of this world. I just want to keep it. It's like a ray of hope for me, you know? If Novak… um… Rasputin was able to create this elixir, maybe there is something else out there that would allow me to bring her back without any consequences."

"Magic always has consequences," objected Yaroslav softly. He got up and headed toward the backdoor. "Just be careful."

He was gone before the door closed behind him. It seemed like he just soundlessly melted into the darkness.

"Vampires…" muttered Gunz. "When is he going to learn leaving at normal speed. Him and Akira, both…"

For a moment, he stood there, staring at the vial. Then he shoved it in the pocket of his jeans and waved his hand, unfolding the fire curtain of his portal.

* * *

Gunz walked out of his portal outside the protective circle of magic that was surrounding Mount Karasova. The desire to be as far away from here as possible overwhelmed him. He grunted, knowing perfectly well that what he felt was the result of the "turn away" spell the Guardians were casting over the large area around the Mount.

He touched the magical dome, sending some of his fire energy through it and a middle-aged man materialized in front of him. He threw one look at Gunz and frowned.

"Mr. Burns, you shouldn't be here," he said dryly. "Not again."

"You're right, Jasper. I shouldn't be here, but this is the last time," promised Gunz peacefully, raising his hand up. "I swear."

Jasper sighed. "I understand. Your beloved is buried there, and you need some kind of closure, but believe me, coming here all the time is not going to help you move on. And that's what you need to do. It's been a year, Zane…"

"Jasper, let me through, please," pleaded Gunz quietly, but his body stiffened as he forced his aggravation under control. "I swear, I'm here to say my goodbyes. I'm not coming back ever again."

"Fine. Last time." Jasper touched the protective dome, opening a small door for Gunz. "I'm going to leave this door opened, so you can open your portal home straight from the Mount. I hope I'm not going to see you any time soon, Zane."

Gunz passed through the protective dome and kept walking without looking back. The vial with the elixir was pressing against his leg and he was trying not to think about what he was going to do once he got inside the cave. He knew he couldn't use it, but at the same time, he felt like he was betraying Angelique.

He reached Mount Karasova and walked into the cool darkness of the cave. Muttering a spell, he sent a few light orbs up in the air and took the passage that led toward the center of the Mount. He didn't stop until he reached a large cave with a tall ceiling that was disappearing into the darkness.

He pulled the vial out of his pocket and carefully placed it on top of the sacrificial table that was situated right in the middle of the cave. The shimmering blue light of the magical orbs reflected off the liquid inside the vial, throwing blue streaks of light on the rough surface of the stone.

Gunz traced the light with his finger and sighed. "Hi Angie," he said quietly, his chest tight with sadness, "this is it… This is the only potion that I know of that can separate you from this evil scum." He fell silent for a moment, swallowing a thick lump that seemed to be permanently stuck in his throat. "And I can't use it... Goddamnit!"

He slammed his fist on the sacrificial stone and the vial fell, rolling off the table to the soft sandy floor of the cave. Gunz dropped to his knees and picked it up, squeezing it in his fist. He glanced up at the cold gray rock towering over him and his eyes welled up with tears.

"Angie," he moaned, bending forward like someone punched him in the stomach, "all I have to do to save you is spill this cursed liquid on top of the sacrificial table. That's all, and we could be together again... But I can't, not without releasing the Zmey." For a moment, he stopped talking and closed his eyes, pinching the bridge of his nose with his fingers. "I love you, sweetheart... You're my life, my perfect world... but you were right – Mount Karasova is one mountain I shouldn't move... not even for you..."

Gunz sat back on his heels, staring up into the endless darkness of the ceiling and squeezed the vial in his fist. The glass cracked, its sharp edges slicing his skin and the clear thick liquid mixed with his blood spilled down his arm, trickling on the floor and quickly getting absorbed by the sand.

He felt a twinge of physical pain and brought his hand up, gaping at the bleeding cuts on his palm. Then he pressed his hands to his face, leaning forward and his whole body shuddered in agonizing sobs. He was tortured, shot and beat up before, but the agony that devastated his soul now was by far the worst pain he had ever experienced.

As the last drops of the potion were swallowed by the sand, all his hopes disintegrated and endless despair drowned him, crushing him with the realization that he just killed the woman he loved. Again. Feeling numb all over, he turned around and rested his back against the cold stone table.

He couldn't say how long he had been sitting in the cave. The clear, human tears were slowly sliding down his cheeks, but he didn't even register that he was crying. After a while, he got up and threw his last gaze at the sacrificial table under which Angelique was lying, forever entwined with their mortal enemy.

"I love you, Angie," he whispered into the unyielding silence of the cave. "I will always love you. Please forgive me..."

He waved his hand, opening the Fire Salamander's portal and passed through it.

* * *

Gunz walked out of his portal into his bedroom and dropped on the bed without undressing. He closed his eyes, allowing exhaustion to quiet down his wounded heart. The night embraced him with the tender touch of a lover, and he relinquished his pain to its warm reassurance and solace.

And there was nothing.

No thoughts. No pain. Just a blissful nothingness. And at this moment, that was what he wanted, what he needed.

He wasn't sure if he was sleeping or if his mind finally shut down, but when he felt a soft touch to his shoulder, he had no strength to open his eyes, his eyelids too heavy to move, his lips too numb to form coherent words.

The touch was gentle and persistent at the same time. He felt someone's fingers moving down his chest, raising his shirt and touching the bare skin of his stomach. He finally managed to open his eyes and sucked in a sharp breath.

"Angie..." he whispered, "but how—"

"Shh..." She pressed her finger to her lips and smiled.

He recognized the very same smile he loved so much, yet he couldn't believe his eyes. He stared up at her, afraid to move or say a word. It couldn't be real and if it was a vision or a dream, he didn't want it to end.

She leaned forward and kissed him, her soft lips pressing against his, as her hands moved down, tugging at the waistband of his pants. Everything inside him flipped upside down. It wasn't just the desire he felt for her. It was a basic need to be with her, to see her, to hear her voice. That was all he wanted.

Angelique pulled away and gazed down at him, her eyes gleaming with love and tenderness. Her hands slowly found the bottom of his shirt and bunched it up to expose his chest. Her fingers traced the shape of his muscles and her eyes got darker with desire.

"Oh, Angie, my love," he exhaled, "are you real? Are you just a dream? I don't care... just don't leave me..."

She smiled again, her finger stopped circling on his chest and halted above his heart. "I'm real," she answered, new, different notes surfacing in her voice, "and I'm your dream... a nightmare to be precise."

Gunz felt a stabbing pain in his chest and jerked up, but she pressed on his shoulder, holding him down, her right hand still above his heart. He glanced down and gasped. Angelique's hand changed. Her sharp, long nails dug into his skin, small pools of his blood rising under each of her fingers.

"You don't want me to leave you? That's priceless! *You* left me! Alone, in the dark, tied up to your mortal enemy," hissed Angelique and Gunz didn't recognize her voice.

He raised his eyes and held his breath. It was still the face he remembered and loved so much, but the eyes... They were gleaming with a sinister yellow light, the serpent-like dark-red vertical slits of pupils, pulsing with hate. They were the eyes of the Skiper-Zmey.

"You're not her, Zmey. Get out of my head," growled Gunz, struggling to get free of the monster's hold to no avail. Just like in any nightmare, his muscles turned into mush, he was slow and weak, helpless against his powerful enemy.

"Oh, I'm Angelique, all right." Angelique's lips stretched into an ugly, terrifying snarl. "You killed me twice, my little lover.

And you dare to ask me for forgiveness? NEVER! You hear me? I will never forgive you, Zane Burns!"

Gunz moaned. With his body filled with lead, he couldn't move, he couldn't even speak. Angelique's right arm went up and he saw a large blade, reflecting the light of the full moon. Her fingers squeezed the handle of the knife, her knuckles white, her tender face contorted with hatred as she plunged the blade down, directing it at his heart...

The loud shrill of the phone slashed his nightmare, shattering it into pieces. Gunz gasped, jolting up and fell off the bed on the floor, panting. The phone was still ringing, and he stared around wildly, searching for it. He picked up the device with trembling hands and answered the call.

"Zane, I'm sorry for the late-night call—"

He heard Aidan's voice and laughed, a dry barking sound. "Aidan, thank God, you called," he managed to say finally.

"Are you okay?" asked Aidan with notes of concern. "You don't sound good."

"I am"—Gunz swallowed, wiping the cold sweat off his face, his mind finally clear—"I'll be fine, Aidan. What's up?"

Aidan cleared his throat. "Zane, I need your help," he said finally. "It's Tessa."

First this terrible nightmare, now this, Gunz thought, getting off the floor and lowering himself on the bed heavily. "What's going on with Tessa?" he asked, dread spreading through him.

"I don't know," replied Aidan. "All I know is that she left the Guardians HQ two and a half weeks ago without telling anyone about it and no one has heard of her since."

"Are you at your penthouse?" asked Gunz, heading toward the washroom.

"Yes," replied Aidan.

"I'll be with you in a minute," he promised, hanging up the phone.

Gunz cleaned up quickly and changed his clothes. His

bedroom was still dark, but the last traces of the distressing nightmare were gone. He grabbed his Swiss army knife and waved his hand, unfolding the smoldering curtain of his portal.

"Fire Salamander – go," he said quietly and stepped through the fire.

BOOK FOUR: EXCERPT

*Read on for an excerpt from
N.M. Thorn's new book:*

The Fire Salamander Chronicles. Book 4

* * *

~ *Zane Burns, a.k.a. Gunz* ~
Modern day
Miami Beach, South Florida

The narrow suburban street was dark and empty. Every single streetlight was out, and nothing was moving in the dead of night. The approaching tropical storm was making its presence known by driving the winds and veiling the dark sky with heavy clouds. The palm trees bent their crowns and the soft hissing of ruffled leaves accompanied every gust.

Even though it wasn't raining yet, Gunz could feel the gathering moisture in the air and his Salamander senses were screaming bloody murder, warning him about the presence of the opposing element.

"Is this the place Akira told you to check out?" Gunz asked, throwing a quick glance at Yaroslav.

The vampire nodded, slowly unsheathing his katana. He was dressed all in black, but his long golden hair was semaphoring his presence from far away.

"I don't sense anything," said Aidan approaching them.

Another one with blond hair, Gunz thought and chuckled. "You guys should wear something to cover your hair. I can see you from a mile away, even in complete darkness."

"So what?" Yaroslav shrugged nonchalantly with a wide grin that showed the points of his long fangs. "Let them see me – I welcome any monster who is fast enough to catch my hair."

"Shh," whispered Aidan, his eyes slightly glowing with the white light of his magic. He extended his arm, muttering something under his breath and a long sword materialized in his hand. As Aidan raised his sword assuming the combat stance, the weapon glistened like an icicle, looking deadly in his hands. "Something is coming."

Gunz expanded his Salamander senses, probing the area and nodded to Aidan, confirming his statement. He reached into his pocket and pulled out his Swiss army knife, turning it into a sword. There was something in the area that hadn't been here just a few minutes ago and its menacing presence was getting stronger with every passing moment.

"Well, that's a new one," murmured Aidan, jerking his chin toward the road as six large SUVs with tinted windows came to a screeching halt in front of them.

"No shit," muttered Gunz, bringing his sword to his shoulder. He squeezed the grip of his sword tighter, wondering why the blade felt heavier than usual.

At least eight men walked out of each vehicle and spread around surrounding them from every direction. The dark energy of their ominous magic overwhelmed his senses and he grunted, channeling his elemental power and magic. As the flames went up in his eyes, he felt Aidan stepping next to him ready to fight.

"Aw, so much fun!" Yaroslav laughed, flashing his vampiric grin as he took his position, back-to-back with them.

A split-second later, the air was thick with the strikes of dark magical energy and the stench of demonic essence as all men charged them at the same time.

"Protect Yaroslav," Aidan hissed into Gunz's ear as he channeled his power.

"Praecidio Amnia," muttered Gunz, manifesting a thick power-shield around the vampire. Then he turned to Aidan and yelled, "Now!"

A blast of white light expanded around Aidan, assailing the advancing enemies. Gunz expected them to fall back as neither demons, vampires nor any other types of supernatural beings could withstand a full assault of Aidan's godly powers. To his shock, the men staggered back just a little, moved by the sheer force of the blast, but none of them suffered even a mild injury.

"What the hell?" Aidan hissed, gathering more of his power. But the second blast produced just as little effect as the first one.

"My turn," growled Gunz, watching Aidan wrap his own protection shield around Yaroslav. *"Ignius Amplio!"*

His sword went up in flames and a smoldering jet of fire hit the advancing men straight in their chests. The fire flowed around them doing no damage whatsoever. Gunz increased the heat and potency of his fire strike to no avail. The fire magic seemed to be useless against them and using his elemental power wasn't an option as he was in the middle of a suburban neighborhood.

"Aidan, take this shield off of me," yelled Yaroslav, his eyes lighting up with a hungry scarlet glow. "Let's do it the old style."

As soon as Aidan brought down his shield, Yaroslav disappeared. He didn't teleport, but he moved so fast it was impossible to see him without using the magical sight. Immediately, his katana wreaked havoc among the opposing party as they recovered from Gunz's and Aidan's assaults and moved forward.

The screams of pain and furious growls accompanied Yaroslav's progress and the stench of blood, mixed with the reek of demonic energy filled the cool night air. Gunz and Aidan exchanged a quick look and joined Yaroslav, putting their swords to business.

Gunz channeled more of his fire through his sword making it burn brighter. He swung it down on one of the men, slicing him in two, and realized that he was just a demon – not even a demon in its pure form, but a human body possessed by demonic essence.

How is it possible that neither my fire magic nor Aidan's godly powers worked against a run-of-the-mill demon? A thought flashed through his mind and quickly disappeared as he had no time to dwell on it. Three men attacked him at the same time, and he spun around, avoiding their direct strikes. His Salamander senses told him that two of his attackers were demons but the third one was a dark wizard, who was wielding not only magic but also a dangerously-looking sword, which meant he wouldn't be easy to kill.

As fast as Gunz moved, he could never be as fast as Yaroslav and today he felt slower and heavier than usual. One of the demons caught his thigh with his sword and Gunz dropped to his knee, a pain-infused grunt escaping his lips. The dark wizard didn't wait for him to recover and blasted him with a powerful magical strike. Gunz cried out and fell on his back. He hit the ground hard, losing his breath, and his fingers unlocked. His sword dropped on the warm asphalt with a loud clang.

The wizard cackled and struck him with his magic again, overwhelming his senses and sending his mind into a wild frenzy. The wizard raised his sword ready to push it through Gunz's chest, and with horror, Gunz realized that he was completely immobilized by dark magic. Helpless and desperate, he watched the blade slowly lowering down, only one thought clear in his mind – if he died now, hundreds of humans would be dead in a split-second.

"No…" he exhaled, struggling against the hold of dark magic.

A second before the sharp end of the blade pierced his chest, the mighty strike of a katana deflected it. One more strike and the head of the dark wizard rolled off his shoulders, hitting the road with a sickening thud. Bright red blood pumped from the headless neck and a second later the dead body dropped to its knees and then collapsed forward. Before the lifeless corpse fell on top of Gunz, Yaroslav's hand jerked him up to his feet.

"What's wrong with you, Salamander," hissed the vampire, thrusting Gunz's sword back into his hand. "You're slower and weaker than usual. If that's even possible."

Gunz rolled his eyes at him and sidestepped the next attacker, allowing Yaroslav to swing his katana one more time, slicing the demon in half.

"Yaroslav is right."

Gunz heard Aidan's voice somewhere on his left but ignored him, engaging the demon who attempted to punch him in the face. Easily avoiding his attack, he seized the demon's arm flipping him over his hip. The demon fell to his side and Gunz twisted his arm up at a painful angle, while running his blade through his neck. The dark shadow of the demonic essence separated from the body and shimmered into the night.

The shrilling sound of police sirens sounded somewhere in the distance and flares of multicolored lights illuminated the air at the far end of the neighborhood. To Gunz's surprise, the remaining men took off. They hopped into their SUVs and a heartbeat later all vehicles were gone.

Gunz lowered his sword, taking in his surroundings. At least

BOOK FOUR: EXCERPT

fifteen dead bodies were sprawled motionless on the asphalt, their dead eyes staring into the dark sky. The severed heads and body parts were floating in puddles of blood. Aidan and Yaroslav stood with their bloodied blades down, their blond hair now more red than gold, their clothes torn and covered in scarlet stains of blood – theirs and their opponents.

The first drops of rain fell from the sky and Gunz flinched from the touch of water to his skin. The police sirens now sounded closer and he didn't think that it was a good idea for local authorities to find the three of them standing with their swords over a pile of dead bodies. FBI agent or not, Jim would have a hard time explaining all of that to the police as well as to his superiors.

"Aidan, Yaroslav, you need to leave," he said, turning to his friends. "I'll take care of the dead bodies. Police can't see this battle field."

"How are you going to do it, Pyro?" Aidan asked, a light smirk playing on his face covered in blood splutters. "You can't use your elemental power here and fire magic won't do the trick fast enough."

"I can't," agreed Gunz, returning his smirk, "but I know someone who can. Now leave, both of you."

Aidan's lips parted, forming the shape of letter "O" and he nodded to Yaroslav. "I'll see you both tomorrow for training in my school." He snapped his fingers and vanished from the street.

"Zane," said Yaroslav wiping his katana on the ripped sleeve of his shirt, "are you sure you're going to be okay?"

"Yes," replied Gunz impatiently, "but I need you to leave, Slavik. Something tells me, you are not going to appreciate the fire show."

A wide grin split the vampire's face and he was gone in a heartbeat. Gunz raised his hand up and tapped his finger on the surface of his wristwatch.

"Mishka, I need your help," he said quietly.

With a light pop, Mishka the wyvern materialized in front of him.

"I'm here, boss, what can I—"

The wyvern fell silent, twirling in the air, circling above the improvised grave yard. As he returned to Gunz, a sarcastic glimmer shone in his igneous eyes.

"Wait. Don't tell me," said the wyvern hovering in the air in front of him. "Clean up on aisle three, Mr. Burns?"

Gunz nodded, guilt swirling through him. But as the bright lights of the approaching police vehicles lit up the street, he forgot about feeling guilty.

"Mishka, please," he hissed, throwing his hands in the air. "I can't leave this Deadsville for police to find! And I can't use my elemental power around humans. So cut the crap and help me clean this mess up, would yah?"

Mishka huffed, rising back up in the air. "Fine, fine, but you'll owe me one."

"I owe you more than one, my friend." Gunz chuckled, turning his sword back into the Swiss army knife and shoved it into his pocket. He waved his hand unfolding the fire curtain of his portal and turned around.

"Now go!" yelled Mishka, the cloud of fire energy surrounding him. "When Mishka the Cleaner is at work, little fire lizards should run." He tittered, spitting tiny fireballs.

"Are you sure—," Gunz started to say, but Mishka waved his wings vigorously interrupting him.

"The police are going to be here in a minute," he hissed, showering him with fire and smoke. "Fire Salamander – go!"

Gunz nodded and walked through his fire portal.

DEAR READER

Thank you so much for reading The Burns Defiance. I hope you enjoyed the book and will join Zane Burns' next adventure in the fourth book of the series.

If you would like to stay up-to-date on the latest information about new releases, special offers, and more, sign up for my mailing list. https://www.nmthorn.com/newsletter

For more information follow me on
  Facebook: www.facebook.com/nmthornauthor
  Instagram: www.instagram.com/nmthornauthor
  Or visit my website www.nmthorn.com.

BEFORE YOU GO...

Your reviews mean the world to me and are greatly appreciated. If you enjoyed the Burns Fire, please take a few minutes to leave a review. It doesn't have to be long. It can be just a few words or stars rating.

Please help spread the word by taking this small extra step and leave your review on Amazon and Goodreads.

ALSO BY N. M. THORN

The Burns Fire
The Burns War

ABOUT THE AUTHOR

N.M. Thorn currently lives in South Florida with her husband and son. Owner of a digital marketing agency by day and a writer by night, she loves spending her times creating new worlds, paranormal planes of existence and anything that could be described as supernatural.

When she is not busy working with everything digital or exploring fantasy worlds, she enjoys spending time with her family, reading, painting and martial arts.

If you would like to share your thoughts, ideas or just send N.M. Thorn a message about the Fire Salamander world, feel free to contact her at: nmthornauthor@gmail.com

facebook.com/nmthornauthor
instagram.com/nmthornauthor

Printed in Great Britain
by Amazon